The words see**if Josh had acc**
about to happe   **there was no**
going back.

He removed her hands and crossed his arms across his chest, tilting his head to stare at the top of hers because she was frightened to meet his hazel eyes. Frightened of the desperation she might see there.

"I made you the guardian of the twins last year."

"Without asking me?"

"Yeah. I was afraid you'd say no." Josh shrugged and lifted the corner of his mouth in a little smile. "You asked what I was willing to do. They're my kids, Tracey. I'll do anything for them, including prison time."

"Just tell me what to do."

"Nothing. You can't be involved in this. It has to be me." She believed him. She had to. But she couldn't promise to stay out of his way. She meant what she'd said about doing anything for Jackson and Sage. And if that meant *she* was the one who went to jail...so be it.

CRIMINAL ABDUCTION

USA TODAY Bestselling Author

ANGI MORGAN

Previously published as *Hard Core Law* and *The Ranger*

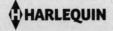

ISBN-13: 978-1-335-42727-4

Recycling programs
for this product may
not exist in your area.

Criminal Abduction

Copyright © 2022 by Harlequin Enterprises ULC

Hard Core Law
First published in 2016. This edition published in 2022.
Copyright © 2016 by Angela Platt

The Ranger
First published in 2015. This edition published in 2022.
Copyright © 2015 by Angela Platt

For questions and comments about the quality of this book,
please contact us at CustomerService@Harlequin.com.

Harlequin Enterprises ULC
22 Adelaide St. West, 41st Floor
Toronto, Ontario M5H 4E3, Canada
www.Harlequin.com

Printed in U.S.A.

CONTENTS

Angi Morgan writes about Texans in Texas. A *USA TODAY* and *Publishers Weekly* bestselling author, her books have been finalists for several awards, including the Booksellers' Best Award, Best Intrigue Series from *RT Book Reviews* and the Daphne du Maurier Award. Angi and her husband live in North Texas. They foster Labradors and love to travel, snap pics and fix up their house. Hang out with her on Facebook at Angi Morgan Books. She loves to hear from fans at angimorganauthor.com.

HARD CORE LAW

There is never a book without my pals Jan, Robin, Jen, Lizbeth and Janie. Lena Diaz, thanks for the brilliant ideas and personal information you shared about raising a child with diabetes. Tim...I love you, man!

Prologue

"It was great to meet you. Night." The last of the birthday guests waved from their cars.

Tracey Cassidy stood at the front door waving goodbye to another couple she barely knew. Two sets of little arms stretched around her thighs, squeezing with an appropriate four-and-a-half-year-old grunt.

"What are you two doing up? I tucked you in three hours ago."

"Happy birthday," they said in unison.

Jackson and Sage giggled until the sound of a dish breaking in the kitchen jerked them from their merriment. Their faces, so similar but different, held the same surprise and knowledge that their daddy was in super big trouble.

"Daddy's going to get it now." Sage nodded until her auburn curls bounced.

"Hurry." Tracey patted them on the backsides and pointed them in the right direction. "Back upstairs before the Major has to scoop you up there himself. You know you'll have extra chores if he catches you down here."

The twins took each stair with a giant tiptoeing motion. It would have been hilarious to watch them, but their dad was getting a bit louder and might come looking for her to help.

"Scoot, and there's sprinkles on Friday's ice-cream cone."

Bribery worked. They ran as fast as their short legs could carry them up the carpeted staircase. Tracey was sure their dad heard the bedroom door close. Then again, he was making enough noise to wake the barn cats.

"Tracey!" he finally yelled, seeking help. "Where's the dustpan?"

Hurrying to the back of the house, she found Major Josh Parker holding several pieces of broken glass in one hand and the broom in the other. A juggler holding his act. Yep, that's what he looked like. He was still completely out of his element in the kitchen. Or the laundry. Good thing he had a maid.

"It should have been in the closet with the broom. Here, let me take these." She reached for the pieces of crystal covered in the remnants of spinach artichoke dip.

"I'm good." He raised the mess out of her reach. "Sorry about the bowl. I thought I was actually helping for once. Damn thing slipped right out of my hand."

"Here, just put it in this." She pulled the covered trash can over to the mess and popped the lid open.

"Hell, Tracey, you don't have your shoes on. This thing splintered into a thousand pieces."

Two forbidden words in one conversation? She'd never seen Josh even the little tiniest bit tipsy. But the group had toasted a lot tonight. First her birthday, then an engagement, then to another couple who'd looked at each other like lovebirds. Then to her birthday again.

"Are you a little drunk?" She ignored his warning and crossed the kitchen to look for the dustpan, which was hanging on the wall of the pantry exactly where it should have been. She turned to tell Josh and walked straight into his chest.

"Well, would you look at that." He cocked his head to the side emphasizing his boyish dimple. "If it had been a snake it would have bitten me."

"Bitten a big chunk right out of your shoulder." She tapped him with the corner for emphasis, but he still didn't back up out of the doorway.

Josh leaned his forehead against the wood and exhaled a long "whew" sound. The smell of whiskey was strong. He had definitely drunk a little more than she'd ever witnessed. Maybe a little more than he should have. But he'd also been enjoying the company of his friends. Something long overdue. Most of his free time was spent with the twins.

"We need a cardboard box or something. This stuff—" He brought the glass from his side to his chest. "It'll bust through plastic."

His head dropped to the door frame and he closed his eyes. This time he relinquished the broken glass to her and backed up with some guidance. She helped him to the table, set a cold bottle of water in front of him and went about cleaning the floor.

Technically, it wasn't her job. She was officially off duty because Josh was home. But she couldn't leave him with his head on the kitchen table and glass all over the place. The kids would get up at their normal time, even if it was a Saturday. And the maid service wouldn't stop back around until Tuesday.

"The way you look right now, this mess might still be here after school Monday."

She moved around the edge of the tiled kitchen avoiding as much of the mess as she could. He was right about one thing, glass was everywhere. She retrieved her sandals from the living room next to the couch. She'd kicked them off while watching the men in Josh's company interact with one another.

The wives hadn't meant to exclude her, but she wasn't one of them. She was the hired help. The nanny. She detested that word and told those who needed to know that she was the child care provider. In between a few bits of conversation, she silently celebrated in the corner. Not just her birthday, but also the achievement of receiving her PhD.

I need to tell him.

She pulled her sandals from where they'd crept under the couch and slipped them on her feet.

"They weren't very…approachable tonight, were they." A statement. Josh didn't seem to need an answer. One hand scrubbed at his face, while the other held a depleted water bottle. "Sorry 'bout this."

"Hey, nothing to be sorry for. The cake was out of this world."

"Vivian ordered it."

"Yeah, I was sorry she couldn't stay." Josh's receptionist had done her best to keep Tracey involved in the conversations. "Would you sit down before you fall down?"

"I'm not drunk. Just real tired. We've been working a lot, you know."

"I do. I've been spending way too many nights here. The neighbors are going to start talking."

"Let 'em." He grinned and let his head drop to the back of the couch cushions. "They can whinny all they want. And moo. Or just howl at the moon. I might even join 'em."

"I think you need a dog to howl."

Josh's closest neighbor was about three miles away. He did have several horses, three barn cats and let Jim-Bob Watts run cattle on their adjoining field. No one was really going to know if she was there all night or not.

No one but them.

They'd become lax about it recently. Whatever case the Texas Rangers were working on had been keeping him at Company F Headquarters in Waco. The case would soon be over—at least their part in it. She'd gathered that info from one or two of those whiskey toasts.

Tracey looked around the room. Plastic cups, paper plates with icing, napkins, forks. How could ten people make such a mess? A couple of the women had tried to offer their help, but everyone had seemed to leave at the same time.

Of course, the man now asleep on the couch, might have mentioned it was late. And if she worked in his office, she might misinterpret that as an order to get out. Tracey sighed and picked up a trash bag. What did one more late night matter?

Not like she had any reason to rush back to her campus apartment. She dropped two plastic cups into the bag and continued making her way around the room. She might as well clean up a little. It was mostly throw-away stuff and it wasn't fair to make the twins help their dad.

After all, it had been *her* birthday party.

Josh had his hands full just keeping up with the twins. The floor would be horrible by Tuesday if she didn't pass a mop across it. So she cleaned the floors and stored the cake—not to mention put the whiskey bottle above the refrigerator. On the second pass through the living room, she took a throw from the storage ottoman and covered her boss.

It might be triple-digit weather outside, but Josh kept the downstairs like a freezer. She draped the light blanket across him and his hand latched on to hers.

JOSH SHOULD BE ashamed of himself for letting Tracey clean up while he faked sleep. *Should be.* He wasn't drunk. Far from it. He was hyperaware of every one of Tracey's movements.

"Tonight didn't go exactly like I planned."

"Oh shoot. I don't know why you scared me, but I thought you were asleep. It was fun. A total surprise." She placed her hand on top of his, patting it as if she was ready to be let loose. She also didn't have a mean bone in her body. She'd never intentionally hurt his feelings.

But Josh had to hold on. If he let her go, he might not ever get the courage again. "You're lying. You were miserable. I should have invited your friends."

"It was great. Really." She patted his hand again. "I better head out."

"No." He stood, letting her hand go but trapping her shoulders under his grip. He lightened up. "I mean. Can you stay a couple of minutes? I didn't give you your present."

"But you threw the party and everything."

Was it his hopeful imagination that her words were a little breathier when he touched her? Touching was a rare occurrence now that the twins walked themselves up to bed and didn't need to be carried. Not his imagination. Her chest under the sleeveless summer shirt was rising and falling faster.

One wayward strand of dark red hair that she tried so hard keep in place was curled in the middle of her forehead. Most of the time she shoved it back in with the rest, but he practically had her hands pinned at her sides. This time, he followed through on a simple pleasure. He took the curl between his fingers and gently tucked it away.

Josh allowed the side of his hand to caress the soft skin of Tracey's cheek. His fingertips whispered across her lips and her eyes closed. It was time. Now. A conscious decision. No spur-of-the-moment accident.

He leaned down as he tilted her chin up. Their lips connected and his hands wrapped around her, smashing her body into his. They molded together and all the dormant parts of his soul ignited.

Four years since he'd really held a woman in his arms. The last lips he'd tasted had been a sweet goodbye. It had been a long time since he'd thought about passion.

Tracey's eyes opened when he hesitated for a split second. He didn't see fear or surprise—only passion waiting for him. He kissed her again, not allowing them time to think or reconsider.

Her lips tasted like the coconut-flavored lip balm she recently began using. But her mouth tasted of the butter-flavored icing from her birthday cake. Lips soft and rich. Her body was toned, yet pliant against him.

Yes, he analyzed it all. Every part of her. He wanted to remember just in case he never got another chance.

Intimacy hadn't been his since… Since… He couldn't allow himself to go in that direction. Tracey was in his arms. Tracey's body was responding to his caresses.

Their lips parted. He wanted to race forward, but they needed a beginning first. He'd worked it all out a hundred times in his head. This was logical. Start with a kiss, let her know he wanted more.

"Okay, that was…surprising for a birthday present."

No doubt about it, her voice was shaking with breathlessness.

"Sorry, that wasn't it. I kept the box at the office so the kids couldn't say anything. It's in the truck." He slipped his hands into his jeans pockets to stop them from pointing to one more thing. One step away from her and he wondered if she was breathless or so surprised she didn't know how to react.

"Josh?"

No.

"It'll just take a sec."

Tracey caught up with him and followed him onto the porch. "Maybe I should go home?" She smiled and rubbed his arm like a pal.

"Right." He slipped his thumbs inside his front pockets. He lifted his chin when he realized it was tucked to his chest.

"It's just… Well, you've been drinking and I don't want…" Her voice trailed off the same way it did when she was sharing something negative about the twins' behavior. She didn't want to disappoint him. Ever.

"Got it." He marched to her car and forced himself not to yank the door off the hinges.

"Don't be mad. It's not that I didn't—"

"Tracey. I got it."

And he did. All he knew about Tracey was that she'd been there for him and the kids. Assuming she felt the same when— Dammit, he didn't know anything about her life outside their small world here.

"I'm going to head out." Purse over her shoulder, she waved from the front door of her car. "Night." She waved and gently shut the door behind her.

Change is a mistake. Nah, he'd had this debate with himself for weeks. It was time to move on. He couldn't be afraid of what might or might not happen.

Tracey's tires spun a little in the gravel as she pulled away. He hoped like hell that he hadn't scared her away. From him, maybe. But she wouldn't leave the twins, right? She was the only mother they'd ever had in their lives.

For a while, he'd thought he admired her for that. But this wasn't all about the kids. He needed her to say that she felt something for him. Because four years was long enough.

He was ready to love again.

Chapter One

Nothing. Two weeks since Josh Parker had kissed her, and then avoided her like the plague. Two weeks and she'd barely seen him. Adding insult to injury, he'd even hired a teenager to watch the kids a couple of nights.

Tracey tilted the rearview mirror to get a better view of Jackson and Sage. They were too quiet. Smiling at each other in twin language. It was ice cream Friday and they'd behaved at school, so that had meant sprinkles. And they'd enjoyed every single colored speck.

The intersection was busier than usual. The car in front of her turned and Tracey finally saw the holdup. The hood was up on a small moving van at the stop sign. She was making her way around, pulling to the side, when another car parked next to the van.

"Tracey, we're hungry," Sage said.

"I know, sweetheart. I'm doing my best." She put her Mazda in Reverse trying to turn around in the street. "Can you reach your crackers, Jackson?"

"Yep, yep, yep," he answered like the dinosaur on the old DVDs he'd been watching. She watched him tug his little backpack between the car seats and snag a cracker, then share a second with Sage.

"Just one, little man. You just had ice cream."

Two men left the moving van and waved at her to back up. She was awfully close to the other van, but she trusted their directions. Right up until she felt her car hit. She hadn't been going fast enough for damage, but the guy seemed to get pretty steamed and stomped toward her door.

Great what a way to begin her weekend.

The men split to either side of her car, where one gave her the signal to roll down her window. She lowered it enough to allow him to hear her, then she unbuckled and leaned to the glove compartment for her insurance card.

"Sorry about that, but your friend—" Tracey looked up and froze.

Now in a ski mask, the man next to her window shouted, pulling on the door handle, tapping on the window with the butt of a handgun before pushing the barrel inside. "Open the door!"

She hit the horn repeatedly and put the car back into gear, willing to smash it to bits in order to get away. But it was wedged in tight. Once she'd backed up, they'd quickly used two vehicles to block her, parking in front and behind, pinning her car between the three.

Would they really shoot her to carjack an old junker of a Mazda?

"You can have the car. If you want money, it'll take a little while, but I can get that, too. You don't have to do this." She kept careful control of her voice. "Just let me unsnap the twins and take them with me."

"Get out! Now!" A second gunman shouted through the glass at the passenger door.

Where were all the cars now? Why had she lowered the window an inch to answer this man's question?

What if they didn't let her get the kids out? Her mind was racing with questions.

They shouted at her, banging on the windows. The twins knew something was wrong and began to cry. Tracey gripped the steering wheel with one hand and blared the horn with the other. Someone had to hear them. Someone would come by and see what was happening.

"Lady, you get out of the car or I'll blow you away through the window." Gunman One pointed the gun at her head.

"You don't want these kids. Their dad's the head of the Texas Rangers in this area."

With a gun stuck in her face, Tracey didn't know how she was speaking—especially with any intelligence. Her hands were locked, determined to stay where they were. That's when she had the horrible feeling it wasn't a random carjacking.

"You're wrong, sweetheart. That's exactly why we want them," Gunman Two said.

"Shut up, Mack!" Gunman One screamed, hitting the top of the car. "You!" he yelled at her again. "Stop blabbing and get your butt out here before I blow your brains all over those kids."

One of the drivers got out of his box truck with a bent pole. Not a pole. It looked like it had a climbing spike on the end.

"No!" She leaned toward the middle, attempting to block what she knew was coming.

The new guy swung, hitting the window, and it shattered into pebble-size glass rocks. The kids screamed louder. She tried to climbing into the backseat. The locks popped open and three doors flew wide.

Gunman One latched on to her ankles and yanked. Her chin bounced against the top of the seat. Jarring pain jolted across her face. Before she could grab anything or brace herself, her body tumbled out of the car. Twisted, her side and shoulder took most of the fall to the street.

She prayed someone would drive by and see what was happening. She looked everywhere for help. Wasn't there anyone who could intervene or call the police? Her small purse was still strapped across her chest, hidden at her hip. Her cell phone was still inside so maybe she could—

Gunman One flipped open a knife and sliced the strap, nicking her neck in the process. "We wouldn't want you to call Daddy too soon. You got that tape, Mack?" He jerked her to her feet, hitting the side of her head with his elbow. "You just had to play the hero."

"Here ya go, Mack." Gunman Two, already in the car, tossed him duct tape.

Gunman One smashed her face into the backseat window, winding the tape around her wrists. Both of the children were screaming her name. They knew something wasn't right. Both were trapped in their car seats, clawing at the straps then stretching their arms toward her.

"It's okay, guys. No one's going to hurt you." She tried to calm them through the glass. "Please don't do this. Jackson has diabetes. He's on a restricted diet and his insulin level has to be closely—"

Gunman One rolled her to her back and shoved her along the metal edge of the Mazda to the trunk.

Oh my God. They knew. She could tell by his reactions. She was right. It wasn't a carjacking. This was a planned kidnapping of Josh Parker's twins. Gunman One knocked her to the ground. The other men cut the seat belts holding the kids, took them from the car in their car seats, grabbing their tiny backpacks at the last minute.

How could men in ski masks be assaulting her in broad daylight and no one else see them?

"Please take me. I won't give you any trouble. I swear I won't. I... I can look after Jackson. Make sure he doesn't go into shock."

Gunman One pulled her hands. "You won't do, sister. It's gotta be somebody he loves."

"Let him have crackers. Okay? He has to eat every three or four hours. Something," she pleaded. "Sage, watch your brother!"

When this had all started, Tracey hadn't paid attention to what the man coming to her window had looked like. An average guy that she couldn't swear was young-ish or even in his thirties. They were all decked out in college gear. She searched this man's eyes that were bright and excited behind the green ski mask, memorizing everything about their brown darkness.

The tiny scar woven into his right eyebrow would be his downfall. He raised the butt of the gun in the air. She closed her eyes, anticipating the blow. The impact hurt, stunning her. Vision blurred, she watched them carry the twins, running to the back of the moving van. Her legs collapsed from the pain, and she hit the concrete without warning.

I'm so sorry, Josh.

Chapter Two

How were you supposed to tell someone you'd allowed their kids to be kidnapped? Tracey would have a doctorate in nutrition soon, but none of the courses she'd taken prepared her to face Josh. Or the future.

When someone found Tracey unconscious on the sidewalk and the paramedics revived her, she'd cried out his name. She could never articulate why she was calling to him. Once fully awake and by the time anyone would listen, the twins had been missing for almost an hour. Tracey hadn't been able to explain to Josh what had happened. The police did that.

"He's going to hate me," she mumbled.

"I don't think he will. I've dealt with a lot of kidnappings. This isn't your fault. Major Parker will realize that faster than most." Special Agent George Lanning had answered her with an intelligent response.

The problem was...

"Intelligence has nothing to do with emotional, gut-wrenching pain. I lost his kids. He'll never trust me again and I don't blame him."

After she awoke in the hospital, she'd only been allowed to talk with one police officer, her nurse and a doctor. The door had been left open a couple of inches.

She'd recognized rangers passing by, even heard them asking about her. But the officer had refused her any visitors. At least until this FBI agent showed up.

Two hours later she was sitting in a car on her way to the Parker home to face Josh for the first time. Where else was she supposed to go? She'd refused to return to her apartment as they'd suggested. "How bad is my face?"

"As in? What context do you mean?"

She flipped down the passenger mirror to see for herself. "Well, I don't think makeup—even if I had any—would help this." She gently touched her cheek-bone that felt ten times bigger than it should. "I don't want to look like…"

"Tracey. Four men yanked you from a car and hit you so hard they gave you a concussion. They kidnapped Jackson and Sage. No matter what you think you could have done differently, those men would still have the Parker twins."

She wiped another tear falling down her cheek. Agent Lanning might be correct. But nothing anyone said would ever make her feel okay about what had happened.

Nothing.

The road to the house was lined with extra cars and the yard—where they needed to park—filled with men standing around. The police escort in front of them flipped on the squad car lights with a siren burst to get people out of the way. Tracey covered her ears.

Everything hurt. Her head pounded in spite of the pain medication the doctor had given her. But she was prepared to jump out of the car as soon as it slowed down. First she needed to beg for Josh's forgiveness. And then find out what the authorities had discovered.

"You really took a wallop," he said. "You should probably get some rest as soon as possible."

She had rested at the hospital, where so much had been thrown at her. Part of the argument for her going home was to sleep and meet with a forensic artist as soon as one arrived. She'd refused, telling Agent Lanning it was useless to draw a face hidden with a ski mask. Then they'd finally agreed to take her directly to Josh.

The sea of people parted and the agent parked next to cars nearer to the front porch. She didn't wait for the engine to stop running. She jumped out, needing to explain while she still had the courage.

Moving quickly across the fading grass of the lawn, she slowed as friends stared at her running inside. She completely froze in the entryway, looking for the straight dark hair that should have towered over most of the heads in the living room. But Josh wasn't towering anywhere. She pushed forward and someone grabbed her arm. A ranger waved him off.

Everyone directly involved in Josh's life knew who she was. The ranger who had spotted her was Bryce Johnson. He put his hand at her back and pushed the crowd of men out of her way.

"You doing okay?" he asked, guiding her through probably every ranger who worked in or near Waco. "Need anything? Maybe some water?"

She nodded. There was already a knot in her throat preventing her from speaking. She'd assumed a lot of people would be here, but why so many? "Why aren't you guys out looking for the twins?"

Everyone turned their attention to a man near the window seat. But she focused on the twins' dad. Josh looked the way he did the day Gwen had died. From day one, neither of Josh or Gwen had felt like employers. They were her friends. She wanted to be there for him again, but didn't know if he'd let her. He glanced at her, and then covered his eyes as though he were afraid to look at her.

The guy in the suit near the window jerked his head to the side and they left. All of them. Except for a woman and Josh, both seated at the opposite end of the breakfast table. They were joined by Agent Lanning, who pulled out a chair and gestured for Tracey to sit.

It was a typical waiting-on-a-ransom-demand scene from a movie. The three professionals looked the parts of FBI agents. The woman sat at something electronic that looked as if it monitored phone calls. Agent Lanning moved to the back door and turned politely to face the window. The other man, who they both seemed to defer to, uncrossed his arms and tapped Josh on the shoulder.

Josh's head was bent, almost protected between his arms resting on the table. He hadn't acknowledged the fact that nearly everyone had left. He hadn't acknowledged anything.

"I don't know what to say. I'm sorry doesn't seem like enough," she began.

Josh's head jerked up along with the rest of him as he stood, tipping the chair backward to the floor. She winced at the noise. She assumed he'd be disappointed and furious and might even scream at her to get out. But feeling it, seeing it, experiencing the paralyzing fear that they might not get the kids back…

"This might sound stupid, but we need to verify that Jackson was wearing his insulin pump," he whispered without a note of anger.

"Yes. I checked it when I picked him up."

"Thank God. I knew you would. You always do."

The woman opened her mouth but the agent at the window raised a finger. She immediately smashed her lips together instead. Josh covered his face with his hands again. What had she expected? That he'd be— *oh, everything's going to be okay, Tracey. Don't worry about it Tracey. We'll find them together, Tracey.*

"Has anyone seen anything? Said anything?" she asked no one in particular.

"Let's step into the bedroom, Miss Cassidy." The agent by the window took a step toward her.

"She stays," Josh ordered, holding up a hand to halt him. "I want to hear everything firsthand. Same for anything you have to say to me. She can hear it, so she stays."

"All right. I'm Special Agent in Charge Leo McCaffrey and this is Agent Kendall Barlow. No, the kidnappers haven't called. There's been no ransom demand." He pointed to the woman at the table and crossed his arms. "Have you remembered anything else that might help?"

"Not really. A van was broken down. Two men came to my car to help me back up. It seems like one purposely let me reverse into the rental van. Then one came to the passenger window and tapped. I thought they needed my insurance or license or something. They looked like college students until they pulled the masks over their faces. I have to admit that I didn't pay any attention to their faces when they were uncovered." Tracey latched her fingers around the edge of the kitchen chair, hoping she wouldn't fall off as the world spun a little on its side.

"You didn't think that was unusual?" the woman asked.

"Not really. Students walk a lot around here. That part of Waco isn't far from downtown."

It was weird what she noticed about Agent McCaffrey. Average height, but nice looking. His short hair had a dent around the middle like Josh's did when he wore his Stetson. Or after an afternoon with his ball cap on. She glanced at his feet. Sure enough, he wore a pair of nice dress boots. And then she remembered the men abducting her had worn work boots.

"Wait. The men who got out of the moving truck. They both wore an older Baylor shirt from about five years ago. And they all wore the same type of work boots. I could almost swear that they were new and the same brand. The man who…who pulled me from the car…" Everyone looked at her, waiting. "He had dark brown eyes and thick eyebrows. Not thick enough to hide a scar across the right one."

"That's good, Miss Cassidy. Anytime something comes to you, just make sure to tell Agent Lanning. Anything special about the others?"

"I wasn't close to the other two. It all happened so fast that I didn't know what to do." She choked on the last word. She hadn't known. Still didn't.

"When you were questioned at the hospital, you had a hard time remembering the small details, but they'll probably come back." The woman spoke again, pushing a pad toward the center of the table. "You should keep a notebook handy."

"I…uh…couldn't get to the hospital," Josh said loudly. He swallowed hard and shook his head, looking a little lost.

Tracey had never seen that look on his face before. "I didn't expect you to."

"It's just... I haven't been there since Gwen..." Josh looked at her asking her to understand without making him say the words. "I guess I had to have been there once with Jackson." He pushed his hand through his short hair. "But I can't remember when for some reason."

"I know. It's okay," she whispered, wanting to reach out and grab his hand. "You needed to be here."

Major Parker was her employer, but she couldn't stand it. Someone needed to help him. To be on his side like no other person would be. This time she shoved back from the table and her chair was the one that hit the floor. She pushed past Agent McCaffrey and covered Josh with her arms. He buried his face against her, wrapping his arms around her waist as if she were the only thing keeping him from falling off a cliff.

Until two weeks ago, they hadn't hugged since Gwen had died. Had rarely touched each other except for an accidental brush when handing the kids to each other. Then there'd been that kiss.

An unexpected kiss after an impromptu surprise birthday party with several of his friends. A kiss that had thrown her into so many loop-de-loops, she'd been dizzy for days. But it must have thrown Josh for a loop he didn't want. He hadn't spoken to her except in passing. Which was the reason she'd accepted the out-of-state position.

She held him, feeling the rapid beating of his heart through the hospital scrubs they'd given her. They had so much to face and right now he needed to be comforted as much as she did.

Someone at the hospital had said she was just the nanny. She didn't feel like *just* the hired help. She'd avoided that particular title and thought it demeaning when Josh's friends referred to her that way. Months when the rent was hard to come by, her friends asked her why she didn't move in to take care of the twins.

At first it had been because she thought it was a temporary job. Eventually Josh would hire a real nanny. Then she'd been certain Josh would eventually date and remarry, so she hadn't wanted to complicate the situation. And this past year it had been because she was falling in love with him.

Now the word *nanny* didn't seem complex enough for their situation. She'd been a part of the twins' lives from infancy. She'd been told to go home and stay there with a protection detail so she could be easily reached if needed. She was *just* the nanny.

Just the person who provided day care—and any other time of the day care when Josh was on a case. But his lost look was the reason she hadn't obeyed the order.

Technically, Tracey knew she *was* just the nanny. Yet, her heart had been ripped from her body—twice. Once for each child.

She held Josh tight until Agent McCaffrey cleared his throat. She sat in the chair next to Josh. Bryce brought the bottle of water he'd offered when she first arrived and dropped back to the living room doorway.

"Is this a vendetta or revenge for one of the men you've put away?" Tracey asked Josh, who finally looked her in the eyes. "I tried to convince them to take me instead. They said it needed to be someone you loved."

Chapter Three

Someone you loved...

Did she know? Josh searched her face, seeing nothing but concern for his kids. It was on the tip of his tongue to tell her they would have gotten it right if she'd been taken.

That sounds ridiculous.

He didn't want her abducted any more than he wanted the twins to be gone. He reached out, touching her swollen cheek.

"They hurt you." Stupid statement. It was obvious, but he didn't know what else to say. "Of course they did. They took you to the hospital."

He noticed what she was wearing, the streak of blood still on her neck, the bandage at her hairline. Hospital scrubs because her clothes had been ruined.

Time to shed the shaking figure of a lost father. Tenoreno had hit his family—the only place he considered himself vulnerable. But he was stronger than this. He needed to show everyone—including himself. Gathering some courage, he straightened his backbone and placed both palms flat on the table to keep himself there.

He knew what McCaffrey was thinking. The agent

had repeated his questions about Tracey's possible motives more than once. Agent Kendall Barlow had been ordered to run a thorough background check on "the nanny." If Tracey heard them call her that she'd let them know she was a child care provider and personal nutritionist.

Definitely not the nanny.

The FBI might have doubts about Tracey—he didn't. First and foremost, she had no motive. They might need to rule her out as a suspect. No one in the room had mentioned Tenoreno by name. But Josh knew who was responsible.

Drawing air deep into his lungs, he readied himself to get started. Ready to fight Tenoreno or whoever he'd hired to take his kids.

"The agents need to know how long Jackson's insulin will be okay. Can you give them more details?" All the extra chatter around him died. He took Tracey's hand in his. "I took a guess, but you know a lot more about it than I do. These guys need an accurate estimate. I couldn't think straight earlier."

"It depends." She drew in a deep breath and blew it out, puffing her cheeks. "There are stress factors I can't estimate. A lot will be determined by what they give the twins to eat, of course. The cartridge can last three days, but he might be in trouble for numerous reasons. They could give him the wrong food or the tube might get clogged. The battery should be fine."

"Hear that everybody? My son has forty-eight hours that we can count on. Seventy-two before he slips into a diabetic coma. Why are you still here?" He used his I'm-the-ranger-in-charge voice.

It worked. All the rangers, cops and friends left the house.

"I'm more worried that Sage might try to imitate what I do with the bolus when he eats. She knows not to touch it. But she also knows that when Jackson eats, I calculate how much extra insulin to give him. She's a little mother hen and might try since I'm not there."

"What's a bolus?" George Lanning asked.

"An extra shot of insulin from his pump. You calculate, it injects." The female agent shrugged. "I read and prepare for my cases."

Josh hated diabetes.

Bryce stayed by the kitchen door. He'd driven Josh and wouldn't leave until he had confirmation of orders that the two of them had already discussed. Unofficial orders when no one had been listening. Ranger headquarters had someone on the way to relieve him as Company F commander. Whoever was now in charge would make certain every rule was followed to the letter and that personnel kept their actions impeccable.

"Everyone is working off the assumption that the Tenoreno family is behind this. Right?" he asked McCaffrey, finally stating what everyone thought.

The FBI agents' reactions were about what he expected. No one would confirm. They zipped their lips tight and avoided eye contact. But their actions were all the confirmation he needed.

The Mafia family connection was the reason the FBI had been called as soon as Josh had received the news. He'd rather have his Company in charge, but the conflict of interest was too great.

Bryce stood in the doorway and shook his head, warning him not to push the issue. They'd talked through the short list of pros and cons about confronting anyone called in to handle the kidnapping.

The more they forced the issue, the less likely the FBI would be inclined to share information. It could all blow up in his face. But it was like a big bright red button with a flashing neon sign that said Do Not Push.

The longer the agents avoided answering, the brighter the button blinked, tempting him to hit it.

"The Tenoreno family?"

Tracey was the only one left who didn't know who they were. She needed to know what faced them because she was certain to be used by the Mafia-like family. No one wanted to explain so it was up to him to bring her up to speed.

Two hours and thirty-eight minutes after Tracey was found unconscious on a sidewalk, his phone rang. Brooks & Dunn's "Put a Girl in It" blasted through the kitchen.

"That's my ringtone for Tracey. They're using her phone. It's the kidnappers."

EVERYONE STARED AT the phone. Only one person moved. Agent Barlow pulled a headset onto her ears, clicked or pushed buttons, then pointed to Agent McCaffrey. It really was like being a part of a scripted movie. Tracey could only watch.

"You know what to do, Josh. Try to keep them on the line as long as possible," Agent McCaffrey said.

Tracey cupped her hands over her mouth to stop the words she wanted to scream. They would only antagonize the kidnappers and would probably get her dragged from the room. She needed to hear what those masked men were about to say.

Agent Barlow clicked on Josh's cell.

"This is Parker." Josh's fingers curled into fists.

"You won't hear from us again as long as you're working with the FBI." The line went dead.

"No. Wait!" Josh hammered his hand against the wood tabletop. But his face told her he knew it was no use.

"What just happened? Shouldn't they let us know how to get in touch with them?" Tracey looked around the room, wanting answers. What did this mean? "You do have a plan, right?"

Agent McCaffrey clasped Josh's shoulder, then patted it—while staring into Tracey's eyes. "That's what we expected."

Everyone's stare turned to Agent Barlow, who shook her head. "Nothing. We've been monitoring for Miss Cassidy's phone, they fired it up, made the call and probably pulled the battery again."

"So we're back to square one." Agent Lanning tapped on the window, silently bringing attention to the suits monitoring the outside of the house.

"We have instructions." Josh stared at the only other ranger left in the house—Bryce.

Tracey was confused. It was as if they were speaking in some sort of code. Or maybe they were stating something obvious and the concussion was keeping her from recognizing it. The others shook their heads.

"You don't want to do that, Josh." Agent McCaffrey kept his cool. He clearly didn't want whatever Josh had just silently communicated to Bryce. "This case is going to be difficult—"

"It's not a case. They're my kids." Josh hit his chest with his fist. "Mine."

"You need our resources." Barlow dropped the head-phones on the table.

"I *need* you to leave. I've told you that from the beginning." Josh stood. Calmly this time, without tipping the chair to the floor. "I've played along for the past couple of hours hoping it's not what we thought, but it is. These guys aren't going to play games. They either get what they want or they kill—"

"You can't do this," Barlow said.

The agent seemed a little dramatic, but what did Tracey know?

"Yes, I can. It's my right to refuse your help." Josh gestured for Tracey to lead the way to the back staircase.

"Look…" Agent McCaffrey lowered his voice. "We'll admit that the kidnapping involves Tenoreno. We assume these men are going to ask you to do something illegal. You're better off if we stay."

"I haven't done anything illegal. You need to go." Josh took the Texas Ranger Star he was so proud of and dropped it in the agent's open palm. "Bryce. You know what to do."

Josh caught Tracey under her elbow and led her up the staircase. They went to the kids' bedroom, where he shut the door.

"What is Bryce going to do?"

"First thing is to get my badge back. I shouldn't have given it to McCaffrey. But the agent wanted it for show in case the kidnappers are watching. I'll surrender it to the new Company commander if they ask me to resign, not before. Then he'll get everyone out of the house. Before the FBI arrived, we assumed we knew who was behind the kidnapping. There's really no other motive. It's not like I have a ton of money to pay a ransom."

Tracey winced, but Josh was looking out the window and couldn't have seen. The twins' kidnapping didn't have anything to do with her. The man said it has to be someone he loves. *He meant someone Josh loves. Right?*

"What if…" She hesitated to ask, to broach the subject that this entire incident might be her fault. She cleared her throat. "What are you going to do without the FBI's help?"

"Get things done. Bryce has already arranged for friends in the Waco PD to watch the agents who will be watching us." He quirked a brow at his cleverness, sitting on the footstool between the twin beds.

His wife's parents had chosen that stool to match a rocker Gwen had never gotten to hold her children in. She'd been too weak. It's where Josh refused to sit. The stool was as close as he'd get. The chair was where Tracey had rocked the babies to sleep.

"Have you told Gwen's parents?"

"There's nothing they could do. McCaffrey thinks it's better to wait."

"The FBI will be following us when we leave the house." He stood again, wiping his palms on his jeans. "They'll wait for me to issue an order to my men. I'd be breaking the law since I've been asked to step away from my command. Then they'll swoop back in like vultures and take control of things."

"Will you?"

"What? Leave? Don't worry." He straightened books on the shelf. "When I do, I'll make sure someone's here with you. Bryce will be close. I won't leave you alone."

"No. That's not what I'm talking about. Will you break the law?"

He gawked at her with a blank look of incredulousness. Either surprised that she'd asked, insulting his ranger integrity. Or surprised that she questioned…

"What are you willing to do to save Jackson and Sage?" She tried not to move the rocker. She was serious and needed to know how far he'd go. "For the record, I'm willing to do anything. And I mean anything, including breaking the law."

Did he look a little insulted as he bent and picked up Jackson's pj's from the floor? Well, she didn't care. It was something she needed to hear him say out loud.

"Don't look so surprised. I've heard about the integrity of the Texas Rangers since the first day I met you. How could I not after listening to the countless kitchen table conversations on the subject? Not to mention this past year when three of your company men might have been straddling the integrity fence, but managed to come out squeaky clean heroes."

"You act like having integrity is a bad thing." He clutched the pajamas and moved to the window instead of placing them back in the dresser.

"Not at all." She stood and joined him, wishing she could blink and make this all go away.

All she could do was wrap her palms around his upper arm, offering the comfort of a friend. Even though they'd been raising his children together for four years, she couldn't make the decisions he'd soon be faced with.

"Are you going to tell me about the Tenoreno family? At least more than what I've heard about them in the news? Are you in charge of the case?"

Josh didn't shrug her away. They stood shoulder to shoulder at the pastel curtains sprinkled with baby farm animals. He stared at something in the far distance past the lake. Tracey just stared at him.

"In charge of the case? No. Company F has prepared Paul Tenoreno's transportation route from Huntsville to Austin. I finalized the details this morning. Now that this…the kidnapping, your injuries…" He paused and took a couple of shallow breaths. "Tenoreno's transport to trial has to be what this is all about. Thing is, state authorities are sure to change everything. It's why they brought the FBI onto the case so quickly."

"Is Tenoreno mixed up in the Mafia like the news insinuates?"

"Tenoreno *is* the Mafia in Texas."

A chill scurried up her spine. The words seemed final somehow. As if Josh had accepted something was about to happen and there was no going back. He hadn't answered her question about how far he'd go. But he wouldn't let the Mafia take his kids. He just wouldn't.

"You need to make me a promise, Tracey."

"Anything."

He removed her hands and crossed his arms over his chest, tilting his head to stare at the top of hers because he was frightened to meet her hazel eyes. Frightened of the desperation she might see in his face.

"Hear me out before you give me what for. I made you the guardian of the twins last year."

"Without asking me?"

"Yeah. I was afraid you'd say no." Josh shrugged and lifted the corner of his mouth in a little smile.

It was Tracey's turn to look incredulous. "Seriously?

When have I ever told you that I wouldn't do something for those kids?"

He nodded, agreeing. "I need you to promise that no matter what happens to me…"

"I promise, but nothing's going to happen to you."

Of course, she didn't know that. This afternoon when she'd headed to the day care to pick up the twins, she wouldn't have believed anything could have happened to any of them. It has been an ordinary day. She'd finally made up her mind to talk with Josh about finding a permanent nanny to take her place.

"You asked what I was willing to do. They're my kids, Tracey. I'll do anything for them, including prison time." Josh still had the pj's wrapped in his hand. "Believe me, that's not my intention, but you have to know it's a possibility."

Was he aware that she was willing to join him? She meant what she'd said about doing anything for Jackson and Sage. And if that meant *she* was the one who went to jail—so be it. And if it came down to it, she'd do anything to keep them with their father.

"Just tell me what to do, Josh."

"Nothing. If Tenoreno's people contact you, tell me. You can't be involved in this. It has to be me." He gripped her shoulders and then framed her cheeks. One of his thumbs skated across the bruised area and settled at her temple. "You got that? *I'm* the one who's going to rescue my kids and pay the consequences."

She believed him. She had to. But she couldn't promise to stay out of his way. She might have the answer. What if money could solve their problem? Even if it wouldn't, now wasn't the time to tell him she'd never let him be separated from the twins.

Chapter Four

Josh pulled Tracey to his chest, wrapping his arms around her, keeping someone he cared about safe. He stared at the green pajamas decorated with pictures of yellow trucks—dump trucks, earthmovers, cranes and he didn't know what else. He used to know.

How long had it been since he'd played in the sandbox with the kids? Since he'd been there for dinner and their bath time?

Mixed feelings fired through his brain. He couldn't start down the regret road. He needed to concentrate on the twins' safety. The overpowering urge to protect Tracey wasn't just because she was an unofficial member of the family.

Tenoreno had hired someone to assault her and steal his children. Her cuts and bruises—dammit, he should have been there to protect her. To protect all of them.

"There has to be something we can do to make this go faster." She pressed her face against his chest and cried.

It was the first time to cry since she'd entered the house today. He fought the urge to join her, but once a day was his limit. If he broke down again, he wouldn't be able to function. Or act like the guy who might know what he was doing.

A knock at the door broke them apart. Tracey went to the corner table and pulled a couple of Kleenex from the box.

"Yeah?" It could only be one of two people on the other side. Bryce or Agent McCaffrey.

"You fill her in yet?" McCaffrey stepped inside, closing the door behind him.

Tracey looked up after politely blowing her nose; a questioning look crinkled her forehead.

"We were just getting there."

"Here's the phone you can use to contact us. We won't be far away."

"But far enough no one's going to notice." Josh took the phone and slid it into his back pocket.

"Anyone following you will see the obvious cars. They'll lose you after a couple of miles, but George and I will be there."

"Josh?" Tracey said his name with all the confusion she should be experiencing. After all, he'd just demanded the FBI and police leave him alone, get out of his house and off the case.

"It's okay, Tracey. All part of the plan. We need the kidnappers to think I'm in this on my own. No help from anyone. Hopefully that'll limit what they ask me to do."

When he left the house he'd have a line of cars following and hoped it didn't look like a convoy. A bad feeling smothered any comfort he had that law enforcement would be close by.

"So everything you just said—"

"Was the truth. Every word." He shot her a look asking her to keep that info to herself.

He knew that stubborn look, the compressed lips, the

crossed arms. It would soon be followed by a long exhale after holding her breath. Sometimes he wanted to squeeze the air from her lungs because she held on to it so long. Each time he knew she wasn't just controlling her breathing. She was also controlling her tongue because she disagreed with what he was saying or doing.

Mainly about the kids.

Lately, it had been about how often he worked late or how he had avoided necessary conversations. Like the one congratulating her on finishing her thesis. Yeah, he'd avoided that because it would open the door to her resignation. What they needed to talk about was serious. She'd most likely accepted a position somewhere—other than Waco. If he could, he'd also like to avoid a conversation about what happened two weeks ago when they'd kissed.

This time, he could see that she didn't believe the lines he was spouting to the FBI. He just hoped that Special Agent McCaffrey couldn't read her like a book, too. Then he might suspect Josh had his own agenda.

"I don't think they'll wait very long to make contact after I leave." The agent unbuttoned his jacket and stuck his hands in his pockets. "My belief is that they knew about Jackson's diabetes and believe it will scare you into following their orders faster. If they didn't, they've seen the pump by now and are scared something might happen to him. Either way, I don't think they're really out to hurt the kids."

Agent McCaffrey stood straight—without emotion—in his official suit and tie. Just how official—they'd find out if he kept their deal to let Josh work the case from the inside.

"But you can't be sure of that," Tracey said. "How can anyone predict what will happen."

Tracey was right about part of Josh's inner core. He was a Texas Ranger through and through. He'd try it the legal way. But if that didn't work, they'd see a part of him he rarely drew upon.

"George said you held up at the hospital exceptionally well, Miss Cassidy."

McCaffrey had a complimentary approach, where George looked like a laid-back lanky cowboy leaning on a fence post. Josh had met George several times on cases. He trusted him. George had given his word that McCaffrey would be on board. But Tracey didn't know any of that history. She had no reason to trust any of them.

"Don't I get a phone for you to keep track of my location?" Tracey asked.

"Actually, yes." McCaffrey handed her an identical cheap phone to what they'd given him. "By accepting this, you're allowing us to monitor it."

The man just didn't have the most winning personality. Josh saw the indignation building within Tracey and couldn't stop her.

"Were you really going to wait for my permission? That seems rather silly to ask. Just do it." Her words seemed more like a dare. She was ready to go toe to toe with someone.

"Tracey. That's not the way things are." Standing up for the FBI wasn't his best choice at this precise moment. Tracey looked like she needed to vent.

"Have you ruled me out as a suspect?" she asked.

Why was she holding her breath this time? Did she

have something to hide? Josh opened his mouth to reason with her, but McCaffrey waved him off.

"I have a lot of experience with kidnappings, Tracey. I imagine you're familiar with the statistics that most children are abducted by someone in their immediate family or life. My people ran our standard background check on you first thing. We would have been reckless not to." He leaned against the doorjamb not seeming rushed for time or bothered by her hostility. "A reference phone call cleared you."

Tracey stiffened. She drew her arms close across her chest, hugging herself, rubbing her biceps like she was cold. Her hand slipped higher, one finger covering her lips, then her eyes darted toward the window. She was hiding something and McCaffrey had just threatened to expose whatever it was.

"Tracey, what's going on?"

"We're good, Josh." The agent looked at Tracey.

She nodded her head. "I don't know why I said anything. I was never going to keep you from tracking this phone." Tracey sank to the footstool. "I already told you I'd cooperate and do anything for Jackson and Sage."

The special agent in charge crossed the room and patted Tracey's shoulder. He'd done the same thing to Josh earlier, but it didn't seem to ease Tracey. There was nothing insincere in his gesture. But it seemed a more calculated action, as though McCaffrey knew it was effective. Not because it was real comfort.

Josh wanted to throw the agent out of his kids' room and be done with the FBI. "Do you need anything else?" he asked instead.

"I can't help you if you keep me out of the loop,

Josh." McCaffrey quirked an eyebrow at Josh's lack of a reaction. "You've got to work with my people to get the children back. We stick with the plan."

"That's all nice and reasonable, but we both know that there's nothing logical about a kidnapping. You can never predict what's going to happen."

"The quicker you pick up that phone and let us know what they want the better."

"The quicker you clear out of here, the faster they'll contact us." Josh's hands were tied. He had to work with the FBI, use their resources, find the kidnappers. Or at least act like he was being cooperative. He sighed in relief when the agent left and softly closed the door behind him.

What the hell was wrong with him?

His twins had been kidnapped. It was natural to want to bash some heads together. But for a split second there, he'd wanted to just do whatever Tenoreno's men wanted and hold his kids again.

Tracey was visibly shaken by whatever McCaffrey's team had uncovered. His background check five years ago when he'd hired her hadn't uncovered it. And in the time that she'd been around his family, she'd never shared it. He had his own five years of character reference. No one else's mattered.

"I don't know what that was about." He jerked his thumb toward the closed door. *Should he ask?* "Right now I don't care."

"I swear I was never… It's just something I keep private. But I can fill you in. I mean, unless it's going to distract you. This shouldn't be about me."

"Will it make a difference to what's going to happen?" Sure, he was curious, but what if she was right and it did distract him? The FBI didn't think it was relevant. He could wait until his family was back where they belonged. "You know, we have more important things to worry about, so save it."

"Okay." Tracey sat straight, ready to get started. "So how is this going to work? Do you think the kidnappers will use my phone to call yours again? Wait!" She popped to her feet. "We don't have your phone. It's downstairs."

Josh blocked her with an outstretched arm. "If it rings, Bryce will let us know. He'll come up here before he leaves and that won't be until everyone else is out of the house."

They stared a second or two at each other. He wanted to know what she was hiding from him. She bit her lip, held her breath, and then couldn't look him in the eyes.

"Tracey, we have to trust each other. If you don't want to go through with this…"

"Of course I want to help. It's my fault they're missing. I don't know how you're being kind to me at all or even staying alone in the same room. I'm not sure I could do it."

"I don't blame you for what's happened. How can I?" He kept a hand on her shoulder. She didn't fight to get away. "I'm beating myself up that I didn't put a security detail on all of you. If anyone's to blame, it's me. Tenoreno has come after three of my men and their families. Why did I think you or the kids weren't vulnerable?"

"We have to stop blaming ourselves," she said softly. "If you have a plan, now might be the time to share it with me."

"It's not so much a plan as backup. What I said before McCaffrey came in, I meant it. But if I can keep the FBI on my side…we're all better off."

A gentle knock stopped the conversation again. "They've cleared out, Major. I've secured all the windows and doors. Here's your phone." Ranger Johnson said through the door.

Josh turned the knob and stuck out his hand. "Thanks, Bryce. You guys know what to do. My temporary replacement's going to have a tough time. The other men are going to resent that he's there. They're also going to want to help with the kidnapping. You've got to make the men understand that none of you can get involved and that those orders come from me."

"Good luck. And sir—" Bryce shook his hand, clasping his left on top of it "—let's make sure it's just a temporary replacement. You know we're all here when you need us."

"We appreciate that."

"I think this is one time that One Riot, One Ranger shouldn't apply. I'll take care of things." Bryce walked downstairs.

Tracey gently pushed past Josh, nudging herself into the hall. "I can't stay in their room any longer. And I really think I need a drink."

Josh followed her. "But you don't drink. And probably shouldn't, with a concussion."

"Don't you have some Wild Turkey or Jim Beam? Something's on top of the refrigerator, right? It's the perfect time to start."

"Yeah, but you might not want to start with that." How did she know where he kept his only bottle of whiskey?

"Actually, Josh, I went to college. Just because you've

never seen me drink doesn't mean it's never happened. A shot of whiskey isn't going to impair my judgment."

She was in the kitchen, pulling a chair over to reach the high cabinet before he could think twice about helping or stopping. He sort of stared while she pulled two highball glasses reserved for poker night that had been collecting dust awhile. A finger's width—his, not her tiny fingers—was in the glass and she frowned before sliding it toward him across the breakfast bar.

"Drink up. You need it worse than I do."

He stared at it. And at her.

She suddenly didn't look like a college student. He noticed the little laugh lines at the corner of her eyes and how deep a green they were. It took him all this time to realize she was wearing a Waco Fire Department T-shirt under the baggy scrub top. Something he'd never seen her wear before.

She threw the whiskey back and poured herself another. "Am I drinking alone?"

He swirled the liquid, took a whiff. That was enough for him. Clearheaded. Ready to get on the road. That's what he needed more than the sting and momentary warmth the shot would provide.

Tracey threw the second shot back, closing her eyes and letting the glass tip on its side. Her eyes popped open as if she'd been startled. Then they dropped to the phone that was resting next to his hand, vibrating.

Her hand covered the cell.

His hand covered hers.

"Wait. Three rings. It'll allow the FBI time to get their game face on."

Ring three he uncovered her hand and slid through the password, then pushed Speaker.

"Time for round one, Ranger Parker. You get a new phone from a store in Richland Mall. We'll contact you there in half an hour. Bring the woman."

The line disconnected.

"Do they really think that no one is listening to those instructions he just gave us?" Tracey asked.

"We follow everything he says. He'll try to get us clear of everyone. We get the phone, but the next time he makes contact—before we do anything else—we get proof of life." Josh dropped the phone in his shirt pocket realizing that the kidnappers had just made Tracey a vital part of their plan. "I hoped they'd leave you out of this. We just need to know both kids are okay before I argue to take you out of the equation."

"Of course." She hurried around the end of the breakfast bar, grabbing the counter as she passed.

"You look a little wobbly. You up for this?"

"You probably should have stopped me from drinking alcohol when I have a head injury and they gave me pain meds." Tracey touched her swollen cheek and the side of her head, then winced.

Josh held up a finger, delaying their departure. He walked around her and pulled an ice pack from the freezer, tossing her an emergency compress. "This should help a little." Then he pulled insulin cartridges from the fridge, stuffing them inside Jackson's travel and emergency supplies bag.

Instead of her cheekbone, Tracey dropped the cold compress on her forehead and slid it over her eyes. "You're right." She took off to the front door. "You should definitely drive."

Proof of life. That's what they needed. He looked around his home. Different from the madhouse an hour ago. Different because the housekeeper had come by this morning. Different because Gwen was no longer a part of it.

Different because Tracey was.

Chapter Five

Josh wandered through Richland Mall with the fingers of one hand interlocked with Tracey's. With the other he held the new phone securely in its sack. No one had the number so the kidnappers couldn't use it for a conversation. He expected someone to bump into him. Or drop a note. Maybe catch their line of sight, giving them an envelope.

"Hell, I don't know what they plan on doing. The dang thing isn't even charged."

"You've said that a couple of times now," Tracey acknowledged. "My head is absolutely killing me and I'm starting to see two of everything. Can we get a bottle of water?"

"Sure."

He kept his eyes open and wouldn't let go of Tracey as he paid for the water at a candy store. She looked like a hospital volunteer in the navy blue scrub top.

"Josh, you are making my hand hurt as much as my head." She tugged a little at his thumb.

"Sorry. I just can't—"

"I know. You're afraid they'll grab me. I get it. But my hand needs circulation. Come on. Let's park it on that bench."

He looked in every direction for something suspicious or a charging station for the phone. Whatever or whoever was coming for them could be any of the people resting on another bench or walking by.

"Here, I'm done. Drink the rest." She capped the bottle and tried to hand it to him.

"No thanks."

"If I drink it, I'll have to leave your side for a few and head into the restroom all alone. I know you don't want that."

"Then throw it away. No one's telling you to drink it." He watched the young man with the baby stroller until he moved in the opposite direction.

"Lighten up, Mack," a voice said directly behind them. "Don't turn around."

Tracey stiffened next to him, the bottle of water hitting the floor. A clear indication that she recognized the voice. The guy behind him tapped on Josh's shoulder with a phone.

"Pass me the one you just bought."

Josh forced himself not to look at the man. No mirrored surfaces were nearby. The guy even covered the phone before it got close enough to see his face in the black reflection of the screen.

"That's good, Major. You're doing good. Now, I know you're concerned about your kids. You can see them when you play the video in about twenty seconds. Just let me get through this service hallway. Yeah, you've got a choice—let me go or follow and lose any chance of ever seeing your brats." The kidnapper tapped the top of Josh's head. "Count to twenty. Talk to ya soon."

Josh had his hands ready to push up from the bench and tackle the guy to the ground.

"No." Tracey pulled him back to the bench. "You heard him. He means it. We have to stay here and let him walk away. You promised to do whatever it took. Remember? So please just turn the phone on and get their instructions."

He listened to Tracey and stayed put. The phone had been handed to them with gloves. Most likely no prints, so he turned it on. He clicked through the menu, finding the gallery.

There were several pictures of the twins playing in a room—sort of like a day care crowded with toys. The video shattered his already-broken heart. Sage was crying. Jackson was "vroom vrooming" a car across his leg and through the air.

A voice off camera—the same as behind them—told them to say hi to their daddy.

"I want to go home." Sage threw a plush toy toward the person holding the phone. "Is Trace Trace picking us up?"

Tracey covered her mouth, holding her breath again.

"Can you remember what you're supposed to say? You can go home after you tell your daddy," the kidnapper lied.

The twins nodded their heads, tucking their chins to their chests and sticking out their bottom lips. They might be fraternal, but they did almost everything together.

"Daddy, Mack says to go to… I don't remember." Jackson turned to his sister, scratching his head with the truck. "Do you remember?"

"Why can't you tell him?" Sage pouted.

"Come on, it has a giant bull." Another voice piped in.

"We've been there, Jacks. It's got that big bridge, 'member?" Sage poked him.

"Can you come there and pick us up, Daddy?" Jackson cried.

"Maybe Trace Trace can?" Sage's tears ran full stream down her cheeks.

"You have twenty minutes to be waiting in the middle of the bridge. Both of you. No cops," a voice said on top of the twins cries.

The video ended. All Josh wanted was to rush to the Chisholm Trail Bridge and pick them up. But they wouldn't be there. Instructions would be there. The guy who'd dropped the phone off would be watching them to make certain they weren't followed.

"Let's go." He wrapped his hand around Tracey's. It killed him to hear his kids like that.

"Are they going to keep us running from one spot to another? What's the point of that? And why have us buy a new phone only to replace it with this one?"

While they were leaving the mall in a hurry would be the ideal time for a kidnapper to try to grab one or both of them. He locked their fingers and tugged Tracey closer to his side.

"Before we get to the car…" He lowered his voice and stopped them behind a pillar at the candy store. He leaned in close to her ear, not wanting to be overheard. "We need to look closely where he touched us. He might have planted a microphone."

He dipped his head and turned around to let Tracey check. She smoothed the cloth of his shirt across his shoulders.

"I don't see anything, Josh." She shook her head and turned for him to do the same.

He pushed his fingers through his short hair. Found nothing. Then ran them through Tracey's short wavy strands and over her tense shoulders.

"If I were them, I'd use this time to plant a listening device. I'd want to know if we were really cooperating or playing along with the Feds."

"Who *are you* playing along with?" She looked and sounded exasperated.

"I'm on team Jackson and Sage. Whoever I have to play along with to get them back home. That's the only thing that's important to me."

"All right. So you think they're planting something in the car?"

"Got to be. Or this phone is already rigged for them to listen. Stand at the back of this store and keep an eye out while I call McCaffrey on his phone." Josh took a last look around the open mall area to see if they were in sight of security cameras or if anyone watched them from the sidelines.

Tracey smothered the kidnapper's phone with the bottom of her shirt. "I hope you know what you're doing."

"So do I." He waited for her to get ten feet away from him then took the FBI-issued phone and dialed the only number logged.

As soon as he was connected he blurted, "They have a new phone listed in my name. Bought it prepaid at a kiosk. No idea what the number is. Handed us another and told us to head to the Brazos Suspension Bridge."

"You can cross that on foot. Right?" McCaffrey was

asking someone on his staff. "You know they'll be waiting on the other side."

Tracey kept watch, walking back and forth along the wall. She'd look out the storefront window, then make the horseshoe along the outside walls again to look out the other side.

Josh kept his head and his voice down. "I can't contact you on this again. It'll be in the car."

"We'll have men on the north side of the bridge waiting," McCaffrey stated. "Trust me, Josh."

"For as long as possible." He pocketed the phone, waved to Tracey.

"Josh, the kidnapper called you Mack. I remember that they all called each other Mack."

"It kept them from using their real names. Helped hide their identities." He didn't speak his next thought—hoping that they kept their masks on in front of his kids.

They both walked quickly from the mall toward the car.

"We just used five of our twenty minutes. Aren't you going to call Bryce and let him know where we're headed?"

"No need. If the Rangers are doing their job, they'll already know."

Josh pointed to a moving van that matched the description Tracey had regarding the vehicle blocking the intersection. If law enforcement spotted it, they'd be instructed to watch and not detain.

The truck pulled away from the end of the aisle as soon as they reached the car. He was tempted to use the phone, but he'd just proved to himself that they were being watched. He couldn't risk it.

Josh didn't wait around to spot any other vehicles

keeping an eye on them. He didn't care if any of them kept up. "Flip down the visor, Tracey." He turned on the flashing lights and let traffic get out of his way. "We're not going to be late."

Tracey braced herself with a foot on the dashboard. "I'm rich. That's my secret."

He slowed for an intersection and looked at her while checking for vehicles. She cleared her throat, waiting. Josh drove. If that was all the FBI could dig up on her, how could that be leverage?

The flashing lights on his car made it easy to get to the bridge and park. He left them on when they got out. Tracey reached under the seat and retrieved a second Jackson emergency kit. He snagged the one he'd brought from the house.

Armed with only a phone and his son's emergency kit, they walked quickly across the bridge to wait in the middle of the river.

"Not many people here on a Friday night." Tracey walked to the steel beams and looked through. "I hope they don't make us jump."

"That could be a possibility." One that he hadn't considered.

"I don't swim well. So just push me over the edge."

"You don't have to go." Josh stayed in the middle, his senses heightened from the awareness of how vulnerable they were in this spot. "How's your head?"

"Spinning. You grabbed extra insulin cartridges and needles. That's what I saw, right? I think I should take a couple, too."

It made sense. He opened the kit. She reached for a cartridge and needle. If the kidnappers took only one of them, they'd each have a way to keep Jackson healthy.

TRACEY WAS SCARED. Out-of-her-mind scared. If today hadn't happened, she would have felt safe standing on a suspension bridge above the Brazos River in the early moonlight with Josh.

But today *had* happened and she was scared for them all.

"What kind of a secret is being rich?" Josh walked a few feet one direction and then back again. "I don't get it. Why is being rich a secret McCaffrey would threaten you with?"

"You really want me to explain right now?"

"You're the one who brought it up." He shrugged, but kept walking. "It'll pass the time."

"My last name isn't Cassidy. I mean, it wasn't. I changed it."

That stopped him. There was a lot of light on the bridge and she could see Josh's confused expression pretty well. He was in jeans and a long-sleeve brick-red shirt that had three buttons at the collar. She'd given it to him on his birthday because she wanted to brighten up his wardrobe. The hat he normally wore was still at home. They'd left without it or it would have been on his head.

"I ran a background check on you. Tracey Cassidy exists."

"It's amazing what you can do when you have money. In fact, I could hire men to help you. My uncle would know the best in the business."

"Let's go back to the part that you aren't who you say you are." The phone in his palm rang. He answered and held it to his ear. "We're here."

Josh looked around the area. His eyes landed on the

far side of the bridge, opposite where they'd left the car. Tracey joined him.

"Whatever you want me to do, you don't need my babysitter."

"No, you need me. I can take care of the twins, change Jackson's cartridge." She held up the emergency pack.

"I don't need any extra motivation. Leave her out of—" He pocketed the phone.

"I'm sorry for getting you into this mess." He hugged her to him before they continued across the bridge then on the river walk under the trees. The sidewalk curved and Josh paused, looking for something.

Another couple passed. Josh tugged on Tracey's arm and got her running across the grass toward the road. If the couple were cops, he didn't acknowledge them. Their shoes hit the sidewalk again and a white van pulled up illegally onto the sidewalk next to Martin Luther King Jr. Boulevard.

The door slid open. That's where they needed to go.

The blackness inside the van seemed final. But she could do this. She'd do whatever it took. Whatever they wanted.

Out of the corner of her eye she saw a man approaching. Then another. The more the two men tried to look as if they weren't heading toward them, the more apparent it was that their paths would. Maybe they were the cops that Bryce had arranged to follow them. If they got any closer, the men inside the van would see them, too.

"What are those guys doing?"

Josh looked in their direction, but yelled at her. "Run. I think they're trying to stop us."

"But—"

"Just run."

It wasn't far. Maybe fifty or sixty feet. The men split apart. Josh dropped her hand. She ran. The van slowly moved forward—away from her. One of the men shot at the van. Then she was grabbed from behind and tripped over a tangle of feet. The man latched on to her waist, keeping her next to him.

"Let me go. I have to get— You don't understand what you're doing."

Another shot was fired. This time from the van. The man's partner fell to the grass. The guy holding her covered her with his body. These men weren't police. The real police raced after the van in an unmarked car, sirens echoing off the buildings across the water.

The man on top of her didn't move and wasn't concerned about his injured partner. She was pounding with her fists on a Kevlar vest trying to get the man off her when a loud crash momentarily replaced the police sirens.

"Oh my God! What have you done?"

Chapter Six

Fire trucks. An ambulance. At least three police cars—maybe more—with strobe lights dancing around in circles. College students edging their way closer in a growing crowd. An angry FBI agent in her face. And a bodyguard who kept insisting that she was too open as she sat on a park bench.

The lights, the voices, the desperation—all made her head swim. Of course it might have been a little remnant of the whiskey. Or possibly the head injury from the kidnappers this afternoon. Maybe both.

Whatever it was, she didn't like it. It was the reason she rarely drank at any point in her life. She simply didn't like being under the influence of anything. Including her uncle Carl, who had taken it upon himself to dispatch bodyguards to protect her. They'd destroyed any chance of getting insulin to Jackson.

The van lay on its side. The driver had escaped before anyone could reach the crash site. Both the guard and Josh had run to the scene, but he was gone. Vanished.

"Miss Cassidy, if you're ready to go. Your uncle instructed us to bring you back to Fort Worth as soon as possible. We've cleared it with the police to pull out."

The guard spoke to her with no remorse for what he and his partner had caused. As if she was the most important person in the entire group.

She hated that. She always had.

"How can you stand there and talk as if nothing's happened? Your partner may have shot someone in that van. The driver's disappeared along with the instructions to rescue the twins. What if the kids had been inside? If anything happens to Josh's son—"

"We were just doing our job." He stood in front of her with his hands crossed over each other, no emotion, no whining—and apparently no regrets. His partner had his breath back—which had been knocked out of him by the bullets hitting him in the chest or him hitting the ground.

Jackson and Sage were missing and now the kidnappers would be angry. What would happen now? She needed these men gone. There was only one way to do that. One man. One man could make it happen.

"Let me have your phone."

"Ma'am?"

"I don't have a phone. I need to borrow yours."

He reached inside his jacket pocket, turned on his phone and handed it to her. She searched the call history and found the number she'd almost forgotten. The phone rang and rang some more, going to voice mail, which surprised her. Unless he was with someone—then nothing would disturb him. Not even the fact that he thought her life was at risk.

Hadn't he sent the guards because he was worried?

A more likely story was that he thought the kidnappers would find out who she was and try to extort money from him. Just the possibility of the family being out any cash would send him into a frenzy to get her safely back inside a gilded cage.

Should she leave a message? She hung up before the beep. What she had to say didn't need to be recorded.

"Where's Josh?" The men standing close to her shrugged in answer. "You do know which man I was with when all this began? The father of the children you just placed in more danger."

The big bulky bodyguard looked like he didn't have a clue. He didn't search the crowd. She followed his gaze to the edge of the people, then across the river where another line of people formed, then back to just behind her where the emergency vehicles were parked.

"Hey. Don't play dumb. I ask. You answer," she instructed, using the power that came with her family name. "And don't think I can't stop your paycheck."

"They moved him to a more secure facility," he finally answered.

"You mean we're trying," Agent McCaffrey corrected as he approached. "I was just coming for you, Tracey. We're heading back to Josh's house. He insists on driving himself but would like to speak with you first."

The agent and bodyguard parted like doors when Josh barreled through them.

"My car's been brought to this side of the river. I'm heading back to my place. You ready?" He extended a hand and she took it.

What would she say to him this time? "Sorry. I should have told you about my powerfully rich uncle who might send bodyguards." Those words didn't roll off her tongue and she'd had no idea he'd send anyone to protect her. Actually, it seemed surreal that he'd found her so quickly.

Josh put his hand on her lower back and guided her through the crowds. Her silent guard followed. The one who hadn't been hit by two bullets in his chest ran toward the road, presumably to get their vehicle.

Josh stopped and did an about-face. "I need to talk with Tracey. Then she's all yours."

"What?" *What did he mean? He was turning her over to her uncle?* She'd been right. Josh wouldn't forgive her this time, but she had something to say about where she went and with whom.

"I can't let her out of my sight, sir." The bodyguard stood more at attention, looking ready to attack. Had he just issued a challenge to a Texas Ranger?

"I don't have time for this. I need to know how you found her." Josh responded by placing his hands on his hips and looping his thumbs through his belt loops. Either to keep from dragging her the rest of the way to his car, or to keep himself from throwing a punch at the bodyguard. She would prefer that he not restrain himself from the latter.

"We tracked her phone. We're assuming it was in the van."

"How did you get the number?" she asked. "I didn't give it to my uncle."

"I have a job to do. And I don't work for either of you."

Josh's hands were pulling the guard's collar together before the man could nod at them both. The guard's hands latched on to Josh's wrists to keep from being choked. Agents who had been watching them closely as they approached the car began running.

If any of them were afraid of what Josh might do,

they didn't shout for him to stop. Tracey couldn't bring herself to call out to him, either. After all, it was this man's actions that caused them to lose their main lead to the twins. It was this guy—she didn't even know his name—who had flubbed everything up.

"If you lift one finger…" she said to the guard. But she couldn't blame him or let Josh take out his frustration on the hired help. She'd lost the kids on her watch. She should have been more careful. She laid her hand on Josh's arm, trying to gain his attention. "It's not his fault."

Josh's strong jaw ticked as he ground his teeth. His wide eyes shifted to hers in a crazy gaze, but his muscles relaxed under her fingers.

"Earlier I asked how being rich could be an awful secret." He released the guard shoving him away when two FBI agents were within reaching distance. "I think I have my answer."

"You don't, but I'd rather talk about it in private."

Josh turned and stomped toward his car—the agents close behind.

"Whatever my uncle is paying you, I'll give you the same to stop following me," she said to the bodyguard.

Tracey fell into step next to Agent Barlow, who held up her hand for the guard to stop and not follow. It didn't work. Josh spun around so fast Agent Lanning nearly collided with him.

"No! I need to be alone. That means all of you." He waved everyone away from him. He shook his head, chin hanging to his chest. Then he looked only at her. "They might need you around, but I can't do it. And I don't have to."

"He doesn't mean that," the agent said.

Tracey stopped. Exhausted from everything but really rocked by Josh's words. Her words had been similar when she'd walked away from her uncle when she was twenty-one. She'd left him, the man designated by her parents and grandparents as her guardian, about the same way Josh had disappeared in his car.

Tracey hadn't only meant every word back then, she'd changed her name and began working for the Parkers. Oh yeah, some hurts just couldn't be fixed with "I'm sorry."

JOSH DROVE, HEADING for the long way home. Flashing lights to warn the cars ahead of him that he was going fast. He was angry. More than angry—he was back to being scared that he'd never see his kids again.

Different than Gwen's last days. That was something he'd prepared for, something he'd known was possible even though he couldn't control it. If those men hadn't shown up, the kidnappers would have given him more instructions. He'd know what he needed to do. Or at least his son would have another insulin cartridge.

There was a blood sugar time bomb ticking away for Jackson, and at the moment Josh had no way to defuse it.

He sped under Lake Shore Drive and realized where his subconscious was taking him—the Rescue Center. He slowed the car to a nonlethal speed and switched off the lights. The phone he'd been given from the kidnappers was still in his back pocket. McCaffrey knew it was there but hadn't obtained the number yet. A true burner that wouldn't lead anyone to his location.

Josh could wait for the kidnapper's next call and instructions. They wanted him to take care of their problem. Right? They had to call back.

Whatever they demanded, he'd do. Alone. No more plans behind the plans or counterespionage. He was on his own and would stay here so no one would find him.

With that decided, Josh parked close to the back door and rang the buzzer. At this time of night there would only be a couple of people on duty. The door opened to a familiar face.

"Hey, Josh. You haven't been around in a while. What's it been, about six or seven months?" Bernie Dawes stepped to the side, holding the door open and inviting him inside.

Six or seven months ago he'd been thinking about asking Tracey on a date. He'd chickened out. Funny how he could be the tough Texas Ranger ninety percent of the time, making decisions instantly that saved lives. But the possibility of asking a girl on a date caused his brain to malfunction.

"Got any dogs that need to be walked?"

"One of those kinds of nights?" Bernie asked.

"Yeah. I'm waiting on a phone call." Josh stuck his hands in his back pockets, willing the phone to ring. Nothing happened.

"Well, I just took 'em all out about half an hour ago. How about I set you up with an abandoned litter of pups? They've had a pretty rough start."

"That'll do the trick."

Bernie led the way to the kennels and pulled a chair into a small room with a box of four or five black fur bundles. Five. They were all cuddled on top of each other.

"What's on their heads? Are those dots of paint?"

"We've got a Lab that just whelped, so we rotate these dudes in. But they're black, too." Bernie laughed and scooped up one of the pups. "We have a chart with their different colors. It's the only way to tell if they've all been fed. These guys are all full. They just need a little TLC."

"I shouldn't stay long. I might not have much time."

"Whatever you give them is more than they have." He leaned against the wall.

Loving on the puppies was easy. Seeing the other animals—the strays, the injured, the unwanted... The tough guy he appeared to be suddenly needed to know how this man survived day after day. "How do you do this, Bernie?"

He shrugged. "I like animals."

Bernie turned to go, but hesitated. He might have realized that Josh was back because there was a problem. It was like he was the bartender, wiping down the counter a little more often in front of the man sipping his third whiskey.

"I got in trouble today," Bernie said, picking up a puppy. "I didn't mention my wife's hair. She told me to find my own dinner because I didn't notice she had highlights. She's always doing something. I didn't think I had to say anything about it. Sometimes it's the little things that cause you all sorts of big problems. Catch what I'm throwin' at ya?"

Josh nodded. He could still see Tracey as she walked into the kitchen. He'd wanted to look into her eyes and reassure her that everything would be okay, but she'd been staring at the floor. He could only see her thick red hair, messed up as if someone had placed angry hands on her. Seeing her hair like that, he knew she'd been hurt and it killed him.

"Tracey doesn't think I notice that she dyes her hair red." He picked up the first puppy and stroked the entire length of its body. He wasn't completely sure why Tracey's hair color was important, but he could breathe again. "She started about three years ago, getting a little redder every couple of months. Further away from the brown it used to be."

The room was quiet. No barking or whining. Bernie kept wiping down that metaphorical bar's counter. Josh felt…relief. There weren't too many people Josh could just talk to. He was the commander of the Company. Being a single dad, he didn't go for a drink with the guys after a case very often. It had been a long time since he'd had friends.

"I should have told her I liked it," he admitted.

"Probably," Bernie agreed. "You get that phone call, just make sure the door closes behind you. You come around anytime, man. We understand. Hey, aren't your kiddos old enough to choose a dog? Maybe one of these will do?" He handed the pup with a green dot to Josh. He brushed his hands and gave up waiting on an answer. "Well, I've got a cat who had surgery today and it's having a hard time so I'm going to leave ya to it."

Bernie left in a hurry. Josh figured he must have scowled at the mention of the twins. Poor Bernie thought his visit was about work. Getting a dog? He brought the pup to his face. It was about time. There hadn't been a dog at the house since before he got married.

A whirlwind relationship, elopement and pregnancy that led to Gwen's diagnosis. There hadn't been time to add a dog to the family. Maybe it was part of the reason these types of visits helped. He didn't know who got more out of them—him or the dogs he comforted.

Admit it. The comfort was for him. The idea had come from Company F's receptionist, Vivian. She volunteered for the shelter, trying to place animals and fostering.

The gut-wrenching pain hit him again like it was yesterday. It had been at least a year since he'd felt the loss of his wife so strongly. He put the puppy down and bent forward knowing the pain wasn't physical, but trying to relieve it like a cramp.

When Gwen had been diagnosed with leukemia, every minute of his time had gone to either the job or research or treatment. There had come a time when he'd protected himself so much that he could barely feel.

After the third or fourth late-night trip out here, he'd realized that his unofficial therapy was working. Petting and walking the dogs made him reconnect. He switched puppies and gently stroked, letting the motion replace the fright. It freed his mind. A couple of minutes later he switched again and realized that's why he'd come to the shelter.

It was also a reason he kept the visits to himself. Vivian was the only person in his life that knew he came here to get his head on straight. And he sure needed a minute to think calmly tonight.

The last two pups were smaller than the others. Each had one white paw—one right and one left. He concentrated on those paws and cuddled both of them together. They both almost fit into his palm.

Jackson and Sage had been small. But when they were born they were strong and hadn't needed machines. Trips here to sit with dogs had been fewer when the doctors attacked Gwen's cancer full force. Some days, just taking the time to hold his kids was an effort that made him sleepless with guilt.

The twins were four months old when Gwen realized she was losing the battle. Somehow that had made her stronger. She'd gotten everything in order—with Tracey's help. Gwen fought hard, but in the end, she was at peace that her family would be taken care of.

Removing the phone from his pocket, he replayed the video of his kids. "Ring," he commanded.

He got on his knees next to the box and arranged the blanket where the pups would be secure as they piled on top of each other seeking sleep.

"It can't be over for them. You've got to give me another chance. This can't be the end. She fought so hard to bring these kids into the world," he told the puppies or God or anyone else who might be listening.

The phone rang and he didn't hesitate. "This is Parker."

"You're a very lucky man, Ranger."

"I'm not sure I share your definition of lucky. Does this mean you haven't hurt my kids?"

The insulin cartridges and needles were on the front seat. *Meet me tonight. Ask me to do something right now. I need to make sure my kids are safe.*

"The deal's still moving forward, no matter where you're hiding out."

He heard the uneasiness in the man's voice. Whoever they were, they had no idea that he was at the animal shelter. That might work to his advantage.

"What do you need me to do?"

"You know what we want. Get it. Keep the phone close and wait for instructions."

"Can I talk to Jackson? Is he okay? He has—"

"Diabetes, yeah, we know. We're dealing with it."

"I need to see him, talk to him. His pump and needle will need to be changed. He has to be monitored closely." There wasn't any way he could talk anyone through all the different possibilities that might happen if something went wrong.

"I said we were taking care of it!" the voice yelled. "Don't forget to bring the woman."

"That's not possible."

"Make it possible. Or they'll die."

Chapter Seven

Josh drove to his second home—Company F headquarters. The lights were on and he recognized the vehicles in the parking lot. They were all there. All of his men.

Bryce met him at the door. "We didn't expect to see you, Major. At least not tonight."

"My replacement here?" Josh waited while the ranger secured things, so he could be escorted through the building like a visitor. "I need a minute of his time."

"How you holding up?"

"Can't take time to think about it."

"Captain Oaks is in your office." Bryce led the way through the men.

All of them stood and offered support. They were the best of the best and working the case with or without him as their leader. He entered his office. Nothing had changed. The lifetime he'd been away was actually less than twenty-four hours.

"Aiden." Josh closed the door and dropped the blinds. He didn't want witnesses to the conversation. Nothing that could hinder the case or put his men at risk of something to testify about later.

Aiden left the chair behind the desk and sat next to Josh. The Captain was much older, but barely looked it. Josh only knew because the "old man," as he was referred to, had been eligible for retirement a couple of years ago. He'd proved his mettle earlier that year when he'd been shot defending the witness of the Isabella Tenoreno murder.

Captain Aiden Oaks had been after the Tenoreno and Rosco Mafia families longer than a decade. It was fitting that he'd take Josh's place as head of Company F.

Even if it was temporary.

"I could ask how you're holding up, but it's obvious. What can I do for you?" Aiden kept his voice low. No chance anyone would overhear them. He also leaned forward, seeming anxious to know what was needed.

There was a chance that Aiden Oaks was the only man in a position of authority who would keep his word. Josh needed to make certain that the captain wasn't going to turn him over to the authorities—state or federal. Or call them as soon as he pulled out of the parking lot.

"They want Tenoreno's transportation route."

"Everyone assumed that's where this was headed." Aiden pressed his lips together into a flat line. "Your men filled me in and headquarters gave me a rough outline before booting me this direction."

"I shouldn't be here." Josh started to rise from the chair, but Aiden coaxed him to sit again. "Just talking to me could get you written up, but I don't have any options."

In his years as a Texas Ranger, Josh had never doubted whether he could count on his partner or the men in his company. If this case was just about him, there'd be no doubt about what he'd do. But his kids' lives had never been dependent on that trust.

Until now.

"I guess the strategy to follow and catch these guys when they weren't looking fell apart when your baby-sitter's bodyguards showed up." Aiden nodded. "Yeah, I'm staying on top of things. But you're here. You obviously have a plan. How can I help put it in action?"

Could he trust this man so intent on helping save his kids?

"I need the route or Jackson dies." Josh watched Aiden's eyes. They never wavered. Never looked away like someone hiding something. "I heard the panic in the kidnapper's voice—both about my son and whatever his original plan was. This character is smart enough to know that he had a short window before everything changed. He's playing it by ear now, just like us."

Aiden nodded again, acting like he understood. "Even if you deliver the route there's no guarantee. Say we give 'em a bit of rope, hoping they might hang themselves, it won't guarantee that your kids will be safely released. Won't mean they'll release you either for that matter."

"But I'll be with them." Josh choked on the words, took a second, then stood. "My kids aren't going to be the victims in this. I know the limits of the Rangers, of the FBI, of the state prosecutors. They're hoping for an easy fix. We both know there isn't one."

Josh stared at the frame hanging above the door. Gwen stitched the Ranger motto when she'd first been confined to bed rest with the twins. It was a reminder every day of what he'd lost, but he kept it there. Over the last year, it had also become a reminder of what he'd gained—the twins. *And Tracey.*

"One Riot, One Ranger," Aiden said.

Strength and truth were in his voice. Josh had to trust him. His plan could only work if he did.

Aiden gripped his shoulder with a firm, steady hand. "I yanked your company into this mess when I sent Garrison Travis to a dinner party and they witnessed Tenoreno's assassin. I owe you, Josh. So what's the plan?"

Eager to help or eager to learn how to stop him? Aiden might be giving him a long piece of rope to hang himself. It was a risk Josh had to take.

"I need a feasible route, you supply a decoy, we bring these guys down like the rest of the Tenoreno family."

"It's a good start. Are you going to exchange yourself for your kids?"

"That's what I was planning, but I'm not sure it'll work. They're insisting that I bring Tracey."

Aiden rubbed his chin and leaned back in the chair he'd reoccupied. "That does throw a kink in the works. Could possibly mean that they'll keep all three as hostages until you do whatever they want."

"Yeah, that's the most likely scenario."

"It seems that the only way to get your kids back is to tell the kidnappers the truth. We'll need to inform them how and where Tenoreno is really being moved from Huntsville to Austin. Company F will just have to be prepared."

"Are you going to run this through state headquarters?"

"They won't approve it—not even as a hypothetical." He winked. "Just like they wouldn't have approved the last-minute operation that brought Tenoreno down to begin with. Might be one of those situations where it's better to ask forgiveness than permission. Of course, there's nothing at all to stop us from talking hypothetical situations. Your experience would be valuable and much appreciated."

"My experience. Right." Josh's gut told him to go for it. *Trust him.*

His friend pointed to the motto. "This is one time, more than one of us might be required."

No more stalling. This fight was bigger than just one man. He had to trust that Aiden wouldn't turn him in.

"If I were still in charge of Tenoreno's transport, I'd arrange for air travel. It would be limited ground vulnerability. At this point the state prosecutor is probably scrambling to even make that a private jet."

"I'm not disagreeing with you," Aiden said. "Hypothetically."

In other words, Josh was right. They planned to move Tenoreno from the state prison via plane to Austin for the trial.

"Since we're just talking here, you know what's bothered me? Why did the kidnappers go to so much trouble to put your situation in the public eye? I mean, they could have kept the kidnapping quiet, but they drew you to a popular, normally crowded place."

"If I were Tenoreno's son, a plane is the fastest route out of the country. Huntsville's just a hop into the Gulf and then international waters. All he has to do is hijack the plane."

"That's a fairly sound guess of what they're likely to do." Aiden tapped his fingertips together, thinking.

"Dammit. Is that what all of this is about? Make the kidnapping public so the transfer is by plane instead of car? I thought it was just about gaining access to my credentials so the kidnaper could get close enough to free Tenoreno."

"They manipulated the kidnapping to force you to hijack a plane?" Aiden nodded his head, agreeing, not really asking a question.

"It would make it harder to recapture Tenoreno. Harder for the FBI or Rangers or any law enforcement not to comply since the twins are at risk."

The kidnapping made sense.

"Did you find out why Tracey's uncle sent the guards? Who notified them?"

Josh shook his head, shrugging.

"Too upset? I understand." The older man stood, joining Josh by sitting on the opposite corner of the desk. "We'll be ready. I guarantee that. And if you just happen to let me see the number you're using on that new phone, then I might have a misdial in my future letting you know what plane and airfield."

Josh turned on the cell and Aiden nodded his head.

"Here's something to ponder while we wait." He jotted down the number. "How did Miss Cassidy's entourage get here? On one hand maybe the kidnappers really want her to take care of the kids. Maybe they just made a mistake not abducting her at the same time. On the other, Xander Tenoreno might have alerted her uncle. That means he knows she's from money. Maybe the kidnappers know too and want a piece of that cash cow."

"How rich is rich?" Josh asked.

"Probably need to have a conversation with the source about that."

Aiden was a wise man. Josh stuck out his hand, grabbing the older man's like a lifeline. It was the first hope he'd had since the van had crashed.

"I can't thank you enough, Aiden."

"I haven't done anything yet. A lot of this depends on you."

Josh looked at Gwen's artwork. "I'll do whatever it takes."

"Just remember, you're not alone."

PULLING A LIGHT throw up to her chin, Tracey curled up as small on the couch as she could get. She closed her eyes, pretending to be asleep, wanting everyone in the house to leave her alone. The FBI agent who'd picked her up at the hospital encouraged her to take the upstairs bedroom.

Josh's room?

George Lanning had no way of knowing she hadn't been in that room since Gwen had gotten very, very ill. It was better to be bothered by people in the living room than to be alone in Josh's bed.

"Miss Cassidy?"

"What?" she answered the bodyguard, who hadn't left her side since coming into her life.

"It's your uncle."

Part of her wanted to tell him to call off these guard dogs and part of her wanted to ignore him—as he'd obviously ignored her for the past several hours. The best thing was to confront the situation and attempt to discover his true motives.

She sat up, tugged her shirt straight and was ready to get to the heart of things. It had been a while since she'd thought of her grandmother's advice when facing a problem. But the words were never truer than at that moment.

Taking the phone, she drew in a deep breath placing the phone next to her ear, ready for an attack.

"Tracey, darling, are you okay?"

"Who is this?" The female voice was a little familiar, but it had been a long time since she'd had contact with her family. She couldn't be sure who it was.

"It's your auntie Vickie, dear. Are you on your way home yet?"

"I don't have an aunt Vickie." At least she hadn't when she'd gone to court to change her name. There hadn't even been a Vickie in her uncle's life. Then again, there'd always been someone *like* a Vickie.

"I know I've met you, dear. I'll admit—only to you—that it's been much too long."

"Where is my uncle? I was told he was calling." She didn't have time to speak with a secretary or even a new wife. She wanted the confrontation over and the guys in the black suits off her elbow.

"Well," the woman's voice squeaked, "he's not really available, but I thought you needed to know that it's important for you to come home."

"Wait, my uncle didn't tell you to call?"

Vickie began a long, in-depth explanation why she'd taken it upon herself to contact her and explain the complexity of the situation in her childhood home. Tracey tuned her out.

Home? The room surrounding her, keeping her warm and safe, was more of a home than any room had ever been in Fort Worth. That place had been more like a museum or mausoleum. Beautiful, but definitely a do-not-touch world.

As a little girl, she'd had the best interior designers. Everything had been pink. She couldn't stand pink for the longest time. Now she had to bite her tongue whenever Sage wanted a dress in the color.

Realizing the phone was in her lap instead of her hand, she clicked the big red disconnect button and put an end to a stranger's attempt to coax her home. Her new constant companion reached to retrieve it, when it rang again.

Tracey answered herself, more prepared, less surprised. "Yes?"

"Listen to me, you spoiled little brat." Vickie didn't try to disguise the venom. "Carl wants you back here pronto. Niceties aside, you should do what you're told."

"Vickie…dearest—" she could make the honey drip from her voice, too "—I walked away a long time ago. There is absolutely no road for me that leads back there."

The red button loomed. Tracey clicked. It wasn't hard. Not now.

The phone vibrated in her hand. She tossed it to the opposite end of the couch. Totally content with her decision. Her uncle wasn't calling her back and, whoever Vickie was, she couldn't do anything to help save the children.

"I only have two things for you to do," she said to the guard. "My first is that you both get in that car of yours and leave. Without me. The second is not to interrupt me again unless it's really my uncle calling. Period. No secretaries. No Auntie *Vickies* that haven't celebrated as many birthdays as I have. No one except him. And don't say that you don't work for me."

"Yes, ma'am." He nodded and backed up to the door.

What he was acknowledging, she didn't care. Just as long as he stayed next to the door and let her wonder where Josh had gone or whether he was coming back. If she were him she wondered what she'd be thinking.

Before she could lean back into the cushions, the man answered his phone and held it in her direction.

"Speaker, please."

He mumbled into the phone, pressed a button and…

"Tracey? You there?"

She raised her hand, using her fingers to indicate she'd take the call. She popped it off Speaker and paused long enough to fill her lungs again.

"Hi, Uncle Carl."

"You okay, Tracey?" Her uncle didn't sound upset. He might even sound concerned. "I heard there was an accident and a car fire."

"I'm good. My head hurts from earlier, but I'm sure you already have the hospital records."

"It's been a while. I have to apologize for Vickie. She sometimes gets…overly enthusiastic."

"She sounded like it." He hadn't called to talk about his girlfriend, which was the category she could safely put the woman in. He hadn't said anything about getting married. The man was in his fifties and had avoided a matrimonial state his entire life.

"I assume you don't want to come home."

"I am home. My place is here and the men you sent— You did send them, didn't you?"

"As soon as I heard you were assaulted."

"You should have asked me first." As if that step had ever been part of his trickeries.

"You would have said no."

"Of course I would have said no. I work for a Texas Ranger who has a lot of law enforcement access. Why in the world would I need two bodyguards to muck things up?"

"Muck?"

"Yes, Uncle Carl, muck. They arrived and everything became a big mess. Josh is gone, the kids are still in danger, Jackson doesn't have anyone there that understands diabetes. Yes, everything's pretty *mucked* up."

"Mr. Parker's children are in danger?"

"They were kidnapped. That's the reason the FBI called you."

"The FBI? Did they tell you they spoke with me?"

"No. I just assumed that's how you found me." Wasn't that what Agent McCaffrey had insinuated?

"That's ridiculous. I've never *not* known where you are. Just because you changed your name doesn't stop you from being my niece and my responsibility. I'm your guardian, but more importantly, we're family."

It sounded good. The speech wasn't unlike the words that she'd heard most of her life. It did surprise her that he'd known exactly where she was. Well, then again, it didn't. She hadn't gone far.

Same city, same school—she only lived four blocks from the place he'd been paying for. That all made sense. What didn't was his statement that he hadn't heard from the FBI.

"Concern for me was never a problem."

"Ah, yes, you wanted your freedom. Well, anonymously donating to your university down there, did keep me informed."

Same old, same old. Carl was very good at saying a lot of nothing.

"Can we stop this? Just tell me what it's going to take to call off your bodyguard brigade."

"I think you need to sit the rest of this out. Come back here where I can keep an eye on you. Better yet, you've finished your presentation, so why not take a long overdue vacay to someplace breezy. You always liked the beach."

"You're wrong, and this time you have no control over my life." She caught the upward tilt of lips—mostly smirk—of the man at the door. Right. Her uncle's money would always have influence over her life. Money always did. "Just call off your goons."

"That won't be happening. They're there for your safety. You need them." Carl's voice was more than a little smug. As usual, it was full of confidence that his choice was the only choice.

"That couldn't be farther from the truth."

Her uncle never did anything without proper motivation. So what was motivating him this time?

"No need to argue the point any longer, Tracey. I returned your call, answered your questions and have informed you what your option is. Yes, I'm aware you only have one. I must say good night."

"You aren't going to win." It embarrassed her to feel her face contract with a cringe. She knew the words were a fool's hope as soon as she said them.

"My dear, I already have. Those men are not about to leave your side. They'd never work anywhere again. Ever. And they know it."

The phone disconnected and she was no closer to discovering the truth of why her uncle sent the bodyguards. Man, did that sound conceited. Josh would want to know the entire story and specifically that answer when he returned. *If* he returned.

Part of the discussion in the past couple of hours was that Josh had a new phone and it was taking much too long to discover the number. Something to do with finding the kiosk owner, then a person who actually had keys to obtain the sales records. Followed by getting permission to enter the mall.

In other words, they had no clue where Josh was. No one could find him on the road. Some of their conversation had been that the kidnappers may have already contacted him. If so, then at least he had the Jackson emergency kit with him. Josh could monitor his son, save both of his kids.

The bodyguard silently retrieved his phone. He stepped on the other side of the door to take a phone call, but she mostly heard manly grunts of affirmation.

Tracey wanted to run and lock the door. Of course, there wasn't a lock, but it didn't stop her from wanting to be completely alone. She could sulk as good as the rest of them. But it felt ridiculous feeling sorry for herself.

What problem did she have? It was Josh's twins who were missing. Josh would have to do whatever it took to get them back. She could sit here and offer support. Be the loyal day care provider. Her role in the family had been made quite clear when Josh had left her behind.

"Your uncle wants you back in Fort Worth in the morning. We'll leave here at eight sharp, giving you time for some rest." He stood with his back to the door as if he were a guard in front of the Tower of London. Eyes front, not influenced by any stimuli around him.

"I'm not a child and you can't force me to get in a vehicle, especially with the FBI here. I'm not going anywhere. I'm waiting here for Josh." At least she hoped he'd return. "And I'm going to help find his kids. Get with this agenda or leave."

The guard didn't answer. He was a good reflection of her uncle, not listening to her. She curled into the corner of the couch again, pulling the blanket over her shoulder. He was right about one thing—she did need some rest. Because when Josh came back, he would need her help.

And she would be here to give it to him.

Chapter Eight

"Where the hell have you been?" McCaffrey burst through the front door, storming across the porch before Josh had the car in Park.

"Not my problem if your guys can't keep up." He didn't care if the agent thought he was a smart-ass. He had barely been thinking when he'd left the river.

During the twenty-minute car ride from Ranger headquarters, he hadn't come up with a way to get him and Tracey out of the house. It didn't help that he lived in the middle of nowhere and there wouldn't be any sneaking off without guards noticing. Men were everywhere again. One of the bodyguards who had stopped Josh from reaching the van sat in a dark sedan parked in front of the barn.

Bodyguards complicated the equation.

What the hell was he going to do?

"Oh thank God! You're all right," Tracey said when his feet hit the porch. "Can we talk? Let me explain?"

Did he want to go there? Then again, when had it mattered what he *wanted*? Life had proven his wants didn't matter. He had to confront Tracey and talk things out. But when? That was the question he decided was relevant. And who else needed to be confronted—the FBI, local PD or Tracey's bodyguards?

Notably absent was the only organization that held the answer he needed. He had to trust Aiden Oaks, but knew the men in Company F had his back. He'd find out the specifics of moving Tenoreno.

He hadn't been able to speak with Bryce. Maybe find out where their tail had been during the bridge incident and why the rangers had been unable to follow the kidnapper from the van.

If they had, Josh would know. First things first. He had to deal with the people back in his house. McCaffrey was standing on the front sidewalk. Looked like he was first, then Tracey.

"You aren't supposed to be here. Pack it up, Agent."

"Did they make contact with you? Is that the reason you returned?"

"I don't know who's out there watching this conversation. Leave." Josh pointed to the empty dark sedans. Then he turned to the cop on his front lawn. "They have two minutes to clear out or arrest them for trespassing."

"I'm not sure I have that authority," he replied.

"Dammit." Josh glared at McCaffrey. "I probably don't have a choice, but I'm begging you for my kids' lives…leave."

"I have my orders."

Josh was dazed to a point that he couldn't speak. No words would form. His mind went to a neon sign that flashed. "Jackson might die."

"Josh, come on inside. You can't do this."

Tracey tugged on his hands. Hands that were twisted in the shirt collar circling McCaffrey's neck. How?

When? The blackness. It all ran together until everything sort of blurred.

He released the FBI agent and let Tracey lead him inside. He thought she pointed at a man who took care of emptying the room. "How do we get rid of him and his partner?" he asked once he realized it was the second bodyguard.

"Are you okay?"

"Sure. No. I just… I don't know what happened back there." Josh shook his head in disbelief. "I can't remember going for McCaffrey."

"You're upset, exhausted. The stress that you're under is—"

"Things like this don't happen to me. I don't let them." He shrugged away from the comfort Tracey might offer. He wasn't a pacing man.

When he needed to think he lifted his feet up on the corner of his desk and flipped a pencil between his fingers. He paced so Tracey wouldn't be near him. What if he lost it again?

The television in the far corner of the room was muted. No news bulletins. He hadn't expected any since the FBI was keeping a tight lid on things. There hadn't been any Amber Alerts for his kids. Special circumstances, he'd been told.

That part he agreed with. They all knew who had hired the kidnappers. Now they just had to find them.

"I owe you an explanation," Tracey said softly.

"Not sure I can process anything." He scrubbed his face with his palms, desperately attempting to lift the haze. His mind screamed at him not to. If it did, he'd have to find a way to save his kids.

Too late. He was thinking again.

He dropped onto the cushions, breathing fully and under control. For the moment.

"I don't know how to apologize for what happened." She nervously rubbed her palms up and down her thighs. Gone were the scrubs, replaced by regular clothes.

"Forget that for now. Before the van showed up, I asked why being rich needed to be a secret. Have your family problems put my kids in danger?" He shook his head as if he needed to answer that himself and start over. He didn't want to blame Tracey, but the words slipped across his tongue before he could shut himself up. "If I wasn't certain that Tenoreno's people were behind this… Go ahead—explain to me why I should trust you again."

Tracey snapped to attention, cleared her throat, then shrugged. "I was raised like every normal millionaire's kid."

Josh was too tired to be amused until it hit him that Tracey was serious. She sat on the sofa next to him, knee almost touching his leg, hands twisting the corner of a throw pillow, bodyguard at the door.

"You're serious."

"My family's been wealthy for a couple of generations. West Texas oil fields."

"Let me guess. You wanted to see how the other half lived so you went to work as a nanny?"

"I understand why you're mad, but—"

"I'm not sure you do." Josh burst up from the couch with energy he didn't realize he had. *Pace. Get back under control.* "I looked into your bank accounts, Tracey. There wasn't money there. You drive a crappy car. You've lived in the same off-campus apartment for four years. Why? If you have enough money to buy the state of Texas, why are you slumming it?"

"I didn't lie and *I* don't have all the money. My family does. At first, I thought you knew about all this. I told Gwen when she interviewed me who my uncle was. I gave you permission to run a background check. Later, when it was obvious you had no idea about the money, it was nice that you didn't want a favor or something from my uncle."

She thought that he'd want something from her family? Second curve… Gwen had kept this from him. He closed his eyes again. The blackness returned along with the thought he had to get moving. He was ready to move past this, leave and find his children. But he had to understand what he was dealing with regarding the bodyguards and Tracey's family.

"Is Tracey Cassidy your real name?"

"Yes. I legally changed it when I was twenty-one. I just dropped the Bass. Not that anyone actually associated me with the Bass family in Fort Worth."

He stared at her after she'd thrown two curveballs at him. She was a Bass? As in Bass Hall and the endowments and three of the wealthiest men in Texas?

"Why now? Why have bodyguards come into your life after you've lived in Waco for this long without them? I know they haven't always been hanging around. I think I would have noticed them."

"My parents divorced when I was six. I went to live with my grandparents. They said it was for my own good. Everyone threw the word *stability* around a lot back then. It might have been better. I'll never know. Both my parents remarried, started new families. By then, I was too old and filled with teenage angst."

He paced until he landed in front of the television screen and the dancing bubbles in the commercial. "Were you hiding from your family?"

"No. My uncle controls the trust fund left to me by my grandfather. With that, he thought it gave him complete control of my life. I decided not to let him dictate who was trailing after me in a bulletproof car, or what I did or when. So I left. I walked away from that life."

He couldn't let the bodyguards or Bass family screw things up the next time he received instructions. "Why didn't Gwen tell me about any of this?"

"I honestly thought she had. Look, Josh, my life changed after I walked away from my uncle. I sold my expensive car and lived on the money for almost a year. I had to keep things simple. I had to find a job. I did that through Gwen. She helped before and after I came to work here."

"I wanted her to hire a nurse. In fact, we argued about it a lot." He swallowed hard, pushing the emotion down. "She was right, of course. It was better to have someone she could be... She needed a friend."

"I told her that—the part about a nurse. But she was insistent that you needed a friend, too. She was a very determined woman."

"Yeah, she was."

"I first came here because a secretary in the department wanted to help me make ends meet. I stayed because Gwen asked for my help."

"Why are you still here? I know about the job offer in Minnesota."

She stared at him. Her lips parted, a little huff escaping before she pulled herself straight. Back on the edge of the couch she shook her head as if she couldn't believe what she'd just heard.

"I've spoken to the men who work for my uncle. They said they work for him and he's the only one who can give them new orders." She ignored his question.

The proverbial elephant was sitting in the middle of the room. Neither of them wanted to talk about her leaving. That's why he hadn't discussed the possibility or their accidental kiss.

He had made it a point to work late to avoid talking to her. "I don't have any control of your life, Tracey."

"Of course you don't. I never thought you did."

"You deserve more."

"I seriously don't believe you. After everything we've been through—are going through." She jumped up from the couch. Her sudden movement caught the attention of her guard at the door. He took a look and didn't react. "More of what, Josh? This is *so* not the time to be thinking about my future. We have to get the twins back before Jackson crashes or worse."

"The kidnappers called me."

"What? Why are we talking about me? Do they want money? I can force my uncle—"

"No. It's not about you." He scraped his fingers through his short hair. "It involves you. I mean, I need your help."

"Anything. I already told you."

"I think they want you to come and take care of Jackson. If they'd known about your family, they would have taken you this afternoon."

"I begged them to."

"It's dangerous. This is possibly one of the hardest things I've ever said, but I don't think you should." *Damn!*

"Why would you even think that? You want me to run to safety while Jackson may be…he might be…"

Control. He needed control. But he wasn't going to get it by ignoring that Tracey needed comfort. Or by pretending she wasn't a part of the situation.

She straightened to the beautiful regal posture he'd noticed more than once. "I'll do it. I'm not hiding. I'd never be able to live with myself."

He stood, wanting to go to her. To hold her. Take as much comfort as he could, possibly more than he was able to offer her.

"If you said that back at the bridge to hurt me…" she sniffed "…maybe to get me back in some way for messing up the exchange at the bridge…well, it worked. I get it. As soon as Sage and Jackson are okay, I'm leaving for Minnesota."

"Yeah." The resignation in his voice was apparent—at least to him. But he hadn't meant it and didn't want her to go. He needed her.

She walked to the window that opened to the back of the house. Sometime in the hour that he was away, she'd gone by her place and picked up clothes. Now she was in jeans, a long-sleeved gold summer sweater over a black lace top.

The boots Gwen had given her for Christmas years ago were on her feet. He recognized the silver toes. She wore them a lot and every time he thought back to that last gift exchange…

So much about her reminded him of his wife. But the strange thing was he'd actually had a longer relationship with Tracey. God, he was confused. Mixed-up didn't sit well. He wasn't a soft or weak guy.

Not being able to concentrate was killing him or

would get him killed. What he wouldn't give for the dependability of his men and a solid plan of action. Give him an hour to be in charge and he should be able to resolve this. But he wasn't going to be in charge. He had to accept that.

Thinking like this wasn't helping. Besides, no one could have predicted that Tracey's uncle would send bodyguards. Or that they'd arrive at exactly that moment.

Whoever was in charge—he stared at the phone still in his possession—a bastard on the other end was dictating the fates of every person he loved.

All he could do was wait.

Tracey sniffed. Her shoulders jerked a little. She was trying to conceal that she was crying. He'd hurt her and been a… Hell, he didn't want to be a jerk.

"I didn't mean it," he said without making a move toward her. "It's just…everything."

"I know. Everything has to work out somehow."

"I need to be doing something."

"Leave."

Josh looked up from his pity party about to ask her where she wanted him to go. But she'd directed her command at the bodyguard still at the slightly open door.

"If you don't leave, I'm going to encourage this… this Texas Ranger to take your head off. Are we clear?" Tracey wrapped her fingers into fists and snapped them to her hips.

With her short hair whipped up like it had just been blown by a big gust of North Texas wind, she almost looked like Peter Pan. Her shapely bottom would never pass for a boy who'd never grown up. But she did look like she was about to do battle.

The bodyguard backed through the door. Tracey took a step forward and slammed it in his face.

"What was that for?"

She spun around and marched across the room. Her battle stance had been switched to face Josh. "No more tears. You think you need action? So do I. What can we do?"

He sputtered a little. The change in her threw him even more off-kilter than he had been. If he'd had any doubts about her, they flew out the window along with the fictional character he'd been envisioning. Tracey was real and very determined.

"When did they contact you?" she asked, hands still on her hips, unwavering.

"How did you—?"

She came in close, taking his hands. "Let's clear the air and get down to business," she whispered. "I understand that whatever might have been developing between us is gone."

Josh wasn't as certain as her upturned face staring at him seemed to be.

"There's only one reason you would have come back here," she continued. "Me."

He deliberately lifted an eyebrow while he glanced at the closed door and searched for the men who'd been passing in front of the windows.

"The only person I've ever worked for is you, Josh Parker. I want to help." She squeezed his hands.

Clarity returned. Her reassurance seemed genuine when he looked into her eyes. As her strength flowed through her grip, sanity returned.

"Whatever it takes. I mean that." The catch in her voice made him want to draw her into his arms again.

Yet, there was something else hanging there, left unsaid. "But?"

She dropped his hands. "We get through this without doubting each other again. But afterward, I'm really leaving. You need to know that."

"I understand." He didn't. Then again, he did.

After knowing her for five years. After trusting her with his children. Yeah, he'd turned on her with a pittance of circumstantial evidence. She was hurt, but there was no going back. He'd lost her trust and maybe even her respect.

Tracey squeezed his left hand—the one where he'd recently removed his wedding ring. Had she noticed? No one in his life had said anything if they had. Another slight tug encouraged him to look at her.

"Now tell me, what do those bastards want us to do?"

Chapter Nine

Tracey had free run of the house. She'd publicly insisted that Josh shower and change, claiming he smelled like dogs. Fingers crossed it made the men watching him less aware of her. She had her fingers on the back door…

"Where are you heading, Miss Cassidy?" Agent Lanning strolled to the breakfast bar, looking as cold as the granite he leaned on.

"I just realized that no one fed the horses yesterday evening." She pointed toward the barn even though it couldn't be seen from the kitchen.

"I'll go with you. It's been a while since I've set foot in a barn." He continued his laid-back attitude and sauntered to the door as if there were no other explanation for her sneaking outside.

He stepped onto the already-dew-soaked grass, paused, lifted the corner of his slacks and tucked them into his boots. "Like I said, it's been a while, but I've done this once or twice."

Great. Just her luck. He really was going to help her. The bottoms of her jeans would be wet by the time they crossed the yard and opened the gate. The agent who'd sat with her at the hospital stretched his arms wide and waved off the bodyguards who would have followed.

The very men she wanted to follow.

"Did Josh leave in the car or his old truck?"

"I beg your pardon?" She tried to look innocent and knew she'd overacted when George Lanning laughed.

"I may not have kids of my own, but I know what I'd do if they were abducted. And that's anything. I've been through this before with my first partner. Josh came back here for a reason. Has to be that the kidnappers decided they need you to take care of Jackson. So is he leaving using the car or the truck?"

She couldn't look directly at him, but saw that his shoulders sort of shrugged. Right that minute, she could see the tall lanky cowboy who seemed to be her friend. But she wasn't easily fooled. Nor was she going to admit she and Josh had planned an escape.

"We've told all of you several times now. That's what the bridge exchange was all about. Or that's what we assumed. And for the record, Josh completely blames me that it got messed up." She tilted her head toward one of her uncle's bodyguards, who followed them across the yard. "I'm not exactly Major Parker's best friend at the moment."

"So it would appear." He waved a gentlemanly hand indicating for her to precede him down the worn path to the barn.

Feeding the horses was a ruse that he'd seen through immediately. She'd had no intention of feeding them at two in the morning, but now she was stuck. At least an extra scoop wouldn't hurt them. And she wouldn't be there when Mark Tuttle came in the morning to clean up and take care of them before school.

George only thought he'd caught her trying to get

free. He'd know for certain in a couple of hours—along with everyone else.

They walked through the barn door and right on cue, the bodyguard followed. Josh had come up with several ways for them to leave. That is, once he'd focused and told her what the kidnappers wanted.

Something had changed for the men who had abducted the children. It might have been the fiasco at the bridge, but their fear was that Jackson's condition had worsened. The faster she got to him, the better.

One thing stood in her way—being confined here at the house. She dipped the scoop into the feed, filling the buckets to carry to each stall. Her hand shook so much that some pieces scattered onto the ground.

"You must be pretty scared." George leaned against the post near the first horse, closely watching her actions.

"Any normal, caring human being would be."

"That's right. So I guess you had to explain your background—or should I call it previous life—to Josh." He rubbed his stubbled chin.

"Is my life as a rich girl pertinent to getting the children back?"

"Isn't it?"

"I don't know what you mean."

He nodded toward the bucket. "The horses only missed one meal, right?"

She'd been intently watching his every move instead of paying attention to what she was doing. The bucket now was overflowing onto the floor, making more cleanup for her. The bodyguard snickered a little at her mistake before he clamped his lips together tight and returned to his stoic expression.

"Let me."

George picked up the bucket, held his hand out for the scoop, then finished putting the right amount into each bucket and then each stall. She let him while she wrapped her hand around the handle of a wooden tail brush. This wasn't the original plan, but it was one of its versions.

Josh had argued against it because they didn't know if the bodyguards would fall in line. She had to risk it. When George bent in front of her to scoop up the spilled feed, she raised her hand and let it fall across the back of his head.

She hadn't rendered him unconscious and hadn't expected to. It wasn't a movie, after all. But he did fall face-first into the dirt. She had seconds. "You! Tie him up. We're leaving."

George grabbed the back of his neck and rolled to his shoulder. The man at the door ran quickly forward, for a man of his size. He stuck a knee in the agent's back, practically flattening one of his hands under him.

"Tracey, stop! You don't want to do this," George called.

She looked around for something, anything to stuff inside his mouth to keep him quiet. The bodyguard yanked George's hands around to his back, looped the lead rope and tied it off. Then he jerked George to a sitting position and tied him to the closest post.

"I don't see anything to keep him quiet."

The guard loosened the tie around George's neck, pulled it up around the man's ears and tightened it enough to quiet any yelling. Then he removed the cell and handgun from under George's jacket.

"Call your partner and tell him to bring the car

closer to the gate." She set the cell inside the bucket and stuffed the gun down the back of her pants. That was what everyone always did, right? It didn't seem to want to stay. "Damn." She couldn't run worrying about where the gun would end up and decided to leave it. She grabbed it again and handed it to the guard. "Unload this. Leave the gun, take the magazine."

He followed her instructions. George didn't struggle. In fact, he hadn't put up much of a fight at all. She locked gazes with him and he quirked an eyebrow, then lifted his chin toward the door. "Be careful," was what she could decipher through his muffled speech.

She flipped the barn lights out and waited at the door for her uncle's hired help to make his call. She could see the outline of the car move toward the fence line without its lights. One more look at the agent left behind and she tried not to debate whether George had set her up or helped.

"You know we can take you to a hotel or to your uncle's, but nowhere else." Her guard placed his hand in the small of her back and gently nudged her forward.

Tracey didn't answer him. They silently moved across the paddock to the far fence. Up and over, then a short distance to where the car waited. Part of her wanted to back out and let him take her to the protection waiting in Fort Worth. Just a small part.

The section of her heart seeking to be fixed needed to find those two kids. It was the half of her that won. She ran to the car and stopped at the driver's door.

"Don't say a word," Josh said, getting out of the car holding a gun on the guard who'd been so helpful. "Your partner's in the trunk. You and I are going to ride in the back. Any trouble, Tracey?"

"George Lanning is tied up in the barn."

Even in the starlight, she could see that Josh was surprised. "Turn around." He cuffed the guard, held the gun until the man got into the car and slid in the back, too.

They didn't need to say anything. She drove to the place off Highway 6 where they'd decided to abandon the guards. It was a long walk back to Waco. She doubted her uncle's men would be picked up by a friendly driver after they'd been forced to strip to their underwear.

"Your clothes will be about a mile down the road." Josh merged onto the road and raised the window.

Less than an hour ago she'd been feeling sorry for herself. "I thought you'd left me behind."

"To be honest, Tracey, I would have. I told you coming back wasn't my choice." Josh shifted in his seat. "I don't want to put you in more danger or ask you to do anything illegal."

"Right. Where to now? They didn't call while I was in the barn. Did they?"

"No."

"So do we need to come up with a plan?"

Josh slowed down on the deserted highway. She dropped the clothes that were in her lap to the edge of the gravel shoulder. The bodyguards would be able to find them easily, and they were far enough off the road not to draw attention.

Josh turned in the seat, facing her.

"Shouldn't we be in a hurry to get away from here?" she asked cautiously.

He tossed the phone they'd bought earlier into the seat between them. "They said they'd call."

"So we wait." She slapped her thighs and rubbed. Nervous tension. She looked around, wondering what he really wanted to say.

The car was still in Drive and his foot was on the brake. No reason to ask if they were going to wait on the guards to catch up with them. Josh kept looking at her and she kept looking everywhere but at him.

"I lied."

"About what?"

"I would have come back. I didn't want to bring you with me to the kidnappers, but I would have come back."

Her mouth was in the shape of an O. She said the words silently and rubbed her palms against her jeans again. *He would have come back.* Despite everything happening to them, her heart took off a little. She needed hope.

He let off the brake, steered the car onto the road and placed his palm up on the seat covering the phone. It was an invitation, confirmed by the wiggle of his fingers. She accepted, slipping her hand over his and letting it be wrapped within his warmth.

"I think I know what they want me to do, Tracey. There are some good men out there on our side. The ones at the house can't help. George Lanning realized that. I owe him a debt. In fact, I'm going to owe a lot of people when this is over."

"Not me. I'm the one who lost the kids."

He squeezed her hand. "I should have anticipated a move like this from the Tenoreno organization. They've been threatening Company F all year. I never thought... Hell, I just never thought about it. I'm sorry."

"Do you have any place in mind for us to wait?

Or are you just driving?" Her stomach growled loud enough to be heard, jerking Josh's stare to her belly. "Have you eaten anything since breakfast?"

"Sounds like you're the one who hasn't." He chuckled. Things were too serious to really laugh. "I don't feel like eating."

"But you need to eat, right?"

"We need to switch cars first." He pulled into a visitor's parking garage at Baylor and followed the signs to park almost on the top floor. Grabbing a bag she hadn't noticed before from the backseat, he pushed the lock and tossed the keys inside before shutting the door.

"You know…it would lower my anxiety level if you'd let me in on whatever plan you've already formed. And don't tell me you don't have one," she finished. He unlocked an older-looking truck. "Aren't you worried about campus security finding the car? Then Agent Mc-Caffrey will be able to figure out what you're driving."

"I'm only worried about Vivian getting in trouble for leaving it. Of course, it'll take them a little while to discover the connection to me. I have high hopes that this is over by then."

"Whose truck is this?" She grabbed an empty fast-food sack and gathered the trash at her feet.

"Vivian's son's best friend. I'm…uh…renting it."

"Not for much, I hope." The half-eaten taco that emerged from under the seat's edge made her gag. "I don't think I'm hungry anymore."

"We should get something anyway. No telling how long it'll be before we can eat again. Looks like we're on empty. Might be good to get Jackson snacks and juice." Josh exited and swung into a convenience store and handed her three twenties without finishing his sentence. "Better pay cash for the gas."

Even with all the media coverage, neither of their pictures had been flashed on the screen—at least from what she'd seen. If she'd had long hair, she would have dropped her head and let it swing in front of her face. Her hair was the exact opposite. Thick and short and very red, but not very noteworthy.

For Jackson and Sage, she picked up some bottled juice, two very ripe bananas, crackers and animal cookies. Not knowing how much gas Josh was purchasing, she didn't know if she had enough money for a full bottle of honey. She looked in the condiments, but could only pick up grape jelly. That would have to do if—if his blood sugar was too low. She'd have to evaluate him and see.

For them—unfortunately—two overpriced and overcooked hot dogs were in their future. She pointed toward the truck and the teenager behind the counter scanned her items. Josh finished pumping the gas and there was enough cash left for a supersized soft drink for them to share.

The clerk popped her gum and sacked everything. "Want your receipt?"

"No thanks."

Tracey lifted the sack from the counter while the girl continued thumbing through a magazine. It hit her that she'd never experienced that kind of work. Normal young adult work. The only job she'd ever had was helping Gwen and taking care of the kids. It was almost as if she got married her senior year of college, but without all the benefits.

Her life, her classes, her study time were all centered

around the Parkers' schedules. That's the reason Josh hadn't known who to invite to her birthday. There wasn't anyone really.

It wasn't his fault. She'd made the choices that had led her to this moment. Josh waved at her to hurry back.

She'd had a very fortunate life. This event didn't seem like it. But they would get the kids back. Josh and the twins would be together again. She took comfort from the way he'd waited to hold her hand. Hopefully that meant there was a place for her in his life, too.

Chapter Ten

"So you have a plan. The Rangers are helping you even though they're not supposed to." Tracey's voice was soft and whispery once the truck engine was off. Josh parked in front of Lake Waco and opened his window.

"The Company isn't involved like you think. I don't have contact with any of them. I won't be sure Aiden is on our side until I get the text with details about the flight. If there is a flight. They might transport Teno-reno some other way."

She rubbed her hands up and down her arms as if she was trying to get warm. Thing was, it had to be ninety degrees outside and he'd cut off the engine quite a while ago. Was she as frightened as he was? Maybe.

He kept his arm across the top of the seat instead of draped over her shoulders where he wanted to put it. Then he extended his hand in an invitation to sit next to him. She took it.

In spite of the trauma and fright, it was a night of firsts. He wanted to hold her because she gave him strength, made him able to face what was coming next. But he couldn't explain that yet. Not while the kids were missing.

He laced her fingers through hers. The tops of her

hands against his palms. His larger hands covered her shaking limbs and she drew them closer around her.

"Want to talk about…anything?" she asked.

"My experience is sort of taking me to the deep end."

"Is that why you're so quiet?"

"I'm quiet?" He never said much. People called him a deep thinker. The Company knew not to interrupt when his feet were up on the corner of his desk. "There's a lot I could tell you. Rain check? It's not the time to think about distractions."

"I look forward to listening and I agree. We need to prepare." She moved their arms as if throwing a punch with each hand.

"Probably. Dammit, Tracey. Do you have any idea how I feel?"

"If your emotions are half as mixed up as mine… Then yes." She squeezed his fingers.

"There's a lot we need to talk about."

"Past, future and present. I know. We've avoided it for quite a while. I understand. I sort of feel disloyal. Then again, I can't help the way I feel."

"You feel disloyal?" he asked, finally looking at Tracey.

"Of course I do, Josh. Gwen was my friend."

He nodded, knowing what she meant. But he also knew that Gwen would want them to be happy…not guilty. When they had the kids back, they'd talk. They'd work it out.

"Do you have any idea what's in store? I know you've worked a couple of missing children cases." She spoke in his direction, but he could only see her in profile.

"Those were more parent abductions. Nothing on this scale."

"But you think they're all right. They wouldn't need me to take care of Jackson if something had happened." She sat straighter, talking to the front windshield. "Wait. You're not sure why they want me, too. Are you?"

"There's a possibility that they've discovered your family has money. They could want that on top of what they want from me. I don't think that's the reason, though."

Tracey relaxed against him, pulling his arms around her like a safety blanket. They shared comfort and intimacy, and the knowledge that they were both scared without having to admit it.

"So everything's just a big mess. I can never tell you how sorry I am about my uncle's interference."

"It wasn't your fault. No need to think about it." In spite of the August heat, she shivered, so Josh hugged her tighter. "I wish there was time to give you some training to protect yourself. It's probably better to get some rest—while you can."

"You think I need self-defense?"

"More like, if you know you're about to be hit—" He had to clear his throat to say the rest. The thought of her being hit was tearing him apart. "Yeah, if that happens, then turn with the…um…the punch. You'll take less of an impact. But the best-case scenario is to keep your head down and don't talk back."

"In other words, don't give them a reason to hit me. I can do that."

"Right." As much as he loved holding her in his arms, they turned until they could face each other again. "Dammit, Tracey. You can't do this. It's too dangerous. When they call I'm going to tell them you refused."

"No. What if it *is* about the money and not just

about Jackson's diabetes? What then? We'll be right back where we are now." She scooted back to the passenger seat. "I totally get why you don't think I can handle this."

"What? That's not it. I have more confidence in your ability to take care of Jackson than I do in mine. It's dangerous, that's all."

"I haven't forgotten how dangerous it is." She rubbed the side of her face that had been hit during the kidnapping.

Josh took her hand in his again. He wasn't going to let tripping over his own words create a misunderstanding. There was a chance that when they faced the kidnappers they may never have another moment—anxious or tender.

"It's not a lack of confidence. I'm just—"

"Shh. Don't say it out loud. It's okay. I am, too."

Afraid. They were both afraid of what was going to happen to them, to the kids, to their world. Changes were coming.

Dawn was still an hour away as Josh watched Tracey sleep. Her head was balanced on her arm, resting on the door frame, window down with every mosquito at Reynolds Creek Park buzzing its way into the cab.

He swatted them to their deaths in between the catnaps he caught. He hadn't tried to fall asleep. Maybe if he had, he would have been wide-awake. He'd drifted to the sounds of crickets and lake waves splashing against tree stumps.

The lakeside park was quiet during the early morning. On any usual morning, he would get up, feed the horses, make breakfast, dress the twins and drop them off at their day care before heading into the office. Normal for a single dad.

He wanted to believe that their life was just as normal as the next family's. He heard the whining buzz of another mosquito and fanned the paper sack from the convenience store to create a breeze. The everyday stuff might not be that much different for the kids.

Who could say what normal really was in the twenty-first century? Not him. If he got his family back, who was to say it would ever be normal for them again? Tracey waved her hand next to her ear.

"Ring, dammit."

"What's wrong?" Tracey whispered.

"I'm willing the phone to ring."

"Is it working?" she asked with her mouth in the crook of her elbow.

"Nope."

Normal? Since it was Saturday, he should be waking his kids up three or four hours from now, searching their room for shin guards and taking them to a super peewee soccer game. He should be standing on the sidelines, biting his lip to stop himself from yelling at the twins to stay in their positions and not just chase the ball.

She stretched. "I know how to make it ring. Take me to the restrooms and it's sure to buzz while I'm inside. You know, that whole Murphy's law thing."

"You have a point." He moved the truck up the road and around a corner, keeping the headlights off so as not to wake the campers.

Tracey jumped out. He watched a possum by the park's trash area. It had frozen when the truck had approached. Would his kids be afraid after this? Afraid of strangers? Cars? Afraid of being alone? Were they being kept in the dark? Possibly buried alive?

"Anything?" She'd been gone less than five minutes.

He shook his head and took his turn in the restroom. His movements were slowing and his thoughts progressing at the horrors his kids could be facing right at that moment. The hand dryer finished and he heard Tracey yell his name.

"Should I answer it?" She was out of the truck running toward him.

"Do it."

"Hello?" she said, on Speaker.

"That's good. Glad you could join the party, Tracey."

It was the kidnapper. If his ears hadn't confirmed it, then Tracey's look of fright would have. Her hand shook so much that he took both it and the phone between his.

"Put Jackson and Sage on the phone." He sounded a lot more forceful than he felt. Inside he prayed that they'd both be able to talk to him.

"The brats aren't awake yet and you don't want me to send one of the boys in their room to wake them up."

"I need to know—"

"Nothing! You need nothing. You're going to do whatever I want you to do, whenever I want you to do it."

He was right.

Tracey stared at him, nodded. He couldn't say it was okay. He couldn't admit that this man threatening to harm his children could ask him to do anything…and he would do it.

"What do you want us to do?" she asked.

His heart stopped just like it had the day the doctor told him there was no hope for Gwen. He couldn't move. Tracey's free hand joined his, pulling her closer to the phone. Whose hand was shaking now?

"Wherever you're hiding from the cops, you have fifteen minutes to get to Lovers Leap. Don't be late." *Click.*

"Do you know where Lovers Leap is, Josh?" Tracey shook his arm. "Isn't it over by Cameron Park?"

"Yeah. Sure. I know where it's at."

"Then let's get moving." She tugged on his arm.

"I can't seem to move."

"What's wrong?" Even in the low golden light from the public restroom he could see her concern. She moved to his side, tugged his arm around her shoulders. "Come on. Just lean on me and I'll get you to the truck."

It was slow going, but she managed it. It felt like they used all fifteen minutes of their time, but a glance at his watch told him they still had ten.

"Shock. I think you're in shock and I'm not sure what I can do." She turned the engine over.

"Drive. I'll... I'll be okay when we get there."

He needed to see his kids. Needed to get Tracey there to take care of them. Needed to do whatever these crazy bastards wanted him to, so they'd be free.

Whatever the price. Whatever it took.

"Are you having a heart attack?" She split her focus from the dark road to Josh's pale face.

"I'm okay. Just drive. You have to get to the opposite side of Lake Waco." Josh braced himself in the truck. He rubbed his upper arm, kept it across his chest.

And he was scaring her more than the phone call.

"I think I know where I'm going. You really don't look okay."

"I will be by the time you get there. Quit driving like an old lady."

"Quit trying to change the subject. Do you hurt anywhere? Is your arm numb?"

"I told you I'm not having a heart attack." His voice was stronger and he pushed his hand against the ceiling as she took a corner a little too sharply. "Whatever it was it's gone. Your driving has scared the life back into my limbs."

Panic attack. Thinking it was okay. Saying it aloud might just make it begin again. She'd never tell. Josh's men didn't need to know that the major of Company F was human.

"Is there any of that soda left? Maybe you need sugar or something?" They were nearing Cameron Park and she had to change her thoughts to what was going to happen. "What if they take me and the kids?"

"Your first priority is the twins. In fact, that's your only priority. Your only responsibility. No matter what they do to me, say about me, or threaten me." Josh shook his head and swallowed hard.

"The same goes for me, Josh. You do whatever it takes to keep Jackson and Sage alive."

"Remember, they seemed a little scared about dealing with Jackson. If you can convince them to drop him off at a hospital, then do it."

"I will." She gave the keys to Josh. He didn't look as pale as when they were at the last parking lot.

"Why did they all call each other Mack? It's confusing."

"Or smart. They call everyone Mack so no real names are used. They wear masks so we can't identify their faces. Hopefully that gives them the security they need not to kill us. So refer to them by body type or what they do. Like the one that gives the orders. He can be In-Charge Mack."

"Is that what you do with the Rangers?" She nervously looked around the park and raced on before he could answer. "No one's here. I wonder if we should get out."

"They're here. There's no vehicle close by. That means they didn't bring the kids. One's on the back side of the restroom building. Another has a rifle behind the north pillar of the pavilion."

The phone was in the seat between them. It buzzed with a text message for her to get out of the car and go with Mack. The second message told Josh to stay.

She tried to brush it off, but admitted, "Josh I'm... I'm scared."

"So am I. I want you to remember this. I'll insist on a video chat when we make contact. They might force you to say whatever they want. I need to know that you and the kids are really okay. So if it's true, then tell me..."

"Something just we know. It'll have to be short."

"Right."

Tracey was nervous. For her, it would be unusual to say I love you. It was on the tip of her tongue to admit that. Thinking like a criminal wasn't her forte, but she understood that they might force her to say those words.

"Let's keep it as simple as possible. Tell me you think you left the whiskey bottle on the counter if you're okay and still in Waco. If you're not okay, play with your ring. If you don't think you're in Waco, then put the whiskey in a friend's house. Can you remember that? Totally off the wall for them, memorable for us."

"What do I say if you can't see me playing with my ring?"

"Say that you wish we hadn't ditched your body-guards." He smiled and took her hand in his and tugged her across the seat. "Come on over here to get out. I can always get back inside if they order me to."

He defied their instructions when his feet hit the ground. Turning to help her from the truck, he pulled her into his arms. Their lips meshed and melted together from the heat of the unknown to come. It was a kiss of desperation, representing all the confusion she'd been feeling for months.

Shoes were hitting pavement behind her. Men were running toward them. She'd already experienced how brutal these men could be.

"You need to be in one piece if you're going to rescue us," she whispered to the man she was falling in love with. Before any of the kidnappers could grab her she got her hands on Jackson's emergency kit, juice and snacks inside.

Josh cupped her face with his hands. "You're the bravest woman I've ever known. There's no way to thank you." He gently kissed her again.

This kiss felt like goodbye. Sweet, gentle, not rushed in desperation or as fast as her heart that was pounding like it would explode.

The men pulled them apart, taking Jackson's bag from her. "Stop. Jackson needs that."

"But you don't. We'll give you what you need when you need it." Tracey fell back a step trying to get out of his way. It was the man who'd hit her. The man who'd been talking to them over the phone… In-Charge Mack.

His cruel eyes peeked through the green ski mask.

But they weren't looking at her. No, they watched Josh. They scanned him from head to toe, sizing him up just before shoving him into the side of the truck. Hard.

"When I give an order you better follow it. Don't push me, Major Parker," In-Charge Mack screamed. "Take her to the van."

Birds flew overhead as the world began to brighten. She couldn't see the sun yet, but it was that golden moment where you knew the world was about to be brilliant. She also knew—before his hand raised—that In-Charge Mack intended to hit Josh. It was part of the man's makeup.

The gloved hand moved.

"Stop!" Her hand moved, too. Directly in the path of In-Charge Mack's arm, catching part of the force and slowing him down. "You put me in the hospital. Don't you need Josh without a concussion?"

In-Charge Mack's hand struck as quickly as a snake taking out its prey. The force sent Tracey stumbling into Mack with the rifle. She couldn't see, but she heard the scuffle, the curses, the "don't hurt her" before Josh was restrained by two other men.

"I'm okay. It's okay," she said as quickly as she could force her jaw to move. She looked back at Josh straining at his captors, then at the man who'd hit her. "You need both of us, remember?"

"What I don't need is you talking at all." He gestured with a nod and thrust his chin toward the bike path.

The man who'd grabbed her, slung the rifle over his shoulder and latched on to her arm again. Jerking her toward the park area, she stumbled often from watching Josh instead of the path. When she could no longer see him, she looked in front of her just in time to miss a tree.

The sun was up. Light was forcing the darkness to the shadows. Fairly symbolic for their journey today. She needed good to triumph. She needed hope because they were on their own. Somehow she'd get the twins out of this mire and keep them safe until their dad came home.

THE INSTINCT TO be free was tremendous. The two men holding Josh weren't weaklings by any definition, but he didn't try. He saw the cloth. Then they poured liquid over it. He jerked to the side avoiding their effort to bring him forward.

Chloroform?

Maybe his hunch about the plane wasn't so far off after all. If they felt like they needed him to be out cold for a while, then whatever he was doing wasn't nearby. One of the extras joining the party was digging around the emergency supplies they'd brought. Tracey must have dropped them when she'd been hit.

"Hey! Jackson needs the stuff in that bag."

"Don't worry about your kid. That's why the babysitter's here."

"Shut up, Mack," instructed the ringleader. "Put the juice back in the bag and take it to the other Mack."

The guy giving all the orders approached him with the cloth and bottle.

"Look, tell me Jackson's still okay. Is he alert? Talking? How's Sage? Just tell me and I'll behave. No problem. There's no reason to knock me out."

"Your kid is fine."

The guy running the show nodded to the men holding Josh. They planted their feet and tightened their grips. It might be inevitable, but he wouldn't just stand there and inhale peaceably.

Chapter Eleven

Blindfolded. Tracey swore the man driving her to wherever the twins were being held was lost. They had to be close by. It felt like he literally drove in circles. No one had mentioned Jackson or Sage. She thought they'd been joined in the van by a second person back at the park, but the one who'd escorted her could have been mumbling to himself.

You're the bravest woman I've ever known.

A lie. Gwen had been that woman. Strong and fearless in the face of death. But Tracey wasn't going to take Josh's words lightly. She couldn't forget that he'd said them, any more than she could ignore that he was saying goodbye.

The van stopped and so did her thoughts about Josh. Now it was about Jackson. Every piece of knowledge she'd learned and could remember about diabetes would be important.

They'd kept such a close eye on Jackson before yesterday, that he hadn't had any close calls since his initial diagnosis. They even monitored Sage regularly to make certain juvenile diabetes wasn't in her future. There was no guarantee, but they wouldn't be unprepared.

"Get out."

"Can I take off the—"

"Just scoot to the edge and I'll take you inside."

She did what they said. She didn't hear anything unusual. It was still very early in the morning, but there
were few natural sounds. She thought she heard the
faint—sort of blurry—noise of cars on I-35. The low
hum could be heard from multiple spots—and miles
throughout Waco. At least she'd be able to find her
way to safety.

*The twins...your only priority. Your only responsi-
bility.*

The men each held one elbow and led her through
a series of hallways. She assumed they were hallways.
She heard keys in locks, dead bolts turning, doors opening and shutting. Three to be exact.

Inside there wasn't any noise. It was like the world
had turned off. Then the blindfold was removed and
she blinked in the bright sun reflecting into a mirror.
She was still blinking when the fourth door was opened
and she was pushed inside. Jackson's emergency bag
was tossed in after her.

Thank goodness.

She expected a dark, dingy place. Maybe full of cobwebs or a couple of mice running around. She'd completely forgotten about the video that showed the kids
playing with a room full of toys.

They were everywhere. Plastic kitchens complete
with pots and pans. Lawn mowers that blew bubbles.
A table where they could build a LEGO kingdom on
top. Stuffed animals piled in a corner.

Where were the kids?

Who would buy all these toys for a kidnapping?
What would be the purpose? She looked closer at them

and noticed they were all clean, but very well-used. They were probably from garage sales or thrift shops. Wherever they'd been purchased, no one would remember the person.

But where were the kids?

She picked up one of the many stuffed animals and sat in a chair made for children. Two mostly eaten sandwiches were on the table. Two bottles of water, barely touched, sat next to them. She spotted Sage's backpack under a giant bear. Next to it, her gold glitter slipper.

Tracey crossed the room and bent to pick it up. There, huddled under the pile of used stuffed toys, with their eyes squeezed tightly shut, were the twins. Relief washed over her, but she had to remain calm. Even a little excitement might overtax Jackson's blood sugar at this point.

"Hey kidlets, it's Trace Trace," she whispered, afraid to scare them.

Stuffed giraffes, dinosaurs, bears and alligators flew in all directions as the kids scrambled to their feet. Their backpacks were looped around their shoulders, ready to walk through the door. Shoes on the wrong feet meant they'd been off at least once.

Grape jelly was at the corner of Sage's mouth. But the most important thing was that Jackson looked alert and safe.

"Are you okay?"

She opened her arms and they flew into a hug. The relief she felt that they were both alive and okay… She couldn't think of words to describe the emotion.

"Can we go now, Trace Trace?" Jackson asked. "Where's Daddy?"

"I want to go, too," Sage said. "Why didn't Daddy come get us?"

"Have you had breakfast? Are you really okay?" She turned to Jackson again, gauging his eyes, looking for any indicators that his blood sugar was too low. "Do you have a headache or feel nauseous?"

"Nope."

"He's been good." Sage lifted her hand to her mouth, trying to whisper to Tracey—it didn't work. "I hid the candy they gave us in the oven."

"Oh, I knew where you put it. But I didn't want to get sick if there wasn't anybody here to take care of me."

"Sage, hon, run and get that bag with Jackson's medicine stuff."

The little girl skipped over and skipped back. Both children seemed okay on the outside.

"Do we have to stay?" Sage whined, deservingly so.

"For a little while longer." Tracey pulled the materials she needed to test Jackson's blood sugar from the bag.

The little darling was so used to the routine that he sat with his finger extended, ready for the testing. She put a fresh needle into the lancing device, and took a test strip from the container.

Sage tore the alcohol wipe package open and handed it to her. They all lived with this disease. They'd had their share of ups and downs, but they stayed on top of it.

"I love you guys. Do you know that?" She wiped off the extended finger, punched the button, dropped the droplet of blood on the strip and placed it in the meter.

Two little heads bobbed up and down. She hid her

anxiousness waiting on the results. He was in the safe zone, ready to eat his breakfast and start his day.

Thank God.

"Have you two been alone all this time?"

"Nu-uh."

"Some guy sits with a mask all over his face. Says he's hot." Sage was the talker, the observant one, the storyteller. "Then he leaves and comes back sometimes."

"Sometimes he tries to play," Jackson added. "That guy came in with his phone one time. 'Member?"

"Yeah, but he wasn't fun. He was angry and mean."

They sat in the chairs next to her at the table. She put a banana on each little plastic plate. Wiped out the glasses as best as she could and poured a little bit of juice in them. She noticed that one of the juice bottles was missing so she kept a third of the bottle, placing it back in the bag.

"So, eat and I'll get some crackers."

"For breakfast?" they said together.

"There's nothing wrong with bananas and crackers."

"Aren't you eating?" Jackson asked, peeling one section and turning the banana sideways for a bite. He left it there, like a giant smile, then posed until she acknowledged him.

He swallowed his bite and laughed, showing the mashed banana on his tongue. Sage said "yuck," and then they all three laughed, making Tracey want to cry. How could any of this be funny? But if she didn't laugh and act as if it was, then they'd get anxious and stressed.

Stress was bad for blood sugar.

Very bad.

Laughing, playing and maybe casually looking for a way out of this room. That's what their day would be. Maybe the man who was scary and mean would stay away.

Maybe if they were really lucky, Josh would haul all the mean Macks to jail. Then the Parker family could all live happily ever after.

"I want to go home, Trace Trace."

"I know, Jackson. And we will. But while we're here, what do you want to play?"

"Princesses. I thought of something first, so we play my game." Sage darted around looking through the toy pile for princess gear.

"I don't feel like playing." Jackson crawled into her lap and rested his head on her shoulder.

She wasn't going to panic. His level was within normal range. He was outside his routine and would be tired even if he didn't have diabetes. "Okay. Sage, would it be okay if I just told you a story?"

"I can't find any princess hats anyway."

"You know, Sage, you don't have to have a princess hat to be a princess."

"You don't? But isn't it more fun if you do?" She smiled and twirled. "What story are you going to tell?"

"Let's go sit on the mattress so Jackson can take a nap. I mean rest 'cause Prince Jackson doesn't take naps." Then she tickled Sage. "Neither does Princess Sage. Right?"

"Right."

They sat down and Tracey created a story about a prince and a princess who lived with their father, the king. When they asked the king's name she told them King Parker. Sadly, the queen didn't live with them anymore. The story went on and of course the kids recognized that it was about them.

"Then one day a horrible evil dragon swooped down and stole the beautiful princess and handsome prince. The dragon..." The kids held on to her hands tightly and snuggled a little closer. "What should we name the awful dragon?"

"Mack," they said in unison.

"Okay. Mack the dragon was tired of flying around burning up all the bridges. So he went back to the cave where he held the princess and prince. 'What do you want with us?' said the beautiful princess."

Tracey changed voices for each character in the story. The kids were nodding off. Both rested their heads in her lap when one of the Macks came through the door, bolted it behind him and sat on the bench.

She stopped referring to the dragon as Mack. There was no reason to antagonize one of them. And no reason to continue the story since both of the kids were asleep.

Tracey left them curled where they were and propped another blanket behind her head. She pretended to rest and assessed the room through half-closed lids. There didn't seem to be any other way out. The next time they left her alone, she'd be bold and just look.

All those years growing up a rich kid, she'd been warned to be careful. Super careful. She was never allowed to go anywhere alone. Not until her second semester at Baylor.

She remembered the guy who looked like a college student and had followed her around campus. He even had season tickets to football games. Probably not the section he wanted, but her uncle's money had bought him access to a lot.

It took begging her grandfather and whining that she had no friends to get him to call off the hounds.

Promising that she'd be overly careful, she was finally on her own. That's when she realized she didn't really know how to make friends.

Then a bad date had shot her overprotective uncle into warlord status. He declared she didn't have any rights and as long as he was paying the bills—blah blah blah. Poor little rich girl, right?

Who would have thought that the first time she'd be placed into real danger would be because she worked for a Texas Ranger? What a laugh her grandfather would have had about this mess.

So there she was, thinking about her grandfather, sitting awkwardly with two precious children asleep on her lap, praying that they'd grow up without being frightened of the world. And then more simply, she just prayed that they'd be able to grow up.

"Trace Trace?" Sage said sleepily. "What happened to the king? Did he get his kids back?" She yawned. "Did he get to be happy?"

"Sure, sweetie. He used his strong sword and killed the dragon. And all the Parkers lived happily ever after."

"Trace…is your name Parker, too?"

"No, kidlet. It's not."

Sage drifted back to sleepy land giving Tracey more time to think about it. She wouldn't be a part of the Parker happy-ever-after. It was time for her to ride into the sunset alone.

Chapter Twelve

Josh lost track of how many times they'd covered his face with the sweet-smelling gauze. Enough for him to have a Texas-size headache. Long enough that his body recognized he'd been in one position too long, lying across the metal flooring of a panel van. And long enough that his stomach thought his neck had been cut off.

The skyline through the van window showed only trees and stars. Definitely not the skyscrapers that would indicate a city. They could still be in Waco, but he had a feeling they'd driven closer to the state prison where Tenoreno was being held.

The men surrounding him were unmasked, but it was too dark to make out any of their faces. Now wearing garb like a strike force—military boots, pants, bullet-proof vests, gun holsters strapped to their thighs. Tracey was right. The idea of calling each other Mack tended to be confusing. He had to admit that it was effective. But they didn't act like a cohesive team.

Josh's hands were taped behind him. Tightly. The hairs on his wrists pulled with each tug he tried to hide. There must be several layers because it wasn't budging. He wouldn't be getting free unless he had a knife.

For the Macks, it had been a good idea to knock him out cold while they traveled. His brain was still fuzzy while he attempted to soak up everything about his situation and process it for a way out. If he'd been awake, the problem would be resolved or at least he'd have a working theory.

Someone kicked the back of his thigh. He held himself in check, but a grunt of pain escaped. He tried not to move. He needed time for the cobwebs to clear. But there wasn't any use trying to hide that he was awake. Even if he wasn't alert.

"Masks on. He's awake."

The thought at the forefront of his mind was Jackson's health and his family's safety. He could only estimate how long his captors had been driving. It might still be early afternoon.

One step at a time.

"I need to talk to Tracey."

If only he could get In-Charge Mack and his men to confirm what they had in store for him. As in why did they need him personally? Whatever it was, they felt like they needed hostages to keep him in line. Once they confirmed, he'd know how to proceed.

Or where to proceed.

"It's time to earn your keep, lawman." The guy who'd kicked him laughed.

They had his phone. Aiden must have texted the location information. Good, they also had his bag from the house. He had a few tricks in there that would help get his family back.

"We're talking to the men that are with her in ten minutes. Behave and you might get an update." The In-Charge Mack didn't even glance back from the front seat.

Laughing Mack looked around, saw where they were, and then pulled a gun to point at Josh's head. "Behave." The gun went under a loose sweatshirt—still aimed at him.

They pulled even with another vehicle, the drivers nodded at each other and separated. He could see the other car lights in the rearview mirror as it did a three-point turn in the road and followed closely behind.

"Where are we?"

"Thanks to you, daddy dearest is scheduled for a private plane ride to get to trial. You're our passport," In-Charge Mack said from up front.

"Daddy? Aren't you a little short to be Xander Tenoreno?"

Laughing Mack kicked out, connecting with Josh's knee.

He'd actually confronted the son of Paul Tenoreno several times. At each encounter he'd looked him straight in the eye. The guy giving the orders here was only about five foot ten. Average height for an above-average criminal.

But he couldn't reject the hunch that these men were regular employees of the Mafia ring in Texas. They were definitely well funded and prepared. The animosity that was associated with their talk about Tenoreno was a bit intense. Why free a man you hated so that he could run the operation again?

"If you'd told me your plans a little earlier, I could have saved you the trouble. They pulled all my authority yesterday when you kidnapped my kids." He wanted to see their reaction. What was their ulterior motive? "I can't get you on that plane."

"Don't be so modest, Major. We have every confidence in your abilities." The one calling the shots turned to show him a picture of Tracey with the kids. "We also have very little confidence that Mack in toy land will keep his cool if you don't get the job done. He's itchy to pull the trigger, don't ya know."

"Isn't it time to stop talking in riddles and tell me what you really want?"

"You haven't figured it out? But you're so good at this. Your Texas Ranger buddies got poor old Mr. Tenoreno moved to the Holliday Transfer Facility. He's waiting to be flown to Austin. We're going to pay him a visit."

"I can't get you inside there, either." Josh attempted to push himself up to a sitting position. His ankles were also taped tightly together. He pushed on a hard-sided case.

"Are you being dense on purpose?" Laughing Mack lashed out with his boot, catching the back of Josh's leg.

"Your kid here is going to make walking anywhere a problem. Call him off. I need my knees." Josh made note of how many guns were in the van.

"Mack, mind your manners." He spoke to the guy still pointing the gun in Josh's direction, but he pointed twice like he was giving directions to the driver.

Josh used the bumps in the road to help shift his position. He was finally upright and could see more of the view. A field, lots of trees, nothing special out the front. But when he glanced out the back, just behind the second vehicle were soccer and baseball fields.

He knew exactly where they were—Huntsville Municipal Airport. He'd assumed that they'd attack here. He'd just expected a little more time to figure out how to throw a kink in their plan.

"Whatever you're planning, I'm not doing a damn thing until I talk to Tracey. And I mean talk, not just see her picture."

"I figured as much. Almost time."

The van started up, speeding down the dirt road, then pulled under a canopy of trees. The second vehicle pulled in next to them.

"They've left the prison. We have six minutes," the Mack next to him said.

"No Tracey. No cooperation."

"Dial the phone. Remember it's face-to-face and you watch," he told Laughing Mack. "Make it quick."

One thing about this outfit, everyone in it obeyed In-Charge Mack without hesitation. Tracey's face was on the phone screen. She reached out toward the phone at her end, looked sharply away and then back at him.

"They won't let me hold the kids so you can see them but they're doing okay. Sage has been watching over her brother, as usual.'"

"And how is Jackson?"

"He's doing okay. I'm sure he's going to bounce right back after this."

"Have they hurt you?"

"Nothing that a shot of whiskey wouldn't cure. Did I leave it in the middle of the house?"

"What was that?" In-Charge Mack asked.

"She said she wanted some whiskey," Laughing Mack relayed to him.

"That's enough. Disconnect."

"Josh? I wanted to tell you that I—"

Laughing Mack got a big kick out of cutting her off. *Tell me what?*

He didn't have time to process. They opened the van doors and Josh could see the airfield.

"Out."

He lifted his bound ankles and the Mack nearest the door sliced them free with a knife Josh hadn't seen. He really did need to clear his head and become aware of his surroundings. Think this thing through.

The Macks moved the hard-sided case that had been near his feet to outside and flipped the lid open. Machine pistols.

"You really think those are necessary?"

"Glad you asked, Major. Obviously, this is the backup. If you fail, we're bringing down that plane."

"What exactly do you want me to do? I thought you were here to free Tenoreno." Josh kept his eyes moving. Trying to remember how each of them stood. If they showed any signs of weakness or additional personal weapons.

"Wrong, Major. You're here to kill him."

Chapter Thirteen

Tracey was taking a huge risk. What if they weren't res-cued before Jackson needed this cartridge? And what if she *didn't* use the insulin on the sleeping guard? It might be her only opportunity to try to escape. What if Josh didn't—

No! Josh was coming back. He'd never give up and neither would she. She put the kids to sleep on the mattress, leaving their shoes on their feet so they'd be ready. Jackets and bags were by the door. They wouldn't leave without them. It was their routine and no reason to argue.

Taking this risk was necessary, not just a shot in the dark. It would work. She knew what the side effects of too much insulin were. In a healthy person, he'd proba-bly vomit, but he'd eventually pass out. She didn't know how many men were on the other side of the door.

The young man watching them had already com-plained about how warm it was while wearing the ski mask. The room had its own thermostat. It looked like an old office space. She switched the cool to heat and cranked the temperature up. It was going to be unbear-able in a couple of hours. Their guard would get hotter, faster—of course, so would they.

The last thing to do while he was gone from the room was to prep the needle with insulin and hide it. They'd take the emergency kit back and return it to the other room as soon as a Mack came to keep an eye on them. Their ultimate weapon to keep her in line was taking away the emergency kit for Jackson.

"I bet your boss wouldn't like knowing that you don't stay in here while I check Jackson's blood sugar. Nope. None of this would be possible if you did," she said to herself, capping the needle. She couldn't keep it in her pockets. They'd see it for sure.

So she arranged toys and the kid-sized kitchen station near the bench where the guards sat. It was simple to keep the syringe with the toy utensils. She snagged one and put it on the table so she'd have an excuse to exchange it later.

She could give the injection without the guard feeling more than a small prick on his skin. Insulin didn't need a vein, just fatty tissue. If he was sound asleep it might not bother him at all. But she had a sharp toy ready as an explanation. She also moved the trash can closer to the bench…just in case.

They should be coming back into the room soon. She'd been wondering for far too long about life and what the next stage held for her. When all this was done and over, there wouldn't be any waiting. It was so much better to find out. To know.

Leaving Waco, leaving her friends, leaving Josh wasn't her first choice. Waiting wasn't, either. She had to stop being a scaredy cat and start living life. That meant handing in her resignation to Josh and telling him how she really felt.

Forty-eight hours ago she'd been ready to give her

notice and walk away. Even if it broke her heart. Well, there was no doubt her heart would shatter now, but it was a resilient organ and she'd manage. She could walk away if Josh didn't ask her to stay.

The locks on the door turned. She dropped her head into her arms on the tiny table and calmed her breathing. She was physically exhausted from a lack of sleep, food and an abundance of adrenaline pumping constantly. Forcing herself to pretend to be asleep might just slow her physical state to let it happen.

Being bent in half like she was wouldn't let her stay asleep for long.

The same guard came straight to the table to collect the emergency kit. She barely saw him through her lashes, watching his silhouette turn off the lamps in the corners, and then sit on the bench.

First step…check.

Rest, rest, rest. She was going to need it to get to safety.

There wasn't a clock in the room and they'd taken her watch—another way to make her dependent on them for Jackson's care. But her body told her she'd been in the cramped position far too long and she hoped her guard was deep in sleep. She pushed her damp hair away from her face.

It was definitely beyond hot.

She took the toy spatula and stood, trying not to make any noise. She'd cleared her path, thinking this through earlier. No squeaky toys, nothing to trip over.

She kept on her toes, not allowing her boot heels to make noise against the linoleum floor. She exchanged the toy gadget for the syringe and removed the needle cover. Still no peep from the kids or their guard. She looked at him; he'd rolled the ski mask up his face, covering his eyes. The smooth chin meant he'd either just shaved or he didn't need to.

The covered eyes meant it would be easier to follow through on her plan. He'd have to move the mask before he could see where she was. She risked a lot by tugging a little at his black T-shirt, but if she could stick this in his side…

Done.

This Mack, sitting on the bench, turned and grunted. He didn't wake. She replaced the cap, threw the syringe away like all the other supplies from earlier and tiptoed to sit on the mattress with the kids.

It didn't take long before their guard moaned, then held his stomach like he was cramping. Before Mack could reach the door, he detoured for the garbage.

Tracey didn't hesitate. She couldn't let herself think about what would happen to the young man. He was a kidnapper. He'd threatened Jackson's life. She was going to make sure the little boy was safe.

No matter the cost. No matter who she had to knock out with insulin to do it. Even in the dim light she could tell he was sweating and disoriented. He was unsteady on his feet and faintly asked for help.

She wanted to. She had to cover her ears, she wanted to help him so badly.

Instead, she got the kids up and sat them in chairs. Jackson was a little woozy and put his head back onto the table. When the young guard began leaning to one side, she struggled with him to put him on the mattress. Then searched his pockets for a cell phone.

Nothing except the keys to the doors.

Before she scooted the twins out of the room, she

checked out the other side of the door. No one was there. She ventured farther, listening before she turned each corner. No signs of the other men. She quietly headed back and saw both of their heads poking around the edge.

Backpacks on, they ran to meet her.

"Are we going home now?" Sage asked.

"First we have to play hide-and-seek. You can't giggle or tell anybody where we're at. Okay?"

Both their heads bobbed. Sage jumped up and down, smiled then got Jackson excited as well. "We get to go home. We get to see Daddy." They said in unison, jumping again.

"Please guys, it's really important for us to be quiet. Shh." She placed a finger across her lips and lowered her voice. "Quiet as church mice. Ready?"

They hurried downstairs, where she used the keys again to get out the front door. Austin Avenue?

They were in downtown Waco? It must be the wee hours of the morning, because this was an area of town that was open until two. She hadn't heard any party or loud music. No wonder they'd filled the room with toys to keep the kids occupied and silent.

Tracey ran. She hoisted Jackson to her hip, holding tight to Sage's little hand. "Come on, baby, I know you're tired, but we've got to run. You can do it."

Where to?

They had to be gone—out of view. Fast. Before someone discovered they'd left their room. She tried the sandwich shop next door.

Locked.

They'd all be locked. Everything closed in this part of town. There was nothing to throw at a window. No alarm she could set off without the kidnappers looking out their window and seeing her.

So close.

They were so close to freedom. If they could just find somebody...

Nothing but parking lots, a closed sandwich shop, more parking lots and the ALICO Building. Maybe there was somebody still there.

It was the dead of night and there were no headlights. No one around to wave down for help. They made it across Austin Avenue and then again across Fifth Street. A door banged open. She dared to look back for a split second. It was them.

"Over there," she heard one of the men say.

"Sage, honey, put your arms around my neck." She'd run for their lives carrying the twins. But where?

The parking garage would be open. She ran between the structures. Garage to her left, fire escape to her right. Fire escape? Then what? Climb twenty-two stories outside the tallest building in Waco with twin four-year-olds?

No. All she had to do was make it up one flight before they saw her. The building was split-level—they could hide on the level that was a parking lot. It was more logical to choose the garage door. She couldn't leave their fate to the off chance someone left their car unlocked and they could hide inside.

What then? Blow the horn until their captors broke the window and carried them back to their downtown dungeon?

It would have to be the fire escape. She set a lethargic Jackson on the stair side of the fire escape, helped Sage over and climbed over herself. They were between buildings where the voices of the men chasing them echoed. She didn't know if it could be done, but it was their only chance.

"Quiet as a mouse, kidlets, we've got to keep quiet. Go ahead and start climbing, sweetheart." She adjusted Jackson on her back moving as fast as she could behind Sage.

One foot, then another. Four-year-old legs couldn't take stairs two at a time. Neither could a twenty-six-year-old with a four-year-old on her back. If she wasn't scared of falling down, she would pick up Sage and make the climb with both of them.

The shouts changed. No longer echoes from the street, they were directly below them. Tracey stopped Sage and slowly—soundlessly—pulled her to the side of the building. Maybe they'd get lucky. Maybe neither of the men would look up. Maybe they'd take the logical path into the garage.

Maybe luck was on their side. Looking by barely tilting her head, she watched as the men took off into the other building.

"More quietly than ever, baby girl. We can do this."

It took time. The one flight was actually a little more than that. Their luck ran out. Just as they made it to the roof so did the kidnappers. They yelled out to each other or at someone else, she couldn't be certain.

They were on the lower roof. She set the twins next to a door and looked around for something to pry it open. No junk in the corner. Nothing just lying around to pick up and bang against metal. She heard the men taking the metal fire escape two steps at a time.

Running to the Fifth Street side of the roof, she

yelled, "Help! Someone help us!" There weren't any headlights, no one walking, nothing.

Then to the parking lot side toward the river. Someone might be hanging out closer to the water, but it was too far away. "Help! Somebody. Anybody."

Chapter Fourteen

The kids were cuddled together. All Tracey could do was join them. They couldn't tackle the twenty stories of fire escape stairs. Even if they did, there wasn't a helicopter waiting to whisk them off to safety.

The men chasing them heard her cries for help. She heard their shoes slam against the metal steps, then across the roof. She braced herself for punches or kicks. The repercussions of running away. Maybe now. Maybe later. But these men would strike out. She'd protect the kids.

She repeated the promise that they'd be all right as the men both angrily kicked her legs. These men would lose. Josh would find them. They *would* lose.

"Stop it! Don't hurt her!" the twins yelled, still wedged between her and the wall.

Their screams echoed in her ears as they were pulled from her arms. One of the men jerked her up by her hair while the other had a hand on each twin. They struggled. She could barely stand.

He dragged her to the edge of the building, threatening to throw her over the side. His hands went around the back of her neck, pushed her to the ledge. She dropped to her knees.

"I wish I could get rid of you," he spitefully whispered. "I'd leave you on that sidewalk along with the jerk who let you escape. Did you hit him with a stuffed unicorn?" He shoved her forward into the concrete barrier. "Get up and get hold of one of them brats."

Limping down the fire escape, she wondered if they'd care that their friend might die from the insulin injection. She carried Jackson, and poor Sage was in the arms of the man to her right.

The men constantly looked over their shoulders, but they weren't followed. No one drove by. No police were in sight. They weren't gentle, especially the blond who held a gun instead of a child and shoved her every third step she took.

"He might just kill us for this. If anybody sees, we're dead. We need to get out of here, fast."

"So we don't tell him, right? He'd just get angry," the man carrying Sage answered. "She sure ain't going to tell him. Mack will never know they got loose. Besides, we got 'em back, didn't we? And we still have another twenty before we're supposed to leave and...you know."

Leave?

Yes, he'd cocked his head toward her. So what did he mean? Leave them or leave with them, taking them to a new location? Or maybe they planned to leave them here after killing them?

Once again she wished that she'd been brave or lucky enough to leave earlier, before the bars on the street had closed. Food trucks were normally one of the last things to leave the now-empty parking lot.

"You need to call 911 for your friend," Tracey told the men, trying to gauge their humanity. "He's very ill and needs emergency care"

"So he's sick. He'll get over it." Gun in hand, he shoved her through the outer door.

Would they call 911? If she admitted why he needed help they'd know for certain that she'd planned her escape instead of taking advantage of their guard being sick. Ultimately, she didn't want the weight of his death on her shoulders.

"I injected him with insulin and he's going into hypoglycemic shock." They ignored her as they entered the building they'd just escaped from. "Can't you drop him at the clinic with a note? He may die."

"That's on your head, lady. You're the one that gave it to him and he was stupid enough to let ya."

They pushed her into the toy room, Sage right behind her. The one holding the gun stuck the barrel under her chin and moved close to her face. His minty breath a stark contrast to the threats. "You listen to me, lady. Stay in line or we're getting rid of you no matter what Mack says."

Then bolted the door.

"Oh my!" She cried out before realizing she needed to control herself for the kids.

"What's wrong, Trace Trace?" Sage asked.

Jackson didn't say anything. He went to the mattress, saw it was full with the young man she'd injected and lay down next to the wall using a teddy bear for a pillow.

"When can we go home?"

"Soon, honey. Soon." She pulled the little girl into her arms and rocked her by shifting her weight from foot to foot. Her long hair was tangled again. She'd finger-comb it after breakfast.

"Did Daddy forget about us?"

"Oh no, baby. He loves you and is doing everything he can to get you back to him."

It took only a few minutes to get Sage to drift off to sleep. She adjusted the children on a blanket and used the secondhand animals to make them comfortable and feel safe.

The young guard wasn't comatose. He roused a little, making her heart a little lighter. He was clammy with sweat, so she used the water from the water bottle to dampen a couple of doll dresses and wiped his brow, trying to make him more comfortable. She would never be able to do that again knowing that the outcome might mean somebody would die.

Sitting still in the predawn hours she remembered something odd about their captors…she knew what they looked like. While chasing her, they'd left their masks behind. She could identify them. This development couldn't be good.

It was her fault for trying to escape. But she had been right about telling Josh the whiskey was in the center of the house. At least she knew they were definitely in the heart of Waco. She prayed that he'd be able to find them.

That line was getting old. Of course she'd hope for that. But she couldn't focus on it, either. She'd do her job and think of another way out of this room. Her life wasn't a series of rescues.

She'd walked away from all that when she turned twenty-one. "Heck, I even changed my name to avoid it." *Pick yourself up and get your head on straight, Tracella Sharon Cassidy Bass.* That was her grandmother's voice talking from her overly pink bedroom. Ha! Years ago Grandma Sweetie had declared that her pieces of advice would come in handy. But Tracey bet even Sweetie wouldn't have imagined this scenario.

She looked at the man in the corner. He was just a man now. Not a creep, not an abductor with a gun—just a young man who needed help. No one deserved to die. And she'd help as best she could. She turned the water bottle upside down and got the last drops onto the cloth.

After she'd cooled their guard's forehead, she decided to talk with the other two guards. She knocked on the door trying not to wake up the kids. Then she knocked a little more forcibly.

"What?" one of them shouted through the wood.

"We need more water."

"Not now."

"Even another bottle for your friend?" She tapped on the door, attempting to get an answer.

"Lady, you need to shut up so we can figure this out."

"There's water in the tan bag you took from me." They'd even taken the kids' backpacks with their toys.

"Yeah, like we're giving that back."

"You have to. It has Jackson's insulin and supplies."

"Isn't that what you stuck in Toby—I mean Mack? One of them insulin needles, right? And you said he could die. So no way. I ain't letting you have it back. Needles are dangerous, man."

There was arguing. Raised voices. Lowered voices.

"Don't matter anyway. We're supposed to head out."

"Are you…are you leaving us? Please unlock the door before—" She tripped backward as the door was pushed open. The gun took her by surprise. When it was pointed at her head, street gangster style, she could only raise her hands and say, "Don't shoot."

"We ain't shooting you, lady. But we don't trust you neither. Get the kids. We're leaving."

"Where are you taking us?"

"Does it matter?" the blond holding the gun in her face said.

"To the airport. He dead yet?" asked the other as he hurried to the corner where the kids were.

"Shut up, you idiot," the blond man insisted. "First you use Toby's name. And dammit, thanks to him," he pointed at the ill man, "she's seen our faces."

She remembered what Josh had said. The kidnappers would feel safe as long as their identities were secret. Would they kill her and the kids now that they weren't? "He, uh, still needs a doctor, but I think he'll be okay."

"That's good I guess."

"No it's not," said the blond, waving the gun like an extension of talking with his hands. "What if somebody finds him? What if he talks?"

"Do we shoot him then?"

"What? You can't— He's unarmed and helpless." Tracey would have pleaded more but the men looked at each other as if she was crazy.

Maybe she was, since they were obviously ready to shoot her and the kids. Now they were going to taking them to a new place? Or could it possibly be...

"Is this an exchange at the airport? Who told you to bring us?"

"We don't do names, lady. We just do what we're told, and then we're gone."

"So there's no reason to kill him." She pointed to the unconscious guy. "You can just leave him here."

"We don't have time, man. If you want to plug him,

go ahead. My hands are full." The second man pulled a sleepy Jackson into his arms.

The blond one lifted Sage. She squirmed and pushed at his shoulders. "I want Trace Trace."

Then she began to cry. For real, not a fake cry to get her way. She was genuinely scared of the man who held her and had a gun pressed against her back.

"Here, let me take her." Tracey held out her arms and Sage threw herself backward, nearly falling between them.

The children were old enough to understand guns. Even at four and a half the twins knew about tension and that guns were dangerous. Their father was a Texas Ranger and had weapons in the house—inside a lockbox and gun cabinet—but they'd already had lectures about how they were weapons and weapons were dangerous.

Sage had watched the gun being waved around. She'd heard the discussion about shooting someone. She could tell things weren't right no matter how many toys were in the room.

"Let's get gone," the blond said. "Mack's expecting us to be there."

Tracey didn't want to draw their attention to the man in the corner, so she grabbed a toy bear for Sage to latch onto and left their backpacks. There were spare crackers and juice in the emergency kit that could tide them over until they received food.

They had almost reached the back door when she asked the blond, "The tan bag with his supplies. Where did it go?"

"Get in the van." He shoved her forward to the back stoop.

"We have to have that bag."

"You ain't jabbin' me with anything."

"No, we can't go without it. Jackson needs it."

"Should have thought 'bout that before you made Toby sick." The second guy put Jackson in her arms after she put Sage in the van.

"Where do I sit?" Sage asked, following with a huge sniff from her tears.

No seats. The panel van had nothing but a smelly old horsehair blanket.

"What an adventure, Sage. You and your new bear friend can help me hold Jackson."

She put the bear on the metal floor and Sage sat cross-legged next to it, then dropped her head onto her hands. Jackson woke up, rubbed his eyes and moved next to the bear, imitating his sister. Sage pursed her lips and Jackson mimicked or answered. Sometimes the twin language was hard to interpret.

The van door closed and they pulled out of the parking lot. It was still before dawn on Sunday morning. Too early for anyone to have noticed them being moved along by gunpoint. A lot of people went to church in Waco, but not *this* early.

Even if someone saw them sitting on the floor of the panel van, no one would think anything suspicious. All they could do was cooperate.

"Trace Trace?" Jackson nudged her leg. "I'm tired and hungry. Where are my snacks?"

"We'll have to wait for breakfast, big boy."

Jackson threw himself backward and stiffened his body. His small fist hit her bruised jaw. She clamped down on the long "ouch" that wanted to escape. It wasn't his fault and she refused to upset him more. When his blood sugar began to get low he became angry and quarrelsome. It was one of the first clues that his levels needed to be adjusted.

"Jackson's always 'posed to have crackers," Sage told her. "He's starting to get a little mean, Trace Trace."

"I know, honey, but they got left with the toys."

Sage leaned closer putting her hand close to her mouth, indicating she didn't want the men to hear her. "Is that man really going to die?"

"No, baby. His sugar's a little low right now, but he's going to be fine."

"That's good."

Tracey held tightly to the sides of the van and the kids held tightly to her. Fortunately, it wasn't a long ride to the Waco Regional Airport. This place wasn't huge by any means. She'd flown home from here several times before she'd turned twenty-one.

Maybe knowing the layout of the airport would be an advantage. If she was given a chance to run, she'd know where to go. But had the Macks hinted at an exchange. Her mind was racing in circles trying to figure it out.

After a few minutes she realized they weren't going to the airport. At least not the one in Waco. The twins fell asleep quickly enough with the rocking motion of the van.

The two men didn't speak to give her additional clues. She couldn't really see scenery out the back window, but it was mainly the black night sky and an occasional streetlamp. She tightened her arms around the kidlets, closed her eyes and concentrated solely on not being scared.

Very scared.

Chapter Fifteen

Kill Tenoreno? Mack wanted him to kill Tenoreno? The person pulling the strings didn't want their leader out of the country? Or who did they bring him here to kill? Less and less about this operation was making sense. He kept coming back to why him and why kidnap his kids? If he could determine the answer to that complicated question, then he might find the solution.

Why tell him to kill the prisoner? Why did they want Tenoreno dead? Why did they bring Josh to pull the trigger? A political nightmare for one. They'd prosecute him and persecute the Texas Rangers. He was thinking too far ahead. The problem was now.

"I'll need a weapon." He was handed a Glock. He fingered the weapon, wanting to pull it on Mack, knowing the man would never hand him a loaded gun. "I prefer my own. It's in the bag you have in the van."

In-Charge Mack shook his head. "Let me say this out loud. Kill me, kill my men, we kill your family. The men holding your kids don't care if they get a call to shoot or get a call to let them go. Understand?"

"Understood."

Thing was, Bryce would be waiting in that hangar, protecting Tenoreno. He wasn't just going to let Josh walk in and shoot anyone. Company F was prepared for an attack to hijack a plane, not massacre everyone. The Mack gang loaded and checked the machine pistols. A lot of men were about to be killed unless he did something.

Or just did what they wanted.

"Your plan doesn't make sense. You can't be certain I won't point this at the wrong person." He aimed the Glock at Mack's head. Three of the leader's men immediately pointed machine pistols at his.

"Hold on, give the Major time to accept the inevitable."

"And what would that be?"

"Mack." In-Charge pointed to the man to his right. "Dial."

Josh aimed his barrel at the night sky. "Point taken."

"You are a useful tool to get us inside the plane…for the moment. Just don't push me again."

Mack waved off the guns and took a step closer to Josh. "Between you and me, I didn't like this plan. Never liked depending on the emotional state of an anxious father. Give me solid logic."

He clapped Josh on the back, took his Glock and removed an empty magazine.

"Then you don't expect me to kill Tenoreno."

"I never depend on anyone with the exception of myself." Mack handed him the gun, nodded to the guy with his phone out and went about his business.

Josh was just a way to get into that hangar. A way to get on that plane. Why? He was tired of asking when the answer was simple—wait and find out.

"They're a couple of minutes out, boss," Laughing Mack said.

In-Charge Mack faced Josh, having to tilt his head up to look at him. "I know what you're thinking. How many of us can you take out if you jump one of the men and take his weapon? But you still have a problem." He folded his arms and looked around him. "Which one of us is supposed to call and check on your girlfriend? Which one of us has the power to tell them to pull the trigger or let them go?"

Damn.

"Now that's all settled. This is where you pull your weight, Major." Mack motioned for his men to come closer. "How many men and where are they located?"

Josh was taller than most of them there. Ten men to be exact. Ten men armed with automatic machine pistols. It didn't matter if they were accurate or not. Just aim close to a human, most likely they'd hit part of him.

Mack waited, his attention on Josh with an expectant look on his face.

"They'll make the prisoner transfer inside the hangar. Less exposure that way. Most likely four men— two rangers, two prison guards. The guards will leave, then the plane. You made this fairly public. They'll be expecting some sort of attack. Additional men might already be waiting."

"So we go in guns blazing and take everybody out," Knife Mack declared.

"Then you don't need me." Josh took a step back toward the van, both hands in the air. He didn't know if any of the guns around him had ammo. But he did know how to use that knife. He just had to get hold of it. "Mind making that phone call before you're all slaughtered?"

"We can get the jump on those guys," one of them said.

Their voices blended together as they spoke over each other. At their backs, Josh could see headlights on the road to the airport. Tenoreno had arrived. But Josh's main focus was on the real Mack. And his focus was on Josh.

The leader lifted a hand. All the conversation stopped.

"Only one person has to fire a weapon. That means only one person needs to get close enough, but we'll take two. Along with the Major."

Tracey had described this man's eyes as frightening. Josh understood why. Black as the dark around them. A color that broke down the walls you thought protected you. Maybe that was a little melodramatic, but true.

The stare was a test. Not just of willpower. It was a test to see who would be giving the orders and who would be taking them. Josh was a leader. It was something that he'd recognized in himself years ago. A skill that mentors had helped him hone. He understood that look. He could also turn his off and allow Mack to believe he'd won.

"I've already told you that I'd do anything to protect my kids. It doesn't matter what happens to me. But what guarantees do I have that my family is going to be okay?"

"You have my word, of course."

"We both know that doesn't mean much to me."

Mack laughed, threw back his head and roared, again halting the conversation of his men. "I knew there was something I liked about you." He turned and waved the men into different directions splitting them into smaller groups that would surround the building on foot. "Put him in the van."

Knife Mack shoved Josh against the bumper. His hand landed on top of his bag, where a smoke grenade and a tracking device were hidden. He just needed to activate the tracker.

"Whoa, whoa, whoa." In-Charge Mack held up his hand. "We still need this guy. Ride up front with me, Major."

Josh was escorted up front, an empty gun tossed in his lap. Empty. The last twenty-four hours had been disturbing to say the least. Sitting here, though, was a bit surreal.

He was in a van with the man who'd kidnapped his family. About to crash through a gate and storm a facility that his friends and coworkers would be defending. When had everything gotten so turned upside down?

"Hopefully this will be really simple," Mack instructed. "We pull up. The Major talks his way to Oaks, Mack takes him out and we take the plane before anyone's the wiser."

"Oaks? Aren't you after Tenoreno?"

"Two for one. We need them both."

Knife had just given him his first piece of useful information. They wanted Oaks and thought he'd be escorting Tenoreno. It sort of made sense now.

"He might not be there, you know. Oaks. There's no guarantee." The gate flew open and their panel van continued toward the hangar. "You could have done all this on your own. You could have taken me out. You didn't need my kids." He was tired of dancing around the truth. "Nothing I do is going to keep you from killing me and…hurting my family."

"You're a sure thing, Major Parker," he said in almost a sad voice. "Smart, too. I always enjoy working with smart people. And I don't think your men are going to just shoot you. You're our element of surprise. Kind of like a flash bang grenade that cops use."

Or maybe that was the answer—he was a sure thing. A sure way to get into the hangar, find Tenoreno and run. Seconds passed in a blur as they screeched to a halt in front of the only open airplane hangar. Handguns were aimed at his chest as he stepped onto the ground.

The other two men stayed in the van with the engine running. It wouldn't be long before eight additional men would be circling the building. They had enough firepower to wipe out everyone on the perimeter before they knew what happened.

"What's the deal, Captain?" Bryce stepped from the back of the hangar. "Trying to make an entrance?"

"I wasn't driving." Josh looked around at his men from Company F. He dropped his handgun—totally worthless anyway—then raised his hands. "There's a couple of guys in this van who want Tenoreno."

"There are a lot of people who want Tenoreno. Sorry."

"They've got the place surrounded, Bryce. Whatever you were planning, it won't work."

"If they're here to hijack the plane they won't get far."

"Change of plans. They say they're here to kill Oaks. Is he on the plane with Tenoreno?" The original plan to overpower Mack's men and discover where Josh's family was being held was a bust.

"Tell the men to drop their weapons," Mack said from the darkness of the van.

"You know they won't do that, but you could lower yours," Bryce answered.

The Rangers were wearing vests. Ready for the shots

Josh should have planned to fire with the weapons he had loaded with blanks. But he couldn't. They wouldn't give him his weapon. Knife Mack jumped out of the van next to him, raised his machine pistol, pointing it at Josh's head.

In-Charge Mack left the driver's seat and stood in front of the panel van. When the Rangers made a move, he stopped them by firing a burst into the ceiling. "Hold it! All of you stay where you are."

"You know I don't want to ask this, Bryce, but they've got my kids. Lower your weapons and don't get us all killed."

Bryce led the way, placing his handgun on the concrete and kicking it barely out of his reach. He squinted, questioning Josh as he sank to his knees. This was *not* the plan they'd discussed yesterday. The one that said it was better to ask forgiveness than permission. They were supposed to overpower these guys, not the other way around.

"Up against the wall, on your knees, hands on your head. Where's Oaks? I don't see him," In-Charge Mack demanded.

"Still in Waco. They were afraid he might get caught up in the moment. Maybe shoot the star witness," the pilot told him.

The first to give up his weapon and the first to give them information. Sort of unusual, but Josh didn't want to jump to the conclusion that the pilot was working with the kidnappers. You could never tell how people would react under stress.

"Get on the plane." Knife Mack shoved the pilot, then shoved Josh toward the others getting on their knees.

"Secure them, tell the others we're a go for phase

two. No reason to panic. We knew this was a possibility." Mack shot beams of hatred toward the plane.

Them? Phase two?

"Join your men, Major."

"What's phase two? You have Tenoreno. Oaks didn't get in the way. You're done here. Just tell me where my kids are or call for their release."

"You are right not to trust me, Major. Looks like we'll have to hang on to them a while longer." Mack smirked.

"The perimeter is crawling with cops." Knife Mack retreated from a window.

The pilot fired up the engine.

"We'll be out of here in a minute. The others will take care of this mess."

Shotguns against machine pistols. How many would be hurt? Would he watch the men on their knees be slaughtered with a single blast? Whatever playbook Mack or Tenoreno had, it wouldn't be discovered here. His family would still be in trouble.

But maybe there was another way.

Josh's head cleared. He instantly knew what had to be done.

"Take me and let my men go. They get in that van and drive away. I give you my word I won't do anything on the plane. I could convince Oaks to meet us."

"Not a chance," Bryce argued. "Headquarters won't go for that. We're not leaving you."

"Nice play, Major." Mack was twenty feet away giving instructions to his right-hand man, then he boarded, turning once inside. "There's only one problem. As soon as I let your men go, they'll warn Oaks that we're coming. Take out the trash, men."

"This is my choice, Lieutenant." He lowered his voice for Bryce, "You know what to do once that plane is airborne. Take these guys out and warn Waco we're coming. Give the signal."

Knife Mack started toward them with crowd-control handcuffs.

"Now, Bryce. Give the order to attack."

Chapter Sixteen

The Rangers outside the hangar made their move. It might have been the last minute before the Macks reached the building, but they were prepared. Most of the gunfire was outside. Bryce rolled, taking cover farther away from the plane, shouting orders for the others. They took their hidden weapons and attacked.

Josh had extra drive that no one else in the hangar did—his need to save his kids and Tracey. His goal was to get on the plane and Knife Mack was the only person in his way.

Josh pushed the adrenaline he was feeling, channeling it to a rage he'd never experienced. All the while gauging that Knife Mack was raising the barrel of his machine pistol. "Get out of my way!"

In a well-practiced gym move—one he had never used in the field—Josh ran and jumped. Both of his booted feet slammed into the chest of his opponent. Josh was prepared to fall hard to the concrete floor, rolling when he hit, keeping his eyes on his opponent. Knife Mack shot backward.

Relentless fire bursts. Shouts. The engine starting. All the noise added to his rapid heartbeat. He heard or felt Knife Mack's "oomph," slamming hard into the wing of the plane. Still, the man got up quickly and moved toward him again.

Josh reached out, grabbed the man's arm and used his forward momentum to spin him into the fuselage. He banged his elbow hard into the man's chin. Then pounded his fist twice into the man's solar plexus attempting to knock his breath from him. He jerked the machine pistol from the man's shoulder, holding the strap across his neck.

Knife Mack didn't stop. Pushing at Josh's hands, he shoved hard enough to force Josh to stumble backward. Josh drew upon a hidden burst of energy thinking about the smiles of his children. He hit Knife Mack with all his strength. The man fell and slid into the back wall, rattling the metal shelves.

Bryce put a knee in Knife Mack's back and yanked his wrist to his shoulder blade.

Josh took in the surroundings. Three of the Macks were defending the runway for the takeoff but Rangers were flanking and about to overrun. Another couple of Mack men were face down in the dirt next to the taxiway.

Josh's only hope was pulling away from the hangar. The Cessna was a single prop engine so there weren't any blades to get in his way. He ran.

"No!" Bryce yelled behind him.

No choice. Josh was running out of time.

Time? Hell, he had seconds. The plane was turning to line up for takeoff.

One more burst of energy and Josh caught the open door. He grabbed whatever he could and pulled himself through as the plane turned revved its engines.

"Very impressive, Major."

In-Charge Mack sat sideways in the seat, holding his machine pistol six inches from Josh's nose. The kidnapper could have pulled the door shut. He could have fired the weapon, shooting Josh. Instead he'd allowed a ranger on board.

Now he extended a hand.

Josh ignored the assist and pulled himself into a seat, shutting the door while the engine roared to full life. He was still alive, on the plane and stuck with a half-ass plan for what he should do next.

Keep himself alive. Get his kids and Tracey released. That was the goal…now he needed steps to reach it. "Is the pilot one of your guys?"

"I believe his name is Bart." Tenoreno, sitting in the seat behind the pilot, raised his voice, competing with the engine. "A new employee. Unlike Vince."

Josh had never met Paul Tenoreno in person. He'd seen the file. Photos of crime scenes. Surveillance pictures Oaks had accumulated off and on for over a decade.

"Vince? Deegan?" Josh couldn't remember the list of crimes attributed to this man, just that it was long. As a criminal, it seemed Vince had avoided pictures. It wasn't a good sign when he took off his ski mask, revealing his face. "I think I'll stick with Mack."

Tenoreno shook his chains. "Can we dispense with these?"

Mack tossed the keys across the aisle to Tenoreno's lap. The organized crime leader didn't look as intimidating in his state-issued jumpsuit. But he still behaved like a man used to having his orders followed.

The restraints were quickly unlatched, dropped and Mack transferred them to Josh.

"Gun." Tenoreno held his palm open and Mack dropped a Glock onto it after pulling it from his belt.

The keys flew back, landing against the shell of the plane and sliding to the carpeted floor. Mack left them there, staring at his employer as he transferred to the copilot's seat.

The confidence that the kidnapper had blustered was no longer apparent. His shoulders slumped. His face filled with hatred. His body language suggested he was tired, but he deliberately kept the gun barrel pointed at Tenoreno's seatback much longer than he should have.

"Change of plans, Bart," Tenoreno said, barely loud enough to be heard over the engine noise. "How much fuel did you manage?"

"I have enough to take you to the rendezvous. You didn't buy anything else. That's as far as this baby and I will take you."

"Unsatisfactory. Come up with a new location not far from Waco."

"That's not the deal," the pilot insisted.

"Your deal is whatever I say it is." Tenoreno pulled the slide to verify ammo was in place.

"What the hell are you doing? Are you seriously going to shoot him while we're in the air?" Mack shouted, sitting forward on his seat.

Tenoreno shot him a shut-up look. "Where are we landing, Bart?"

"Hearne."

"Get us there." Keeping his weapon trained on Bart, Tenoreno looked at Mack. "Call your men with the new location."

"That's taking an unnecessary risk. My men can easily bring Oaks to you later. How do you plan—"

"Do it! We'll exchange him and his kids."

Josh crushed his teeth together to keep from interjecting. He'd played right into Tenoreno's plan more than once. Mack removed a satellite phone from the bag at his feet and made the call.

"I want Oaks discredited and dead. He's supposed to be chained back there, not Parker." Tenoreno spoke to Mack who shrugged. "You've gotten sloppy, Vince. There are too many people involved. Too much has been left up to chance."

"I follow orders. It wasn't my plan that went wrong,"

"I suppose it was my idiot son, then. Why didn't kidnapping his kids work? Didn't the Rangers replace him with Oaks?" He pointed to Josh.

"That part of the plan worked fine." Mack smiled as if he'd regained the confidence he'd lost for a moment. "Maybe they thought Oaks would kill you himself if he was on a plane with you."

"Ha." Tenoreno put the headset on and turned to the front of the plane. Mack and Josh sat silently next to each other until Mack leaned forward and added the ankle restraints, locking Josh to the plane.

"I never underestimate the power of emotion. Especially that of a father. I told my employers that, but they insisted on this ridiculous revenge plan. Wouldn't listen to me." Was he bragging that he had predicted Josh's behavior?

"Smart advice for someone dumb enough not to follow it." They could talk without either of the other men hearing. "You know this exchange this isn't going to work. Right?"

"You Rangers are so full of pride that buying you off isn't an option. Fortunately, killing you is."

"You kidnapped my kids so you could kill Oaks?"

"No, Major. We did all this to free Paul. The only way to get Oaks off his back is to kill him." Mack pointed the gun at Josh. He raised and lowered the barrel as if it had just been fired. "You see, you guys just don't stop. We can buy off other agencies, bribe or blackmail some types of guys...like Bart. But Rangers? None of that works."

"So you're telling me that if the Texas Rangers had a history of corruption, my kids would be safe at home?"

"Kind of ironic when you look at it that way." Mack leaned back in his seat, machine pistol in his lap.

There wasn't any reason to keep a close eye on Josh. He wasn't going anywhere cuffed hand and foot. No chance to attempt anything.

"Before I waste my time trying to convince you I'm not important, tell me why you let me board. And don't say it's because you wanted to see if I could make it through the door."

"I've got to say that I admire the way you don't give up. You're here because I can use you for a hostage. Nothing more. Nothing less."

"Use me all you want. Just make the call that will let my kids go." Josh swallowed hard.

"We both saw the mess back at the airport. It won't be long before the Rangers are calling Oaks and the entire state is after us. I have some leverage with you here."

"I'm a nobody. They won't negotiate because of me."

"We'll see." Mack dropped his head back against the headrest and closed his eyes. At this point, Josh shouldn't and didn't trust anyone except himself to save his children. Except Tracey. He trusted Tracey. For one moment, it was nice to imagine what she might have been about to tell him. One moment when he hoped she knew exactly how he felt about her.

Chapter Seventeen

They pulled to a stop and Tracey felt the van settle into a parked position. She kept her eyes down, pretending to be asleep. She sneaked a peek out the windows. It looked the same as the rest of their ride. The sun was just dusting the treetops and highlighting the surrounding fields. Whatever was going to happen, it didn't seem like there was anyplace close to hide.

The two Macks looked at the phone, said things under their breath and got cautiously out of the van. Tracey rose quickly and looked out all the windows. They were at a small airport. One smaller than Waco and not large enough to have a terminal or control tower.

The van was parked a long way from any building or aircraft hangar.

"Listen to me, Sage. There might be a chance that you can run and hide without these men seeing you. If you can, you do it. Don't look back. This is important. Just run as fast as you can. Okay?"

"By myself?"

"Yes, baby." She lifted the little girl to look out the back windows. "You see those hay bales across the road?" She pointed. Sage nodded. "Can you run that far?"

"Is it important?" Sage whispered.

"Yes, baby. Very important. Somebody will find you. Promise."

"I want to go home," Jackson insisted. "I don't feel like running. I want to eat colors 'cause it'll make me run faster."

Tracey looked closely at Jackson's eyes. She hadn't monitored his blood sugar levels in several hours and had none of the necessary tools now. She had to completely rely on her experience of the last year.

Acting out, anger, lethargy, not making sense with his words—those were all sure signs that his blood sugar was dropping. She got up front as quickly as possible. Why hadn't she thought of that first? There weren't any keys in the ignition, but she locked both the doors.

"Sage, lock the back and the side doors. Quick!"

The van rocked back and forth a little when Sage moved. She made it to the side door while Tracey searched for a spare key or food. Nothing but ketchup packets and trash.

The van moved again, but this time it was from the rear door being yanked open.

"I told you she was up to something."

"It didn't matter. I had the keys to get back in." Blond Mack dangled them like candy in front of her.

Tracey huddled with the kids again, not trying to explain herself or reason with them. They were tugged from the vehicle. Tracey held Jackson on her hip and he put his head on her shoulder.

"You sure that's them, man?"

"You think there's more than one plane sitting on this out-of-the-way runway?"

"Then what are they waiting for?"

The men whispered behind her. Maybe they were using her and the kids as a shield. She didn't know. She held Jackson's forty-four pounds tight against her and wanted to pick up Sage. Instead she held tight to her hand and the little girl held the secondhand bear against her own little chest.

There was no movement from the white Cessna.

"What's going on?" she asked. "Who's in the plane? Do we have to get on board?"

Her thoughts were considering the worst-case scenario. The one where awful things happened in an isolated basement where no one could find them. The bodyguards suddenly seemed like a really good idea.

Neither of the men answered. Neither of the men moved.

"I got a creepy feeling about this, man. You get me?"

Tracey thought it was the blond guy talking, but it didn't matter. They both were armed and the only place close where she could protect the kids was back inside the van.

She'd never make it carrying Jackson, who was more lethargic than just a few minutes ago. He needed food and she didn't know how much.

"What does the text say?"

"I don't care what it says anymore. Get back in the van."

It was definitely the blond Mack giving the orders. She could tell that they faced each other and had a phone between them. She inched Sage toward the corner of the van, ready to make a run for it. She desperately wanted her hunch about this to be right.

A hunch that told her Josh was on that plane waiting

to see if she and the kids were released. But that would mean someone—like the FBI or police or Rangers—was here somewhere, waiting.

The men continued to argue behind her and she loosened her hold on Sage. She arched her eyebrows, questioning if she should run, and Tracey nodded. She looked so young and yet so much older than two days ago. Tracey didn't have to guess if she understood the danger—she did. Josh's little girl squeezed her hand, then tiptoed along the length of the back of the van and ran.

The arguing stopped. Tracey turned around, keeping her hand behind her back. Hoping the two Macks would think Sage was hiding there. She stared at the men, one arm cramping from holding Jackson, the other waving his sister to safety.

"Where's the girl?"

"She's right—"

They both took a step in Tracey's direction. Blond Mac's hands were out to take Jackson from her. She turned but only made it a couple of steps. The van doors were still open. Blond had a hold of Jackson; the other guy pushed her inside the van, climbing in on top of her.

She couldn't see if Sage made it across the road. Based on the cursing and slamming fists against the van, then the running to get in the driver's seat, she assumed Sage was out of sight.

Thank God.

THEY HAD LANDED about five or ten minutes earlier. Mack had been surprised and Tenoreno had been rather pleased. Neither had said anything loud enough to let

Josh determine what was going on. But it had something to do with meetings and putting them at greater risk.

Tenoreno was in the copilot's chair and Mack was busy sending an in-depth text. Neither paid attention to the activity at the van. The plane was far enough down the runway to make the van visible to Josh. He yanked against the chains when Tracey and the kids had been wrenched from it. He managed to cap his panic when he saw his little girl run. He didn't want to draw attention to her.

"Did your heart stop there for a minute?" Bart the pilot asked. "I know mine sure did. That's this guy's kid. Right? Man, you've got a brave little girl."

Josh nodded. He might have gotten out a yes or confirmation grunt, but he couldn't be certain. As soon as the relief hit that the men weren't following Sage and she might be safe, the anxiety had doubled as Jackson and Tracey were pushed back inside the van. Tracey hadn't run. He'd seen Jackson's form. He was practically limp in Tracey's arms. Something was wrong with his son.

"What are you talking about?" Tenoreno shouted as Sage disappeared behind a hay bale. "Tell them to go get her. Why didn't you say something when she ran?"

"Man, I didn't sign on to hurt any kids. Disengage the transponder, fly the plane, get my payoff. Sure. Hurting kids was not included and won't be."

"If we didn't need a pilot, you'd be dead now." Tenoreno turned an interesting shade of explosive red.

"We don't need the girl. We didn't need additional hostages on the plane. I tried to tell you that."

"This is not a debate. You work for me."

Tenoreno screamed his lack of control. Bart shrank

a little more toward the pilot's door. Mack's body stiffened as he deliberately sank back into the leather seat. The muscle in his jaw twitched. He let the machine pistol's barrel drop in line with his boss's head. Accident or deliberate?

Josh didn't want Mack to open fire. Not when he didn't have a weapon and no control over the men still holding Tracey and Jackson.

"It doesn't matter now. Here they come. Open the door, then tell the men to bring the woman on board."

Josh couldn't see who was inside the darkened windows. Mack did as he was instructed—opened the door and called his men on the phone.

If he made it through this, someone might eventually ask him what he'd hoped to gain by allowing himself to become a hostage. Originally there'd been a lot of adrenaline involved. But it came down to being there for his kids. He couldn't let anyone else make decisions that involved their lives. And if that put his at risk.

So be it.

Chapter Eighteen

"This isn't going to work." George was compelled to voice his thoughts one last time. "There's only one reason they'd want you here, Captain Oaks. Paul Tenoreno wants to kill you."

"We have a sound plan."

"Hardly. It's our only plan. Might be a good one for Tenoreno. You get out of the car, they shoot you. Period. They have no reason to release any of the hostages."

Crouched in the backseat of a small sedan wasn't the most comfortable place George had ever held a conversation. It definitely wasn't the worst, either. At least he wasn't shoved in the trunk like last year. He shook the random thoughts from his mind and concentrated.

Aiden Oaks had parked the car next to the Cessna. His plan to accommodate the kidnappers and escaped prisoner hadn't included the FBI. George was coordinating the teams surrounding the airstrip.

Of course, the entire jumping-in-the-car-at-the-last-minute thing had caught him slightly unprepared. He was only carrying his cell phone and Glock. The ammo he had in the magazine was it. The team was communicating through a series of group texts.

"No one asked you to ride along," Aiden said.

"No, sir, you didn't. I have a lot of experience with kidnappings and abductions. Did you know that, Captain?"

"I wouldn't say you've had any experience with this kind. Those kids are still in danger because the men who outrank me wouldn't allow me to escort Tenoreno's flight. He's a vindictive son of—"

"I know why we're waiting, but what do you think they're waiting for? Is the van with Tracey and Jackson still sitting on the road? Damn, that was a brave move Tracey made, sending one of the kids to safety."

The cop who picked her up had her safely in his squad car.

"Good thing the Hearne PD picked up Sage as she ran to hide behind the hay. Sweet thing argued that she had to stay there and wait on her daddy." Aiden chuckled. "Van's been creeping up behind us at a snail's pace. Everybody seems to be in a holding pattern. Are the men in place?"

"Three more minutes, sir."

Just before they'd arrived in Hearne to rendezvous with Tenoreno, he'd kicked the rearview mirror off the windshield. It was propped on the backseat headrest so he could see the plane. The door opened but he couldn't make out anything inside.

"Van's speeding up. I'm getting out and leaving the door open for you, Agent Lanning."

"We have eyes on Parker. He's handcuffed and manacled to the seat behind the pilot. Tenoreno is in the co-pilot chair." The team kept him up-to-date with a text. "You have your handcuff key ready?"

"Got it," Oaks said as he swung his legs from the

car. He left the door as a bit of protection between him and the plane.

George dialed Kendall's number, ready to get the advance started with his men. He'd pass along information, but his phone was on silent, just in case the perps got close enough to hear him. Then he angled the mirror, attempting to find any guns pointed in their direction. They knew from looking through the windows that at least two hostiles were aboard, maybe three.

The Rangers in Huntsville had stated that only the kidnapper who gave the orders was on board. Bart Temple, the pilot, already had an open investigation about his suspicious activities. The report from the airplane hangar suggested that he had supplied information and had voluntarily gotten on the plane.

"Air traffic has been diverted. We have a helicopter standing by in case we need it."

The van squealed to a stop.

"Where are you going?" a man shouted.

George turned the mirror. "One man, armed with a Glock. Nervous. Anxious. Unpredictable. No eyes on Tracey or the boy."

"Move to the door, Oaks," a voice inside the plane said.

"I ain't no rookie. Release Parker and the other hostages."

"The Major is cozy and staying where he is."

"Then so am I." Oaks sat on the seat.

George knew what the captain was doing. It didn't make it any easier to wait on the kidnappers' next move.

Tracey screamed and George could only imagine what the kidnappers had done to elicit her reaction. Damn, he hated being blind. He whipped the mirror around to see the driver pulling Tracey past the steering wheel. Soon they were joined by his partner, who carried Jackson.

"The kid looks ill. I repeat, the kid looks ill and won't be able to run on his own."

"Hey, you guys in the plane." The driver pushed the barrel of his handgun under Tracey's chin. "Or inside the car. Whoever cares about this woman! You better give us a way out of here or she and the kid are going to get it."

"Yeah," the one cradling Jackson said. "We want our own plane. Or you can kick these bastards out and we'll take this one."

"I can get another plane here. Why don't you give me the kid to show good faith?" Oaks tried to negotiate.

"Oh no. No way! We keep both of them." They argued.

The man holding Jackson started waving his handgun, then smashed it against his own forehead, proving that he was losing it. If he touched the kid, nothing would hold George inside the car.

Everyone on the team hated unpredictable kidnappers. The ones who began to panic. The ones who were sweating buckets, were probably high as a kite and who made everything about his job high risk.

"That's a shame." Oaks raised his voice to be heard over the Cessna's engine. "We have a sweet private jet not too far away. We could have it here in ten minutes."

"Call 'em!"

"Sorry, can't do that until I have a hostage."

"Man, I just want to be gone." He pushed Jackson into Tracey's arms and climbed back into the van.

"Ron, what are you— Hey! Hey!" he screamed into

his phone as the door swung halfway shut. "We're getting on that plane no matter what you say!"

He placed his gun at Tracey's throat and started her moving, carrying Jackson toward the plane.

Whether it was their intention or not, they'd parked the van partially in the path of the Cessna. To reach the open door, they had to walk close to the sedan. The men now calling the shots, hidden on the east side of the buildings, sent instructions.

"Captain, if there's an opportunity to rescue Jackson, McCaffrey wants us to take it."

"Are they seeing what we're seeing?" Oaks asked in a low voice. "The kidnappers are panicking. We can't startle these guys."

George wasn't certain if McCaffrey had a good grasp on the situation or not. He could hear the chatter in the background. Hear the arguing over what the best move might be. When the best-case scenario came up, he thought they'd back up his plan.

Jackson looked unconscious and unaware that he was being carried to the plane. Tracey stumbled because the remaining captor's gun was still at her throat and pushing her chin upward. George watched behind him with the help of the mirror. Feeling as helpless as Josh Parker.

The phone buzzed on his chest with another message from his partner. McCaffrey was about to blow a gasket because he hadn't burst out of the car and done anything. George rolled to his side, hiding behind the dark-tinted windows for a better view.

The two men were met at the plane door with a machine pistol. "Send the boy up. Then the woman."

"You dirty rotten son of a bitch! You ain't leaving us here to go to jail." The man holding Tracey turned in circles, always bringing her between him and any of the men who might have a shot.

"Take me." Captain Oaks moved slowly from behind the car door with his hands in the air. "Leave the kid in the car and take me. They'll let you on the plane if you bring me."

George was ready to spring into action. "That is not the plan."

JOSH LOOKED THROUGH the open door and saw Tracey stumble. Whatever was being said outside, he couldn't hear because of the yelling in the small plane.

"Give me the gun so I can shoot him myself." Tenoreno held out his hand, expecting Mack to drop his weapon into it. The older man climbed between the front seats and stuck his hand out again.

"Buckle in, Paul. Bart, get this plane in the air."

"Oaks is standing right there, dammit." Tenoreno pointed. "Shoot him."

"So are the FBI and more Rangers. Even if you can't see them, they have to be here. Oaks isn't stupid. He wouldn't come alone."

Mack was right, but Josh wasn't going to agree with him. He kept his head down and his mouth shut, continuing his search for something he could use to free himself. Unfortunately, the plane had been checked for that sort of material before transporting a prisoner.

"I want him dead. It's the reason we're here."

"I could have taken care of this. I had men in Waco ready to do the job after they got rid of the hostages." Mack explained. "But you had to detour and involve the kids again, making everybody on edge."

"Those incompetent jerks." Tenoreno pointed to the men holding Tracey.

"Someone has confused them." Mack pointedly looked at Tenoreno. "Now they believe they've been double-crossed. Their position is kind of natural."

"Don't take that tone with me, Vince. I know where your kid lives."

Vince, Mack, whatever the hell his name was, didn't like Paul Tenoreno. His knuckles turned a bright white, fisted as they were around the machine pistol grip. The plane shifted slightly to the side as someone climbed up the steps.

The blond guy who had been holding Tracey backed onto the plane—slowly, sticking his foot out behind him while he wrapped one arm around someone's throat. Josh had to pull his legs and feet out of the way. He didn't want the man to fall and choke… Aiden.

A shot of relief hit Josh. He didn't want anyone else on the plane, but knowing Tracey wasn't gave him a little hope she and Jackson might make it out of this situation alive.

"Good to see you alive, son," Aiden said to Josh as the new guy shoved him onto the empty seat.

"Captain Oaks." Tenoreno was halfway between the seats.

"Fancy meeting you here, Paul," Aiden taunted. "You okay, kid?" he asked Josh in a lower voice.

Tenoreno's fists hit both of the seat backs. "Shut up before I shoot you dead. Your blood would be splattered against this white leather in a heartbeat if we didn't need to leave."

"You don't trust that they'll let you?" Aiden taunted. The result was another beet-red rise in Tenoreno's color. The man definitely didn't have control of his temper. And Aiden definitely knew what buttons to push. Tenoreno slammed Aiden forward.

To Josh it seemed that Aiden sort of threw himself forward, then he knew why. He dropped a handcuff key into his hand. His eyes must have grown wide with surprise because Aiden frowned and shook his head.

Josh recovered and tried to shrink into the seat. Let Aiden have all the attention and he could free his feet and hands pretty quickly. Or at least he thought he could.

The plane dipped slightly again as someone began climbing the steps. The second man was pushing Tracey up, and in her arms she held Jackson.

Escaping was complicated before. Now it was closer to impossible. Was he willing to risk a machine gun blast through the plane with two people he loved occupying seats?

Tenoreno continued to yell. "Get us out of here!"

Bart started the engine. Josh held out his arms to catch his son as Tracey handed him through the opening, before falling to her knees on the carpet as the plane jerked forward.

"Wait! No!" the man on the bottom step fell away.

"Pull the door shut, Tommy, so we can get going," Mack ordered.

Tommy laughed at the man—his partner three minutes ago—being left behind on the runway. He reached for the rope to pull in the steps and the slam of Mack's weapon firing hit Josh's ears. Gunpowder filled his nostrils before he turned his head and caught a glimpse of Tommy falling through the door.

Mack leaned across, fired his weapon again—

presumably at the man he'd left behind. Then he pulled the stairs up and secured the door.

"Damn. What now?" Bart yelled.

It seemed like Josh had constantly asked himself the same question again and again for the past forty hours…

Chapter Nineteen

Jackson had barely been noticed by anyone on the plane since they'd tossed him back to Tracey. The sudden firing of the gun had made him scream. She was certain he hadn't seen any part of the cold-blooded murder. She'd had his face buried against her shoulder. His hands had already been over his ears.

"Just stay still and keep your eyes closed," she whispered to him.

She desperately wanted to be next to Josh, or better still not on the plane at all. But they were, and they'd survived another hour.

"Get us in the air, Bart, old buddy." Mack grabbed a pair of handcuffs. He pointed to an older gentleman sitting across from Josh. "Put those on Captain Oaks. And loop the seat belt through them so you can't get up and retrieve a gun."

After he had Aiden's hands locked into place, Mack took the open seat and buckled up. They kept taxiing to the end of the runway. The plane turned around and not only was the van still there, a row of patrol cars and SUVs were side by side, cutting off half the tarmac.

"Same question, second verse," the pilot said. "What now?"

"Can't you run them over with this thing?" the man sitting up front said, like a minion who didn't really think.

After her time in the van, she realized these men were more like lost boys than criminals. Young men who got used by people like Mack. She couldn't let herself have too much sympathy. If it came down to it, she'd choose the Parkers every time.

"Let's try some diplomacy. Paul, get on the radio." Mack raised his voice to be heard over the prop engine.

She recognized his voice. That was the man who had hit her Friday. It seemed a lifetime ago, but she would never forget. He was the In-Charge Mack, the man who'd given all the orders.

Sitting practically in the tail of the plane, she had a clear view of everyone except the pilot. The fidgets of the men in restraints. The toe tapping of Aiden Oaks. The cavalier words that didn't match the tense, upright stiffness that Mack's body shouted.

And Josh. His glances kept reassuring her that it would work out. He'd come up with a plan. Then he caught her eye and sharply looked at her lap. There was only one seat belt for both her and Jackson. As inconspicuous with her movements as she could be, she buckled the seat belt around her waist.

She'd use her last ounce of strength to hold on to Jackson if something happened with the plane. She was prepared. Tenoreno picked up the microphone to radio the FBI, who was certain to be listening.

"Tell them about our situation. We're taking off or someone's dying. Starting with Daddy Dearest." Mack pointed the gun at the back of the copilot's seat.

"What are you talking about? Is this a joke? You

work for me. Or—" Realization hit Tenoreno. "Who hired you? My son will pay you double to escort me to safety."

"Your son is the one who wants you gone. As in forever, never coming back. It would have simplified everything if I could have killed you in Huntsville. Or even right now. But Xander insists on seeing it happen." He kicked the empty seat across from him. "You stupid old man. Did you really think he would forgive you for killing his mother?"

"You've got Special Agent in Charge McCaffrey." A voice boomed through the radio.

"They're threatening to kill me. You have to save me. It's your job! Don't move the vehicles! Don't clear the runway."

"Who is this? What's going on in there? Stop the engine and exit the plane."

Mack placed the barrel next to Tenoreno's temple. The man in the orange jumpsuit tried to squirm aside, but there was no place for him to go. Tracey covered Jackson's ears and eyes.

"Trace Trace, that's too tight."

"That's unacceptable. Didn't you see him shoot one of his own men? He's not bluffing. He won't negotiate." Josh tried to shout loud enough for the agents to hear him.

"He's not going to back down," Aiden shouted at the same time.

Was Josh's fellow ranger talking about Agent McCaffrey or Mack? Josh looked first at her, then in the direction of Mack. She could see the murderer's jaw tighten. The muscles visibly popped.

"If you don't do anything, then you've just killed us." Tenoreno laughed like a crazy man.

"Do you think I'm going to fall for that? If you're the one holding our people hostage, you won't get far. We have helicopters in the air waiting to follow you to any destination. We know there's not enough fuel on board to get you out of the country. Surrendering now is your only option."

"I don't think he's joking." Tenoreno sat forward looking out the windows.

Aiden seemed more uncomfortable. He'd moved his hands from above his head to closer to the top of his shoulder. "Why set up this elaborate prison break if you just wanted him dead?"

"He's about to pull the trigger." Tenoreno's voice shook into the radio.

Was Mack about to shoot? Tracey couldn't tell. One message had been crystal clear—Josh wanted her wearing the seat belt. And now it looked like they were going to take off.

"To hell with this standoff," the pilot shouted.

He pushed what she assumed was the throttle because the engine roared louder and they moved forward. Fast.

As the plane gained speed, she looked out her window and saw men with guns pointing in their direction. But in a blink they had pointed toward another target. There was gunfire—tiny pops to her ears which drowned in the airplane engine's hum.

The young man she'd dubbed as Simple Mack. The one left alive on the tarmac was firing his weapon. Not at the FBI, he was shooting at the plane. They were dangerously close to the SUVs before dramatically dashing into the air.

The bouncing up and down stopped, but the dipping

didn't. Tracey loved roller coasters, but now there were no rails connecting her seat to the earth. It was several seconds before they stabilized in the air. And several more before anyone released their breaths.

Jackson was in her arms. No seat belt. If they crashed, would she be able to hold on to him? *No.* The takeoff was just a couple of bumps and she'd nearly lost the death grip around his waist. She had no more illusions about keeping Jackson safe. He was kicking and crying out and hitting her with his small fists.

"Keep that kid quiet."

"It's the diabetes." She knew that. He didn't realize what he was doing and after his blood sugar stabilized he wouldn't remember his actions. It hadn't happened often, but since it had, the family recognized the signs.

There was a lot of tension surrounding them and a lot of noise, even though she could hear better after popping her ears. Josh and Aiden seemed to be communicating by looks. They were going to do something. She just didn't know what or when.

She quickly rose a little and switched the seat belt from around her waist to tighten around Jackson's. It was a close fit to sit on the edge of the seat next to him pressed against the side of the plane. He didn't like it at all.

"Please, kidlet. We've got to do this to keep you safe," she said next to his ear, scared to death that he'd lift the latch and not be safe at all. She worked with him to get his ears popped and relieve some of the pressure.

"What now, Mack?" Josh asked.

"Don't you mean Vince Deegan?" Aiden smiled. "Yeah, I know who you are. Jobs like this aren't normally your forte. You're more of a…bully. Aren't you?"

From her new position, she could barely see the front of the plane. She heard a jerk on Josh's chains. She could imagine that he wanted to stop Aiden from antagonizing the man holding a machine gun. She hated not knowing what was going on. It made the fright level just that much higher.

"Bart, take us to the landing strip. Somebody's waiting." Mack's attention was on the front of the plane. Maybe on the pilot or Tenoreno.

He seemed to have forgotten that she wasn't tied up or restrained—with the exception that it was a tight fit between the seats. She reached forward, touching Josh's arm. He didn't whip around, but took a look at her slowly around the edge of the seat.

She leaned closer to him and said, "I can do something."

"No," Josh mouthed.

"Daddy! Daddy!" Jackson kicked the seat, and Tracey. "Take me home."

"It's okay, Jack. Everything's okay. I bet you're tired. Maybe try to take a nap." Josh said it loud enough for Jackson to hear. One sincere look from his father and he was leaning his head against the side of the plane.

But the outburst caught Mack's attention, causing him to look and stare at her.

Did he realize she wasn't secured? It was the first time that she hoped she appeared insignificant in someone's mind. And maybe that's how he saw her—insignificant or not a threat—because he turned his attention back to his phone.

Josh looked around the edge of his seat again. He winked. She smiled back in spite of the anxiety speeding up her heartbeat. She wasn't alone. He was there and he was not helpless.

Jackson's breathing evened out. She liked it better when he was awake. Even if the diabetes turned him into a tiny terror, she knew he was awake and not slipping into a deep sleep or diabetic coma. They didn't have long before Jackson was going to be severely ill.

At the risk of Mack noticing her lack of binding, she called out, "Where are you taking us?"

"Yeah, Vince, where are you taking us?' Tenoreno echoed.

"Not far."

"That agent said they're tracking us," the criminal said from the front, his tenor-like voice carrying to the back of the plane.

"We got rid of the transponder. You!" Mack lunged across the short distance between seats.

Tracey heard his fist hit Aiden. She heard him searching through pockets and patting him down. She could see the ranger's hands tighten on the seat belt, heard him release a moan of pain.

"How are they following us?" Tenoreno screamed.

"They don't need much but their eyes. The FBI wasn't bluffing about a helicopter." The pilot pointed to the right side of the plane. All heads looked. Tracey's view was blocked by a compartment of some sort but she could tell the pilot was telling the truth.

"If the FBI knows where we're going and can tell when we land," she said, leaning forward to be heard, "how did you plan on getting away?"

She was genuinely confused.

Mack's dark eyes, which she'd memorized the moment he'd raised his fist to hit her, went dead again.

He was filled with blackness that looked so empty...
so soulless. "I didn't."

"What the hell does that mean?" Tenoreno asked.

Tracey saw the concerned look on Aiden's face and
knew it was mirrored on Josh's. She squeezed back in
next to Jackson, dabbing some of the sweat off his forehead. There was nothing for her to give him. No juice,
no water—nothing. All she could do was hope.

It wasn't long before the pilot circled an even smaller
runway from where they'd left. The engines ebbed and
surged as he lined up to set the plane on the ground.

"This isn't going to be pretty, people." The pilot
gained everyone's attention. "Those gunshots must
have hit something important and the controls aren't
handling like they should. So grab something steady.
It's going to be a bumpy ride."

Aiden, handcuffed to the seat belt, settled more
firmly into his chair and braced a long leg on the seat
across the short aisle. Josh couldn't brace himself at all,
not manacled to the floor.

"Can't you unlock his feet?"

"Dammit, Mack. Let her have a seat belt."

Tracey's heart raced. Good or bad. It shouldn't matter what side you were on when a plane was about to
crash. Mack didn't acknowledge them. He fingered the
phone, then put it in his pocket.

There was nothing to grab. She sank between the
seats and braced herself between the bulkhead and the
closet. As she did, Mack noticed and didn't make a
move to stop her or let her move to the open seat in front
of him. Jackson was unconscious. None of the shouting woke him up. At least he wouldn't be scared out of
his mind like she was.

"I love you," Josh said as the plane dipped and shot back to gain altitude. He didn't have to say anything. She'd known he loved her as soon as he'd held her hand in the bodyguards' rental car. That moment had changed everything for her.

Seconds later the plane bounced against pavement and was airborne again. She kept her eyes glued to Jackson.

It wouldn't be long. Sage was safe. At least there was that.

"Hold on tight, baby." Only Jackson could have heard her, but she said the words for Josh, too.

Chapter Twenty

Josh braced himself as best he could. Mack was finally sitting straight in his seat and not watching his every move. There hadn't been an unobserved moment to retrieve the handcuff key from where he'd hidden it—between his cheek and teeth.

Once on the ground, they'd need the weapons that should be stored in the small closet next to Tracey. He couldn't give Mack time to recover from the rough ride or realize what was happening. He had to be ready. He had to be fast.

Spitting the handcuff key into his hands, he twisted his wrists until he could reach the latch. Key inserted, turned, one hand was free. The plane's power surged, trying to gain altitude, pressing his body into the seat. He fought gravity and leaned forward to release his ankles from the manacles.

"This is it!" Bart shouted, cursing like a sailor.

Josh sat up. There was no time to grab and hold Tracey like he wanted. Then it was apparent that Bart didn't have control. The plane was on its way to the ground. Crashing.

"Hold on, Tracey. We're going to be okay. Just hold on." He could see her boots in the aisle next to him.

He wanted to comfort his son. There was just no way to be heard.

Nothing was fake about what the plane was doing. There was a radical shimmy when the wheels touched down again.

Noise from every direction assaulted him. At first there were huge vibrations, bounces and slams. He thought that was bad until the plane made a sharp pull to the right, tipped, and he knew they were flipping. His neck felt like it snapped in two from the concussion of hitting the ground.

Stunned. He hung upside down, unable to see around him. Then he realized he couldn't really see his hand heading to his face, either. Stuff was floating in the air. Smoke or steam—he couldn't tell.

"Josh! Josh! You still conscious?" Aiden called.

"Yeah, I'm… I'm okay." His ears were still ringing.

Mack seemed to be unconscious next to him. His arms were hanging about his head.

"Tracey? Jackson?" No sound from either of them.

"The kid's still buckled. The girl looks like she's out cold."

Pulling his heavy arms back to his chest, Josh stretched his legs so he could push his feet against Aiden's seat.

"Hold on, Josh!" Aiden yelled. "I'm pinned in here just as tight as a bean in a burrito. My leg's busted up and caught between these things. Can you get out the door? Or see the machine pistol?"

"Give me a sec."

Bent in half and still a bit disoriented, his mind refused to adjust and accept that the plane was upside down and not just him. He managed to unclip his seat belt. There wasn't room to fall. It was just a jolt. The windows had shattered and the space around him had shrunk.

"Tracey? Jackson? Can you hear me?" He could finally see her, boots pointed toward him, lying on the ceiling. He shook her legs as much as he dared. He couldn't get his shoulders through to the area behind him. His seat was wedged in the way.

"Josh, you need to get the gun, son."

"Yeah." He did *know* that he needed to find the weapon. Logic told him that. But his heart wanted to free Tracey and Jackson first. They were both hurt, or worse.

Mack was hanging from his waist, seat belt still in place, arms swaying with each move that Josh made. He looked around on the ceiling—no weapons.

A pounding at the front of the plane made him jerk around. He hit his head on something fixed to the floor. There was a small triangle of space left where he could see the instrument panel. He carefully got closer, trying not to cause Aiden more pain.

The pilot was strapped in but it looked like his injuries were severe. Tenoreno kicked his door and it was almost open. Josh saw the gun. The strap was caught and it hung just out of his reach near the pilot.

Tenoreno stared at him and followed the direction he was reaching. An evil grin dominated his face. He moved like he was no longer in a rush. He casually lifted the machine pistol, moved the radio cord farther from the opening, then kicked the door a final time.

It sprang open and Tenoreno escaped. Josh pushed on the seat back until beads of sweat stung his eyes. It wasn't budging.

"Josh?" Aiden spoke softly, as if he were in pain. "Try the other door, son."

Crouching, he checked Tracey, giving her a little shake. He reached up and felt a pulse at Mack's throat. Then he checked the door next to his seat. Jammed. Their side of the plane had settled mostly in the field.

His head was beginning to clear a bit. His vision along with it. He checked Aiden, who had passed out. He had lost the handcuff key in the crash, but could get Aiden free with a knife. To get to Tracey and Jackson, he'd need a crowbar or tools to release the seat back. And to get either of those things he needed out of the plane.

"Hello?" a voice from the outside called. Knocks on the outside of the plane. More voices. And light. Lots of light as the door opened.

"Are you all right?"

"I'm fine but there are injured people and a child. Have you got a knife?" Josh asked the man who was at the door on the far side of Mack. Josh's ears were ringing badly and making it difficult to hear. He was catching every other word or so and letting his mind fill in the rest of the answer.

As much as he wanted to sit and let someone else take care of things, his son needed him. Tracey needed him. He wouldn't quit.

"My daughter, Jeannie… Hand me the knife. I think we can get everyone out. Paramedics are on their way."

"Let me get inside here." The man kept the knife.

Without too many words, they worked together and released Mack. The rescuer climbed out and Josh passed Mack through the door to him.

"Make sure you use these." Josh tossed the handcuffs

that had been around his wrists a few minutes earlier. "Anchor him to something so he can't get away."

"You can come out," the man helping said. "I can free them."

"Not leaving until they do. You'll need me in here." Josh began moving debris, trying to get to Jackson and Tracey.

The stranger had seen what tools they needed to release the others, retrieved them and they went to work. "Start moving the dirt from the pilot's window," the man instructed someone who had just arrived.

This time another teen jumped in with him, rocking the plane just a bit.

"Where are the rescue crews?" Josh asked.

"We're in the middle of nowhere here," the teenager answered.

"They're probably another fifteen minutes out." The man moved carefully to Aiden. "Your friend has a broken leg, let's get this wreckage off him."

"The boy first," Aiden said.

"Boy?"

"My son's in the back along with Tracey. He has diabetes. They're both unconscious."

The man didn't need more of an explanation. He went to work removing the seat blocking Tracey. It was a tight fit and Josh felt in the way until they got some of the bolts removed and the seat needed to be held in place. His shoulder kept the seat on the ceiling while they finished and moved it in front of the door.

"Tracey?"

Josh needed to be in two places at once. But he let their rescuer check Tracey while he released his son.

"How long have I been out?" Her voice was breathy and tired. "Where's Jackson?"

"He's okay." Josh looked at his watch. "It's been seven minutes since the crash."

"It might be the diabetes keeping him knocked out."

The man called to someone outside the door to come get Jackson. Josh handed him to another stranger and leaned down to get Tracey. Her eyes opened.

"I didn't find anything broken," their rescuer said. "Can you climb out of here?"

"Is it over?" she asked, looking at Josh.

"Tenoreno's out there somewhere," Aiden answered behind him. "Watch yourself."

Josh looked at the Ranger Captain. "I'll be back to help. Just let me check on Jackson."

"You stay with your boy. These guys can handle me."

Josh helped Tracey through the door. She was already at Jackson's side by the time he was halfway out.

"Do you think it's too high or too low?" Agent Barlow asked, running around the tail of the plane.

"He hasn't eaten today, but he's been getting the basal dose so that should—" She turned Jackson on his side, checked where his insulin port should be. "The cannula is still here but no tubing and no insulin pump. So now there's a chance it can be clogged. The ambulance may have one."

Tracey took the information a lot more calmly than he did. He was feeling that intense uncertainty again. But watching Tracey thoroughly check his son brought him stability and reassured him. "He's going to be okay. They've called an ambulance. They'll have what we need."

"Jackson." She shook his shoulder. "Can you hear me? Wake up, baby." Tracey pulled up one eyelid and then the other to check his response. Jackson moaned.

"His skin is clammy to the touch," Josh said, knowing that they didn't have much time. "Where's the ambulance? They can test his level and will have a glucagon shot. That should bounce him back."

"We can't wait on the ambulance. We need honey." Tracey searched the people. "Does anybody have honey in their car!" she called out. "He needs his blood sugar brought up fast."

A woman ran from the other side of the plane. "I have what you need at the house. Our grandson is diabetic. I sent someone to fetch it."

Josh had been absorbed in helping his son and hadn't noticed that there was a small group of buildings about a football field away. Sky High Skydiving was written on the side in big bold letters.

"No! Wait!" Out of breath, a teenager stumbled into Josh. All he could do was shove a bottle of honey and a blood testing kit at Josh's chest. "This will work faster."

Josh popped off the top to open a honey bottle and handed it to Tracey. She squeezed the honey onto the tip of her finger and rubbed Jackson's gums, tongue and the inside of his cheeks.

The people who had gathered around were being moved back. Agent McCaffrey's voice was in the background giving instructions to another agent.

"Don't be too low…don't be too low," Tracey chanted.

Tracey went through all the steps they'd done several times a day in the last year. When this all began Friday afternoon, he couldn't remember the date he'd been to the hospital with Jackson. He knew it had happened, but his mind had just gone blank.

The memories and feelings came rushing back like a jet taking off. His son had looked a lot like he did now. Tracey had held him in her arms. He'd had a hard time talking and staying awake.

Everything a year ago had happened so damn quick. Jackson had gone from a healthy little boy to almost dying. He was an amazing kid who bounced back and took it all in stride. Diabetes was a part of his life—their lives—and he never let it stand in his way.

The details crowded his thoughts, trying to block out everything else. Four days in the ICU while the doctors slowly, carefully brought Jackson's electrolytes, potassium and blood sugar into balance. If they did it too fast, he'd die. If they did it too slow, he'd die.

The memory recreated the raw fright of that drive to the hospital emergency. His heart was pounding faster now than it had throughout the past two days.

He'll be okay. He has to be.

"What's she doing?" an onlooker asked.

"Trying to get his blood sugar up." Kendall Barlow answered for them, then knelt next to Josh and Tracey. "I wanted you to know that Sage is safe. We took her to a hospital near Hearne. She's a brave little girl and is talking up a storm about what happened. If you're uncomfortable with that…"

"You're sure she's okay?" Josh asked.

Agent Barlow patted him on the shoulder. "No reason to worry. Rangers arrived to escort her home. Bryce Johnson said he won't be leaving her side. I'll call and have him bring her to Round Rock."

"Round Rock?"

"It's the closest hospital. Agent McCaffrey gave the order for our helicopter to evacuate you guys." The agent stood and withdrew her weapon. "Can he be moved?"

Josh saw the weapon out of the corner of his eye. He scanned the area around them and saw Mack being loaded and handcuffed into the back of a truck. He didn't want to move Jackson until the digital reading came up, but they were about to be sitting ducks.

"What's going on?" Tracey asked from the ground. "His reading is only at forty. I'd like to see if we could get some juice. I'd hate to be in the air if he doesn't bounce back."

"We should take cover. Tenoreno escaped when we crashed. He grabbed the machine pistol before he got out of the plane."

"Does Jackson need juice or is he stable to make a twenty-minute flight to the hospital?" Kendall asked. "Or do we need to take him to the house?"

"No, we can't risk it. Not unless we can get him to drink something, get his levels a bit higher. This kit doesn't have glucagon." Tracey stood with Jackson in her arms. Josh reached for him but she shook her head. "Tenoreno is out there, isn't he? Do you think he'll try something?"

She'd lowered her voice so none of those watching or helping get Aiden and the pilot out of the plane could hear.

"Agent Barlow, I don't suppose you have an extra weapon for Josh? He's a better shot than I am."

Kendall reached down to her leg, unstrapped her backup pistol and handed it to him.

He nodded his thanks. His mind suddenly became clear, remembering something that had bothered him about their landing. "How did our pilot know where he was heading?"

"What are you saying?" Kendall turned in a defensive circle, keeping her back to Josh. "Like they meant to come here all along? This rough landing strip is a legitimate skydiving school. You sure? Why land at a field with no planes that could get fugitives to Mexico?"

"Dammit. Not Tenoreno. It's Mack who knew where he was heading. He was hired to bring Daddy to the vindictive son. Not set him free."

Josh searched the perimeter of the field again and nodded as they headed toward the buildings to the west. Tenoreno was out there—both father and son. The plane crash had been less than ten minutes ago and a man could get a long way on foot in that length of time. But Josh's gut told him that their escaped prisoner was close.

"So you think Xander Tenoreno wants his father dead?" Kendall seemed as surprised as he'd felt earlier. "And he's here waiting to kill him?"

"Is it such a far-fetched idea that the son would want revenge for his mother's murder? Or even to keep the power he's had since Paul was locked up?" He kept Tracey and his son close between him and the agent leading the way. "Maybe we should see if Mack's awake and find out."

Josh trusted Tracey's judgement about his son. He also trusted his own again. He shook off the insecure blanket he'd draped around his shoulders for letting these events happen. Jackson stirred a little, still displaying symptoms of low sugar, but he was a strong kid. He'd make it.

Hard Core Law

And Josh was a Texas Ranger because he was good at his job. He'd seen the hatred Mack—or Vince Deegan—had for Paul Tenoreno. It was possible Xander could hate him that much, too.

Chapter Twenty-One

Agent McCaffrey nodded to them, standing guard at the plane as the volunteers continued to free the men. Tracey carried Jackson, protected by Agent Barlow and Josh. Whatever her armed escort was discussing, her only concern was getting Jackson to safety. That meant to get him stable, then on that helicopter to Round Rock.

For the middle of nowhere, there were a lot of people gathered under a shed where Agent Barlow stopped. Parachutes. They were packing parachutes for skydiving.

Tracey could see the FBI helicopter on the opposite side of the road. Mack now sat in the back of the truck next to the helicopter. One of his hands was secured to a rail along the truck bed. The pilot was armed with a shotgun, standing guard.

"Ma'am, you mentioned you had juice?" Josh asked the woman who seemed to be the owner. "Is it in the house?"

"Yes, I've sent someone for it," said the woman who'd arranged for the honey and testing kit. "Do you want to take him inside?"

Tracey sat on a stool, balancing Jackson on her legs. She shook her head not wanting to be out of sight of the helicopter.

"No, thanks. We'll head out as soon as Tracey says." Josh kept turning, searching for something or someone.

She could tell that he was anxious but not just for Jackson's welfare. "I can wait on the juice if you need to talk with that man, especially if they might come back and hurt the kids again."

"The FBI can take care of it."

"Looks like they're a little short-handed. Go on. You can tell the helicopter pilot we'll be ready in five minutes." She was confident it wouldn't be long before Jackson was his normal self. Looking down the hill, they were loading the injured ranger on board. "You need to make sure everything's safe. I can wait on the juice."

"I'll be right back." He kissed Jackson's forehead.

Then he brushed his lips against Tracey's and ran to catch up and interrogate Mack.

Agent Barlow was behind her getting names and asking why each person was there. Jackson kicked out and Tracey almost lost him from her lap.

"You could lay him here. If he's not allergic, this is all fresh hay." A young woman stretched a checkered cloth over a loose bunch. "None of the animals have been near it yet. I just set it out this morning."

"Thank you." Tracey moved to let Jackson stretch out.

"Is he okay?"

"I think he will be. Do you live here?" Tracey wiped Jackson's forehead, now dry and cool. Definitely better.

"Oh no, this is a skydiving school. I'm taking lessons and help out with the animals. They're so adorable."

Tracey didn't normally have bad vibes about people. And after the past two days, she didn't really trust the one she felt from this woman, who seemed to be

nice. There shouldn't be anything "bad" about someone trying to help a sick little boy get more comfortable. And yet…

Tracey stood. "You know, he is better. We should
probably join Josh." She bent to pick him up, but
stopped with a gun barrel in her ribs.

"Wow, you caught on real quick," the woman whispered. "Now, we need to leave the kid and back out the
other side of this place. Got it? And if you make a move,
then somebody else is going to be hurt."

Where had she come from? No one seemed to be
alerted that she was there. It was barely dawn for crying out loud. So why wasn't anyone surprised that she
was leaving?

When exactly was this sick nightmare going to end?

"I'll come with you." Only to keep anyone else from
getting hurt. Tracey tried to get Agent Barlow's attention. No luck.

The woman holding the gun waited for the agent to
walk to the opposite side of the structure. She giggled
as they walked around the corner and through another
shed with long tables.

The gun continued to jab her ribs as the woman
picked up her pace and forced Tracey to the far side of
all the buildings. They darted from a huge oak tree to
a metal shed. Then another. Then another. This side of
the skydiving facility couldn't be seen from the plane
crash or where she'd left Jackson.

"They're going to know something's wrong. I
wouldn't leave Jackson like that. Not voluntarily."

"We don't care if they come looking for you. The
more they look, the more they'll flush Paul from his

hiding place," a man in his midthirties answered from behind a stack of hay.

The twentysomething woman, actually about the same age as Tracey, sidled up next to the man and lifted her lips for a kiss. And, of course, she lifted the gun and pointed it in Tracey's general direction.

"Why in the world do you think you need me to help you find your father? You are Xander Tenoreno. Right?"

It was hard to be scared. Too much had happened in the past two days—she'd barely been conscious half an hour. She'd changed or she was just plain tired. The reason was unimportant, but these two didn't really seem threatening to her.

"You know… I might have a concussion. Even though I feel totally fine." She crossed the lean-to and plopped down on a hay bale. "Or I might be quite confident that Josh won't take long to find me. But I am going to wait. Right here. You can do what you want. I'm waiting."

She was the one who sounded a little scary. Sort of delusional or exhausted. Maybe it was shock. Once she sat, she realized her entire body was shaking and her mouth had gone completely dry.

Xander Tenoreno acted like he was ignoring her, as if she wasn't important. But she'd been watching men and their body language closely for hours. And his was tense, ready to pounce if she moved the wrong direction.

"This is ridiculous," Tracey continued. "Your father is long gone. Probably stole a car and headed out while everyone else was running to the plane crash."

"You can shut up now." The chick—she'd lost the right to be referred to with respect—pulled the rather large gun up to her shoulder again. "Xander knows what he's doing."

Tracey nodded and began looking for a weapon or for something to hide behind when the shooting started.

Wow. She really did feel like help was on the way. Josh wouldn't let anything happen to her. She was more concerned about both of them being separated from Jackson. He needed juice and was barely coherent enough to swallow.

Xander took out a telescope that fit on top of a rifle. He searched the fields and turned his body in a semicircle. He paused several times but didn't do anything except remove his arm from around the woman.

"Why not just let your father go to jail for the rest of his life?" She was legitimately curious. But it also occurred to her that if he was distracted, Josh would have an easier time taking him by surprise.

"My father wasn't going to jail. He wasn't even going to stand trial." He cocked his head to the side. "He was headed to Austin to make a deal. Screw me and our business over so that he could what? Get away with murdering my mother. That's what. His deal would have put him in witness protection. I have a right to take care of this the way I see fit."

Now she was scared.

"Where's Tracey?" Josh sat Jackson upright and made sure he could swallow some juice. A little dribbled down his chin, but he didn't choke. He'd give him a couple of minutes and then repeat the blood test.

"I thought she followed you. I checked the west side of the house, came back and she wasn't here." Kendall placed her palm on Jackson's cheek. "His color is better. Are you ready to transport now?"

"I…" He looked at his son, looked around for Tracey, then stared at the armed pilot. "Something's wrong. She wouldn't leave him alone like this."

They asked the family members and the instructor if they'd seen anything. Their answers were no.

"Maybe you're overthinking," Kendall said.

"Call it in."

"We only have three agents here, Josh. We can't cover each of these buildings until backup arrives."

"She could be dead or miles away from here by then."

"Ma'am?" He tapped on the shoulder of the home owner. "You said your grandson has diabetes, so you're familiar with it?"

"Oh yes, I'm sorry that we didn't have everything your wife needed."

Josh didn't correct her. Moving forward was more important. "Do you mind sitting with Jackson?"

"No. I'd be glad to."

Josh walked away and caught the end of Kendall's phone conversation.

"He's not going to stay put. Tenoreno's out there, sir. I can at least find out where." She hung up and faced him. "Do people always go out on a limb for you, Josh?"

"Not sure how to answer that, but I am grateful."

"Excuse me, you asked about the woman in the plane." A teenage girl holding a dog waited for an okay to finish. "Shawna's gone, too."

"Shawna?"

"She's taking lessons and wanted to feed the animals this morning."

"Has she ever wanted to do that before?" Kendall pulled out her cell again.

"No. Today's the first time."

"Do you have a picture of Shawna and a last name?" Kendall asked.

He battled with himself over whether he should go. Jackson needed him, but so did Tracey. His son was able to swallow. It wasn't his imagination that Jackson's color was better.

"Kendall, I need you to climb out on another limb for me." Her eyebrows arched, asking what without saying a word. "Five minutes and you take Jackson to the hospital."

"But he's—"

"My gut says yes he's better, but I have to be certain. I can't choose one person I love over the other."

"Better idea. You get on the chopper and I'll do my job and track down where Tracey is. Go. Take care of your kid."

While Kendall got the information necessary for her report or an APB on the missing woman, Josh looked for an exit route. Not because he was trying to ditch the FBI agent. If he could find the best route to leave the shelter, he might be able to find Tracey.

"Can I borrow your phone?" Josh asked and the young man nodded. "That's your mom sitting with my son over there, right? Can you tell her to call this," he shook the phone side to side, "if Jackson's condition changes?" He nodded again.

The boy went to his mother, pointed at Josh. He had to try to take care of them both. He'd track down Tracey. When he was gone, Kendall would take his son to the hospital. He focused.

Where would he… There. To keep out of sight they would have headed toward a tree with a tractor parked under it. It was the only place from that side of the shelter. He ran that direction and sure enough, his line of sight to the helicopter pilot was obscured.

He zigzagged across the property using the same logic. If he couldn't see anyone behind him, they probably didn't see him. Then it wasn't a matter of where he'd come from but what was right in front of him.

Tracey.

Along with Xander Tenoreno.

Tracey didn't seem in immediate danger. He could get Kendall or McCaffrey, surround the man ultimately behind the kidnapping of his kids. He felt the emotion building. He shouldn't burst in there with no plan to rescue the woman he loved.

The lines between logic and emotion blurred as he debated which path to follow. Xander looked through a scope toward the far tree line. Josh moved close enough to hear the conversation.

"Predictable. I knew he'd head for a vehicle after walking away from the plane. A shame I wasn't ready for the crash, but that surprise caught me off guard and I missed."

"It's okay, baby."

The girl, Shawna, who had been at the shed earlier, wrapped her arms around Xander and he shrugged her off, uncovering something on a hay bale. Yeah, it was a rifle. Mack had been telling the truth about Xander wanting to kill his father.

The decision about leaving had been made. The son was scoping the dad like it was deer season. Josh didn't have good positioning, he didn't have backup and he only had a peashooter revolver.

What could go wrong?

"Step away from the rifle. Hands on your heads, then drop to your knees." Josh revealed where he was and stepped from behind an animal feeder.

"Well if it isn't Major Joshua Parker here to save the girl again." Xander fingered the rifle trigger. He was not dropping to his knees with his hands on his head.

The girl got closer to his side. She didn't bother listening to Josh, either.

"Don't be an idiot, Tenoreno. I'm not going to let you hurt anyone. Even your own father." Josh stepped closer, but not close enough to give Xander any advantage. Swinging the rifle around to point at Tracey or himself would be harder at this range.

"She has a gun," Tracey informed him as she slipped off her seat on the hay.

"And she knows how to use it." Xander shifted and the gun was in his hand. "But I know to use it better."

"Give it up. You're not getting away from here."

"Funny thing about revenge, Josh. I'd rather see my father suffer for what he did. He murdered my mother. All she wanted was to live somewhere else. Someplace where he wasn't. After forty years with him, she probably deserved it."

"So you kidnapped Jackson and Sage, and set up this entire game to get back at your daddy?" Tracey moved another step away from Tenoreno.

Josh could tell she was heading for the back side of the lean-to. All she needed was a distraction. "All this because you have daddy issues."

"Seriously? You think I'm going to fall for a question like that?" Xander aimed the gun at Tracey. "I'll let my girlfriend keep your girlfriend occupied while I take care of my business."

"You know I can't let you pull that trigger."

"You're not on the clock now, Ranger Parker. You can let me do anything you want."

"Thing is…he doesn't want to." Tracey answered for him, her shoulders rising with every frightened breath she took. "It doesn't matter how deviant you are or who your father murdered." She pointed to Josh. "That man is a good man. He'll give his life to protect you both. You'll never understand what makes him decent."

Josh's heart swelled. No two ways about it, she loved him. His hands steadied. His feet were firm and fixed. He was ready for whatever came next. But she was wrong. He loved her and would protect her before doing anything else.

Xander ignored them and put his eye to the scope again.

"I'll say this one more time. Drop the gun, kneel and put your hands on your head." It was a small backup revolver. "I have six shots. That's three for each of you. No warnings. Center mass. I won't miss."

"Xander? Baby, what do I do?" The weight of the big gun or the nerves of the young woman caused the gun to wobble in her hands. Xander ignored her, too.

Shawna looked from Tracey leaning on the hay, to Josh pointing a gun at her. After he didn't answer or acknowledge her, she didn't look at her boyfriend. The gun dropped from her hands, she fell to her knees and began crying.

For a couple of seconds Josh thought it was over. He wanted to be back with Jackson and Sage. He wanted to talk about everything with Tracey. He wanted all this to become a memory.

Xander Tenoreno pulled the trigger. Josh squeezed his.

Shawna screamed. Tracey fell to the ground.

Josh leaped across the space separating him from Xander. Encouraged by the love he'd heard in Tracey's words and scared to death that something had just happened to her. Shawna was up and running but she was someone else's problem. Tracey needed to find the gun that had dropped from the woman's hands. The man fired and she'd hit the dirt herself, not certain what would happen.

Josh was fighting Xander. She was sure he felt like he needed to eliminate the threat. The man was crazy. He'd shot his father in front of a Texas Ranger.

Where's the gun? Where's the gun?

Tracey scooted on her hands and knees looking for the silver steel in all the dirt and pieces of hay. Her head was down and she looked up only to see Josh winning the battle.

She got knocked backward when Xander tripped over her. Josh came in to land a powerful blow to the man's abdomen.

"Give it up." Josh watched as his opponent fell backward.

Tracey didn't need to search for the gun anymore. It was over. Xander Tenoreno didn't get up. He was done. Knocked out cold by the time Kendall and the other agent got to the lean-to.

"We heard shots."

"I'm not sure, but Paul Tenoreno might be at the other end of where that rifle is pointed."

"You okay?" Tracey asked. "Can you make it back to the house?"

Josh took a deep breath and stood up straight, wincing. "As long as you're here… I'll be fine. Let's go get our boy."

"TENORENO JUNIOR'S WOUND isn't serious. We'll ride with the emergency unit and transport him and Vince Deegan to Round Rock." Kendall joined them at the helicopter as they watched a now alert Jackson let the pilot settle a headset on his ears.

"And Tenoreno senior?" Josh asked.

"We were too late. Bullet hit the lung."

"I didn't think he'd do it."

"You aren't the murderer, Josh."

"Aiden and Jackson are set and ready. Unfortunately, the pilot didn't make it. There's room on the helicopter for one of you. Who's going?" McCaffrey asked, tapping Josh on the back of his shoulder with whatever papers he had in his hand.

It was his son. His place was beside him. Tracey didn't hesitate, she gently pushed Josh forward. "I'll find Sage and be right behind you, even if I have to steal a car to get there."

Josh stepped on board, watching her, acting as if he was about to say something.

The corners of Tracey's mouth went up and down. She couldn't keep a smile as the door began closing, separating them. She lifted her hand, then covered her mouth to hold back the tears.

"Hold it." Josh pushed the door aside and held out his hand. "She's with me."

They all moved out of his way and an agent got off, not bothering to argue. Once again he showed everyone around them that she wasn't *just* the nanny.

Chapter Twenty-Two

Bouncing back from the low blood sugar levels was a breeze for Jackson. What they hadn't realized was that his right ulna had been cracked in the plane crash. He'd been so out of it at the time that he didn't begin complaining until much later in the day.

Instead of sending them home to sleep in their own beds, the FBI put them in a hotel suite in Waco. They claimed it was easier to protect them there. And since it didn't matter where they slept, Josh agreed. They were all together. Exhausted but very much alive.

"Didn't they catch all the people involved?" she'd asked him once McCaffrey had gone.

Josh had pulled her into his arms and kissed her briefly. "They're playing it safe. Think of it this way, no cooking. No commuting back and forth to your place."

And no talking about how—or if—their relationship had changed. The suite had two bedrooms. She had to admit that room service and not making her bed had huge appeal.

Sage drew pictures that were full of Jackson's favorite things and asked for a roll of tape so she could cover the walls. There were a couple of times where she ran to the bed where Jackson was on forced rest and

Tracey thought there might have been a hint of twin talk. Just long looks where they were communicating, but no words were exchanged.

They were back to their regular twin selves.

Whatever happened between Jackson and Sage, they didn't share it with her, but they did involve their dad. Josh had stepped into the hall for several phone calls she assumed were official Ranger business.

Tracey went to bed after watching Josh hold his kids close, tucked up under each arm. A beautiful sight. His look—before he'd fallen asleep—had invited her to join them, but it wasn't time. Not yet.

One day soon, they'd talk about the way they felt. Right now, they all just needed rest and assurance that nothing else would happen.

Day two of their protective custody, under a Ranger escort, Tracey took Sage home to clean up and grab art supplies. She thought Josh would want something clean to wear and headed to his bedroom when she caught Bryce coming from there.

"Oh, hi." He turned sideways in the hall so she could pass. "I was just grabbing him… He asked me to pick up—I even remembered his toothbrush."

He lifted a gym bag. She assumed it was filled with Josh's clothes and she didn't need to worry about picking anything out. But Bryce looked extremely guilty. What was up with that?

"Okay. So I'm just going to grab Sage some snacks, then we'll be ready to head back. Is anything wrong?"

"Nope. Nothing's wrong."

"I got Jackson's stuff." Sage came from their bedroom and Bryce scooped her up to carry her downstairs, making her giggle all the way down.

Everything shouted that the man was lying. She'd let Josh deal with whatever that was about. One short stop by her place and they were ready to head back to the hospital.

"Sage, honey, can you wear your headphones for a little while?"

Bryce waited for the little girl to comply, then her escort took a long breath. "That doesn't bode well for whatever you're going to ask."

"I need to know what's going on. Has something else happened? We're being guarded twenty-four-seven and you're acting very suspicious." Not to mention Josh's compliance with everything Agent McCaffrey suggested.

"Nothing that I know about. It seems that Xander Tenoreno bribed the pilot. They aren't making a big deal about that because he died."

Even with Bryce's assurances, Tracey has a feeling something was being kept from her. Everyone was acting so...different. Bryce drove into the parking lot and she saw the two men who had been her bodyguards standing at the front entrance.

"Oh, that's just great! Just when I thought everything was settling back to normal my uncle strikes again."

"You want me to get rid of them?"

"No. I can do it. Will you take Sage back to Josh?" She walked up to the guard who had at least spoken to her and stuck her palm out. "Your phone, please."

"No need for that, miss. Your uncle's inside. We're waiting for him here."

The demise of the Tenoreno family, the dramatic recovery of the twins. All of it made good television and press for the state and the Rangers. But all of it put the Bass family in the limelight, too. She'd expected a phone call from her uncle, not a visit.

She entered the lobby, expecting an entourage to be surrounding Carl. He sat in the corner alone, a cup of coffee on the table next to him. He acknowledged her, she overheard some business lingo and expected to have to wait.

"There she is. I've got to go. Call you back later." Carl dropped the phone into his pocket—totally an unusual move for him. "You look tired, darling. Getting enough rest? Do I need to secure the entire floor so you can get a decent night's sleep?"

"I'm fine. It's been pretty hectic lately. So what do you need? If it's about the reporters, my name change is public record—there's nothing I could do about them finding out our family history."

"Same Tracey." He pulled her shoulders, drawing her to his chest for a hug. "But you're all grown-up now, right?"

When he released her, she took a couple of steps back, looking at him. "What's going on?"

"I needed to see that you were okay. Completely okay. And here." Wallet now in hand, he reached inside and took out a check. "Spend it on whatever you need. Buy a new electric fence or a security system or even bodyguards for a while. No, don't argue. You've discovered there are some seriously bad people in the world. Those kids need to be protected. Oh, and I'm here because I was invited."

He wrapped her hand through the crook of his arm and escorted her to as if it was Buckingham Palace. She might actually enjoy being an adult around him, but why would he say he'd been invited? By whom?

Carl stepped aside just before they reached the door to the suite. Bryce handed her a handmade princess hat Sage had decorated that morning. "I think you're supposed to put that on."

She followed instructions and entered. The room was overflowing with friends and relatives. Everyone was wearing either a crown or a princess hat.

"My lady." Carl placed her hand on his and took two steps.

The room was silent, people practically held their breath. Asking what was going on would ruin the entire effect. Carl joined Gwen's parents, who were steadying Sage and Jackson on chairs next to Josh. Both children had towels draped around their shoulders as if they were acting out one of their stories. Sage even had the wand they'd made together months ago.

Josh formally bowed. He raised his eyebrows and carefully took her hand.

"I was hoping for a moment alone before this happened," he whispered, "but I got outvoted." Josh cleared his throat. "Before we have an audience with the Prince and Princess Parkers, you need to know that their father—"

"The king," the twins said together.

"The king, loves you with all his mind, soul and heart. So… Tracey Cassidy…" He dipped his hand in his pocket and knelt on bended knee.

"Would you marry us?" they all said together.

Josh opened his palm where a sparkly diamond solitaire was surrounded by multicolored glitter. She cupped Josh's checks and kissed him with her answer as he stood.

Everyone began clapping.

"That means yes!" the twins shouted,

Epilogue

Two weeks later

"Let me get this straight. All you have to do is wait around until you're thirty years old and you get control of your own money. That sounds like a plan. You're already set for life," Bryce told Tracey. He had one arm around the waist of his girlfriend and the other wrapped around a bucket of Bush's chicken strips.

Tracey nodded like the ten other times she'd answered the question for Josh's men. Josh thought she'd lose a gasket if she discovered Bryce was teasing a fellow silver-spooner. She needed rescuing and this time he didn't need a gun.

"Did he tell you that I had to collect that rock and get it to the room before you?" Bryce said, pointing to her ring. "So you really don't have to work—"

"She does if we want to eat." Josh jumped in and stole the chicken from his computer expert. He whisked Tracey away to a corner of the kitchen not occupied by a ranger or significant other. "Sorry."

"You said you wouldn't tell anyone."

"I didn't." He shrugged. "They are investigators, you know. They all worked on different possibilities of who had the kids even when they were told to stand down. It's just one of those things that happens at my office, Mrs. Parker."

He took a chicken tender from the box. Gone in two large bites. She laughed.

Life still hadn't settled into something resembling normalcy. Maybe it never would. Maybe normal didn't exist. But here they were—husband and wife. Had he been romantic? He couldn't wait that long. He'd asked. She'd replied, "Yes. Let's not wait."

So they hadn't.

Two weeks later, the Company was throwing them a surprise party. Tracey's uncle had flown Gwen's parents in the previous week. They all encouraged them to have the courtroom ceremony while they were visiting.

"Don't you think you should put the chicken on the table with the rest of the food?" Tracey asked, making a lunge for the box.

He plucked another tender and shoved it in his mouth. "We could feed a starving nation with what's on that table. They aren't going to miss this little bit of bird."

"Bryce will. You should have seen his face when you stole it from him."

"Ha. You should see yours now that you can't reach it."

"Oh, I don't want the chicken. I want your hands free. I'm getting kind of used to them touching me. But if you'd rather hold deep-fried chicken, then…" She shrugged and spun out of his arms.

"Okay, okay. You've made your point." He followed Tracey to the table, where she picked up two plates and filled them with munchkin-sized portions.

"I thought Gwen's parents were taking the kids to dinner?"

"They said they'd take them for chicken and since it's here—"

"You feel kind of weird letting them leave the house?" Josh took the plates from her hands and set them on the bar. "I get it. I'll take it up and explain."

"I'll go. They're really nice and I think they'll understand."

"Yep. And you're right." He wrapped his arms around her body and pulled her to him for a kiss.

The door opened and Josh watched from a distance as Aiden Oaks entered. White hat in hand—at least the hand that wasn't holding a crutch, blue jeans ripped up to the knee, leg in a cast, badge over his heart. "May I come in?"

"Sure."

"Need a beer?"

"Here, take this chair." The men of Company F made their commander comfortable.

Aiden swung the crutch like a pro and made himself comfortable. Josh squeezed Tracey's hand and kissed her for luck. That uncertain future might be resolved in the next couple of minutes.

"Hello, Captain."

"Major." He adjusted the crutch to lean on the chair and hung his hat on top. "How are the kids, Tracey?"

"Physically they're great. We're working on the kidnapping slowly. But I think we're all getting back to normal."

Josh threaded his fingers through hers. She knew why Aiden was there. Most of the conversation had stopped. There was the lull of a baseball game in the background. They'd all been expecting a decision on his reprimand at any time. Maybe it was appropriate that they get the news tonight.

They were celebrating the start of a new life.

"A couple of decisions came down the pipe today. Xander Tenoreno's been indicted on racketeering, kidnapping and everything else the attorney general's office could come up with. An operation to free the families of men who worked for him was successful. And before you begin clapping, the thing you've all been wanting to know…" he paused while the crowd came closer. "I'm returning the reins of Company F to Major Parker."

Cries of laughter and relief echoed through the house from the men and women surrounding him. Claps on the back and congratulations should have distracted him, but all he could see was Tracey's joy.

Their relationship had begun with a tragedy, and then adversity had brought them closer. His bride had the right to ask him to walk away from the Rangers after the kidnapping. Her uncle had told them he'd make arrangements for her to access her inheritance. Unlike what he'd told Bryce, neither of them needed to work.

Seemed like all he wanted to do was make up for the time they'd been waiting on each other to make decisions. He knew how much support he had from her. Seeing it now, all he could do was pull her to him and kiss her.

One kiss that turned into a second and a third. It might have gone further, but a couple of fake coughs started behind him.

"Do we have to stay upstairs, Daddy?" Sage crooked her finger several times, then just waved her hands for him to bend down so she could whisper in his ear. "What am I supposed to call Trace Trace now? Grandfather told me she's our stepmother. Is she going to get mean and grow warts like in all the stories?"

Josh laughed and picked up his little girl. "What do you want to call Trace Trace?" he asked, using the kids' nickname.

"Can it just be Mommy?"

His eyes locked with the woman who'd been there with him through the darkest part of his life. Her eyes brimmed with tears ready to fall. "I think she'd like that."

Tracey nodded her head, quickly whisking the tears from her cheeks before letting Sage see her. "Hey, kidlet. That sounds like a perfect name. No one's ever called me that before. You two will be the first."

Cast banging on the rails, Jackson flew down the stairs and into her arms. "They said we needed to ask, but I knew you'd like it."

Tracey kissed both of their cheeks with lots of noise. "I don't just like it. I absolutely adore it." Her eyes locked with Josh's. "Almost as much as I love all of you."

And just like kids that subject was settled and they ran back to their grandparents on the stairs. Their grandmother declared there was enough food to feed all five companies of Rangers. He felt Tracey's sigh of relief as she relaxed within his arms. The kids went up and Gwen's mother came for their dinner.

Before they handed her the plates, she gathered them both close for a hug, then wiped away a tear. "I want you to know how happy we are for you. We had begun to wonder if Josh was ever going to ask you after what he said last Christmas."

Tracey looked confused. "What did he say?"

His mother-in-law pushed forward. "Josh told us how he felt and that he wanted to remarry. You were a blessing to our Gwen, Tracey. If she can't be here to raise her children, I know she'd be happy you will be. Welcome to our family."

Tracey looked happy as they watched his mother-in-law return upstairs. "I meant to tell you about that."

"Did you change your mind or something?"

"Obviously not. I thought I should probably ask you on a date first. I intended to on your birthday," Josh whispered.

She twisted around to face him. "Get out of town. Really? What changed your mind? Get a little too tipsy instead?"

"I wasn't tipsy. Just lost my nerve."

"You? The man who ran and jumped into the small door of a plane with machine guns firing all around him?"

"Yeah, I know, hard to believe. But a wise man once told me never to ask a woman a certain question you didn't know the answer to. I thought I did. Only to realize the only thing for certain I knew was that I loved everything about you. But you might not necessarily feel the same."

She swatted at him as if he was totally wrong. He knew better. He'd messed up her birthday and he'd messed up the romance. He'd spend the rest of his uncertain future making it up to her.

Every day was precious. They knew it better than most. And he wouldn't take life for granted.

"Do you think those two will even notice that I've moved in?"

Josh seized the opportunity of her upturned face to kiss her again. Slowly, gaining the notice of their surprise guests and family. He came away with a smile on his face.

Happy. Satisfied that Tracey, Jackson and Sage were the normal he wanted.

Josh whispered his answer so only his wife could hear. "There will be a heck of a lot of sleepovers to explain if they don't."

* * * * *

THE RANGER

Thanks to everyone in the magic room:
Jan, Janie, Lara, Jodi, Tish, Jen, Gina, Tyler Ann
and Robin. Tim, thanks for doing the dishes.
And Kourtney—who consistently amazes me—
thank you so much for your help with this series.

Chapter One

Mitch cracked one eyelid open, staring at pavement. The last thing he remembered was palming his .45 and soundlessly skirting the back wall of Junior's garage. He'd been about to open the office door, tripped and then nothing but stars. God bless 'em, but he'd seen enough pinpoints of light in the past couple of minutes to last a lifetime.

Texas Ranger Mitchell Striker had been an undercover mechanic in Marfa going on six months. Too long in his humble opinion, but no one asked him. He couldn't see a blasted thing from his position on the cement. He concentrated on the sounds around him. Shuffling of smooth-soled shoes inside the office. Papers falling to the floor. Excited breathing.

It didn't make sense that he'd fallen. If anything was out of place where he worked, he would have been the one to leave it there.

Nothing was ever left out of place. He hadn't tripped.

He'd been hit on the back of his head. If he concentrated any harder, he'd hear the lump pushing through his hair. Inching his left hand, minutely extending his arm, he tried to find his gun.

A noise like someone bumping the chair, followed by

muffled voices awakened him from a light sleep in the back room. He'd come to the office but must not have been as quiet as he'd thought. The guy with the smooth shoes had gotten the drop on him.

"You didn't have to hit him with a wrench."

Mitch froze, recognizing the woman's voice. Daughter of the garage owner and his boss, Brandie Ryland. She should be at home with her son, not rustling through files in the middle of the night. Files she had access to anytime she asked in the daylight.

"What if you've seriously hurt him?"

"Good. We told you to clear him out for a while. Why's he here in the middle of the night? You got something on the side?"

Male voice with a bit of a northern nasal. Clearly not from south of the border or Texas.

"He's my mechanic and sleeps in the back room." Brandie moved next to him. Tiny bare feet, he could see she'd painted her toenails herself and had missed a spot on the outside of her pinky. The color was her, calm blue with festive glitter. She knelt beside him, and her toes were replaced with cartoon characters covering her knees.

"Where do you hide the cash around here?"

She wanted to rob her own garage? She didn't need muscle for that.

Cool, shaky hands gently parted the hair where he'd been hit. Just a lump or she would have hissed at the sight of blood. Mitch had seen her practically pass out when Toby had gashed his shin falling from his tricycle. She stroked his longish hair covering his face to tuck it behind his ear. He was forced to completely close his eyes and couldn't see where her partner was located.

"I don't keep cash here." Brandie was lying. Mitch knew she put it in the safe overnight and drove it to the bank after the breakfast crowd thinned out.

"I can't get it to work," the male voice accused, shaking something.

"I told you it wouldn't. We got rid of the phone line back here," she whispered. "Help me get Mitch to my car. I should take him to the hospital."

"You ain't for reals. For a bonk on the head? I ain't helping you do nothin'. You're lucky I didn't give him a kick or two in the face. What a waste of my time."

Kicking anywhere would wake him up and warrant a reaction.

"You need to leave. Tell him I was right and you shouldn't come out here."

Mitch risked cracking his lids again.

The points of well-polished, expensive shoes came toward them. Nice, not supermart quality and definitely not from around here. He was ready to take this guy down. But Brandie's fingers curling his hair around his ear didn't seem frightened, just nervous.

"I think he's waking up," fancy shoes said, inching closer.

If Mitch moved, would he put Brandie in danger? Was it worth potentially blowing his cover? His superiors would say no. He'd been Mitch the Mechanic for going on two years now. Yet, his personal answer was an emphatic yes. He couldn't let anything happen to Brandie.

She stood, her bare feet right next to his torso. He didn't need to open his eyes to know what she looked like. Tiny compared to him, she was a redheaded spitfire on most days. She stood up to problem customers by sweet-talking them into agreeing with her.

"You aren't going to touch him. I said leave and I meant it."

"It's amazin' anything gets done out here in this Texas hell hole. Back home we wouldn't think twice about gettin' rid of this guy. Anyway, a stinkin' mechanic ain't worth the trouble you'd cause me. But you should think about the next time you's asked for something. Maybe be more serious tryin' to get hold of it," the unidentified man threatened. "You know I'll be back when he needs somet'in' else. Oh, and, Brandie, you've got a really gorgeous kid. His blond hair really makes him easy to spot."

A light step over Mitch and the man—and his shoes—were clip-clopping out the back door and down the gravel drive.

"Leave my son out of this," she threw out the door behind him. "You can tell your boss if he has something to say, he can come here and deliver the message himself."

She paced a couple of times in the small office. On the trip away from him, he looked to see where her arms were. Yep, fingers digging into the side of her neck. She was worried.

As she should be.

"Threatening him was such a dumb move. What am I going to do if he does show up? And how am I going to explain this to you?" She vented, faced him and flung her hands toward him. "Or anyone else for that matter? At least you aren't bleeding. But I can't just leave you lying there. I'll be right back with the first-aid kit from the café."

Did she know he was conscious? He'd remained motionless, kept his breathing regular. She didn't stick around for confirmation, popping to her feet and running through the dark garage.

He rolled to his back, searching for his weapon. He took a quick look around the office. The bastard walking away must have taken it. He rubbed the lump on his head, cursing that a runt who threatened kids had gotten the drop on him. *He did have to use a wrench.* He heard Brandie's feet slapping against the concrete of the garage and quickly drew the door closed, locked it and then sank, resting against it.

The night sky actually lit up the outside more than the cloaked dark inside the shop. It was all those dang stars. Over two years undercover along the border and he still couldn't get used to the millions and millions of them.

"Thank God, you're awake," Brandie said, dropping to her knees again and riffling through the first-aid kit. "Are you okay? Maybe we should get you to the hospital in Alpine?"

"I should be asking you that. You don't look so good. How did you know you needed to come rescue me?" He rubbed his head and watched her carefully for any type of reaction. "Got any ice in there?"

"Let me get some from the café." She put a hand against the ground to stand.

He covered it, keeping her where she was. "Naw, it can wait. Tell me what happened and why you're here. Was there a break in? I thought I heard a noise, got up and then there's nothing."

"I…um…" Her eyes darted everywhere except directly at him.

Sign of a guilty conscience?

"Brandie? Did you see anything? Have you called

the sheriff? And you still haven't said what brought you to the garage?"

"How hard did they hit your head? Those are the most words you've ever said to me at one time before."

"Sorry."

"Don't be. I like the sound of your voice. Makes me feel safe." She twisted her fingers in the bottom of the loose skimpy pink shirt. "I got a phone call that the door was open. When I pulled up you were unconscious."

"Where's your cell?" he asked, hiding his disappointment that she had to lie.

"Why?"

She had to have gotten a call or visit from the mystery man. She was barefoot and still in her pajamas. His superiors could get a warrant for a phone dump, but it was just easier to take a look. He couldn't alert her to why he wanted to know.

This entire time, he'd had his ear to the ground listening for pertinent news about someone helping the Mexican cartel. He'd never suspected he might be working for that very person. Brandie Ryland was a liar? He couldn't trust her. Didn't want to believe she'd been fooling him with a struggling single mother routine.

"I'm going to call the sheriff," he answered.

"Is it really necessary? I mean, it doesn't look like they took anything."

"It's up to you, but someone did hit me over the head. Knocked me out cold."

"Are you going to sue me or something?"

"Hell, no. I want to press charges when they catch the guy. What if he does it again? Let me call 9-1-1 and I'll deal with it."

She slid her hand away from his and stood. Her

phone had been tossed to the back of the desk. While she searched for it she destroyed evidence by picking up the papers and putting them back exactly where her *friend* had shoved them aside.

He held his hand out for the phone.

"I can make the call. I'm the manager. It's my responsibility." She dialed. Left a message with the sheriff's department. "It'll be a little while before someone gets here. I should get you that ice."

He reached out and snagged her hand. "What's really going on, Brandie?"

"I don't know what you mean."

"If you're in trouble, I can try to help."

The phone rang. "Great. My parents. I should take this. I'm fine, Dad. Mitch got hit on the head. He's fine, too." She placed the phone between them and pushed speaker. "Mitch is here in case you'd like to ask him anything."

"What happened? Peach just called from the police station and said there'd been a robbery. What did they take?"

"Nothing that we can tell, sir." Only his pride after that runt of the litter got the drop on him.

"I don't know what you're doing at the café at this hour, little girl. Who's watching Toby? Oh, he's here? Well, how was I supposed to remember that?" he mumbled to someone in the background, probably his wife, Olivia. "We'll be right there."

Her parents would interrupt them in less than five minutes.

"I should get a shirt."

"That's probably a good idea. Mom hasn't seen that much muscle since we went to the car show in Abilene," Brandie teased.

"We were robbed and the lady makes jokes." Her hands circled her neck again, protecting herself or maybe a subconscious sign she felt like she was choking?

She waited at the garage entrance. He had to turn sideways through the door to pass. She looked so worried that his hands cupped both of her petite shoulders before he remembered she was now his primary suspect. She tilted her head back to get a look at him and he saw a tear silently fall before she brushed it away.

"What if something had happened to you?" she whispered.

"It'll take more than a lug wrench to keep me down." He wasn't good at joking or conversation. And exceptionally not good at being cared about. "I guess I better get that shirt."

She nodded. "How do you know they hit you with a lug wrench?"

Damn, he was slipping. "It's on the floor."

"Oh. Everything's just gotten so weird. I'm just really glad you're okay. I, um—"

The red and blue of police lights spun just outside the window.

"Brandie! You in there?" Bud Quinn shouted from the parking lot.

"Your dad got here fast." Mitch pointed toward the old storeroom where he bunked. "Hey, do you need a…a shirt?"

"Oh, my gosh. I…" She wrapped her arms across her breasts, hiding the pert nipples. "Yes, please."

"I'll be right back."

He grabbed two shirts and his shoes, hanging back while Brandie explained things to her father. After their initial hug and his "thank God you're okay," Brandie's dad was all business and confronting the deputy and then the sheriff before he made it through the door.

Sheriff Pete Morrison had been on Mitch's back from his first day in town, keeping a close eye on his movements. Admittedly, Mitch had come into Marfa a self-proclaimed drifter looking for a job. This incident wouldn't make it easier to get around unnoticed. At least Morrison didn't look the type to try to run him out of town.

The deceit was a necessary evil. No one could know he was a Texas Ranger. Mitch would find the rat—or rat*ette*—and move on without anyone knowing. It was his job and he'd move up and down the border as long as the cover held.

He watched the men in the parking lot from inside the garage. The window opened toward the main road. Just a standard-looking gas station with a two-bay garage.

"That pole you're leaning on used to be covered in grease." Brandie handed him ice wrapped with a bar towel.

He shrugged, knowing it had taken a full day to clean it up. "I didn't have a lot to do until word got around I could tune an engine."

"I wish I could give you a raise."

Would she offer him money to keep his mouth shut? Was that dread creeping into his mind that she might actually be the cartel's contact? His job would be over if she was supplying the information. He could move on to the next assignment. Leave.

There was no way she was responsible for the drug and gun shipments getting across the border without detection. She couldn't be. His head was ready to memorize her words and something else grounded him to the pole he'd worked hard to clean up.

"I like it here." The word *amazed* passed through his mind. First that he'd admitted it out loud and second that it was true.

"That's good because I'm paying you more than I can afford as it is. Dad and I argue about it all the time. Thank goodness nothing was stolen or I'd never hear the end of it." She pulled the T-shirt over her pajama top and greeted the sheriff.

Funny, he didn't remember handing it to her. Just like he didn't remember exactly when he'd realized he was glad she wasn't married. Damn, he needed to catch this informant and move on before something emotional happened to him.

Chapter Two

Brandie was dead on her feet. The only real crowd the café had was at breakfast and, of course, it was her morning to open. Between Rey's threats and his minion's visit, she hadn't caught a wink of sleep. Zubict's name and northern accent was enough proof for her that Rey had expanded his association.

Her feet were dragging, and she felt emotionally bruised. Mitch, her father and the sheriff had spoken to her like she should know more than she'd told them. It didn't matter that she did. She'd never given them reason to doubt her before.

"I can handle the café if you want some shut-eye," Mitch said just behind her.

Rey and his men had bothered her with infrequent phone calls until two weeks ago when the visits began. Her parents hadn't picked up on the additional stress. She thought she'd hidden it from everyone, but the concern in Mitch's expression made her doubt she could hide anything from him for long.

"I'm fine. Really." She had just enough time to pick up Toby, get them both dressed, drop him at day care and head back for morning setup.

Mitch put a hand on hers as she unlocked the café

door for the cook. "I can take Toby by the day care then. That is, if you trust me."

His hand was strong and oh so warm—even through two T-shirts earlier. They'd probably touched more in the past couple of hours than the entire time he'd been working there. His touch had a calming effect on her that she was really enjoying.

"He's at my mom's, remember? Besides, you're the one who should be getting some rest. Is your head okay? Why don't you keep the garage closed this morning or take the entire day off? I'll get Sadie to bring you a breakfast special before she opens." He'd already saved her once, whether he knew it or not. Even lying unconscious on the floor had stopped Zubict from acting on what his eyes suggested each time he showed up. It gave her the creeps.

She slowly withdrew the key from the front bolt, her hand still covered by one of the most mysterious men she'd ever known. *Wait!* Tobias Ryland had been mysterious once and look where that had landed her. She glanced at her hand, and Mitch dropped it.

"I appreciate the offer, I really do. But this is my responsibility and I'll see it through."

"You got it. I'm going to hit the shower and grab a protein drink. Don't bother Sadie's routine. I'd rather— She's sort of— Seriously, I—" He walked to the gas station entrance seeming a bit flustered at the thought of meeting her newest waitress.

I sure do hope they aren't a thing. She got another whiff of his wonderful scent.

How? Oh, yes, she had his shirt around her. Extralarge and yet there wasn't an ounce of fat on the man. At her average height she felt like a midget next to him.

He was well over six feet. She hadn't figured out if he dwarfed men by his height or just his presence.

Whatever it was, she wasn't alone. Sadie and the rest of the staff had taken notice. The high school boys she used for dishwashers never opened their mouths when he stood guard at the door. *Stood guard?* Yes, that's how he presented himself. He never really appeared... casual.

Mitch didn't seem to talk much and offered his opinion even less. Maybe that was why when he did offer, she listened. He made suggestions about the garage and waited for her to respond, to think about it. Unlike Glen Yost, the last mechanic who went to her father with every problem and potential scheme to get customers.

When her dad gave orders, Mitch responded that she was the one who had hired him and had stated—not bragged—that it was his skill that brought in business. And he was right. The garage was no longer a liability. She was grateful to him, but she couldn't take advantage of his kindness to drop Toby at his school. The old-fashioned cola clock above the café door was straight up on the hour. She'd be late, but no, she couldn't impose even when it would clearly help.

She wouldn't ask her parents to drop Toby at day care, either. She'd hear endless advice about how to manage her life better. Most likely they'd keep him at their house instead of taking him to day care. But the most important reason was that she honestly missed him and wanted that morning connection with her son. A brand-new day presented itself with enormous possibilities. Neither of them were normally bogged down with problems or frustrations. So she'd pick Toby up and desperately try to get her morning under control.

"Hi, Brandie. I heard you had some excitement around here this morning. Did they get away with anything?" Sadie stowed her purse next to the safe in the storeroom. She sashayed to the coffeemaker, now perking and gurgling the first of its many pots for customers.

"Mitch seems to have interrupted them before they could make off with something important." She hated lying, but this was only half a lie. He really did interrupt Zubict.

"Oh, that poor man. Does he need someone to take care of him today? So is Mitch a dream without his shirt on? I heard he got caught in just his boxers."

Sadie popped a hip to one side, flipping her dress and showing off her legs. She constantly said her calves were her best feature and that she could give anyone a pair if they attended her aerobic classes in Alpine. Brandie had tried to find it one day while she was shopping, but hadn't had any luck. It wouldn't have mattered, she couldn't afford to attend anyway.

"It's amazing that you've already heard anything. But please don't repeat that rumor. He was wearing jeans."

Brandie was lucky to have Sadie Dillon, even if it was for only three days a week. A flirty thirtysomething who was an adequate cook. She could make a lot more money anywhere else, but said she enjoyed the company here. Thank goodness they all got along. Competent help was one of the reasons her dad had turned the management of the café and garage over to her.

"Did you count to see if he had a six-pack? Were his abs as yummy as I think they are?"

"I did not look at his chest," she lied terribly, giggling like a teenage girl behind her hand.

"Oh, yes, you did. Brandie Ryland, you are such a

tease." She switched legs, popping her opposite hip, smacking a piece of gum and twirling a dark brown curl just below her ear. "I guess you didn't have time to take a picture."

"Of course not. Oh, gosh, it's getting late." She accepted a to-go cup of coffee from Sadie. "I've got to get Toby."

"Good thing he was with your parents last night."

"If he'd been at home, I would have gotten Dad to come up here and I wouldn't be late. I better run."

Almost to her parents' home, her mother phoned and volunteered to take Toby to day care. Brandie didn't ask for favors, but when her mother volunteered, she accepted. She hated not to see him. He always put her in a good mood. Getting back to the café earlier would help.

Not making the stop at her parents' would speed up her timetable tremendously. Dropping Toby would only take twenty minutes, but she always allowed a good half hour to pick her son up. She'd answer her mother's questions and listen to her advice on how she'd run the café until her father's heart attack had changed everything.

Brandie had too much to think about and didn't need to dwell on how her life had changed in the blink of an eye.

At the moment, all she had to do was shower and get back on the job. She didn't have to worry about anything or anyone. She sighed a deep release and was immediately surrounded by Mitch's manly scent. She'd gone an entire four or five minutes without thinking about him. He could have been hurt much worse and it would have been her fault.

She had a good life and no one, especially Rey King, was going to take it from her. She'd drawn a line in the sand this morning. It wouldn't take long to see who he'd send to cross over.

Had she really thought that she had nothing to worry about? Whatever was in the garage, those scum buckets needed Mitch to leave. The suggestion this morning was for Brandie to ask him to stay at her place.

That was absurd. She was his boss. They didn't have any attraction to each other…at least none she could act on. Stop. It would do no good to lie to herself. She was strongly attracted to Mitch Striker. Who wouldn't be?

She'd counted his abs all right. It had taken a great deal of willpower to caress his head for injuries instead of his chest.

MITCH COULD BE in the middle of nowhere five minutes after leaving most of the towns where he'd been stationed for undercover work. It made it easy to meet handlers and made it difficult to find the bastards breaching the border.

After refusing Brandie's offer of a day off, he'd contacted his counterpart on this operation. They could meet at noon instead of the dead of night.

Mitch had worked with a different Ranger in each of the cities where he'd landed a job. Most places he stayed two or three months, tops. Presidio County's problems were bigger.

Officially a part of a task force set up by the Homeland Security Customs and Border Protection Office, he was the member no one knew about. With the exception of Cord McCrea. This task force had been attempting to bring down a well-organized gun-and-drug-smuggling operation for several months.

The West Texas task force had already caught two

criminal leaders and stopped two major gun shipments to Mexico.

The Rangers believed someone had picked up the pieces of those organizations. So quickly that it seemed he'd planned their demise. Each successful takedown was important, but within weeks the smugglers had another operation up and running. And now the new principal player wanted something from Brandie.

He'd never seen this place in the daylight and didn't think Cord would use his truck—one that everyone in the county could spot. But he still watched the road instead of the trail behind him. Then he heard a horse galloping toward him.

"I've been looking in the wrong direction. For some reason, I didn't think you'd be riding up on a horse."

"I do live on a ranch," Cord said, dropping the reins next to the car. "Didn't you know this was Kate's property?"

"I figured. Did you bring it?"

"Your conk on the head has made the rounds about town. Kate even asked me about it." Cord took a holstered weapon from his saddlebag. "I only had a spare SIG. I have to report your Glock missing."

"I know. It's one of the reasons I didn't mention it to our friend the sheriff. Sure wish you could let Pete in on this soiree. He might threaten me less with a jail stay. It might even make our conversations a little more productive." Mitch leaned on the old car he used while undercover. He'd worked on the engine until it purred.

"I will when the time's right. I'd like to keep the fact you're on the task force under wraps as long as possible. You need anything besides the gun?"

"Some background on Brandie Ryland and her family."

"What's Brandie— Wait a minute, are you saying that Brandie hit you over the head with a pipe?"

"It was a lug wrench and no. She let a guy into the shop, and *he* hit me over the head. I heard a noise and was eating concrete before I saw his face." He rubbed his chin, which had begun to feel as bruised as his lump. "I did manage a good look at his shoes. Not boots. Real nice, not local stock if you know what I mean. Had a bit of a northern accent."

Mitch had met Cord in street clothes many times. This time, he looked more the part of a cowboy. A Stetson that had seen better days, but he wouldn't retire. He'd overheard stories at the café about that hat and how even a winter blizzard couldn't blow it off his head.

"This guy threatened Toby just before he left," he added. "I don't think it's the first time, either."

"That's not good. You think Brandie's the informant we're trying to find?" Cord asked while patting his horse's thick neck.

"I don't know. Maybe. There are a couple of other new people in town. The Dairy Queen took on a new face and Brandie's waitress would hear a lot of talk."

"Anything pointing you in their direction?"

"Not anything I can pinpoint." He didn't care for indecisiveness.

The more he looked away from Brandie, the more it seemed he shouldn't.

Every instinct in him told him to protect Brandie, that she hadn't been capable of fooling him for six months. Yet he had to be truthful. If Brandie was guilty, there was nothing he could do to save her.

"I'll add that I agree Brandie doesn't seem the type. Not from what I've picked up on. It sounded like the cartel might have found a way to force her to cooperate with threats or something in her past."

"I'll check with headquarters." Cord flipped the end of the reins he held and dismounted.

"Is there a *but* in that statement?"

"I don't see her betraying all the people around here. This is a close community. I've known Brandie's parents a while now. Kate's known the Quinn family her whole life."

"I'll remind you, sir, of what you wrote when you requested someone to come in undercover. You wanted a new set of eyes to look over the people out here—including your friends. That's why I'm here. A new look. I'll stay close to her and see if I can pick up on anything."

"You've been darn close to her for six months. Hell, you live there." The horse nickered and tossed its head at Cord's tension. "Take it easy, Ginger. Wait. Don't tell me you're going to saddle up next to her. As in date Brandie? She hasn't dated anyone since moving home."

"It's the only way. She was on the verge of telling me something before the sheriff showed up this morning. I think she'll confide in me if I can get her away from the café."

"Just be careful. I like Brandie. She's bounced back after a rough go of it when her husband died. If she's involved… Honestly, I just don't believe she is." Cord dropped his head enough that his hat covered his face.

"That's the rancher, not the Ranger talking." But it was good to know his instincts about Brandie weren't just because he was attracted to her. "I'll get to the truth. You're aware that I don't prejudge."

"Fine." He mounted, his feisty horse kicked up dust

as it turned in a circle then settled down. "You sure you're okay and don't need to have your head checked out?"

"Naw, two aspirin took care of the pain." Mitch had his hand on the door handle of his old sedan.

"If you're going to *date* Brandie, I'm officially reminding you not to sleep with her. You shouldn't get involved with a suspect."

"What kind of a man do you think I am?"

"One with eyes. That young woman is attractive in more ways than you can count, and her kid has a serious daddy crush on you. I mean that in a good way, Mitch. He needs an authority figure. I don't think you meant to, but you're providing it when you spend time with him." He pushed his hat lower on his forehead. "Just be careful. For both your sakes."

"Careful. Got it."

Mitch had never thought of the way Toby liked hanging out with him as a *daddy crush*. But come to think about it, he'd done exactly the same thing with his father on more than one occasion as he'd grown up. His dad had taught him everything he knew about repairing a car. It had been their thing every other weekend. The only thing that got them through the first years after his parents divorced.

He could act the role of a concerned boyfriend without blowing his cover. He did need to be careful, though. He could really get into playing both roles—temporary daddy and boyfriend.

Chapter Three

"What a day." Brandie wiped the last booth and dropped the wet vinegar-soaked cloth over her shoulder. *Exhausted* seemed like a word with too much energy. She had none. "I've never had the stamina to pull all-nighters, back in college or when Toby was an infant. I feel terrible."

The evening cook had finished his cleanup and headed for home. Brandie looked through the serving window where her mechanic put the last of the dishes away.

"I sure am glad you could help out this afternoon, Mitch. I had no idea we'd get busy after I sent the staff home. But I think we made bread money this month."

"Not a problem. Do buses normally just pull up outside with no warning?"

"I gave the driver our number. He's going to check with us next time. He said he thought his charter company had called. Thanks for suggesting some of the customers shop before eating."

She gathered the bills from the cash register and went to the back room to place the bag in the safe. She'd make the deposit on her day off or take a break when one of the part-timers worked.

"For a morning that started out questionable," Mitch said from the front of the café, "it turned out well for you." He stepped away from the jukebox and her favorite song started playing.

It brought a smile to her lips every time she heard it. Tonight was no exception. Especially since Mitch had chosen something she liked. So he'd noticed what music she played when she was here alone? *Duh. He could hear it in his room at the back of the garage.*

"You're absolutely right. A bad start but an awesome finish." She took the hand he extended and swung into his arms. When their fingers touched she thought about Rey wanting her to get Mitch away from the garage. Only a split-second thought because she was ready for a moment of not thinking at all. A moment to let her mind rest and just feel nice swaying to the music.

Feeling Mitch's arms around didn't hurt, either. He was an expert dancer and it was so easy to lean her ear against his chest and let him weave them between the tables. She could sweep and mop early in the morning.

Right now, it felt wonderful being held by someone taller than herself. She loved having her son's arms around her and missed him terribly on days like today when she worked from open to close. But there was something about a man guiding you around a dance floor, trusting him to protect you.

"I can't remember the last time I went dancing. Probably before Toby was born."

"No talking. Just enjoy the music."

Brandie relaxed and let him lead with confidence. The next song was country swing. With gentle nudges at her waist, his strong hands had her performing fancy dance moves she'd never dreamed of before. When the song was over they were both laughing, and she leaned in to hug him.

"That felt so good." She craned her neck backward to look up into his eyes.

"Then we need to do it again." He leaned toward her.

Brandie didn't dodge him. His lips were amazingly soft for a man, but still firm. Tall, lean, comforting, protective, strong…all were good words to describe him. The scruff from his five o'clock shadow teased her cheek, and she kissed him back, drinking in his taste and trying to remember the last exciting thrill she'd had.

Then it hit her. The last dance and intimate kiss had been saying goodbye. She jerked back, bumping into a table and scooting the chair a little across the floor. "I…um… I'm afraid I've given you the wrong impression, Mitch."

"It was just a kiss. I doubt your boyfriend will get upset."

Not a boyfriend. But Rey would be more upset that she hadn't let the kiss continue and progress to an overnight stay at her house.

"Oh, I'm not dating anyone. I can't. I don't have any intention of dating at all. I have a son to raise. There's just no time for a relationship."

"I wouldn't think a dance and kiss meant we had a relationship. But let's say it does. What's wrong with a man in your life who understands your commitments and doesn't want to take you away from them? I like Toby. He's a terrific kid. You've done a great job." He took a step, pushed his hand through his hair.

He had a very frustrated look on his face that didn't match the complimentary words he spoke aloud.

"Thanks, that means a lot. I better lock up now." She

fished the keys from her pocket and was ready to think more about their moment once she got home.

He snagged her hand and twirled her back in front of him. "You didn't answer my question. What's the big deal about having a little fun? I'd love it if Toby could come, too."

"It's going to just break his heart when you leave." Hers was going to ache a little, too. "I can't do that to him." *To us.*

"Here I am asking you on a date and you've got me leaving town, breaking a kid's heart. How did that happen? You firing me for asking the boss out?"

"No, of course not." The bell over the door rang, letting them both know someone had walked into the café. Mitch released her.

"Sorry, we're closed, man. I must have forgotten to turn the sign," Mitch said.

She froze in her tracks. She hadn't seen Rey King in three years and then only for a passing moment while she'd been in Alpine. Even bothering her like he had for the past six months, he'd never made the trip to Marfa. He'd always sent one of his men with a message of veiled threats about divulging the secrets her parents wanted desperately to keep.

"Hey, buddy," Mitch said from over her head. "Really, we're closed. Cook's gone home. Not even a slice of pie left."

Mitch took her arm and gently pulled her behind the counter.

"How about a latte?" Rey requested as he sat on one of the bar stools.

What was he doing here? *No. No. No!* He couldn't invade her business. Fright, powerful and swift, forced the happiness of a few moments ago into the recess of her everything. What could he want with her? Even if she said he should ask her himself, she never imagined that he would. Especially here. Now.

"If we served latte—which we don't—I just told you we're closed," Mitch said with force.

She watched as his hand moved under the counter to a bat they kept there for emergencies. She, on the other hand, could only watch. Words... Movement... Both had temporarily left her paralyzed.

"Mitch, I don't think Mr. King is here for coffee."

The man on her side of the counter jerked his head her direction, surprise on his face. The man responsible for her current problems tipped his head toward the door where two men stood, hands inside their jackets, staying their actions. She could only assume their fingers were ready to pull guns and shoot.

"How's your head?" Rey asked Mitch.

Mitch's eyes narrowed, his eyebrows drew into a straight line as his fingers wrapped around the grip of the bat. She crossed over to him and patted his hand, moving the bat into her possession and giving him an assuring smile. Or at least she hoped she did no matter how stiff it felt.

"It's okay. Can you make sure the rest of the doors are locked?"

"Yeah, Mitch, go away like a good boy. Brandie and I have some catching up to do."

After a threatening glare directed toward first Rey and then his men, Mitch left. It surprised her that he left so quickly. But she had asked him to secure the other doors. Rey might have brought more than just two thugs with weapons, and Mitch seemed like the sort of man who would think that direction.

"Why are you here?"

"What? An old friend can't come for a visit?" He nodded toward the door, and one of the men left. The other turned the lock and watched the lot out front.

"You aren't my friend. I don't know how many times I have to tell you that." She said the words as bravely as she could, but didn't feel very courageous. She couldn't predict anything about this man and had no way to stop him.

"Don't push my patience, girl." He grabbed the front of her apron across her breasts and tugged. "You sent an invitation and I accepted."

The apron loop behind her head kept her from getting free. Her face inched closer to him across the counter. The bat bounced to the floor at her feet. Now painfully on her tiptoes, Rey kept pulling until she could smell the wretched onions he'd had with his dinner.

"I don't know what you mean," she eked out, trying to be brave and not turn away.

"Weren't my instructions clear to get your *boy* out of here so my men could reclaim what's rightfully mine?"

He smashed his lips against hers. She jerked back as much as allowed, far enough to get the word *stop* out before he jerked her lips to his again. His hard, punishing mouth took everything wonderful about kissing and turned it into a horrible experience.

"Enough. Let her go."

Mitch shoved Rey's shoulder with a thick pipe, and Brandie slid back to her feet. Rey stood and held his hand in the air, signaling for the man behind him to stop.

"No need for violence, friends. Stand down. I will

come back another time when you aren't entertaining."
Rey winked at her and straightened his expensive suit.

"That's not about to happen while I'm here," Mitch
said. "I imagine you sent the guy who hit me on the
head this morning. Tell him I'd like to know where he
got his shoes."

Rey perked up. He tried to look casual about it, but
Mitch made him nervous. It was evident in the way he
buttoned his jacket and gave directions to his guards
in Spanish.

"Sweet Brandie...*au revoir* until next time."

"There won't be a next time, buddy. Or your face
will be on a wanted poster. Got it?"

Rey didn't acknowledge Mitch. Just turned his back
and left. Mitch followed to the door and secured it.

"What the hell did that guy want? Is he trying to
shake you down?"

"No. I need to warn my parents. Rey isn't the type
to walk out of here and do nothing." She picked up her
cell. Her hands were shaking so much she could barely
tap just one number. She should just go, but she couldn't
think. What did she need? "My keys. Is the door locked?
Yes, I saw you lock it behind him."

"Brandie." Mitch caught her between his arms and
pulled her to his chest. "Catch your breath, then we go.
I can't help you if you don't tell me what's going on."

"Mom's not answering. You don't think he'd really
kidnap or hurt them, do you?" She saw the answer in
his eyes. "You do." She shoved at his sturdy chest. "I'm
leaving. Right now."

"And I'm going with you. No discussion." He dangled her keys in front of her face. "Who is that guy, and

don't give me any bunk about not knowing him. You're scared of him."

"I'll tell you on the way."

"You're not waiting on me. Cars are out back."

He pointed to the rear garage entrance. Mitch stopped her before she turned the knob. He tossed her the keys and pulled a gun from the top file drawer.

"Has that been on the premises all this time?" She couldn't imagine Mitch owning a gun or that he'd been playing with Toby in this very room.

"Shh. Let's get to the car. Then we'll talk." He held the gun and searched through the windows like a professional.

Professional what?

Something had changed, and suddenly she could definitely picture him with a gun. There was Mitch the silent mechanic and Mitch the fun guy twirling her around the café. Then the almost shy Mitch who'd asked her on a date. Then there was this version. He pivoted around corners like the cops on television. At any point she thought he'd start giving her hand signals to stop and advance.

It wasn't funny. Nor was it supposed to be. She was confused by meeting all of this man's personalities on the same day. She watched his eyes looking everywhere. How he tensed at the sound of a car passing on the street.

"We go through the door. You lock it and I've got your back. Is your car locked?" She answered with a shake of her head. "Great. Just great. You're too dang trusting, Brandie. We'll take my car. They might not have known which one if they were going to rig something to blow or break down. You're driving. The keys are in my front right pocket."

Back to her, he blocked her from any potential threat, holding the gun down, but ready to shoot. He turned his hip for her to have access to his keys. She couldn't dig in the man's pockets.

Forget what she'd normally think or normally do. They might already have Toby. Brandie followed his instructions.

In other circumstances, fishing in his pockets would be an intimate gesture. He remained silent, cocking his head to the side when a car slowed and its occupants looked closely at the gas pumps.

"We move to the car, you keep the alley on one side and me between you and the street. Got it?"

"Sure." Her insides started jumping. Whoever this man really was, he was there to protect her. The frightening thing was that she needed protecting at all. She lived in a sleepy little town that probably wouldn't be there if not for the phenomenon of lights in the sky.

Hands shaking, she unlocked his old four-door sedan and got behind the wheel. As soon as he was in the car, she spun gravel as she left the garage lot, totally not expecting the powerful engine.

"Take it easy there. We don't need the locals pulling us over," he directed, placing the pistol in his lap. "Start talking, please."

"Are you an undercover cop?" That had to be the only explanation.

"No."

"Is Mitch Striker your real name?"

"Almost. We don't have much time, Brandie. I need to know everything."

"No. I appreciate the help. But if you aren't a cop you

may be working for Rey to see if I'm going to spill my guts the first time he walks through the door."

"First time for him? But there have been others. Like the guy with the fancy shoes this morning."

"Nope. I'm not talking." She shook her head and turned off the main road. "I think someone's following us." Brandie had seen the lights in the rearview mirror. On the highway through town she might not have paid attention, but this car hung back just far enough to make her wonder.

"Yeah, it's waiting to see which way you turn—right to your parents' or left to your house. We should get to your dad's place."

They turned the last corner, and the car following stopped half a block behind them.

"Pull over. Now."

She jerked the wheel right and slammed on the brakes. "Why did you want me to stop? What if— Just the possibility of something happening to Toby is making me sick."

"I know what I'm doing, Brandie, but I'll need your help."

Mitch slid the car into Park and switched off the ignition. Something in the calm directness of his voice made her listen when all she wanted to do was throw open the car door and run to the house to see if her family was okay.

She nodded and dropped her head to the wheel. "Why aren't they answering the phone? Are his men already inside?"

"I need you to do two things. First, you call 9-1-1. Ask them to dispatch Pete and tell him some of the men he's looking for are at your parents'. That's it. Hang up after." He reached into the backseat and raised a blanket, pulling a backpack from the floorboard.

"You *are* a cop. Where are you going? You're leaving me here? What if they already have Toby?" Each word dried her throat a little more, making it difficult to sound confident. Her insides knotted, her hands shook with fright and anger. Holding on to the steering wheel was the only thing keeping her inside the car. She removed her foot from the brake, finally realizing the car wouldn't go anywhere.

"I'm giving my word. If something's happened to Toby, I guarantee that I'll find the bastards and make them pay. If he's gone, I'll find him and bring him home." He covered her hand with his left and pulled a second gun from the glove box with his right.

Until she knew her son was safe, her heart would be controlling her actions. She searched his eyes. He meant every word and then some. She didn't care who he worked for as long as he'd defend Toby.

"What's the second thing?" she whispered, afraid with every second that she'd break down, melting into a puddle of hysteria.

"Whatever's happened, I need you to keep quiet about this Rey guy."

"That doesn't make sense. Rey King is the only person who's threatened me. If something bad has happened, he's the prime suspect. The sheriff will need to know."

What would she tell them? That a respected man from Alpine had been sending men for unknown reasons to her café, searching for something she wasn't aware existed? She could just hear the conversation with Pete where every answer she provided was a resounding *I don't know.*

"I need this guy to think his threats have worked. Trust me."

"Just admit that you're a cop."

He shook his head. "I'll explain everything later. Right now—" the engine varoomed to life as he turned the key "—we need to find out who's following and why."

"So what do I do?"

"Act natural and trust me."

It had been a long time since she'd done either. The last time she'd trusted someone hadn't worked out. At all. In spite of her instincts screaming at her to do otherwise, maybe her heart wanted to believe that this man was different.

"I'll trust you, Mitch." *Until you give a reason not to.* "But if Toby's injured or gone, I'll keep Rey's name out of it for my own purposes. I know how to use a gun, too."

Chapter Four

I know how to use a gun, too. Mitch knew that calm, kill 'em with kindness Brandie Ryland didn't make that threat lightly. She meant every unspoken word and would kill Rey King—whoever he was—if anything happened to Toby.

Nothing was going to happen to the kid. Mitch wouldn't let it. As he thought the words, he knew how futile they were. Many times fate stepped in no matter how many precautions you took to prevent it.

He watched her reverse his car in next to her dad's truck. Good idea, they could leave faster if things went sideways. The car that had followed them idled at the corner. If Brandie looked at it, no one could see her eyes from this distance. Surprise had to be on his side. He needed to make this quick.

Mitch had several sets of zip cuffs in his back pocket, two extra clips for the weapon in his palm and enough adrenaline for a battle. These guys didn't act like they'd seen him get out of the car. He'd left under the cover of darkness, having disconnected the dome light as soon as the vehicle had been issued to him.

Run! He did. Leaving his spot on the opposite side of the road from Brandie, he was able to catch these guys while they watched her walk into her dad's home. If someone was inside, he'd deal with them next.

Right now, he jerked the passenger door open, slugged the goon dressed in black in the jaw, knocking him into the driver. The driver honked the horn twice. *Damn it.* That probably was a signal for whoever was making a move on the house. He shoved the passenger onto the driver to keep him from putting the car into gear and taking off. Both men went for their weapons inside their jackets.

"Hold it. You don't want to pull on me. I'm not used to this SIG. No safety. I'm a Glock man, myself. I hate it when guns go off sooner than I anticipate. Now, push your hands through the wheel and lace your fingers under the steering column."

The driver followed his directions. The passenger pushed off his friend and tried to head butt Mitch, but Mitch was faster, shoving the man's ear into the dashboard.

"I didn't give you permission to move. Behave yourself." He stuck the barrel of the SIG next to the man's head, tossing him the zip cuffs. "First your friend, then you."

Neither man had said a word. Not a complaint or a curse. They were more concerned with watching the house. He grabbed a cell phone, which had landed on the floorboard, and their guns, adding them to his bag. Then he took the keys and yanked the nylon circles tight against their hairy wrists until they winced.

"I don't suppose you're going to tell me what's waiting in that house." Silence. "I didn't think so." He took the roll of duct tape from his bag, tore two sufficient pieces and silenced both men. "The sheriff will be here shortly to collect you."

Mitch covertly ran the block to the Quinns' house. He expected the lights and sirens of the sheriff or a deputy at any moment. He was counting on the distraction. As long as he got into the house and prevented any harm from coming to Brandie's family, he'd feel successful.

The house had plenty of large windows for him to get a good glimpse of the situation inside. He'd been correct. The car horn had been a signal to let Mr. Fancy Shoes know Brandie had arrived.

Bud and Olivia were tied to kitchen chairs, blindfolded. Safe. If they didn't witness him in the house, his cover could be saved. No talking. No contact with the Quinns. He needed to make certain Fancy Shoes couldn't identify him, either.

A complicated rescue. Where were the cops?

Brandie stood just inside the front door. Fancy Shoes held her at gunpoint, but from his position near the hallway he would be able to see movement at both the front and rear doors. If Mitch entered either way, Fancy Shoes could shoot all three adults.

Where was Toby? Just as he asked himself, he could hear Brandie asking the same thing. He had to get inside that house. He walked the perimeter, looking for an open window. Bingo! He lifted and removed the screen, then shoved the old four-pane window up without a lot of sound or trouble.

And the cops? Marfa wasn't big enough to take more than ten minutes to get from anywhere to anywhere. So where were they? Mitch slid his bag to the floor. He could hear a muted argument and pulled himself over the windowsill.

He cracked the bedroom door open enough to see a hallway and sitting right on the edge of the pool of light from the living room, just beyond the line of sight of a machine pistol, was Toby. His little thumb was stuck in his mouth, something Mitch had never seen the five-year-old do. His bedroom was at the end of the hall where a projection lamp still spun, shooting images of airplanes on the wall.

Mitch still wasn't in a position to charge into the room, guns ablazin'. He wouldn't be saving anyone. He needed the distraction he thought the arrival of the police would cause. Then it hit him. For whatever reason, Brandie hadn't called 9-1-1. He couldn't, his phone was in the car.

He was on his own.

As he inched through the door, Mitch put a finger to his lips. Hopefully, Toby would see it and remain quiet. When he went past the hall entrance, Brandie would see him. Her reaction could give him away, and Fancy Shoes could react badly.

"Come on, Zubict. I want to make sure Toby's okay. Can't you do that?"

Fancy Shoes had a name—Zubict. Had to be real; who would ever call themselves that?

"The kid's asleep. I ain't touched him. Don't mean I'll keep it that way. So you best behave yourself." Zubict leaned against the wall.

"What does Rey expect from me?"

"Anything he needs. Like getting rid of the new guy. We calls, you tell us what Rey needs to know. Then no more problems and we don't go through this again."

Mitch wanted the conversation to exonerate Brandie. He wanted her to be an innocent bystander in whatever plan was going on around her. The more he listened, the less it seemed like she was an unwilling participant.

"Are they at the garage now? Aren't you worried about Mitch?"

"The other fellas will take care of that jerk. Don't worry that pretty little red head about none of it." The gun relaxed in his hand a bit, drooping, pointing toward the floor. "Just relax. It ain't none of your business."

"Until the next time."

Toby stood, acting like he was going to his mother. Mitch put up his hands, indicating for the little boy to stop. He had to get across the wooden floor without making any sound. He inched himself into Brandie's view. Half his face could be seen before he made eye contact. The woman didn't miss a beat.

"If you tell me what you're looking for, I could tell you where it's at and maybe they won't tear my place up. Just like I told you this morning."

Mitch cleared the hall entrance and scooped Toby up. He had to cover the kid's mouth to keep him from talking.

"That's up to Rey and he didn't seem much interested in any deals," Zubict said.

Mitch couldn't see anything as he squeezed through the opening to Toby's room and continued to the closet on the far wall.

"I can't go in there, Mr. Mitch. Gramma Ollie will pank me."

"Your Gramma wants you to hide in the sewing closet. No spankings. I promise." He whispered, then opened the door without a creak, dumped the laundry basket of scrap material onto the floor and set Toby in the basket. "We're going to hide from the bad man.

Okay, Toby? Can you stay as quiet as a mouse?" The little boy nodded. "Great. I'm going to cover you up and it's going to look like your Gramma's sewing. Don't be afraid. I'll be right back. Promise."

He left the closet open a crack so it wouldn't be pitch-black. *Time to kick some bad-guy ass.* He was about to swing around the corner and eliminate the threat when Brandie's tone changed.

"You know, Zubict, I've never said I wouldn't help Rey," Brandie whispered. She and her captor had switched places. She was close enough to put her hands behind her and wave her fingers in his direction, as if she'd heard him close Toby's door. Then she flattened her palm in a signal to stop.

Mitch was inches from handing her a gun. Conversation ceased and the floor creaked. He knew which board from the couple of times he'd visited the Quinn house. Knew that his opponent was two feet from the hallway. And knew that something had alerted him that Mitch was there.

He grabbed Brandie's hand and pulled her into the hall, launching himself into the living room. He landed in Zubict's chest. The man's gun fired wildly.

Mitch caught the gun hand and squeezed until it dropped to the floor. Brandie stood in the hall, searching. He couldn't tell her to get to Toby. Talking would risk completely blowing his cover. Her parents would hear him.

"Brandie! What's happening?" yelled her mother.

"Untie me, Brandie," Bud said at the same instant.

Without his gun, Zubict darted for the door. Mitch had height and weight on the shorter man with fancy shoes. Those same pointy posh loafers slipped like a dog from a cartoon spinning in one place.

Mitch barreled into him from behind, tackling him to the floor. The little man let out a pathetic squeal. It might have been funny, but he'd held Brandie's family hostage and threatened Toby more than once.

He yanked the man's left hand behind his back. This really wasn't a fight at all. He raised himself to a knee and heard Zubict moan.

"What the hell's going on in there, Brandie?" Bud yelled from the kitchen.

Mitch looked up just in time to see a lamp crashing to the top of his head. Flaming red hair swirled, cool blue nails held on to the base. It took a lot to bring him to his knees. Brandie had managed it twice in one day.

Chapter Five

The police had arrived, and Brandie's guilty conscience was working double time. She was the reason Mitch had not one, but two lumps on his head. The spiraling red-white-and-blue lights entertained Toby and a host of neighbors from a couple of blocks. Marfa was a small town and everyone knew what went on. But she was in the dark.

Something had been happening at her garage and she needed to get a clue. And it all hinged on Mitch's timely arrival. Four days after their mechanic of six years just disappeared, Mitch had driven up looking for work. It was also about the time the phone calls from Rey had started. Maybe *Mitch* was the connection to Rey King that she didn't know about.

When she'd quit school, she'd spoken to her former college advisor about what she could do. He'd implied that she might be able to help with a business venture. So it didn't take much imagination to conclude the reason he was interested now had something to do with drugs if he was involved.

The paramedics continued working on Mitch. Taking his pulse, attempting to revive him with smelling salts. She had to get closer and fill him in as soon as he woke up so their stories matched.

Or rather her lies.

Mitch attempted to sit up on the rolling stretcher. The paramedic lost the battle as he swung his legs over the side, rubbing his lumps. "Again?"

"Looks like your head came into contact with a lamp. A wrench this morning and a lamp tonight." Pete stood at Mitch's side, notepad in hand, bad look on his face.

"I think it's heroic how he tried to save me from those horrible men." She moved from behind Pete, took the cold pack from the paramedic and gently held it on top of Mitch's head.

"He doesn't seem to be very good at it," Pete said. "Your dad's sawed-off shotgun was a better weapon than Mitch's head."

Mitch's eyes narrowed. His wonderful lips compressed shut, the vein in his forehead was prominent so she let the cold pack slip a little. She took the opportunity to move in closer as Mitch's hand grabbed her wrist.

"What happened?" he asked through gritted teeth.

"Don't you remember, Mr. Striker?" Pete raised an eyebrow along with a corner of his mouth. Did he have the same suspicions as her? That Mitch was somehow involved with Rey's men?

"Brandie needed a ride. I got tired of waiting in the car. I went to the door. Then nothing. Did someone try to break in like at the shop?" It was a question, but his horrible attempt at sounding innocent made her stand straight. Pete faced him again instead of walking away.

"Just like at the garage." Pete wrote another note then put his pad away. "You're lucky they used a lamp instead of just shooting you. Any idea what they were looking for?"

"I just work at Junior's, Sheriff. How would I know?" The cold pack slipped again.

"Thanks, Brandie, I got this. Toby? Your mom?" he asked. His eyes spoke volumes. He was going along with her lies for some reason on his own agenda and she'd hear about it later. The grip on her wrist let her know that.

"They're fine. Toby curled into a basket and slept through the whole thing. It took a while to find him under the quilt squares."

"Don't worry, Mitch, I showed that SOB who tied us up what's what." Her father had grabbed the shotgun as soon as she'd untied him.

The sheriff was still much too close for Brandie to tell Mitch why she'd hit him.

"Bud nicked one with his shotgun. We found traces of blood on the porch." The sheriff crossed his arms and didn't seem in a hurry to head anywhere else.

"Pellets, not a real shell. But I yelled at him that a real bullet was waiting if he set foot inside our door again," her father bragged. "Damn. Now I have to replace the screen."

"Can I ask why no one here thought to call me until a shot was fired?" Pete asked.

"Olivia dialed 9-1-1 as soon as we got to the phone."

"Why didn't you use *your* cell phone?" Mitch asked her, turning his face up and letting the ice pack fall to the portable gurney.

She kept glancing at Pete who waited for her answer, pencil in hand, ready to make note of her answer. Should she tell him that she knew who had ordered his gunman to come and threaten her family?

"I think it's in the car."

"Any clue as to who these guys are, Sheriff?" Mitch asked after an outward sigh and slight shake of his head.

"Bud took off after the guy and got a partial plate," the sheriff explained. "Fool thing to do. But it's a start on catching them and finding out why the Quinns' place is being targeted."

"Did the men say anything to you, Bud, or give a reason?" Mitch asked from just behind her. "Did you get a look at any of them?"

"I only saw the backsides of those three when they took off. Ha." He slapped his knee, then slapped his hand in a loud clap. "The last stupid dope isn't from around these parts if he didn't think I already had a gun aimed at his privates."

Her dad was laughing about a man threatening his life. He seemed to have forgotten all about being tied up when she'd arrived.

"I'm so glad you're okay." She hugged her father, and he hugged quickly then set her away from his chest. But that was okay. The return hug was more than she'd expected. "Do you think they'll be back?"

"There's no way to tell why he chose your parents' home. Maybe it had something to do with the break-in at the garage this morning. Maybe not." Pete shrugged. "We may never know."

But she knew. Mitch knew. Even though he'd taken care of two of the men waiting in the car, they'd be back because Rey said they'd be back. They'd force her to cooperate by threatening her family. She'd been lucky this round. Just lucky.

Her mechanic would be extremely angry if he'd seen that she'd slammed him with the lamp. Maybe he hadn't, but she should explain anyway. If he'd followed the men, he probably would have caught them. And then where would she be? Tangled in another lie.

Whatever Rey wanted her to do. Whatever he wanted from the garage that he hadn't told her about. He hadn't found it and was angry that Mitch had sent him on his way tonight. He would definitely be back.

"Do you think the highway patrol will find them?"

"There's no telling, Bud. They may stay away." Pete looked at Mitch with some hidden message one man shoots another. "I'd be afraid to face your good shooting."

Her dad began to laugh and leaned on the car near him. Mitch's car. He gave it a long glare, squinted his eyes at her and then Mitch. He must have finally realized they had arrived together. "Something wrong with your car, girl?"

"I—"

"Flat tire, sir. I'd already closed the station and offered to just bring her home." More lies and this time one her father wouldn't easily believe.

"See that's all you do."

"Got it." Mitch leaned closer, his breath a light warmth on her neck. "Right after we discuss who really hit me over the head," he whispered.

"Mind if we go, Sheriff? I want to get Toby to bed." She heard Mitch's harrumph behind her. He remembered the lamp and wasn't happy.

"Go ahead. If we need anything else, I know where you live. And Mr. Striker, don't think bad about our sleepy little town. Crime isn't the norm here."

"No plans to leave a good job, Sheriff."

Brandie hugged her father again, just because she

could get away with it. One of the deputies was dusting for fingerprints so she led the way to the back door. Out of earshot, she did an about-face and poked Mitch in the chest.

"I do not like lying to my parents."

"I didn't much care for you lying to me this morning. Or lying to the sheriff about who hit me on the head. That might come back to bite you in your tush."

"You are definitely a cop. Go ahead and admit it. Anyone could tell by the way you moved in the house during that fight. Both of Zubict's men complained about you. They wanted to kill you. At least you don't work for them."

"Let's get Toby and go to a secure location." He turned her by her shoulders and gently pushed hard enough to get her walking.

"Really? A secure location? What kind of talk is that for a noncop?" She stopped on the first porch step and faced him again. This time a little closer to his face. Too close not to notice his deep-set eyes that were the perfect shade of brown. "You don't think my house is safe?"

"Do you?"

She wanted to kiss him. To celebrate that they'd survived a hostage situation. She fisted her hands into the sides of her apron. Realizing she still had it on for a reason. A reason shaped like a gun.

"You've got a heck of a lot of nerve coming in here and trying to take over my life. I've taken care of myself for a long time and don't need your help." She verified they were alone and pulled his gun from under her apron where she'd stuffed it while her dad had scared Zubict away.

Mitch threw his hands in the air and took a step back. "You don't want my help, I can understand English. I'll wait in the car before you shoot me."

"Wait. Here. It's yours. I didn't think you wanted Zubict to take another one from you." She handed him his weapon, and he stuffed it under his shirt in his waistband. "Do you think they'll come back or might already be at my house waiting?"

"It's a strong possibility. King has threatened you and your son twice. I'm taking him seriously. I just need an hour for you to hear me out."

"Okay. I know I owe you an explanation for this morning, but nothing more." He rubbed the knot closer to his forehead. "Right, I need to explain why I hit you tonight, too. But my life is my own and whatever agency you work for—since you say you aren't a cop—you need to remember that my past stays *my* past."

"Don't you think we should call Cord and Kate before we just drop in?" Brandie asked from beside him.

"It's not too late and I don't think they'll mind. I'd rather not use the phone." He pushed the gas, speeding down the highway whether another car was in sight or not.

"I hit you with the lamp, but you already know that. You couldn't see the gun. They looked so mad, I thought it was the only way to get everyone out of there alive."

Mitch was still digesting her declaration of her past staying hers. What could she have done that was so terrible she didn't want it mentioned? Hell, he was still digesting the fact that she'd hit him over the head to save him from being shot.

"Telling me there was a gun to my head might have been easier."

"I didn't think you'd listen." She twisted in the seat to face him and placed her hand on his upper arm. "Look, Toby's asleep and I'd rather not walk in on the McCreas blind. Care to start talking? And start by telling me why I need to stay overnight out in the boonies."

"I need two answers first," he said, fingers tapping on the console between them.

"Okay."

"Why should I trust you? For all I know you're working for Rey."

It was hard to judge her reaction. She was so full of contradictions. Her words and actions did not support the woman he'd known as the café manager.

"Fair question. I'm not working for him. I don't know who he is."

"That's not an answer and I'll just keep my information to myself." She crossed her arms and looked at the window away from him.

He could see a wall going up between them. She'd slap down the mortar and he'd throw on another brick. It was up so fast and strong that unless he took drastic measures, it would be permanent.

"Okay, okay. What I'm about to tell you can't be shared—" Cord would kill him.

"If you aren't a cop, then you're a Ranger. Right? That's why you're taking me to the home of a Texas Ranger?" She was too smart for her own good.

"Hey, if you knew, then why the drama?"

"I didn't know for certain, but it's better that I guessed, isn't it? I mean, now you won't be lying when you tell Cord you didn't tell me."

Brandie was completely at ease. No signs of stress. It was like they were out for a Sunday picnic and heading back to town.

"So you were awake this morning," she continued. "No wonder you wanted to spend time with me. Either you think I'm working with Rey King or you feel responsible for our safety."

"It wasn't like that at all." It had never been, even when he told Cord it would be kept professional. A small part of him had been looking for an excuse to twirl her around the jukebox. A big part of him had been wanting to kiss her from day two.

"At all?"

He normally could have shrugged it off. He'd done it hundreds of times. He was pretty good with nonverbal communication. But this time, his face held on to the lie he'd told Cord.

"That's what I thought." She crossed her arms, holding tight to her sides.

He couldn't straighten her out. Not only was it his career, but if she knew he was deeply attracted to her she might forget. A little mistake could get her killed. "What was the second thing you needed to know?"

"It doesn't matter. You're just doing your duty."

"Man alive." He felt like cursing at how she could get to conclusions he was trying to hide. "If I were just doing my job, I wouldn't have blown my cover on the very afternoon I got a lecture about blowing my damn cover."

They rolled to a stop outside the McCreas' house.

"Maybe I should have left you with your parents. I think your dad has a handle on protecting his home."

The porch light flipped on, and Cord slowly came

through the screen door, dressed only in his jeans and sidearm.

"Then why did you bring me here and admit you're undercover?"

"Basically, I want you to disappear. Stay someplace safe, away from Marfa or Presidio County. King is out for blood and it's too damn dangerous for you to stay working in the café."

"Mitch?" Cord used a knuckle to tap on the window, waiting for it to be cranked down. "This better be good."

"It is, sir."

"Were you followed?"

"Not to my knowledge, and I turned Brandie's phone off."

"When did you do that?"

"Car seat fiasco. Who knew moving a car seat from one vehicle to the next took three adults?" Mitch couldn't look Cord in the eye. He was disobeying a direct order, several by coming here.

"I did. Enough times that I bought a second car seat. You better come inside. Need any help?" Cord turned back to his porch after Mitch shook his head.

"I'm not going anywhere." Brandie crossed her arms and flattened her lips into a straight, determined line. "I have a home and I have a business to run. You guys can't force me to leave."

"Are you willing to sacrifice your family for the café?"

"That's not a fair question. Of course, I don't want anything bad to happen to them. But the café's the only living I have. If I leave there's no telling what will happen to business. Surely there's another way?"

"There is and I'm certain my superiors are going to

ask it of you. I want you to refuse. It's not safe…for either of you." How could he get her to understand?

"We should get inside. Your real boss is waiting at the door."

Mitch reached out, securing her hand in his until she looked at him. "I'm deadly serious. It's too dangerous."

"I made a mistake several years ago and have worried ever since that secret would destroy my life. I hate that feeling as much as seeing everything I've worked for being taken away from me." She wiped a fast falling tear off her cheek with the back of her knuckle. "I'm staying here. You should go inside and talk things over with Cord. He looked pretty upset."

"Whatever you did—"

He left the rest of the words unsaid. She didn't know him. He had no way to convince her of anything. He had no proof that King had any connection with the Mexican drug cartel or the gunrunning into Mexico. He just felt it down deep. Maybe because he'd watched her for the past six months and this was the first lead they'd had.

No logical road to deduction, just a gut feeling. Not the most intelligent way to convince the Texas Rangers.

Chapter Six

Mitch dreaded the earful he was about to receive from Cord who could report back to his captain at any time. But there was no denying that he deserved it. He'd let down his guard and blown his cover with his prime suspect.

Now a suspect—at least according to the Rangers. He still didn't believe it.

"You know about our fight with the Mexican gangs. Do you think the men trying to hurt Brandie's family are their associates?"

Cord and his wife, Kate, had a history with the people King worked for. Even a closemouthed mechanic heard the stories how the couple fought off one of their vindictive leaders. Maybe they could do a better job of explaining the gravity of the danger to Brandie.

"How long have you known that I work with your husband?" Mitch asked Kate, avoiding her question.

"You just told me this minute." She laughed. "Cord said repeatedly that there was something off about the mechanic at Junior's. That's how he explains all your private conversations at the garage. I'll never trust him again." She smiled at her husband as he came in from the kitchen. "I can't believe he kept the secret."

"You'll have to excuse us, Kate." Cord had two beers, handing one to Mitch.

"I can help get Toby inside if you guys want to talk in Cord's study." Kate pointed to a door on the opposite side of the house.

"If you can get Brandie out of the car." Mitch didn't think he'd have any luck doing it. That was one of the reasons he'd come in alone. "She needs a little convincing."

Cord led the way to his study, shaking his head, scratching his chin. Once inside, he closed the door. The only window in the room didn't open to the front of the house so it didn't matter that the wooden blinds were tilted to where Mitch couldn't see out.

"She'll be okay. You can hear a car coming for half a mile at this time of night." Cord sat. "So you blew your cover."

"Yes, sir."

"I'm a Ranger, just like you. My name, you know it? Use it. Don't start *sirring* me when you're in trouble." He tipped the bottle to his lips, not looking like a superior about to give someone the ax.

"My captain at Border Security Operations is a little more strict."

"Bet you don't come to his house at midnight, either. It's okay, I appreciate that they loaned you to the task force. But I told you this morning the situation with Brandie wouldn't end well. You're too involved."

Mitch hadn't been invited to sit down. Manners or nerves let him take advantage and walk the perimeter of the room. Listening for signs that Kate had coaxed Brandie inside.

"You warned me about Toby. I'm keeping that in

mind. Circumstances have changed. She was threatened."

"I believe you mentioned that this afternoon."

"A man from Alpine, Rey King, paid us a visit after we closed. He threatened her family."

"She's working with King?" He sat forward.

"No. I don't think she's working with anyone. Do you know about this guy? Who is he?"

Cord tossed a folder his way. Just glancing through it, Mitch could tell the Rangers had been keeping tabs on King awhile. He had ties to more than just the south side of the border. "Chicago, New York, Philly…why isn't the DEA more involved in this operation?"

"They've been kept up-to-date and are waiting on evidence. No one's talking and we can't prove a thing. If you think Brandie may know something—"

"I don't."

"But you seem certain she needs protection. That doesn't justify that you've blown your cover."

"I didn't have much of a choice. Okay, I did. You're right. But when Brandie accused me of working for King I saw her shutting me out, and we need her. I know she has valuable information. I just don't know what it is. Maybe you can talk some sense into her about going back to the café— It's too dangerous for her and Toby to—"

"Ever have this happen before, Mitch?"

The front door closed, but he didn't hear the kid or noises in the other room. Was Brandie really going to just sit in the car until he pulled her out kicking and screaming? He would. She needed to be protected from her pride.

"Have what happen?"

"Do you make it a habit of getting seriously involved with your suspect when you're undercover?"

Cord's accusation faded with the sound of an old engine purring to life.

"What the hell?" Mitch banged the beer bottle down on the desk and shoved his hand into his empty pocket.

"Nothing personal, you know I have to ask."

"No way." He pulled open the office door and heard tires spitting up gravel and turned back to face Cord. "She's stealing my car."

TOBY WAS TUCKED in his bed and still sound asleep. It took Mitch longer to get to her house than she'd thought. She would have cleaned up or even gotten her shower out of the way if she'd known it would take that long. When the car pulled away, she realized Cord had dropped him off and Mitch would need his keys.

Surprisingly, he didn't bang on the front door and he didn't try to burst inside. He stood on her porch stoop for a couple of minutes, pinching the bridge of his nose as if he had a headache. She opened the door before he moved again.

"What do you want, Mitch? Besides your car." She tossed him his keys and crossed her arms, waiting for his rant.

His lips flattened as he shoved the rabbit's foot and two keys into his pocket. He had a very simple life living in the garage's back room. "Two keys. One to my garage and one to your car. I don't suppose you have some in storage somewhere? Some other home that you'll go to when this is over?"

She was angrier than she'd thought she'd been when she took his car and sped back from Valentine all alone.

Always alone. She should know and be used to that frame of mind by now.

"I'm not leaving town and my job. I'm not staying out at the McCreas' place," she said for emphasis.

"I realize that," he said softly, acting sort of withdrawn or reverting to his short-sentenced mechanic routine.

"I also won't tell anyone who you really are—as if I actually know."

"I really am Mitch Striker."

"Oh." She took a step back inside the house, her anger deflated by the sorrowful look in the brown eyes staring at her. "Well, it's been a long day, I should get some sleep."

"Agreed." He sat on the porch, leaning back against the vinyl siding.

"I said I'm hitting the hay. See you tomorrow." Brandie had to go farther on the porch to look at his face.

"Understood." His head was leaning next to the front window, his eyes closed.

She plopped down next to him. "What are you doing?"

"Making a statement."

"To me? It's not necessary." And yet, her heart did a little flip-flop in her chest, excited that he'd sit on her porch to do so. "No one's sitting across the street ready to break in and tie me to a chair. Zubict did that to make his own statement. So there aren't any threats."

"Damn straight. Not while I'm here. You should go inside." He hadn't looked at her, completely at ease leaning back and staking his territory.

She stood, feeling like she was talking to her son. "Okay then."

She shouldn't ask him inside. It would be all over town. Her dad would find out. But couldn't she explain that he'd been worried about her? It was the truth, after all.

She saw the curtains next door be pulled back and dropped quickly back into place. Her neighbors were already paying too much attention to her. "Good grief, Mitch. You can't sleep out here on my porch."

"I agree. I'll get a nap back at the garage tomorrow." He shifted uncomfortably on the cement porch.

"You can't stay here all night. People will talk. Marfa's a real small town. They don't overlook things like this."

He opened his eyes, zeroing in on hers, catching her to him without a touch. "I'm not leaving you alone."

"Come inside." She cleared her throat that had become all warm, making her voice like syrup. A little stronger she said, "You can stay on the couch, but don't get any ideas."

"None that weren't already there."

She gasped. That was the word that specifically described what her mouth did with the air she almost choked on.

"New or old," she coughed out. "Nothing's going to happen."

"Tonight." He nodded once. "I agree."

"Ever. Not ever." She marched to the hall closet, completely off-kilter and much too warm after Mitch's brazen statements. She had to squash the idea. She couldn't get involved with anyone, especially a cool Texas Ranger who had been lying to her for six months. He wasn't who she thought he was. She grabbed sheets and a blanket for the couch.

"I don't have any extra pillows so the couch cushion will have—" He wasn't in the living room. She poked her head into her small kitchen that was still empty.

"Mitch?" Turning around he was directly behind her. "Oh. Wow. You scared me."

"Just checking the windows to make sure everything's locked and secure." He took the linens. "You ready to explain to me what's going on with King?"

Could she trust him? She was in this mess because she'd trusted the wrong person. And if she explained one part of her problem, she'd have to explain the other. And if that came out, she'd be out on her ear. Everything she had been working for would be gone.

Toby would be homeless.

"I take that look to mean no. Might as well get some shut-eye, then. It's been a long day and I have a lot of catching up to do at the garage tomorrow."

"That's it? No interrogation or coaxing my secrets from me?"

He tossed the sheets on the chair nearest him and did an about-face. "I could live with some coaxing." He waggled his eyebrows. "You want me to…coax your secrets?"

She laughed at his silliness and felt her body blushing at his suggestiveness. "I was thinking more along the lines of thumbscrews."

"Naw, we gave that up in the last century."

She was so confused. He wasn't upset and yelling at her that she'd taken his car? Or arguing about staying in Marfa. He had plans to work tomorrow and was content to sleep on her couch. She did feel safer and she'd probably sleep sounder knowing anyone was in the next room.

Who was she fooling? She felt better because it would be Mitch on her couch.

"Okay, so, my bedroom's on the right."

"I know." He smiled by tilting up the sexy corner of his mouth and winking.

"Sure, you'd know that because…ah…"

Whoa. The image that popped into her mind wasn't of him sleeping on the couch alone. And it was no longer of her sleeping in her bed all alone, either. *Oh, my.*

"Because Toby's door has his favorite superheroes taped on it."

His T-shirt came off over his head, and this time she counted the defined and rigid abs. He sat and pulled his boots off. "'Night, Brandie."

She didn't—couldn't—look at him any longer. She was slowly closing her door and heard Mitch on the phone with someone. She used the lock for the very first time, keeping her mysterious mechanic out and her nosy curiosity in. She wasn't about to eavesdrop on his conversation. She had enough secrets to keep.

The T-shirt she'd borrowed from him during the morning embarrassment was still on her pillow. She changed into it just because she could and got under the covers. She inhaled deeply, loving Mitch's male scent as she drifted into dreamland.

Chapter Seven

Little fingers pried at his eyelids. Mitch had peeked at Toby a couple of minutes earlier, as the little boy had poked at Mitch's puffed-up cheek to get him to make a popping sound with his lips.

It was still early, still dark. He hadn't slept much. The couch was too short and his mind too uneasy. First with the threats from King and his men. Then the accusations Cord had made about his personal life.

It was a revelation to Mitch that he had a personal life at all. Popping the air from his cheeks was a game he and Toby played often. The kid had been excited to find him on the couch, but not freaked out. Mitch expected Brandie to come in at any minute and tell him he needed to leave.

Funny thing was, he didn't want to leave. He was fine keeping Toby occupied and letting his mom get some extra sleep. He let the little fingers poke his air-puffed cheeks one more time, made the noise the kid loved and popped his eyes open at the same time.

Toby jumped and giggled. A sweet sound Mitch never got tired of.

So he was involved. So what? It reminded him what he was undercover for. He was protecting women and children like this family from the threats of men like Rey King. There wasn't anything wrong with that.

To which Cord had replied there was if it interfered. So was it?

Mitch tickled Toby, who squirmed on the beige-carpeted floor. "You ready to eat, kid?"

"Scrambled eggs?"

"Sure, I can do that."

"I'll get mom."

He took off, but Mitch's arm got him around the middle. His little feet kept running like a cartoon and his giggle filled the room. Another trick they did when Toby visited the café and he was running when he should be walking.

Cord had warned him to hang in the background, to let the situation with King happen without interference or rushing in to save the day.

Maybe he was ready to let those close to him know he could save the day. It just seemed like he smiled a lot more in Marfa—at least when people couldn't see him.

He had the eggs scrambled in the bowl and the pan hot when Brandie wandered into the kitchen.

"Morning."

"Nice shirt." He noticed his T-shirt and the blush that crept up the fair redhead's neck and cheeks. She crossed her arms and did a one-eighty from the room.

Mitch had also noticed her pert nipples and her long curls messed up like she'd had a restless sleep, too. He cooked Toby's eggs, gave him chocolate milk and buttered toast, then sat at the table with him.

"Mitch?"

"Yup, that's me."

"Are you gonna live here now? 'Cause if you did, we

could get bunk beds and share my room." Toby was all eyes and seriousness, milk-stained lip and all.

Mitch didn't have the heart to tell him it wasn't a possibility. Then again, what was stopping him? He remembered the way his T-shirt had looked on Brandie earlier. Sharing a room with someone wasn't such an unpleasant idea.

"Eat up, kid. We'll talk about those bunks later."

He was scooping the last bite of eggs in his mouth when Brandie emerged. Her plate had grown cold before she returned completely dressed and ready for another day at the café.

She put the eggs between two pieces of bread and wrapped it in a napkin. "I laid out your clothes, buddy. Go brush your teeth and get dressed."

"Does Mitch have to brush his teeth?"

"Sure I do, kid. But mine's at the garage."

"You need one here then, 'cause you gotta brush before you leave the house." Toby pushed in his chair and scampered from the room.

"You shouldn't encourage him," she said while washing up his mess.

"I was going to do that."

"It's okay. You cooked, I'll clean." She stretched on her tiptoes to peek out the high window over the sink. "Better get your boots on. Mrs. Escalon's on her way over to stay with Toby. I have no idea how I'm going to explain this. Maybe you can leave without her seeing your car."

"How about the truth. I stayed here because of the attack on your family. And your car's at the café. Remember?"

"I'm afraid you staying here will be gossipier news

than my dad filling an intruder's behind with buckshot."
She dried the pan, looking away again.

He didn't know what to say. He'd put her in a compromising situation. His first thought was that he didn't care. It had been the right thing to do. Then again…he cared. Enough to blow his cover and tell her the truth about himself. Something he'd never thought of doing before.

"I KNEW I HAD some catching up to do in the garage." Mitch pushed hard to get the door open. "But this?"

Supplies were everywhere. Shelves had been overturned. Invoices, estimates and receipts out of their file folders and on every surface.

"Why didn't the alarm go off? I thought you said the sheriff would have extra patrols?" Brandie said right behind him.

He'd had a great morning, sharing a homemade breakfast with the kid who had been superexcited to see him. Until a reminder that the real world would see his staying overnight as wrong. Then a phone call from Brandie's dad had shifted all the good to bad. Mitch heard him yelling through the cell about a certain car parked all night in her driveway.

He hadn't set the alarm. "I think we were in too big of a hurry last night and left without turning the blasted thing on."

"You're right. All I did was lock the door." She scooted paperwork out of her path with her toe. She looked up to see the vandalism to his immaculate garage. "Would you like me to call Ricky in to help you clean this mess up?"

"I'll take care of it after the sheriff finishes."

"We're not calling Pete."

He spun around, letting her walk into his chest. He secured her balance and quickly dropped his hands because in spite of all the distraction, he was still thinking about her in his T-shirt. "Why not? What are you afraid of them finding?"

"We already know who did this. There's no reason to bring the sheriff's department into it. It's not like I'm going to tell them anything." She pointed a finger at him. "You can't, either."

"No, we don't. I know you've been threatened by King. Your family's been threatened. And now you've been robbed. I also know you're too frightened to go to the police."

"I'm not afraid, Mitch. I'm angry." She dug her phone out of the piece of luggage she called a purse, scrolled and dialed. "There's a huge difference."

She passed through the garage to the café, growling as she tripped on a ratchet extension and slid in some spilled brake fluid. Mitch followed, picking up Jacob's radiator replacement hose that he'd been waiting a week to arrive. He didn't have time to think about garage customers and yet he was.

"Hand him the phone, Zubict. I want to talk with Rey." She waited at the café entrance, not moving into the room.

He could see over her head and it wasn't a pretty sight. Everything was trashed. He heard a sniff, saw her fingers swipe away a tear. Then he saw the irreplaceable jukebox…smashed, the records thrown around the room, destroyed.

He thought he'd been mad seeing the garage. This was senseless and clearly a threat. The cost of repairs and replacing everyday items they needed for the café would be astronomical.

"I'd like to listen." He stood behind her while she pressed Speaker without asking why or telling him to mind his own business. He wanted her to bury her face in his chest so he could comfort her completely. Instead, he stiffly put his hand on her sweater-covered shoulder.

Mitch had given his word to Cord that nothing was going on between him and Brandie. The teasing last night had been fun, but that's all it was. The needless destruction hit him deep in a place he didn't know he had. He wanted to find Rey King and rip his head to shreds.

"*Hola*, baby."

"I hope you found whatever you were looking for," she demanded. "But you went too far tearing my place apart."

"You know we didn't find it, Brandie. Moving the package somewhere else won't help you. We'll get everything back. But this is your last warning, sweetheart. Give us what we want or someone's going to pay the price. Might even be that new boyfriend of yours. Thanks for getting him out of there so we could have a looksee."

"I didn't—"

"You're forgetting our agreement. You return my property or your parents will be in for a shock."

King disconnected. Mitch nudged Brandie forward into the room, flipped over a chair that was still intact and made her sit. He took another of the old-fashioned café chairs and straddled it so they were facing each other.

"You ready to tell me what's going on now?" he asked.

Tears filled her when she looked up at him. "The staff will be here in a few minutes."

"We tell them to come back after the sheriff has processed the scene."

"But—" She swiped at another tear. "Fine. It'll look weird if I don't let them."

"More than weird, Brandie. At the moment you're connected with a known criminal organization."

She shook her head. "Rey King is an Alpine college professor in the Spanish Department. He's got his mind set that my former mechanic hid something of his here."

"Like what? Money? Drugs?"

"At first I thought he was kidding around. But then I assumed Glen had been selling weed. I didn't realize that he even knew Rey."

"And you haven't moved anything from the garage? Did King get in touch with you after Glen disappeared?"

"You mean after he left. You found a note in the desk, remember? Was that a lie, too?"

"Look, Brandie, you have to remember that I've been undercover. I wasn't allowed to tell anyone why."

"Just how long have you been lying to everyone you know, playing Mitch the Mechanic?"

He recognized that she needed a place to vent her anger at the situation as much as she was hurt by finding out he'd been lying to her. They needed to stay focused on one problem at a time. Right now, it was her problem with King.

"We don't have time for my life story. I need you to tell me how you know Rey King and why he has control over you."

"I can't trust you with that."

"Brandie, you either trust me or you spill it to the

Texas Rangers' captain who will be showing up when you're arrested for obstructing justice. It's that simple. I've already been told I don't have much time."

She jumped up. "You're leaving?"

He'd just threatened to arrest her and she asked if he was leaving. At any other time, he might think that was a good sign. Hell, it was a good sign.

"I've already been here too long." He tugged her to the office chair. "But the main thing is that the Rangers think they have enough for a real investigation. We need solid connections to bring in the DEA or more Rangers."

"About me? I haven't done anything. Why would they want to look into my life?"

That was the second time she'd flinched about her past. This was about Rey King. He needed anything she'd spill. "You've got to give me something to hold them off."

"I...can't."

The pain in her eyes was genuine. It wrenched his heart and his gut, but he pulled his phone out and got in touch with Cord. "Yeah, another break-in. They smashed the place up pretty good."

"Do you know what they're looking for?"

"She won't tell me." Mitch looked at a fiery redhead determined to keep her secrets.

"Something's not adding up. You said she was angry at King. I just have a hard time thinking that she'd be in business with him. What about the former mechanic? Think he was the problem?"

"Didn't everyone have a hard time believing the last informant you found who worked with Bishop? What about the one who worked with Rook?"

"I'm not an informant," Brandie said with a huff. "Rey wrecked the place because I'm *not* telling him anything."

"I get it," Cord stated in his ear. "Brandie's listening to your side of the conversation and you're trying to scare her into telling you? I can tell you that the only people I've seen scare her are the Quinns themselves."

"So you think I should talk with her parents?"

"Don't go there, Mitch," Brandie said softly.

"Good advice. You might need to run interference with the locals." He disconnected and called the sheriff's department, reporting the break-in.

"From what I can tell, you have less than ten minutes to convince me." He hated threatening her. Hated it.

Once Cord heard that Rey King was involved, he explained that he was a new major player in gun running across the border. All law enforcement agencies were under pressure to take this guy off the streets.

"Are you a man of your word, Mitch? Are you trustworthy?"

He took her soft, shaking hand in his. He was the person responsible for the uncontrollable tremor. King had destroyed her place and she'd grown angry. It was his threat of talking to her parents that made her tremble. His threat.

"You don't have any reason to trust me, Brandie. But I swear to you, I want to help. I want to get you out of this mess. But I can't unless I know what's going on. You have to tell me."

"This—" she pointed to her wedding ring "—is my mother's. I've never really been married."

"I don't understand. Isn't there a picture of you with your deceased husband at your parents' house? What about Toby?"

"The picture is really Toby's dad, but we were never married. My parents were embarrassed that I went away to school and came home pregnant. I had nowhere else to go." Her hands twisted in the edge of her shirt. Tears fell down her cheeks.

He couldn't imagine being alone and going through something like that. "What, were you eighteen?"

She nodded. At eighteen, he'd been a senior in high school, stealing beer and partying 'til dawn. One thing his dad had been blunt with him about was using protection to prevent early fatherhood.

"What about Toby's dad? I haven't seen anyone around in six months, so I assume he's not in the picture? Does he know?"

"My dad said I couldn't live here, that it would shame them with the community. So my mother came up with the story that I married a man in the Army, he shipped out and was killed in action. So, you see, I'm a liar, too."

She hadn't answered his question about the father.

"He should know people don't think that way about unwed mothers anymore."

"Don't you see? It didn't matter what people would really think. It only mattered what my dad thought they were thinking. In his eyes, his friends pity me now."

Mitch had heard Bud talking about Toby's war hero father more than once. He told the story like it really happened. "King thinks you have his property and is going to expose your secret if you don't give it back. How does King know?"

"He was my advisor in college."

Their attention was drawn to the garage door before he could ask more details. Great, not a deputy. It was the sheriff himself. Again. The man was always on duty.

"Anybody here?"

"We're in the café." Mitch dreaded another confrontation. In fact, being the town drifter and the first place the police looked for answers after trouble happened was getting sort of old.

"So Pete doesn't know you're undercover?" she whispered.

"It's better that way."

"Funny meeting you here again, Striker." The sheriff leaned against the door frame. "I'd say good morning, but I don't think that would be accurate."

"You work a lot of hours, Sheriff. Late last night, early this morning. You must be exhausted." Mitch looked at his watch, wondering how soon he could call Cord. "Looks like they came in the back garage window."

There was no way he'd share all of the story. His captain would kill him if he didn't give over all the details. It wouldn't change how they went after King, but if it got out, it would really destroy Brandie.

"My dispatchers have been instructed to call me whenever there's a problem concerning you." Pete started to push his fingers through his hair but stopped before they got caught in his hair gel. "I saw the broken glass. The extra patrols I had by here last night didn't see a thing. Any working theories?"

"Sure," Brandie answered before Mitch could take a deep breath. "They didn't find what they wanted yesterday morning, so they tied my parents up as a distraction last night and came back while all your deputies were on our lawn?"

"Makes sense. It would be a reason why they harassed your parents." He walked around along the wall to the jukebox. "Now that's a downright shame. That smash looks like someone was angry. Any idea what they were looking for?"

"Not a clue," Mitch answered quickly. The look of relief he received from Brandie was worth all the ear chewing he'd receive from his captain.

Chapter Eight

"Mind if I take a look around, Brandie?" Pete asked, seeming to look at whatever he wanted anyway. "I'll need a list of anything that's missing. Hardy will be here to take pictures and document the damage for insurance. His shift starts at seven."

"Thanks, and go right ahead. It all looks the same, though."

"Have you told Bud yet?" he asked as he sifted through chairs toward the garage.

No two ways about it, her parents were going to freak. How would she break the news?

Mitch steadied her shoulders again and said, "You were the first call today. Surprised they aren't here already considering your 9-1-1 gossip line."

"Mitch, can you help me look at the storage room?" She had to get them away from each other. She gave a tug on his arm. Once in the back room she went to the wall and they cleared the shelf in front of the safe. "I bet you'd be best buds if he knew you were a Ranger."

"I doubt that. I haven't been a fan of small-town cops for the past two years. They've had every right to distrust a drifter like me."

"Is that how long you've been undercover?"

"You know I shouldn't answer that, Brandie." He politely turned his back as he did every time he watched her put the money in the safe.

"Thank goodness. Two days' proceeds still here."

"That doesn't make sense. I mean, I'm glad it is, but why wouldn't they think you were keeping the stash in the most secure place you have?" he whispered. "Unless…"

"Unless what? I told you I have no idea what Rey is even looking for."

"Whatever it is, it won't fit in your safe."

"Mitch?" Pete called from just outside the door.

"That's great. Just great. I recognize that tone. I should have checked my gear before calling him. Damn it." Mitch squeezed his forehead. "Whatever happens, don't call Cord. Promise me."

"What? Why?" Brandie was completely confused as she watched Mitch put his hands up and back out of the storage room.

"You know the routine. Lock your fingers behind your neck and drop to your knees. Mitch Striker, you're under arrest for the illegal possession of a firearm and illegal substances with the intent to sale."

"Great." Pete hooked handcuffs on Mitch's right wrist.

"Tell him," she mouthed when Pete's face was turned. "Tell him who you are."

Mitch kept his lips pressed together tightly, wincing as his second arm was jerked behind his back.

"Hey, take it easy. This is all a mistake." She tried to make Pete see reason.

"The mistake is that I gave this guy a chance to begin with. There's something off about him, Brandie."

"You've got this all wrong. He's—"

"Don't argue with the sheriff." Mitch glared at her, shaking his head.

Pete lifted Mitch's arms backward. "Up. Come on."

"Are you really arresting him? Everybody owns a gun in this town." Should she go against what Mitch said and stop him from being arrested?

"Brandie, go home and get Toby. Keep him with you until I'm back. Go to your dad's."

"Why do you think she needs protection?" Pete asked, being none too gentle with his prisoner.

"I'm not going anywhere. I have to clean up this mess."

Mitch jerked Pete to a stop, causing her mechanic to hiss a little in pain.

"You need to get to Toby. Don't you see why they've done this?"

"Stop talking. Sorry, Brandie, but this is a crime scene and you'll need to hold off cleaning while we process everything."

"How long will that take?"

"At least today. Just depends."

"Oh, good gravy. I don't know why you're doing this. Mitch doesn't use drugs." She followed them through the garage office entrance. "They came in here and planted that stuff."

Pete shook his head. "Regardless, I have to arrest him. Let's go."

"Wait," Mitch said. "Take the sedan home, I haven't checked your car. Will you let her take my car? I'll save you the trouble of a warrant. Check it out. It's not locked."

"I can't let her do that."

"Come on, Sheriff. She needs that car."

A deputy pulled up in a second Tahoe. Pete put Mitch in his truck where the window was already cracked.

"Mitch, you're scaring me." She kept her voice low while Pete spoke to Deputy Hardy.

"They set me up, Brandie. They want me out of the way for some reason. Be overly cautious and spend the day at your mom and dad's with the shotgun."

"Will Cord get you out?"

"Someone from headquarters will let him know. I don't know who will post bail. They've invested a lot in this cover. That's how it normally works. Not my decision. Stay safe."

Pete climbed into his truck. "Hardy's going to watch the place. You good driving home? If you're worried about your car, I can drop you or have another deputy stop by to drive you wherever you need."

"I'll be okay." She looked at Mitch through the back window. The look she'd seen on his handsome face was back. Concerned, worried, analyzing…brows drawn into a straight line, he'd looked like that for most of the six months he'd been here. Yesterday had been different. She liked the man from yesterday and had really enjoyed breakfast this morning.

As soon as Pete was out of sight, her father drove up. He got out of his car, took one look at her tires—none of them flat—harrumphed loudly and started toward the café.

"Sorry, Mr. Quinn, um, this is a crime scene and we have to wait for the sheriff to get back."

"Nonsense, I own this place and you can't keep me out."

The deputy stepped in front of the door. "Sorry, sir, but I have to."

"It's a real mess inside, Dad, and there's nothing we can do today. Will you take me home? Toby's waiting."

He nodded grumpily. "Something wrong with your car?"

"Mitch thinks it's better if I don't drive it 'til he has a look."

"That drifter's taking on a lot of responsibility around here." Her father didn't hint at animosity. It dripped from every word.

"Drifter? I thought you liked Mitch." She was a little confused at her father's hostility until she remembered that Mitch's car had been at her house all night. Her father had probably already had an earful of questions from her neighbors. Some about yesterday's break-in at the shop, lots about how he'd rescued everyone last night with his shotgun.

Fending off questions of why Mitch had been at her house had taken him off guard. In the five years she'd been back after dropping out of college, no one had ever stayed at the house she rented from her father.

"I like him fine as the hired help. He's a drifter. I expect him to move on any day. Maybe we should advertise for another mechanic."

"Why would we do that if he's good at his job? None of this is his fault. He stayed to make sure we were all right last night."

"I could have done that if you thought it was necessary. And if he's the hero in all this, then why did they arrest him?"

"It's all a mistake." She couldn't tell him Mitch had been framed by Rey King. That would lead to a host of other questions she wasn't prepared to discuss at the moment.

"I don't know why you hired him without a criminal background check."

She had taken care of verifying everything about Mitch Striker. Her dad was going to argue with her no matter what she answered. It was more important to consider what Mitch said. Why wouldn't he want her to call Cord? Because if he showed up then Pete would wonder what was so special about Mitch.

Stay with Toby, he'd said.

"Oh, my gosh, he thinks Toby is in danger." Chills rippled down her back and across her body. "Something's wrong, Daddy. I've got to get home."

Chapter Nine

"I hate small hick towns. The door was unlocked like I said. Good." Rey King directed his men through the hands-free mic on his cell. "The cops took the mechanic so she's on her way home. Stay on the phone and stay ready."

He and his men had been in Marfa all night—ransacking and watching. If the mechanic hadn't slept over at Brandie's, Rey would be at his home with Patrice having breakfast and...other things. He was stiff from sitting in the car. Each time he'd caught some sleep at that run-down café, one of his men would wake him with the news they hadn't found anything. He'd thrown a chair into the jukebox during his last frustrated rage.

A car pulled up and parked in the driveway of Brandie's house. She ran to the front door. Before her father was out of the car, she stood on the porch with her son in her arms. They waved, and the old man returned behind the wheel of his faded Buick and drove away. An old lady joined Brandie, blew kisses at the boy and took the steps carefully back to the house two doors down.

"Five minutes for Brandie to get relaxed and we go inside. She must know where the package is. The only person that hurts her is me. I am not losing everything because of this bitch or because one of you gets trigger-happy."

Rey adjusted his suit along with the new gun holster as he got out of the car. He loved the feel of the holster and secretly practiced drawing his new Glock 21 .45 ACP. He liked the sound of the name and firepower of the bigger caliber.

It was a shame he couldn't use it today, but it had been easier to get the mechanic thrown in jail instead of confronting him. Drug charges were taken seriously in this little town.

Brandie came to the door at his knock. She was smart enough to keep it closed. Her son looked like he was still on her hip. His eyes were wide and as bright blue as hers. Most people would think he looked like his mother, but Rey could easily see the resemblance to his father.

"Come on, Brandie. Open up. We need to talk."

"I can hear you just fine." She twisted the dead bolt in an attempt to keep him outside.

"What? I'm not sure what you're saying." He lowered his voice and put his hand to his ear. He could see the ruse wasn't working. No sane person would open the door to a threat.

"It'll go better for you if you open up voluntarily," he said in his regular tone.

"When did you start acting like a gangster? You were my history professor and advisor. I can't believe I shared anything about my life with you."

"I still teach, Brandie. You know that." Then, just loud enough for his hands-free, he gave the go-ahead to break in the back door. "Now."

"I don't know what you want. I don't have anything of yours. So go away and leave us alone before I call the sheriff."

"We both know you won't do that. And why." Rey tugged on the bottom of his jacket again. The bigger gun definitely made the jacket more snug. He watched the neighborhood for signs that someone had noticed him walking there or that they heard the muffled screams inside the house. The dead bolt turned again and the door pulled open.

No drapes moved across the street and no sounds escaped from Brandie as he shuffled into the living room.

"How do you live like this?" he asked, not expecting an answer. "This reminds me of the place my mother rented when I was young like your boy. I do prefer the home I have her in now."

The little boy hadn't started crying yet. Although, he looked like his lungs were about to explode in Zubict's arms. Brandie's mouth had been quickly taped shut as he'd instructed. Zubict's partner had her arms pinned behind her back. She spoke volumes to her son through her expressive eyes.

"Let's be clear. You stay quiet and nothing happens to either of you. Nod if you understand." He waited for the reluctant agreement. She really had no other choice and finally moved her head. "Take off the tape, but one word and your son will disappear. You believe me?"

She nodded again, and he signaled his men. Zubict took the boy to the back of the house, and Rey enjoyed the panic in Brandie's eyes. Then the shock of pulling the tape made her wince in pain. To her credit, she closed her lips and swallowed any sound.

"I guess the next time I ask to come inside for a visit you'll allow it?" He shooed her backward with his hand until the back of her legs met the old chair in the corner. "I need my package. No more pretending you don't know what I'm talking about."

"But I don't. Really. If you would just tell me what to look for I—"

His palm slammed against her cheek to shut her up. The sting didn't hurt as much as it empowered him. It dimly compared to the ecstatic surge he felt at being in control and slicing through her excuses.

"You can hit me all you want. If I don't know, I'll never have the answer you're looking for." She stuck her chin out, eyes closed, ready for another slap.

Rey unbuttoned his jacket and pulled his .45 from the shoulder holster. He stuck it under her chin. When the metal barrel connected with her skin, her eyes popped open with the knowledge that he could—and would— kill her.

"If you are of no use to me, then I could leave that boy in there an orphan." He leaned in closer so only she could hear him. "At least an orphan in everyone else's eyes. You and I know the truth. I will pull the trigger. Don't ever doubt that. I might reunite father and son."

He stood straight, twisting the barrel a little harder to make his point, then putting the pistol away.

"Was Glen working for you? If he left something at the café, it must still be there or someplace close. Tell me and I'll find it." Brandie's body showed her relief even if her words weren't grateful.

He believed her. He had her son, had control of her world. He looked around the four walls she called home. If their product had been sold, he would have heard about it. And there was nothing to indicate she'd come into cash. If she had, she would have ditched this town a long time ago and headed to a real city. She'd written about it in essays enough. Romanticizing history. It was the reason he'd given her a B in his class.

"Out." None of the men in his employment ever hesitated. He liked that. He heard the back door shut. "Cocaine. Thirty-five bricks of cocaine. It's been missing for seven months."

He could see the question in her eyes, but she didn't voice it. Why was he looking for the shipment now? Why wait so long? Because it hadn't been his problem before last month. The organization made it his problem and promised more if he recovered it or the man who had stolen it.

"You don't need to know anything else. The less you know about this the better. If you do good, we might be able to use your place and give you a cut. I doubt your mechanic would have a problem with extra cash flow."

"I don't want your drug money. All I want is for you to get out of my life and leave us alone."

He slapped her again. Harder. This time silent tears fell across the bright pink staining her left cheek. She'd hold her tongue if she knew what was good for her.

Yes, he preferred for people to jump when he said jump. Give a directive and have it obeyed. He wouldn't tolerate anything else no matter who he ordered. His men were grateful to be employed and a part of his organization.

When he returned the cocaine to the men behind the curtain, he wouldn't need to hide behind boring history any longer. He would be making it. He'd say farewell to snotty college students.

"You seem to be forgetting that I'm the man who knows your secret, Brandie. The man who could destroy your world with one simple truth. I know the father of your child."

"So what? Why would anyone believe you? You don't have any proof."

"But I do." He sat on the broken-down couch. "Since you've been so reluctant to help me this past month, I decided to do a little research. You remember that research is my specialty, seeing that I'm a history prof and all."

"You're lying." She closed her eyes and stiffened, prepared for the slap he didn't deliver.

His cell notification let him know his men had successfully left the city limits. Time to let Brandie in on what they'd accomplished. "Test me and find out if I'm bluffing. It's a calculated move allowing you this much knowledge. I'm confident you'll come through for me."

"You are an arrogant bastard. I will never work for a drug dealer. You can never pay me enough."

He opened his cell to the picture sent by his men. Toby was lying on the floorboard. His distinctive blond hair sticking out beneath a greasy blanket.

"You're misunderstanding me, Brandie." He flipped the screen toward her. "Currently, the return of your son is the only payment I intend."

She leaped forward, and he recoiled quickly, but her short claws still managed to catch his neck. He pulled back his fist and hit her in the side of the head. She fell and was unconscious when he left her house.

Rey controlled himself and leisurely walked to the car, his fingers tapping the sting of scraped skin. Served the bitch right that he'd hit her. The feel of his gun reminded him how close he'd come to pulling it and ending her life. She had one chance to redeem her place in his game.

If she failed, his new weapon would get some practice.

Chapter Ten

It wasn't the first time Mitch had spent a day—or two—in jail. If he continued working undercover with the Rangers, it wouldn't be the last. He'd had a lot of interesting days for the past two and a half years as an undercover agent. His skills under the hood of a car made it easy to move up and down the Mexican border and Texas coastline.

If there was one thing Mitch had learned it was that there would always be more scum out there ready to step in and fill the gap of an organization that law enforcement brought down. He didn't know how Cord could work this job year after year. It seemed hopeless. Take out one bad guy, up pops another.

What was the point? People like Brandie and Toby were the point. He needed to get them someplace safe. Convince her that leaving was better for her and the kid. If only they knew what the former mechanic had hidden and where. He could return it, letting Cord know the details and maybe—just maybe—King would stop threatening Brandie.

"Bail's been posted, Striker," a deputy called from the hallway door to the holding cells. "Never had someone go to the trouble to post it anonymously before."

"About dang time," he muttered to himself, knowing that headquarters had come through.

The deputy took him through processing. The sheriff impatiently waited on the other side of the cage, pacing, scrubbing his hand across his lower jaw. Something had happened. It couldn't be good if Pete was waiting to ask him for help.

Mitch stuffed his wallet into his back pocket and faced the barred door. The look of dread on his opponent's face made explanations unnecessary. Mitch's gut kicked acid into his throat. Toby. "They have the kid?"

Pete nodded, leading the way out of the jail. Just outside the door, he grabbed Mitch's arm. "If you have anything to do with Toby's kidnapping..."

"I don't." He looked the sheriff straight in the eyes. The urge to tell him he was one of the good guys was on the edge of his tongue. But he couldn't. Especially now. Keeping his cover was the only way to help Toby.

A craving to wring Rey King's neck overtook his thinking on the short ride to the house. He had no doubts that the wannabe mobster was behind the abduction.

"Can't help notice that you aren't curious about what happened, Striker." The sheriff put the car in Park and twisted in his seat, facing Mitch. "That might make me a bit suspicious."

"I was locked up in your jail. Might not have happened if I hadn't been."

"I figure you'd more than likely be dead before you let Toby be carried off." Pete scratched his chin with his thumb. "See, I have a feeling that Brandie's mixed up in something. We've had our fair share of excitement around here recently, but I'd have to be blind not to see that she's had more than the normal citizen."

"Meaning?" Mitch pressed his mouth shut tighter than before to keep his occupation a secret.

The house was surrounded with county vehicles. Deputies, the Quinns and neighbors were standing in the yard.

"She asked for you because she thinks you can help. You should convince her that I can help, too. I want to call in the Texas Rangers or the FBI."

He'd already decided to convince Brandie to use anyone who could help get her son back. His undercover position would be an asset, but they needed more eyes, more people searching for Toby. "What does she want?"

Pete shook his head. "I gather Brandie knows more about this situation than she's willing to tell. Brandie insisted you were the only person who could help her and magically bail is posted." Pete looked as angry as Mitch felt.

Brandie pushed open the screen door. Her body physically relaxed a little when their eyes met. He could see the reaction across the yard along with a swollen cheek where she'd been hit.

He wanted to shout who was to blame to every cop in the yard. To Brandie's father. To the town. They'd speed down the highway, find Rey King, get Toby back and the kidnapper would pay. He'd hurt. A lot.

They needed a case against him to put him away for good. Not just a trip to the hospital.

"I know you want explanations from me before we walk inside, but you won't get them." Brandie's eyes pleaded with him to remain silent. "It's not my story to tell."

"But you're admitting there *is* a story." Pete used a couple of four-letter words before he shoved open the Tahoe's door and stomped to the porch, waving off every question thrown his direction. "I need the family inside."

It was a hard call to make. Protect Brandie's right as a mother versus the need for the extra man power to find her son. Pete wasn't a dumb man. He knew something was going on and he'd figure it out sooner or later. He'd be more helpful and cooperative if Cord told him there was an undercover Ranger working in his town.

Revealing that was Cord's call. Mitch had already been reprimanded for telling Brandie. The family went into the living room.

"What are you doing to find my grandson?" Bud demanded from Pete, ignoring that Mitch slipped inside behind him to stand by Brandie.

"We've issued a statewide Amber Alert. To be honest, I wish you'd reconsider calling in the FBI. We don't have a lot of experience with kidnapping cases in Presidio County. We also have no idea what we're dealing with or why."

He and Brandie both knew who had her son. They both knew why. He needed to get her away from everyone so she could tell him the details.

"What do you mean reconsider the FBI? They haven't been called? What have you been doing for the past two hours? They could be across the blasted border with my grandson by now." Bud yelled at everyone, aiming his anger at Pete who was man enough to take it. Then he marched across the room finger pointing at his wife. "Did you know about this? How the hell are we supposed to find Toby if we don't know—"

The older man stopped himself, something clicking in his head. Mitch could see the gears turning and shoving information together. Bud looked over his shoulder and his eyes locked onto Mitch. The fright was masked with a desire to blame someone.

"Is this your fault?" the frantic man asked.

Brandie's hand swung out and caught Mitch's. He'd taken a step forward without realizing it. Pete came across the room to intercept him. He'd never felt the urge to defend himself from such an accusation before. People could normally call him every name in the book and he was able to ignore it. But Bud's question had insulted him like nothing he'd experienced.

Mitch drew a deep breath to calm down. Somebody needed to talk Bud into doing the same. But nobody else seemed willing.

So Mitch would. "I don't believe anyone here is responsible. We should let the sheriff explain what's being done and what they need from us."

The veins in Bud's neck might burst if they didn't get him calmed down. Six months working in the garage and he'd never lost his temper like this. And yet, no one in the room seemed very surprised.

Time for Mitch to keep his mouth shut and return to his role as the silent type staying on the edge of conversations, listening but not participating. He released Brandie's hand, crossed his arms and tried to look relaxed before he looked at the angel at his elbow.

Her eyes beseeched him. For help? For restraint? For…? She simply took his breath away and all thoughts along with it.

Brandie's mother cried softly into a handful of tissue.

The conversation continued in the background between Pete and Bud. The only person who could change its direction was Brandie. She was exhausted and probably terrified. And unfortunately, she was as silent as him.

Mitch was getting lost in the blue of her eyes, trying to comfort her without a word when he heard his name pretty much taken in vain again.

"I still don't know what good you think this bum is going to do," Bud criticized, looking at Brandie. "You let him into your bed and he becomes the all-important person in your life."

"That's enough." Mitch's fingers balled into fists. He was conscious of the tense muscles in his arms. More aware that he was ready to take someone's head off as much as Bud. But he couldn't let anyone hurt Brandie more than she'd already been today. One look and a stranger would know she was a tear away from her breaking point.

"You ready to leave?" he asked her. Well, sort of asked her, since it came off more as *We're leaving whether you like it or not*. She nodded, then he turned to Pete. "Got a car to take us back to the garage? I don't think it's a good idea to walk."

"I'll do it myself."

"Good. We'll wait outside." He extended his hand and Brandie took it. Her parents watched, both silent until the door closed again and Bud continued his tirade. Harsh words. Mitch quickly got Brandie out of earshot.

"He doesn't mean anything. He's just upset and needs to do something." She tried to justify.

"I disagree with his methods. I'm also keeping my mouth shut. So should you until we know we're alone."

She waited on the Tahoe's backseat, looking older than she should with her thick hair pulled in a ponytail. The tiny studs in her ears were brightly colored rainbows. The earrings seemed at odds with their situation, but perfect for Brandie on a normal day.

She twisted the fake wedding ring on her slim finger instead of knotting the edge of her frilly shirt. It didn't make sense to wear a shirt like that to cook and serve customers at the café, but she liked them. She must since that's almost all she wore. That was it. It was the dang shirts that made her look older than twenty-four.

Personally, he enjoyed seeing her in funny T-shirts and faded torn jeans—even her cartoon pajamas. He also liked the glittery blue polish on her toenails that were currently covered by practical tennis shoes.

He'd never given much thought to what a woman wore. A distraction from Toby's kidnapping? Maybe. Or a concentrated effort to keep from jumping in a car and heading for his kidnapper. If King's people hurt him, if he were traumatized in any way… Mitch wasn't normally a violent man. But the anger surged through him again. He felt his insides shake with the rage.

The emotional swell took him by surprise. Maybe Toby wasn't the only one with a crush. Cord had mentioned how the five-year-old was used to Mitch being a part of his life. Maybe it worked both ways. Maybe Mitch was used to the kid and Brandie being in his life, too.

"Nothing's going to happen to Toby. I promise you."

"You can't keep that promise, Mitch." The full pools in her eyes overflowed down her cheeks as she tilted her face toward his.

The bruising had begun. She needed ice to keep the swelling down. Someone had hit her. Didn't matter who, he'd make them pay at some point. He gently stroked her jawbone with his fingertip.

"Then I'll make one I can keep. I swear if he's hurt, the person responsible won't live to regret it."

Before she could object—which he assumed she would do by the O shape of her lips—the sheriff gestured for him to get in the truck.

PETE DROPPED THEM at the garage side door, but not before asking them again if they were ready to share their secret. Brandie kept her face turned away and stayed silent, fingers crossed that Mitch would do the same.

Pete told them that two deputies would stay at her house waiting for a call that wouldn't come from the kidnappers. The phone from the café had been forwarded there, as well. They were finished dusting for prints and searching inside.

Maybe this was so hard on Mitch because he had sworn to uphold the law. A big part of her was grateful he had to keep secrets for a living. There was no one else she could turn to. If he was unwilling to help, she would be lost.

"Pete knows, doesn't he?" she said, but Mitch had stepped back into the garage. He hadn't heard her, but she already knew the answer. The sheriff might not know specifics, but he knew she was mixed up in something horrible.

He'd be watching as much as Rey's men.

With shaking hands, Brandie added coffee to the filter and cleared the broken glass from the pots. She found the extra carafe stashed deep on a shelf under the counter, rinsing, drying, then turning it on.

Black and blacker. That was the way Mitch liked his coffee. She didn't mind making him a cup while he inventoried his personal possessions.

Looking around the café depressed her. It wasn't just the overwhelming cleanup challenge that they faced. Its topsy-turvy shape represented her business and emotions…everything was so overwhelming.

Toby was gone. She'd put him in danger by being defiant to Rey. She dropped her face in her hands and cried. It was all her fault. If they didn't find Toby, no one else could be blamed. The decision was solely hers and it was too late to change her mind.

She had to pull herself back together. Fake composure. She heard Mitch's footsteps. "What doesn't kill ya makes you stronger. Right?"

Mitch's strong palm rubbed her back, patting it a couple of times like a guy completely uncomfortable with a crying female. But even in a pat, his strength was there, penetrating through the blouse she hated.

"What have I done? He's just five years old. He has to be scared and wondering where I am. Oh, God. They might have told him I was dead or don't want him. What if they hurt him? What if you can't find him, Mitch?"

"I assume you have a message from King," he finally said, completely ignoring all her doubtful thoughts. There was no accusation in his voice or touch, just comfort. "Are you sure you don't want to bring in outside help?"

"You are my help. Rey thinks you're just a mechanic. He might believe you're still in jail. Won't that help us get Toby back?"

He pulled a stool over for her to sit down.

"You know you don't have to rely just on me. One phone call and the Texas Rangers will be searching for Toby. Are you worried about your past coming out?"

"No. Nothing matters except Toby. Rey said he's watching, that he'll know if I do anything except bring him the stupid package." Should she tell him that the package was cocaine? Would he still help her?

"Did he tell you what's in this *package* or how big it is?" Mitch took a clean bar towel, filled it with ice and held it to her jaw.

"Wow, that really hurts."

"I'm guessing you haven't seen it yet?" Mitch's eyes darted to the side of her face. "It should hurt awhile."

"No."

"You need to tell me the whole story."

Her body was stiff and sore from falling to the floor when Rey had hit her. But the thought of telling Mitch everything had her squirming on her stool. She'd shared much more than she was comfortable with already.

"I told you—"

"Start with what's in the package. I can guess the rest." He removed the ice and gingerly drew his knuckle along her cheek.

"Is it really bad?"

He grimaced and didn't need to answer. She took the ice pack and hoped it would help keep the swelling to a minimum.

"At least you don't need a straw. They could have broken your jaw. Want coffee or a milk shake? The freezer's messy, but they at least closed the door."

"Thank goodness. Coffee please. I made it strong so—"

"I know. You want it half with creamer." He shook

the powdered mixture they used on the tables into a half-filled cup. He measured a spoonful of real sugar and then stirred.

Brandie realized it wasn't the first time he'd prepared her coffee. And it hit her that she hoped it wouldn't be the last. She wanted him to stick around—undercover Texas Ranger or true blue-collar mechanic. She liked Mitch. Period.

So why was she hesitating telling him the truth? Because she was afraid his secret profession would have to make the call to the authorities that they were looking for thirty-five bricks of cocaine. She didn't even know how much that meant.

If they found it—and they had no choice but to find it—he'd know what it was. She'd still be faced with convincing him to turn it over to Rey no questions asked.

"Stop debating with yourself and spill it. I've given you my word that I'd help. Before you think about how to ask…just ask me."

"What?"

"You want to know if I'm calling Cord if I find something illegal." He arched his eyebrows, asking the question with his face.

"Will you?"

"My first priority is to get Toby back. Second is to get the both of you to safety." He held up his hand. "Don't argue. Admit you're in danger. That's the deal. I find Toby and you both leave."

She hated to leave everything, but they'd have to. They just wouldn't be safe here anymore. She'd seen what happened to families that ticked off the Mexican cartel. Cord and Kate McCrea had lost their unborn child and nearly lost their lives. The illegal activity was higher now, putting more people at risk.

"You're right," she reluctantly admitted, dropping the cold pack to the counter. But what Mitch didn't know was that she and Toby had nowhere to run.

"After I see to both of those, then I'll settle the score with King." Mitch barely touched her chin, taking another look at her bruise. "You hungry? How 'bout a grilled cheese and then we get started looking for that package."

"Sounds like a plan. I'll get the stovetop cleaned up if you get the cheese from the walk-in."

Mitch led the way as she fought more tears. It had been a long time since anyone was so completely on her side. She swiped at the wetness trickling down her face before turning on the flattop. Nothing happened. "Great. I need to flip the breaker."

"I can get it. Stay there."

She cleared a work area, wiped off the cast iron and found the bread.

"Brandie!" Mitch called.

She ran to the back of the garage where the breaker box was located. Mitch stood in front of the shelf, staring at the wall, rubbing the back of his neck. Brandie picked her way through the old boxes of car parts that had been brushed off the shelves.

"All the breakers are marked. So what's the problem?"

"Do you know what this box is for?" He pointed to one that had been hidden behind the car parts. "It's disconnected."

"It must be to the old pit bay. Dad sealed that up years

ago when he bought the lift that you use now." She'd been eleven or twelve. Her mom ran the café and her dad ran the garage. They couldn't afford sitters—she'd insisted she was too old for them anyway. So she'd sat in the corner booth finishing homework, listening to the jukebox and overhearing all the town gossip.

"Makes sense to disconnect it. But this is newer wiring than the rest. It looks like it's been used recently. Maybe just before I arrived?"

"You mean Glen tried to repair something. That would be unusual for him. He hardly did anything without Dad's instructions."

"Maybe he didn't want your dad to know."

"You mean, you think he's hiding something down there. But why wouldn't he come back to get it?" She sank to a stack of tires as the realization hit her. Glen couldn't come back. "He's dead. Rey killed him. That's how he knows his drugs are still here at the garage. You knew. That's why you came to work here and have been tricking me."

Mitch searched through strewn tools. She stared at him as he found and connected a power drill, then began unscrewing the metal plating that covered the pit bay.

"Yes, he was murdered. Yes, his death presented an opportunity for me to observe. I didn't want to trick you. I hope you believe me."

Brandie was stunned. "There's too much to take in. Toby has been kidnapped and is being held for the ransom of thirty-five cocaine bricks that my murdered former mechanic hid in my father's garage. Oh, and let's not forget that the mechanic I could have very much become involved with—and who I've admired tremendously—

has been lying to me for six months. Because he's one of the good guys, an actual-to-goodness Texas Ranger playing undercover and sleeping on my couch."

Chapter Eleven

Mitch stopped retracting screws from the steel plating.

"Thirty-five? King told you there's thirty-five bricks of cocaine down here?" He wanted to react to her slip about the possibility that they could become involved. It wasn't the time. He had to let it go and only think about Toby.

"Rey didn't know where it was, just that I have to find it if I want Toby back. We don't know that it's down here."

"That's around a million dollars street value. That's more than enough evidence to put him away for a very long time."

He continued removing the screws, pretty certain Brandie hadn't realized she'd even spoken her complaint out loud. He would deal with it later. He had to finish one job before starting another. Toby, drug smugglers, then a possible relationship with Brandie. He was looking forward to that.

"It's not evidence. It's ransom. We have to turn it over to them."

"I need to call Cord to document—"

"No!" She jumped to her feet, hands karate-chopping the air. "We play this completely by Rey King's rules and we get my son back."

He stood with every intention of going to her, calming her down, assuring her that he'd never do anything to put Toby in jeopardy. Instead, he just stood there. Holding on to the cord, he let the electric impact wrench slide and clang on the floor.

"If you can't do this my way, then you need to leave. Right now. Just go." She bent to pick up the wrench.

"That isn't an option." He pulled on the cord, drawing her close enough to wrap in his arms and rest his chin on the top of her head.

The tears that had threatened fell again.

She clung to the electric wrench and buried her face in his shirt. Completely lost, he just held Brandie tight. Unlike the last time he'd been around a woman crying. Not since junior high when his dad had moved out. His mother had cried for days even though it had been her yelling for his dad to get out. All Mitch had done was cover his head with a pillow.

That wasn't an option at the moment.

"I'll get Toby back," he said softly across her head after the tears had lessened. "I have to do my job, too."

Her body and cheek were flush with him when she said, "What happens when this is all over and Rey finds out you're a Ranger? What do you think he'll do then?"

"No one will know."

"I can't risk it. He'll kill us. All of us. That's what monsters like him do when they get angry. We see it all the time."

"That's on the other side of the border." He bent his knees to look her in the eyes. "The Rangers can relocate you, put you in protection. Would it be such a bad thing?"

At the moment, Mitch couldn't imagine walking back

into the same room as Bud Quinn. After the things he'd said about Brandie, how would she ever forgive him?

She shoved him away and gripped the wrench tighter, dragging the cord across the concrete floor. "This is my home. Do you really think I could just walk away from everything I've ever known? Or take Toby away from his grandparents?"

"But you just said a minute ago—"

It didn't make sense and wouldn't. No one should go through the stress she was under at the moment. One of the strongest people he'd ever met turned from him and stared out the rear window. No one was out there. Just a small gravel lot where their cars were parked.

She needed a minute to come back around. He was glad they were here instead of at her house with the Quinns. Her dad reminded him of his own father.

His parents hadn't had a pleasant divorce. Years of screaming were followed by years of complaints about each other. It made undercover work all that more appealing. Like Brandie, he hadn't had any siblings. No one else shared the burden of their constant bickering. It fell on his shoulders and he learned real quick to not give either parent ammo about the other.

But Brandie's parents were essentially blackmailing her as much as King was. If she stepped out of line, she'd lose everything. Why didn't she see it that way?

"You should leave. Before you find out if anything's under those pieces of thick steel. Go." She stared out the window. Not facing him.

"Is that what you really want?"

He wasn't leaving. There was no way he could leave her to face King by herself. But something in him pushed her for an answer. He wanted to hear her decision and wanted her to need him to stay. That particular emotion had never crept to the surface before.

Need? Want? Desire? These weren't normal emotions for an undercover Ranger.

Damn.

"You shouldn't go against your principles, Mitch. If you have to tell Cord about the missing drugs, then so be it." She was killing him with kindness. "But I'm afraid you'll have to come back with a warrant."

She was working him like a problem customer. That's what she did, and he admired her ability to be gracious and disagree at the same time.

"It hasn't escaped me that you are still holding that impact wrench. I imagine it's to keep me from using it. So I'll ask again. Do you want me to leave?"

Her hands shook as her knuckles turned white. She clenched her jaw and visibly swallowed. All signs of someone trying hard not to say what they really want.

"Brandie, honey." He crossed the short distance to her again. "I'm here for you and Toby. I might get fired for my divided loyalties, but I heard of this great mechanic's job, room and board included. Sounds like heaven."

The little spitfire hugged the wrench to her chest, shaking her head, sort of laughing and crying at the same time. "I can't ask—"

"Doesn't seem like you did." He squeezed her shoulders with his hands, squelching the desire to pull her to his chest yet again. "I volunteered. Now if you'll give back the wrench, I can see if we can stop looking for King's cocaine."

He extended his hand, and the power wrench was popped into his palm. That same look of relief she'd displayed on her porch at the sight of him this morning relaxed her features and her body. It was crazy, but he felt the same way. If she'd kicked him out, he might have thrown away his badge to stay.

Insane was a better word that came to mind to describe his decision. Or maybe stupid. Like he'd said to her inside the café, one phone call and the resources of the state of Texas would be at their service.

He knelt by the steel plates to remove the last few screws. "I must be crazier than I look."

"Well, I don't know, Mitch. You're acting about as crazy as me." She began clearing the floor, picking up parts, setting them on the shelves.

"Last one. Brandie?"

Her hands encircled her neck, and she looked toward the ceiling. "Change your mind?" She dropped her hands, slapping her thighs before she looked at him.

"Nope. I'm not calling for backup. I'm not going to stop the exchange and we're going to get Toby back. I'll be with you a hundred percent of the time. No exceptions."

"Great. Can we see if it's even there?"

He knew it was the only place it could be. "I'm going to document the money. Rey King is going to jail and this will put him there."

Her eyes closed as she took in a deep breath. "So be it. I just want my son back safely in my arms."

He took his phone from his pocket, took pictures and then removed the last screw. The plating had been screwed to a wooden frame first covered in plywood to make it safe to walk in the shop. The length and weight of the frame should have been impossible to lift. But under the metal cover, the plywood had been cut. Two finger holes made it possible to lift, revealing the ladder underneath.

"This is it." Mitch took a couple of pictures and lifted the wood, then took a few more of the pit. "Empty."

Brandie was just behind his shoulder. "Glen wouldn't have gone to all this trouble to hide nothing."

"There's no guarantee that whoever killed him doesn't have the cocaine."

"It's kind of dark down there. I'll grab a flashlight." She ran into the café.

There wasn't a question of whether he was going or not. He just didn't want Brandie to fall apart when they didn't find anything. He was already on the top rungs when she handed him a tiny penlight from her key ring.

"Take pictures, will ya?" He held out his phone.

She slid his cell into her pocket and sat on the side, ready to come over the edge. "Don't even argue with me. You might miss something."

She shimmied down the ladder faster than he could figure out how to turn the flashlight on by twisting the end cap. It was close quarters, barely enough room for a man his size to maneuver comfortably. And man alive was he uncomfortable with Brandie down there with him.

"Looks like you should have connected that wire. Then maybe these fluorescents would come on." She flipped a switch up and down but nothing happened.

It was dark, so looking at all the notches on the wall would take a few minutes. Brandie stuck out her hand, and he gave her the light. She immediately walked to the far end.

"Oh, my gosh, Mitch. That's a handle. Can you reach it?"

"Stand back. If it's a block of cement then I'm going

to control where it lands. Doesn't make sense, though. It would be too heavy for one man to move."

He yanked, and a square board smeared with concrete pulled away. Along with a stack of cash and a couple of .38 Specials, there was a duffel filling the entire back of the hole. The light flashed on his cell. Brandie was taking the pictures, documenting what they found.

He reached for the bag but hesitated. The urge to call Cord grew. Along with a very bad feeling. Nothing tangible. He just knew something was going to go wrong if they didn't bring the Rangers on board.

"Aren't you going to see what's inside?" She stretched her hand toward the bag.

"Wait. Did King tell you when to meet?"

"Yes. I'm supposed to call and meet later today if I find the package."

"Then we're going to need proof."

"Of what?" she asked as he tugged her back toward the ladder. "No. You're trying to convince me to call the law. To let your friends handle this. Rey said I'd never see Toby again. Do you want that on your head?"

"You came to the conclusion that Pete knew what was going on. He didn't hang around and he didn't leave a deputy to stay with you. Your son's been kidnapped and he didn't leave anyone here to see if you would be contacted. That's not procedure in any law enforcement agency." Mitch's jaw muscle twitched as he ground his molars together.

"That…that doesn't mean anything."

Mitch took her hand in his. Her hands were chilled from the coolness in the pit or maybe holding the ice earlier. "He knows something's up and he's trying to trap us for some reason." He released her hand and rubbed the back of his neck.

As dark as it was, he could see the slight shake of her head as she acknowledged his idea, but still tried to ignore it. At the bottom of the ladder, he waited for her to grab the rung. She shrugged off his hand.

"You're wrong. He wouldn't do that. We've known each other forever."

"Brandie, he's a cop. He's doing his job and he wouldn't be worth his salt if he couldn't figure out someone's threatening you."

Her hand covered her cute little O-shaped mouth. She got it and he hated springing it on her. Right then in a car repair pit, with the smell of a decade of grease, oil and other smells…all he wanted to do was comfort her. Make her believe everything would be all right. Convince her beyond a shadow of a doubt that he had the answers.

He did. But she wasn't going to like them.

"What do we do?" she asked softly.

"First, I'm putting everything back the way it was. Wait for it." He pressed a finger to her lips at the first inhaled breath or objection. "Then we make a video of coming down here and finding everything. We document our movements. You admit that you're being forced to cooperate in order to get your son back."

"You're treating me like a criminal."

"We can't prove these drugs aren't yours. We have to do this my way to protect you." And put Rey King in jail.

"Why don't *you* believe they belong to me?"

"The thought never crossed my mind." Mitch handed her the penlight. "Hold that, will ya?"

She stayed put while he put the wall cover back in place. She didn't wait for instructions after he was done. Flashlight off, she climbed out of the pit. He followed and put everything back in place while she searched for something on his phone. She wouldn't find anything except a few random pictures of Toby or a car.

It seemed a little ridiculous, but he put every screw back in place. He wanted her name squeaky clean. The way he felt about her, having already been reprimanded for blowing his cover—to her... Yeah, he had to think about protecting her from future accusations.

"We need his fingerprints," she said out of the blue. "Do you know how to lift prints? It's okay, I've looked it up on the internet. We've got everything we need here."

"That's a smart idea." He stuck out his hand for the cell, switching it to video. "If something goes wrong. Hey, I'm not saying it will. But if something goes wrong, this may help find Toby. You ready?"

The video captured all the raw emotion Brandie was experiencing and the purple-colored jaw from where she'd been hit. She explained everything pertinent to the case. She didn't need to mention that King had threatened to expose her son's parentage. This would be enough.

When they were done, he sent the file to a secure email account. "You're positive you don't want to involve anyone else for help or even backup?"

"We can't." A simple statement of fact this time.

"Then let's get started."

Mitch opened everything again while Brandie held the phone, recording. They found a regular-sized flashlight, which brightened everything once they were down the ladder. And this time, he took the money and gun out of the homemade wall safe and wrapped them in his shirt until they could secure a substitute evidence bag.

Back upstairs, Brandie found his charger still plugged into the wall so they could continue recording. He set the duffel on the bed. She stayed his fingers on the zipper.

"What if this isn't the drugs?"

"Only one way to find out."

There was no reason to second-guess themselves. The bag was stuffed to capacity. If King was missing thirty-five bricks of cocaine, this was probably it.

"Let's make that fingerprint powder and get this over with." She turned off the camera on the cell and dropped it to the mattress.

As she sorted through the rubble in the café for what she needed, Mitch swiped the video record button, switching the image to record himself.

"Cord, this was the best I could do. If the exchange for Toby goes wrong or if something happens to me… For the record and without a gun to my head, this video should serve as my last will and testament. I want Brandie Ryland to receive my benefits and savings. I'm counting on you, man, as one Ranger to another, that you'll get Brandie and her son out of this mess here in Marfa. Make sure she's safe for me."

Chapter Twelve

"Patrice, my love. I missed you last night." Rey waltzed into the kitchen as if he didn't have a care in the world. At least not the version he lived in. Patrice had already learned about how he'd messed things up.

The Amber Alert on her phone had awoken her hours ago from a sound sleep, notifying the entire state of Texas of Toby Ryland's disappearance.

Patrice's world had been missing thirty-five bricks of cocaine for far too long. The filthy mechanic had managed to hide it from them, and Rey had been too quick with his death. The drugs had to be at the café. It was the last possible place they could be hidden. Rey had complicated everything with this kidnapping.

The buyers had expected the cocaine in their hands weeks ago and were becoming impatient. She could placate them for only so long and it looked like time had run out. But kidnapping the boy had never been part of their strategy to find it.

Rey kissed her on the cheek, greeting her much like a longtime boyfriend should. They'd been together for three very long, tedious years. She took a sip of her coffee, and as was his custom, he swung around to her back, dropping his hands to caress her bare breasts beneath her robe.

"Slow down." She shrugged away and pulled the robe closed. "What happened last night?"

He leaned on the kitchen bar next to her and snagged the last piece of her bacon from her plate. She absolutely hated when he ate her food. She hated a lot of things about Rey King. Too many to think upon at the moment.

It had been months since she'd been satisfied— sexually or in her everyday routine. She loved variety in her life and bed. It was definitely time for a change. Time to make her move and prove who'd been running the show all along.

"We snatched the kid. So I figure we'll have the blow by this afternoon."

He'd purposefully deviated from her plan. She was furious and couldn't show it. The time wasn't right. He might get the wrong idea and realize that the Chessmen organization was as fictitious as his brains.

"Rey, baby." She laid on the thick accent he liked that was a very sad Marilyn Monroe. "Do you think the men in charge are going to get mad, sug? I mean, they said to bust some stuff up, but what if the kid's mom lets the police help find him? Things could get real complicated. Will there be extra cops and state troopers on the highways?"

"Their way was too slow. We got the kid. I guarantee we'll have the cocaine by tonight."

He kissed her and slid his hands under the silky material again. The Marilyn imitation always got him turned on. And if he was thinking with one certain piece of his anatomy, he wouldn't be thinking with any other. Some men were so easily manipulated. And even more loved the dumb blonde she could imitate so well.

"There's nothing to worry your pretty head about. The guys and I got this covered. They have true incentive to find that million in cocaine now. It'll be in their hands before we're finished in the other room." He tugged her up and with him toward his bed.

Patrice followed. Sex allowed her time to think. They passed through the door, he stripped off her robe and threw her to the mattress.

"Are you high, Rey?"

He ripped the buttons, pulling his shirt apart. "Yeah, baby, want some? I got more in my pocket than what you're craving."

Craving? He couldn't give her what she craved, but he'd do. "I'm fine like this." She grabbed his belt before he could toss it away.

"Oh, yeah, baby. You're always fine." He buried his face between her breasts and rolled on top of her.

While she let him have his way, she'd put together a new strategy. Then she'd have her real fun.

Chapter Thirteen

Brandie paced, turned circles, tapped her toes and then a pen, waiting on Mitch to finish fingerprinting the bags. She'd obviously been distracting since he'd set his phone in a place to record him without being held. She didn't mean to be in such a hurry but not doing anything to get her son back was more nerve-racking than handling the drugs themselves.

"I think I should call Rey and tell him we've found the bag." Brandie watched him carefully brush away the fingerprint powder that they'd made. "We can at least set up a time for the exchange."

"Not until I'm finished with this." He waved his fingers over the cocaine. He wore two layers of food service gloves, trying not to mar any prints left behind. And not leave his prints to confuse police officers later.

"Wasn't twenty-five of those brick things plenty? You've said they must have been wearing gloves. You haven't found anything but a smudge so far." She picked up the second paintbrush they'd found with Toby's art supplies. "I could do a couple."

"It's better if I do them all."

"So you said. They won't question anything if you're

the only one who attempts to lift the prints. But you're taking hours. I want my son back. Today."

Mitch didn't say anything. He stopped the recording, saved it to the cloud and began everything again.

"Do you have enough candle soot?" She'd blackened a plate more times than she could count with their emergency candles. If he needed more, she'd have to go to the gift shop on the corner.

"I think so."

"I'm going to clean up the front then."

"Good idea."

She'd tried several times to clean up the café dining room without success. Usually a very patient person, today she wanted to get her son. Nothing else mattered. Looking at the mess in front of her dampened her spirits again. It was so overwhelming.

One thing. Concentrate on one thing and finish it.

She gathered all the condiments that belonged on the tables. Two were missing so she began in a corner and searched methodically. She felt like Mitch as he had checked each inch of the plastic wrapping on each brick of drugs. She found them under the fourth booth.

The blouse that her mom had given her caught on something and ripped. She kept a spare set of clothes in the back and changed. Getting into comfortable jeans and a T-shirt shifted her attitude. Then her stomach growled.

The thought of her little boy going hungry curled her fingers into fists. She didn't want to think about being comfortable or about food. But if they were going to meet drug dealers it should probably be on a full stomach.

At least the kitchen wasn't torn to pieces. She tied

a cook apron around her waist and wiped the remaining flour off the flattop. While it heated, she picked up pans from the floor and stacked them near the sink, then gathered her ingredients. Just as she put the sliced turkey and buttered bread on the hot surface, she heard a knock on the front window.

Her heart raced, and she couldn't breathe. Her first instinct was to run to the garage and to Mitch. Rey had to be back. Then logic kicked in. He wouldn't knock and wouldn't be seen coming through the front door. She kept the metal spatula in her hand and slowly peeked through the service window.

Pete stood at the door, knuckle rapping against the glass again. "Mitch!" she called loudly. "The sheriff's here."

She had to let him inside. She didn't have any choice. Did she? No. She flipped the dead bolt and prayed Mitch had enough time to put the drugs away. "We're not open."

"I know you're not open, Brandie. We thought you needed to know what could be happening." He turned sideways, and she could see Cord standing a few feet behind him. A café regular walked down the sidewalk, peering into her window to get a peek at the wreckage.

"I appreciate you coming by but today's not— I'm just really not up to…um…company."

"Any news, Sheriff?" Mitch asked from over her head.

"We need to come inside." Pete said the words, but Cord arched an eyebrow and nodded his head slightly.

Mitch must have received the message from his boss and pushed open the door. Brandie shot him a look, silently asking if he were crazy but he missed it. He shook the hands of the two men and flipped undamaged chairs around for everyone to sit down.

This was not how her afternoon was supposed to go. What if Rey had men watching the café?

"Mitch, will you help me with the sandwiches?"

"Sure."

"You guys help yourself to some coffee. You might have to rinse out a cup but the pot's fresh." She took her mechanic's hand and kept him next to her so he couldn't even hint at or tell either man about the cocaine.

"The bread is practically burned." She flipped the sandwiches and turned off the flattop.

"It's okay. I just need to shove something into my stomach. It doesn't matter if it tastes good. I'll find some plates."

"Just grab the box of to-go wrappers." She accepted the thin aluminum sheets he handed her and scooped the sandwich onto it. She lowered her voice. "What do you think they want?"

Mitch shrugged with a mouthful of turkey and cheese. "Why don't we ask 'em?"

He ambled comfortably into the other room, seeming completely at ease facing two law enforcement officers with a million dollars' worth of cocaine in the next room. There was no way she could look as calm and collected as he did. She was more nervous than words to describe it. But she should be. Her son had been kidnapped.

Mitch was right. All they could do was ask her and all she had to do was not answer. So she followed him. He inhaled his sandwich—burned bread and all—while she nibbled, too sick at her stomach to think anything would actually stay down.

Mitch stopped and got them both glasses of water. Brandie stayed at the counter watching three lawmen sizing each other up. Who would break the silence first?

"Why are you here?" she finally asked. The little bit of sandwich in her tummy turned to a rock waiting on the answer.

"To try and talk some sense into you." Pete flattened his palm on the table.

Cord pressed his lips together into a thin line and flicked some imaginary crumbs on the table. Mitch twirled the bottom of his glass in a circle after he sat down and used that patience thing where he never seemed in a hurry to get anything done. Which was so opposite to all that he accomplished every day.

"So talk." Mitch leaned back, and the front feet of his chair left the floor. He looked totally relaxed with his arms crossed, his pointer finger tapping on his biceps.

Pete leaned on the tabletop, his head quirked to the side looking at her mechanic. Not knowing that Mitch was much more than his outward appearance or his calm collective.

"Don't convince *me*," he said, nodding his head in her direction. "She's calling the shots."

Yep, Mitch was a man of his word and definitely her friend.

Silence. The bite she was chewing turned into a piece of dried-up jerky. And they all waited. Mitch's finger didn't miss a beat to whatever rhythm he was tapping on his arm. She finally swallowed but still didn't know what to say.

"I thought you came here to talk." She gulped some water to get the awful flavor of burned toast from her taste buds.

"I brought Cord out here to convince you that you need help with whatever you're supposed to do with the people who took Toby. You've got to realize it's too dangerous to work on your own."

"Why do you assume I'm supposed to do anything?"

Pete pushed away from the table, slapping it at the same time he stood. "I'm not a fool and I'm not your father who's too upset to see straight. I'm the sheriff. And he's a Texas Ranger."

It took her a second to realize he meant Cord, not Mitch.

"You can't do anything—"

"And yet you've chosen the help of a drifter mechanic with anonymous friends who post his bail."

"There's nothing—"

"If he's a part of whoever's threatening you, or working with whoever has taken Toby, I swear, bail or no bail, I'll get him behind bars. Nobody should mess with a kid." He yanked Mitch to his feet with two fistfuls of fabric.

"Pete, please stop." She was speaking to the sheriff but pleaded silently with the Ranger who still sat there with an unconcerned expression. "Cord? Do something."

He fiddled with the hat that Rangers were so famous for, changing its angle on the table, then scratching his chin as if he weren't concerned. Mitch's hands slowly wrapped around Pete's wrists, tilting them backward. They were about to have it out.

"Just stop!" she yelled to prevent the all-out fight that was bound to happen.

"What's he forcing you to do, Brandie?"

"Oh, for goodness' sakes. This is so ridiculous. I

should be taking care of my son, not supervising grown men acting his age."

"Tell me what he's making you do and I'll help you get Toby back," Pete said with a grimace of pain.

"You can't. Mitch knows what he's doing. Please let him go."

Cord jumped up, his chair falling backward to the floor. "You win, Pete. Mitch works for me. He's an undercover member of our task force. I'm not sure how this relates to Toby's kidnapping, but Brandie found out last night. That's probably why she wants his help."

"I knew it!" the sheriff boasted.

Pete and Mitch dropped their hands, both taking a step in retreat, both mumbling under their breath.

"Dammit. I said you were getting too involved." Cord turned to Mitch. "What the hell's going on and why does Brandie need your help?"

Mitch shrugged. "Not my story to tell."

"Will someone tell me why we've blown the cover on a major operation?" Cord commanded with authority. "Is someone going to explain why? And it better be worth it."

"Oh, my gosh. You all just need to stop. Please just stop." She stomped as loud as she could to the door and put her hand on the knob. "I get that this reveal allows you to be the best of pals. We can schedule a playdate for later. Get out. Now. Before someone sees you here."

"Who?" Pete and Cord asked together.

Mitch pulled her away from the door to whisper in her ear, "We're good. It's still your decision. You're in charge and I'll do what you want even if they order me not to."

They looked at each other, and she shook her head. She couldn't risk never seeing Toby again.

"I know someone's forcing you to do something il-legal." Pete was quiet and firm and sounded sad. "Let me help you."

"I'm waiting on the kidnappers to contact me. You know why I couldn't do it at the house. Dad would have just kept getting worse."

Pete and Cord nodded their heads.

"I'm not saying that I've been contacted. But if I am, I'll do exactly what they say to do. I want my son back and I'll do anything to hold him again. Period. End of story."

Mitch laced his fingers through hers and the steady-ing strength she'd felt so many times in the past day filled her being. She could calmly take a moment and believe everything would be okay.

"They don't know I'm undercover. Our operation hasn't been blown. Yet." His fingers tightened around hers. "If they're watching this place, it's going to be hard to explain why you've been here so long. So maybe it's time for you both to leave?"

"You going to leave this alone, Pete?" Cord asked, settling his hat on his head, ready to leave.

"I don't have too much of a choice. We haven't had any hits from the Amber Alert."

"You think I'm making a mistake. I have to trust my-self, Pete. How many times have these men attacked our town? How many times will they hurt someone in our future? I know you want to put them away forever, but I can't risk Toby's life with that possibility."

Chapter Fourteen

"You can make your call now, but use my phone." Mitch told Brandie as he zipped the duffel, mentally retracing his entire process. He'd been painstakingly slow and careful. Driving Brandie nuts while she waited, but still methodical. He hadn't messed it up.

Granted, he wasn't a fingerprint expert, but he'd found no useable prints or even smudges. He'd finished up after Cord and Pete left, cursing under his breath that there was nothing to tie King to the drugs or Glen's death. But more so that his cover had been blown.

He was a professional who had been undercover for more than two years. He'd never blown it before. Then again, a five-year-old's life had never been at stake. Or someone like Brandie.

How many people did he know who could come through this ordeal without falling apart? Very few individuals had the rare inner strength that he admired in her. There wasn't anything about her he didn't appreciate.

Maybe her stubbornness to trust him, but even that was explained by her past. He'd find out that entire story someday. A barrier would be crossed when she shared that part of herself. And for the first time in his life he was willing to see what was on the other side.

"We've got a lot of hours ahead of us to get both places back up and running." Brandie stretched on his cot, waking from a short nap while she'd waited.

He looked around the garage, seeing the needless destruction but it didn't compare to the café. Amazed that she still thought she could come back here and take up her life as if nothing happened.

"Where's your phone?" she asked, pulling hers from her jeans pocket.

He handed her the cell from the shelf and waited for her to tap in the number. Then he covered her hand, delaying the conversation with King.

"Look, Brandie, my cover's done here. I'm taking this money and getting Toby back." He was starting to like that cute little O shape she made when she was taken by surprise. "Don't try to argue. You'll tell King you're being followed. This is the deal. He wants the cocaine, he gets me."

"Whoa, now—"

"That's the only way." He squeezed her hand, fighting the urge to take her in his arms.

She stood and took a couple of steps away from him. "I appreciate that you want to keep me safe, but you're mistaken if you think you have the right to order me to do anything. I thought I made it perfectly clear that we'd do everything the way Rey tells us to. I'm following his instructions to the letter and that's it."

"I wasn't trying to order you."

"It's okay." She patted his chest as she passed by and crooked a finger for him to follow to the garage office. "We follow his instructions."

A petite fireball. That's exactly who Brandie Ryland was. First the phone call, then he'd tie her up and leave her on the cot in order to prevent her from being in danger.

Too involved. Yep, Cord had called it right. Brandie and Toby were more important to him than the case. He knew it and it didn't matter.

She dialed the cell. Someone answered and immediately hung up. "That's the number he gave me to call. Should I use my phone?"

"Give him a second, then call again and tell him your name. He should realize that you can't use your own phone because of the cops."

She did. Someone answered and she put the call on speaker.

"Brandie, Brandie, Brandie. My men tell me you had visitors and haven't left your pathetic café all day. Are you calling to tell me you can't give me what I want?"

"I found your bag of drugs. Tell me how to get my son back." Brandie shook the phone like it might be King's head.

"We tore that place apart. Glen must have had a real good hiding place."

Mitch silently moaned, realizing he should have recorded the conversation. It would have cleared Brandie of any wrongdoing and would have given the Rangers enough for a warrant. He was definitely off his game.

Sharing that he was undercover with—at the time—their prime suspect. Then staying and protecting Brandie and leaving this place wide-open… He had to set the emotional attachments aside and perform like a true professional.

"Enough with the nice stuff!" she yelled. "I want my son."

"Simmer down. You and your mechanic take his car.

Drive around so you know no one's following you. Be at the south end of Nopal Road at five o'clock. Then start walking east." King disconnected.

"Do you know where Nopal Road is?" He pocketed his phone, knowing that he had to notify Cord about the drop and send him access to his secure account.

She nodded. "We won't have cell service since it's out in the middle of nowhere."

"What *is* out there?" He put the location into his cell.

"Nothing. I don't think there's even a tree large enough to hide behind."

"That's not in our favor. It's also not good that they want the both of us in my car. He's smart enough not to want any surprises, like me surprising them after we have Toby."

"If we're supposed to drive around for a couple of hours, maybe you should fill the gas tank."

"Just in case they strand us out there for a while, would you get together some water and food? I'll move the car inside the garage." He lifted shelving and took a push broom to make a clear path for both cars.

Before turning the key he looked under the carriage and hood of his car. He removed a false bottom and took out his satellite phone and a tracking device. He wouldn't notify Cord until the last minute, but he had sworn an oath to uphold the law. Letting King abscond with a million in cocaine wouldn't work for the state of Texas.

The part of him that still had brains wanted to know why King had specifically said to use his car. As far as his eyes could tell, there weren't any explosives or a tracker. He cranked the engine, moved to the pumps, filled up and moved inside the empty bay.

He repeated everything with Brandie's car, reversing it over the steel plates he hadn't secured back in place. Brandie had a box of fruit and sandwiches. On top of the sleeping bag she'd taken from his cot, she set Toby's backpack with his toys and crayons inside.

"I need my cell." She extended her palm. Determined. Not waiting for him to ask what for.

He had an idea that she was calling home. Her dad could yell and be full of bluster. He could lay down extensive rules and limitations. But bottom line, he was still her dad. Her parents loved her and Toby.

He put their emergency supplies in the backseat, paying close attention to the phone call behind him.

"Hi, Dad. Yeah, sorry about this morning. Everything's crazy. I know you love him. And me."

There was a long pause when Brandie listened and was more patient than Mitch could ever have been.

"I called to check in and let you know that…that Pete is keeping me up-to-date here at the café. I love you, too." She turned to Mitch, her eyes once again brimming with tears. "I couldn't risk telling him. I wanted to, but couldn't. I hope they'll both forgive me."

"You're going to bring Toby back and be a hero. No one will question what you had to do to achieve that."

"I hope you're right because at this exact moment, looking at that bag and the secrets it has… I feel like a lowlife drug dealer." She crossed her arms, pushing her breasts up under the T-shirt.

"You remember what you told me earlier today. You'll do anything to get your son back. Most good parents would, too."

"If we head north, getting back to Nopal Road will

take a couple of hours. Should we grab a map?" She gestured to the garage office where they were sold.

"I have a detailed map of the area under the seat. You ready?"

"Yes. Everything's already locked up. We just have to set the alarm."

"Then let's go get Toby."

Chapter Fifteen

Rey looked so pleased with himself. It had been easy for Patrice to get his consent to come along. Normally, she let someone else take care of the mundane deals. But today was exciting.

Today, all her patience and bowing to inferior partners would pay off.

Today, Patrice Orlando would become queen of her world by taking control of the board and all the chessmen. That was a logical assumption.

Nothing would stop her. Especially not Rey King and his insignificant kidnapping exchange. He thought recovering the cocaine would set him in the sights of the bigger distributors. No, the cocaine was a distraction to keep him sidetracked.

All it did was square them for the next and biggest delivery they'd attempted. But she hated to be rushed. Hastily laid plans were how she normally took out an opponent. Rey had set her plan in motion earlier than she'd wanted, but she'd deal with it. She always dealt with it.

She smoothed her stocking as she formulated a plan around at least two questions. First, whether to keep the couple alive or not. And secondly, to return the boy or keep him for leverage. If she kept him, she'd need to use that leverage within twenty-four hours. Waiting any longer would just bring the law breaking down her door or whatever door she hid the kid behind. No matter what branch of the police it was, she couldn't afford to have her operation slowed.

Yes, today was her new beginning, and she wouldn't let Rey screw it up with this unplanned kidnapping exchange. He'd end up bragging to someone about how easy the entire debacle was to pull off. They in turn would bring the police into the picture. Now that they'd arrived at the drop, step one would be to goad him into handling things himself.

Sitting as close as they were, it was easy to turn her body into his, to sensually cradle his bare arm between her breasts and scoot his hand into her lap.

"Rey, this is so exciting. In all the years that we've been together, I've never really seen you so in charge." She grazed her nails across the knit shirt he wore, drawing a pattern to his slacks and then back up. "It's so… sexy."

"You want to see me more in charge than just talking about it?"

"Baby, you've got men to pick up the money for you. What if something goes wrong?" she deliberately pursed her lips. She wanted the fake tears so none of Rey's crew would suspect anything. So she thought back to when she had nothing. A run-down shack of a house. A father who loved to smack her around. She rubbed her cheek, remembering the sting.

"Brandie's easily manipulated, barely a challenge to me. She just wants her kid back. The guys have been watching her all day. They haven't made a call or contacted the police."

"Are you sure?" She smiled as big as she could manage and threw her fingers to her chest. "I would be thrilled to watch you in action. Absolutely thrilled beyond measure if you think it's safe."

"Then you got it." He flipped the switch to roll the passenger window down. "I'll be collecting myself. Get me a weapon and get the kid ready."

"Yes, sir."

"There's one more thing, baby. Do you think you should take the boy with you?"

"Why not?"

"I mean, most of the men will be up here. What if they have a gun and... I can't imagine what they might do. Isn't it less risky for you, sugar, if we send the kid somewhere they can't find him?" She needed to get the boy away before they found the inevitable tracking device that would be hidden with the drugs.

"You're right. I love the way you think and want to take care of me." He kissed her, long and sloppily. She was so over being attracted to him. Definitely ready to talk in a normal strong voice that people listened to instead of rolling their eyes.

It took very little effort to get Rey out of the car and walking down the incline. It was as easy as dangling a carrot in front of a jackass.

The men she'd dealt with always liked their egos stroked along with other parts of their bodies. Easily manipulated without knowing they were controlled at all. She gave instructions to one of her men who left immediately with the boy. The brat would be kept in a safe place for later use. She couldn't risk the FBI swooping in with a last-minute rescue.

Soon, she was standing in the wing, watching Rey hike down a steep hill with two of his men. The valley was getting darker, but she could see him with the binoculars. He strutted across the field like absolutely nothing could go wrong.

She rolled down the window, crooking her finger toward her secret right-hand man. The shoes she'd bribed him with were on his feet—another item Rey had never questioned. His man had switched from roughneck work boots to Italian loafers and the man "in charge" had never asked why or how he could afford them.

"When we head back, move the boy to a secure location. Did you give the two men their instructions? They grab the bag and run without looking back."

"Yes, ma'am. They'll run like the devil's behind them. Or me."

She laughed. "I'll be free tonight. Stop by the house."

Zubict stood straight. She watched Zubict's crotch swell under the black jeans. He was an adequate lover. She could teach him a few ways to make the sex more enjoyable. Until the next man came into her sights.

Get a man to fall in love with your body and he'll do anything for you. She'd learned that lust was a powerful tool at a very early age.

"They dropped the bag and backed away. Our man is in place and has the shot," Zubict whispered over her shoulder.

"Take it."

Chapter Sixteen

Brandie heard the rifle shot at the same time she saw the impact of the bullet. The blood on Rey's chest was absorbed by his baby blue shirt, soaking into a larger and larger circle.

Rey was dead.

A look of surprise was forever locked on the dead man's face as he fell to his knees, creating two small puffs of dust she would never have noticed at another time. But she witnessed every nanosecond of his demise.

The puddle on his shirt got bigger and bigger as he fell. A dark red rip taking over the baby blue of the fabric like a sunset disappearing behind the Davis Mountains.

She was locked in place. Shots rang out around her, but she stood in the same spot staring, unblinking. Just like the open dead eyes of the man who had kidnapped her son. He stared at her from the ground. Eyes open wide. Mouth now full of West Texas dirt.

She'd never forget the dead man's look as his own men shot him in the back. It was the last thing he had expected.

"Come on!"

Mitch grabbed her arm to get her to move. It didn't work. Toby was with those murderers. She threw off his grip and ran toward the hills, heading straight toward the shooting.

"Are you crazy?" Mitch shouted. "We've got to get out of here!"

The man who had shot Rey could pick them off. She didn't know if it were easy for him to kill like that. Yet they were alive and the two men next to Rey were dead. She kept running toward the hills after the remaining man carrying the drugs. Faster. Watching the ground for anything that might trip her. She had to reach her son. Her vision blurred. She couldn't focus on the rocks or cactus or anything in her way. She just kept running.

Shots peppered the ground to her left.

"Brandie!" Mitch yelled.

More shots popped dirt into the air in front of them, causing her to shield her face and stop. Trying to protect her, Mitch pulled her into his chest, turning his back to their attackers.

"That's far enough," a woman's voice called from the top of the steep hill. "They won't miss again."

Whoever the woman was, she was still a long run away from where Brandie and Mitch had stopped. Far enough that her face was a blur next to the man clearly outlined holding a rifle. As tall as him, with blond hair past her shoulders that blew free in the breeze.

"Give me my son." Brandie heard her voice crack, already hoarse from screaming she hadn't heard. "We had a deal."

"Your deal is with a dead man."

Mitch laced his fingers with hers, tugging to get her to move. "We've got to get out of here."

"Not without Toby."

"You'll be contacted. I've got your number," the

woman shouted, sounding smug. She disappeared behind a dark car.

Brandie collapsed to the ground. All of the fear she'd been pushing away cut through her defenses and stabbed her heart. She'd failed. She couldn't go on. The last bit of light disappeared behind the mountaintops along with her last bit of hope.

Strong hands encircled her shoulders. She felt like a rag doll as Mitch lifted her into his arms and carried her. She cried into his denim jacket, unable to think, unable to stop.

"Stand up for me, sweetie." Mitch set her on her feet. "I've got to get my bearings and make a call."

She really tried to stand, but ended up in a pool on the ground. Face on top of her arms, the tears just kept coming. Then Mitch's voice cut through the fog. He was talking to someone.

"...to the southeast. Have you got a fix on the duffel?"

She turned her head enough to find him. He was using his cell, which shouldn't have been working. No one had reception out here.

"Roger that," the voice on the other end answered through the speaker. "Are you in need of emergency evac?"

Mitch looked all around them. "Negative. Will return on our own."

Brandie lifted herself to her elbows, then to her hands and knees before standing just behind the man she'd trusted with her son. They were surrounded by stars and darkness. Her eyes had already adjusted and she could see the brush and outlines of prickly pear. What she couldn't see was his black heart of betrayal.

"You lied to me."

"I had a backup plan."

"I told you to play this out by their rules, their instructions to the letter. That's what I said and that's what I meant. What part of our instructions said to put a tracking device in with the drugs?"

"Rangers are moving in and might have Toby back any minute. That's what you want. That's what's most important, right? Nothing we did caused King's death or some crazy witch taking—"

"Do you know who has Toby?"

When Rey had her son, she'd been worried and scared. But she'd known he'd keep his word. Or she'd wanted to believe it so badly, she hadn't let herself believe anything else. This was different. They didn't know who had her sweet little boy. It was more real somehow.

"The car's over there. I marked it with my GPS." He pointed, looking at his glowing phone. They walked in silence. She prayed for his cell to buzz good news letting them know Toby was safe.

By the time they sat in the front seat, she knew the Rangers had been unable to rescue him. There was nothing to do this time other than wait. They had given up their leverage when Rey's men had disappeared with the cocaine.

Toby was truly kidnapped.

"Why did they keep him? Are they the same group? Did Rey's men kill their boss just to get him out of the way? What could they want us to do now?"

"I don't know, Brandie."

He started the engine, driving them back to Marfa on the long, deserted road. His cell still hadn't rung. At the stop sign, she put her hand on top of his.

"I know they didn't find Toby."

He shook his head, lips smashed flat into a straight line, frowning with his brows just as straight. "I can call to see what happened."

"He's gone. I assume they would have let you know if something had gone wrong. Or if they'd found him."

"I'm pretty sure Cord would have. He was there."

"I see. Would you take me home now?"

He squeezed her hand, and she didn't react. Ten more minutes and they were at her home. Her parents' car was still in the driveway along with two Presidio County vehicles.

He parked his car, and she stopped him after he cracked his door open. With the dash lights on, she got a good look at his worried, anxious expression. It didn't matter. She'd made up her mind.

"I know I couldn't have done any of this without your help, Mitch. I wouldn't have found the drugs. I'm not even sure I could have pulled myself together to deliver a million dollars' worth of cocaine to drug dealers. But as much as I appreciate your help, you need to stay away from me."

"I don't understand."

Swirling beams shooting Christmas tree colors across her humble home pulled up behind them. The sheriff had arrived. The lights bounced around the neighborhood and off the rearview mirror, blinding her a bit. But she looked at Mitch, her heart more than a little broken at how he'd disregarded her feelings.

"It's not just you. I'm telling Pete the same thing. And if Cord comes around, he'll be next."

"You're in shock or something. You can't send all of us away. You need us to get Toby back."

"You're the reason he's gone!" she shouted, unable to control herself. Stopping. She laced her fingers together to stop the nervous habit of twisting whatever material was available around her finger. She wouldn't be calm until Toby was safe and back in her arms.

"You need to rethink this."

She quickly stared at her hands instead of the confusion on his face. "I know I'm perfectly within my rights. I'm listening to the kidnappers. You already know I'll do anything they want in order to get Toby back. Kicking you all out will prove that."

"Okay, we'll get rid of the cops, but you can't do this by yourself, Brandie."

Pete tapped on her window, and she pushed open her door. "You okay?" he asked. "We need to ask you about what happened out there."

"I've got nothing to say." She pushed by him and ran up the steps. Her dad already had the door open. "Out!" she yelled at the deputies. "Everybody get out of my house."

Her father held open his arms, and she ran to them. No matter what, being held by family was a sure way to feel protected. She needed that. Her mother joined them, encasing her tight in another set of arms. They all cried in the one living room corner free of gadgets.

She cried until she couldn't stand any longer. Her parents helped her to the couch. When she looked up, the three men she wanted to see the least stood in front of her. Almost identical in stature and mannerisms with their arms crossed.

"You aren't going to change my mind."

"You need everybody working on your side. Don't send us away." Mitch stood in the middle. His eyes looked a few years younger, but they also seemed a lot angrier.

She looked straight at him, hoping she could match his anger even with her eyes puffy. "You broke your word to me. You promised you'd do things my way without their help. Trackers, Rangers following them. They knew. They shot Rey."

"I kept my word. No one knew until the last minute. I already had everything I needed and let them know the tracking frequency through a secure email." Mitch took a step forward. Each arm was locked in the grip of the lawmen on either side of him, preventing his advancement.

"What's going on here?" her dad asked. Her mom was as silent as ever, but still had her arms protectively around Brandie.

"Mitch is—"

"Wait," Cord cut her off. He turned to the deputies who had been monitoring for a ransom phone call. "Give us the room." Once they'd gone outside and the Ranger had shut the door he said, "There are three people other than our captain who know Mitch is undercover."

"What?" her parents asked together.

"Mitch is an undercover Texas Ranger," Brandie said with a little too much glee in her voice. She was proud of his hidden occupation, even if she didn't want him around any longer. The surprised look on her father's face seemed like vindication somehow. He was far from an authority on people and it gave her a spark of happiness that he had to rethink his opinions about her mechanic.

"Did they do something that caused Toby not to be

released?" her mom said quietly. "Pete came and told us where you were. Is that why you don't want them here?"

"Yes."

"No."

Mitch had answered at the same time. Her mother looked at her, another tear fell from the corner of her eye. "Bud, get them out of here, please."

Her father stood, pointing to the door.

"This is a mistake," Mitch said again. "I can help. They can't know—"

"Get your stuff out of the garage. Lock the keys inside."

"Brandie?"

She made the mistake of looking into his pleading eyes as the other men physically hauled him from the house. She covered her face, replacing the memory of his pleading look with Rey's death stare. She'd never let that happen to Toby. Never!

Chapter Seventeen

"Hand over the impact wrench." Mitch used a low, threatening voice, but he didn't think the sheriff was listening.

"The owner instructed you to collect your things and lock the place up. I have to make sure that happens." But Pete slapped the wrench into Mitch's palm, then turned to Cord. "I assume you'll be watching Brandie and her parents. You'll keep me in the loop?"

"As much as I'm allowed."

"I'm. Not. Leaving." Mitch stated each word, securing a screw into the steel plates between each. The garage floor was safe to walk on again. He finished with more determination to retrieve Toby unharmed.

The look of disappointment on Brandie's face had cut him as surely as any blade.

"You've been ordered to return to Austin for reassignment." Cord pushed his worn Stetson off the back of his head with one hand and clawed at his hair with the other.

Mitch stowed the tools he'd been using. He ignored his two escorts and picked up parts lying on the garage floor from the break-in, stacking them on the shelves. It bugged him to see his garage in such a sloppy state.

Several boxes later it hit him that he thought of this place as his. That was, his and Brandie's. He clutched an air filter in his right hand and grabbed the metal shelving with his left trying not to fall as the enormity of the situation hit him.

The pain in his chest was from holding his breath. The pain in his jaw was from gritting his teeth. The blurring of his vision couldn't be from his eyes watering. He dropped the box and used the back of his sleeve to wipe his face.

A friendly couple of slaps on his back got a regular beat back to his aching heart. Toby was kidnapped.

"There's not a damn thing I can do," he mumbled. "I never thought he'd…"

The emotion crushing down on him like a vise was more than an undercover Ranger should feel. It was more than a friend felt for someone's missing child. That instance was full of the realization that Brandie and her son meant more to him than anything else.

And just like Brandie, he was willing to do anything to get him back. He'd fight to stay in Marfa. Even knowing that Brandie would never forgive him, he knew he had to stay.

"Look, man—" Cord's voice was full of empathy "—we've both been where you're at. Pete, you should know that my source who helped find your fiancée was Mitch."

"When those bastards took Andrea, I thought I'd go insane before I found her. Can't imagine it being a kid."

"You know we'll find Toby," Cord said.

Mitch clapped his arm on his superior's shoulder, locking gazes with him. "Get me reassigned here. I need to see this through."

Cord shook his head. "There's nothing I can do. Your work on the border is too important."

"Then I resign."

"You don't want to do that," Cord said.

Mitch caught Pete's uncharacteristic tension with his peripheral vision as the sheriff paced behind them. Would he have to fight both of them off to get back to Brandie? Or would they bend the rules to get back her son?

"I don't have a choice. I have to get Toby back."

IF HER FATHER didn't find something to occupy his time now that the deputies were gone, she might have to go stay at the café by herself. Every few minutes he had another question about Mitch that she didn't know the answer to—or at least she knew very few truths about him.

Once she'd convinced him that she'd only known since the night Rey's men had come to his house, her father withdrew to the kitchen to bother her mom awhile.

Brandie watched her mother fold the last of Toby's clothes and stack them in the laundry basket. The house was spotless. That's what her mother had been doing while waiting. Cleaning, cleaning and cleaning some more.

Now they were all back in her tiny living room wondering what to do. Brandie kept activating her cell screen, expecting a call any minute. She tried to convince herself it was the mystery woman she wanted to hear, but that wasn't the truth. She wanted Mitch to be on the other end.

She'd brought up his face several times on her screen

and was one swipe away from asking him to come back. "What do I know about kidnappers or getting Toby back? This is all my fault. I can't think straight long enough to figure out how to fix it."

"I'm sorry, Brandie." Her father's voice was extremely soft, but it wasn't her imagination.

Her mother stopped smoothing Toby's clothes and stared at the other end of the couch where he sat. "What are you sorry for, Bud? You've been sorry a long time and need to actually tell her what you're sorry about."

Her dad's Adam's apple bobbed up and down in his wrinkled neck. "I should never have treated you like I did, Brandie. I was so scared for you when you came home from college. We had such hopes that you'd get out of this little town and do something big with your life."

So had she. For five years he'd blamed her for ruining her life. And now? Why talk about it now?

"At first I was scared people would treat you bad. Then when Toby was born, I was afraid of how they'd treat my fatherless grandson. I wanted everybody to be as proud of him as I was. That's why I started making up stories about his father being a war hero. Can you forgive me?"

"I understood, Dad. I knew I disappointed you."

He knelt by the old rocker, taking her hand in his. "Honey, you've never been a disappointment. Never. You're a hardworking, kind and caring young woman. You're more than an old fart like me deserves."

Her father had always been a man of few words. Other than instructions on how to run the café and garage, this was the longest he'd spoken to her at one time in years. She knew how hard apologizing was for him, so she leaned forward and hugged his neck.

She'd loved him in spite of the hard words he'd said over the past few years. Part of being a family was loving each other no matter what. Both her parents had taught her that. It was something she lived by. A way of life that had kept her going no matter how ugly life got.

Soon they were all in another family hug. She felt happy, frightened, loved yet alone all at the same time. She realized her cell had slid from her lap to the floor when it began vibrating. Her mother picked it up and answered.

"Yes?"

Brandie could make out a deep voice, but not words. She stuck out her hand, but her mother shook her head and continued the conversation.

"That would be fine. We'd appreciate that." She disconnected. "Mitch offered to bring hamburgers from the DQ."

"I don't think that's a good idea."

"I didn't feel like cooking, so I agreed. I'll keep this—" she pocketed Brandie's phone "—so you can't call and cancel our dinner. I'm quite hungry." She lifted the laundry basket to her hip and moved into the short hallway.

"But Mom—"

"Let her go. This is the way she copes."

"Dad, Mitch will try to talk us into doing things his way. And his way involves law enforcement. I have to do whatever the kidnappers say."

"Then we won't let him stay. But like your mother, I

haven't eaten and I'm beginning to feel kind of peckish. A burger sounds good while we're waiting." He winked, then followed her mom to Toby's room.

Waiting for Mitch to pull into the driveway didn't make her anxious. She was relieved for the very reason the talk with her dad had begun. She didn't know what to do. And she didn't know how she'd wait not doing anything at all.

Confused and conflicted. She wished she had someone to talk everything over with, but Mitch had become her best friend. Sadie worked with her almost every morning but they weren't close. Her high-school girlfriends had moved. And she hadn't been in college long enough to make lasting friendships.

She'd grown more dependent on Mitch the past six months than she'd realized. And that's why she felt alone. She recognized the sound of his car's engine a short time later. Prepared to tell him to leave as soon as she said thanks for the burgers, she stood in the middle of the room, ready for his knock.

"Come on in," she called out.

The door opened, and he extended his arm through. His hand held two white sacks. "I didn't have a white flag. You ready to discuss a truce?"

Unable to send him away again, she took one of the sacks and walked it to her son's room. She wanted to cry, but held herself together as her dad took two burgers and proclaimed they were fine where they were.

Brandie had to face him. Her stomach growled at the smell of mustard and onions. She didn't want to be hungry while her son wasn't home, but she hadn't really eaten all day and needed the fuel to function.

Mitch had pulled the burgers out onto the table and opened two bottles of water. "Mind if I join you?"

"Go ahead and sit." Brandie forced every bite down, hoping she wouldn't be sick.

They ate in silence. Then he waved a napkin. "I should have thought of this when I came inside. I didn't know if Bud would have his shotgun ready or not."

"I think Pete took it this morning so he wouldn't accidently shoot someone. I guess if they'd contacted you or you had any news you would have told me when you got here. Right?"

"I would have called you. I wouldn't have waited."

"Was Pete civil when you got your stuff from the garage? Dad asked him to follow you and make sure you left."

"Yeah. But I didn't get anything except a change of clothes and my toothbrush. Everything's locked tight. Alarm's on." He finished his last French fry and licked the salt from his fingers. He must have caught the way she was looking at him because he arched those normally very straight brows.

"Did I really have to say you're fired?"

"Well, that is what I came to talk to you about. See, I sort of quit."

"You can call it anything you want. Hand over my keys." She stood with her hand out, waiting.

"No. Wait. I mean that I resigned from the Texas Rangers. If you still need a mechanic…"

"Why?" she asked, plopping back onto the hard wooden chair.

"I knew you wouldn't keep me around if I didn't."

"But Mitch—"

"We need to find Toby. I can help. I can't if they send me back to Austin." He sat back, crossed his arms, looking firm in his decision to end his career in order to find her son.

"Thank you." He was right. She couldn't think beyond finding Toby. "Where do we start?"

"We wait for a call. In the meantime, we go back to the beginning and see how all these events mesh together. They have to have something in common or be some kind of pattern."

"What if it's days before the woman on the hill calls?"

"Then we'll have longer to think this through, maybe figure out who she is. King couldn't have that many associates. With or without your permission, Cord and Pete are still working on Toby's case. They just aren't working with us."

"Am I wrong? I don't think they'll contact me if they see deputies hanging around the house. I just want him home safe and sound." She just couldn't imagine what might be going through his young mind. "He'll probably toss a fit if he can't take his big boy shower before he goes to bed."

"Big boy? I haven't heard about that."

"Mom was at choir practice when he spent the night a couple of months ago. Dad didn't want to bathe Toby, so he taught him how to take a shower. That's what he's done every night since."

"I don't think he'll get his shower, but I don't think he's being mistreated. King was a blowhard." He gathered the paper and ketchup containers pushing them back into the sack, then tossing it into the waste bin like any man would.

Such an ordinary thing.

"Toby loves you," he said. "He's not going to blame you for this. We'll get him back and he'll be fine."

"I hope you're right, Mitch. I'll never forgive myself if he doesn't come home."

"Neither will I."

Chapter Eighteen

Zubict waltzed through the front door using a key. His audacity made Patrice want to shoot him. Unfortunately, she needed him and would have to play along with his imaginary importance.

"The child is where we discussed?" she asked.

"Of course. Kid cried the whole way. I hope that woman has better luck with him than me. Does Rey got two large sitting under the mattress? She was more expensive than you said."

"I think I can handle a reimbursement. I've made a list of things you should take care of— What are you doing?"

He slipped the last button through its hole. "Taking off my shirt. What's it look like? I figured you'd want some of this." He flexed his slender muscles.

"We have things to do. There's time for that later." She brushed him aside and crossed the room for her notepad. If it weren't for sex the men she knew would have no reason to accomplish anything.

"Hey, ain't you afraid the cops will be showing up here?"

"Why?"

"Rey's dead." He used an incredulous expression as if she were the dumb one.

But she wasn't. She'd convinced Rey to put everything in her name several years ago. "This is my house. No one can trace anything back to me through him." She extended her hand. "You should give me his set of keys."

"Why should I do that?" He shrugged, letting his shirt fall to the carpet.

"Zubict, I could use your assistance." She reached into her handbag on the counter, removing Rey's gift to her. Rey's new Glock 21 .45 ACP was heavier in her hand than she remembered. "But I will shoot you between the eyes if you don't put your shirt back on and give me the keys to my house."

"You are some real piece of work," he said as he followed her instructions.

"Yes, I am. You'll get your cash back when I say you'll get it." She watched him as he tucked the shirt back into his pants. "Let's get on with things, shall we?"

"Your wish is my command."

"Are you familiar with decoys? You are my decoy. While you're in San Angelo, I'll be setting us up a huge score. Bigger than anything I've moved this past year."

"You mean the Chessmen has moved. What you's got to do with it? Rey said we worked for the Chessmen."

"Think whatever you want, Zubict." She flipped her hair over her shoulder and tapped her nails on the counter next to the handgun. "I've made all the arrangements and have a job for you tonight."

Her suppliers had taken notice of her accomplishments. She didn't need the praise of the pawn in front of her. She handed him a piece of paper, ready for his role in this game to end.

"Take the trunk of cocaine to this address in San Angelo."

"That's gonna take me hours. I won't get back 'til late tomorrow." He whined. "You's sure ya can live without me that long?"

"Believe me, I'll make do." His whining reminded her of the character she'd played for Mr. Rook. She loved the burnt orange leather skirt she'd worn. Just watching the games of chess he played improved her game. It would have been fun to pit herself against him. Then again, she had a much riskier game that she'd won—considering he was awaiting trial. Another loose end she'd tucked away.

"How much we chargin' for the bag?" he asked, crossing the room and dropping the strap on his shoulder.

"Nothing. We're returning it. No lip or I'll—"

"Right. I gotcha. Take it. Drop it off. Come back here. No problem."

"Great. Once you do that, we'll be ready for the shipment from Mexico."

"And I suppose you's got it all figured out and don't need no help. So what's in it for me?"

"I chose you over Rey. You know what you'll get when this is over." She pulled his face to hers and kissed him until she felt him harden against her. "Business before pleasure, darling."

"That's right. You just wait until I get back." He staggered backward when she released the sides of his face. His slick-soled Italian loafers slid across the carpet, back farther until his hand found the knob. He left with a fool of a grin on his drooling face.

She turned the dead bolt. Zubict wouldn't be returning. The buyers in San Angelo had agreed to take care of that loose end for her.

The organization she'd been working with for the past year had offered her a position. She was leaving Alpine and West Texas for good. Leaving the dust, the emptiness, the morons who were Rey's friends and hit on her every time his back was turned.

This paltry little house was a shack compared to what she'd be living in next week. Just one thing was in her way. She glanced at the chessboard and the unfinished game that Rey had been playing against an unknown opponent.

Switching the CD player to her music, she twisted the knob as loud as her ears could stand it. The neighbors were far enough away and used to the loud bass reverb powering from her speakers. She reset the Civil War chess pieces on their squares. The silver-based pieces representing the south called to her. It was illogical—everyone knew that the south lost.

This time, in her game, they would definitely win. She removed three pieces from the north. After all, she'd removed them from her game board in real life. Just a few more details and everything would be perfect.

Now what had she done with that leather skirt and jacket?

Chapter Nineteen

"Why haven't they called?" Brandie chanted from the bed. She clasped her cell between her palms as if she were praying with it, then twisted the small blanket as she flipped to her other side.

Mitch watched her grow more upset as the sun rose higher in the sky. She hadn't slept and as a result of her staying awake, he'd been awake all night, as well. He wasn't taking any chances with her safety.

Not after that unknown witch on the mesa had shot King before he could say a word. One second the man opened his mouth to speak and the next he fell to the ground with a hole in his chest. Mitch didn't try to convince Brandie to leave her house for a safer venue. Nope, she needed to be close to her son's things. Even he could see that.

She'd curled up on Toby's bed, and he'd set his butt on a cushion with his back against the bedroom door. He faced the window, ready for an intruder. No one was getting to her and that included her parents who had stayed over and slept in Brandie's room. She didn't have to face anyone until she was ready.

If they hadn't already been awake, the texts and messages from Cord would have awakened him every hour.

He'd ignored them all along with an occasional text from Pete asking for updates. He'd wait, talk things over with Brandie and see if she wanted them in the loop. Or if she wanted their help.

At the moment the answer was a decisive no.

"Do you still have eggs in the fridge? Since we're up, might as well make breakfast."

She rolled over to face him, one of Toby's stuffed dinosaurs in her arms. "Mom and Dad get up early. They'll take care of things."

"You ready to get up, then?"

"No. Not yet." Her eyes slowly dropped to a half-closed position, then all the way shut.

He took out his cell, responding once to each lawman that he'd get back with them later. He wanted a note-pad and pen because something important was at the edge of his memory. There was something about this puzzle that he couldn't piece together. If he wrote down what he could remember from the case files, maybe he could put questions together that Brandie could answer or allow him to ask Cord about.

"Aren't you tired?" Her words were mumbled into the fuzzy brontosaurus. "You could squeeze in behind me if you want to stretch out."

"I'm fine." He'd be curled much too close to her on that junior-size bed.

"Oh." She shifted closer to the edge next to the wall.

"There's no way I'll fit on that short bed."

"Okay. It was just a thought. Might have been nice."

"Do you want me to hold you?" He was surprised. Totally willing and very surprised. Wait. No way. He was staying put. Not that he couldn't use a few minutes of shut-eye. But Bud Quinn was on the other side of that wall and could come into this room at any moment wanting an update.

"It's probably safer to stay where we are," she whispered.

Bud might have apologized to his daughter, but he still had a hot temper and didn't need to be provoked. Mitch stayed exactly where he was, satisfied that Brandie had thought him holding her would be nice.

They'd get Toby back and send her parents to their own home. Then he'd hold her exactly how he wanted. And that would be skin to silky skin. It wouldn't happen straight away, but when things were back to normal...it wouldn't take long.

He rubbed his eyes, attempting to get the image of a naked Brandie out of his head. It just got more vivid. He needed to think about the case.

First objective—get Toby back. Then figure out how to tell the spitfire hugging a stuffed green fur ball that he was head over heels in love with her.

Yep. One-hundred-percent in love. It was the only thing that explained his actions. Toby might have a daddy crush, as Cord put it, but Mitch definitely had a sexy Brandie crush.

"How long have you been a Ranger?"

He looked up from his phone into her brilliant wide-awake blue eyes. "Just under three years. Almost all that time has been undercover. I was a state trooper before that. And four years with the Austin PD narcotics unit—I joined the force straight out of junior college."

"I don't know anything about you. As often as I wanted to know, I never asked before. I didn't consider it any of my business. Do you have family?"

"No brothers or sisters. My mom and dad are still

around. But they split when I was young. They also fight a lot and it makes it easy to avoid them." Real easy after years of practice.

"So where did you go for Christmas? Did you spend it with friends? When you left for that week, I didn't really think you'd be back." Brandie squished the stuffed toy closer to her breasts.

"I said I would be, but I get it." He had a sudden urge to be a stuffed brontosaurus. "I haven't kept up with many friends. They do most of their talking through social media and in my line of work, that could get me killed."

"So where did you disappear to then?"

"A hellish week of training in Austin. Didn't sleep a wink on that soft hotel bed. Two months on that army cot in the garage and I'm spoiled for life."

"Was it the cot or the smell of grease? So no permanent address?" She smiled softly.

How she could still have a normal conversation with what she'd been through in the past couple of days was beyond his understanding. But that was one of the things he loved about her. One of the reasons he was in love period. He'd never met anyone like her.

"Nope. This is the longest I've been in one spot since I stopped wearing a trooper uniform."

"Do you like it here?"

He liked her. Would go anywhere she wanted to go. Take her and Toby away, or find a quiet, safe place to stay here in Marfa. "Very much."

"You look surprised."

"I sort of am." Now wasn't the time to explain just how surprised he was that he'd fallen in love. "I grew up in the city. But these last three years working in smaller towns has been okay. I like the people here in Marfa. For all the turmoil behind the scenes, it's pretty quiet. Working on a car wins every time if put up against being undercover with dope dealers. I like the challenge of finding the problem and fixing it."

"Did you really walk away from your job last night?"

"Let's just say that I didn't gain any points by not reporting back to headquarters."

She swung her legs over the edge of Toby's dinosaur bedspread. She began to say something several times. Indecisive wasn't her norm. "I, um, need to tell you about Toby's dad. His name was Private Tobias Ryland."

"Okay." Not that it mattered to him. It had never mattered.

"You see, we weren't serious or anything. In fact, we'd only gone on a couple of dates while he was visiting one of his friends in Alpine. I told him I was pregnant after he returned to Fort Hood. His unit shipped out soon after. He was supposed to have added us to his will and stuff like that. Guess he didn't get around to it."

"Did you contact the military? How did you find out he was…dead?"

"His best friend in Alpine called me. I was already back here by then." She paused, smiling with the slightest upturn of her lips. "Thank you, Mitch. I don't have many friends. You coming back to help, well, it just means the world to me."

She stood and put a hand out to help him to his feet.

"I couldn't run back to Austin."

She completely caught him off guard with the kiss. Her hands caught his cheeks and brought his lips to hers, holding him in place. Why his hands cupped her slender fingers against his stubble instead of wrapping around her body, he'd never know. Sooner than he wanted, it was over and she was sinking back to the pads of her feet from her tiptoes.

"Thank you for coming back. I can't ask you to go away and leave us. Toby needs your help." She dropped her arms against her jean-covered thighs. "I need your help. I wouldn't be able to get out of his bed if you weren't here."

"Of course you would." He hooked a strand of her gorgeous red hair behind her ear. "You're the strongest and bravest person I know, Brandie."

She dropped her head to his chest, wrapping her arms around his waist. "What are we going to do if they don't call, Mitch? What are we going to do?"

He tilted her chin back so he could look into her eyes, which were filled with tears again. "We won't stop looking. We'll bring him home. Don't doubt me, Brandie. We will find him."

She stepped back, shoving her hair out of her face, and blew out a long breath. "Tell me how long we wait. *You* make that decision. Do you think we need to bring Pete and Cord back? Just tell me what to do and don't make me decide. It's too hard to think."

"I can do that." Convincing her parents that he was capable of making decisions might be another story. "But to be honest, Pete and Cord didn't stop because you told them to. They're still looking. Ready to get started?"

"I'm going to grab a quick shower before I face my parents."

"I'm grabbing coffee."

The smell of bacon and eggs filled his nostrils. He was a lot hungrier than he wanted to admit.

Olivia was in the kitchen, her apron on top of her

clothes. She'd made a breakfast casserole and was scooping out the first spoonful for Bud.

"Good morning, Mitch. I can fix you regular eggs if you prefer them."

"Is that the recipe they serve at the café?"

"Sure is."

"I can't get enough of that stuff. Load me up with as much as you can spare."

"You're a lucky young buck not having to worry about cholesterol." Bud forked a bite into his mouth. "No real bacon. No fried eggs. How'd you sleep?"

Brandie's father didn't pause between bites or questions.

"I didn't, sir."

Olivia set his plate in front of him along with a large cup of coffee.

"That going to be good for my daughter if you're called into action today when you find my grandson?" Bud set the fork down and crossed his arms on the edge of the table, leaning forward.

Mitch could finally see through the rough edges. Bud Quinn's eyes were just as puffy as Olivia's. They'd been crying. They were worried and scared. Everybody was doing the best they could.

"I've gone without sleep before. I give you my word that I'll bring Toby home."

"I'm going to hold you to that, son."

"So am I, sir."

He'd finished half his plate when Brandie joined them wearing the worn jeans he loved. The old T-shirt was worn through in places but she had a tank on under it. Bud harrumphed, letting Mitch know that he'd seen the way he'd looked at his daughter.

"Are you really going to wear that, sweetheart?" her mom asked. "What if someone stops by?"

"Don't worry, Momma. I'll be working at the café getting it cleaned up. I'll go nuts if I just sit here waiting."

"We'll hold down the fort here, then," she announced.

"You ready?" Brandie asked.

The last bite went into his mouth, he gulped the last sip of coffee and they were soon climbing into his car.

He shifted into gear and teased, "So much for me making the decisions."

Chapter Twenty

The cleaning was going well. Most of the broken stuff was in a pile at the back of the garage. Two hours of physical labor and no sleep had Brandie ready for a nap.

"I have no idea how I'm going to work repairs into the budget." She barely got the words out before a yawn overtook her.

"I can help."

"Oh, no. Dad and I will figure it out with the insurance company." She picked some of the glass pieces out of the jukebox. It crushed her heart to lose this antique. "Did I ever tell you that this jukebox is how my dad first spoke with my mom? She was looking at the songs and he asked her if she liked traditional rock or country."

"I wonder if someone can restore it?"

"Oh, I can't afford that. You know we're barely treading water around here. I have to get this place open again soon or there's no reason to try." She sat in a clean booth, suddenly so tired she could barely move.

"Why don't you lie down awhile?"

"There's so much to do. And what if that woman calls?"

She checked the volume on her cell again to verify she hadn't switched it to vibrate or mute. It was as loud as it would go. The background picture of Toby with his favorite dinosaur made her choke up. She wouldn't cry again. She didn't have the strength.

"Don't worry, I'll wake you up." Mitch scooped her from the vinyl seat and carried her to his comfy cot.

The lack of sleep had definitely caught up with her. Her arms were too heavy to lift. She barely got one crooked under her head before the faint sounds from the café faded into complete silence.

Brandie woke with a start. Voices—lots of them—broke into her dream of pushing Toby on his swing in the backyard. In the dream she'd gone from laughing with her son to having her numb hands tied to the posts. Fighting the pins and needles shooting through her arm, she pushed herself to a sitting position, her arm waking from sleep a second later. She recognized those voices.

"Why's he being so stubborn? He's put his entire career at risk. Does he plan on confronting the kidnappers alone?" Cord answered from inside the café.

"They wouldn't be here if they'd heard from the kidnappers. Any word on the missing drugs?" Pete asked.

"Never even found the device Mitch put inside the duffel lining."

"Did you try tracking them the old-fashioned way?" Nick Burke's voice was as quiet as usual, but she knew what they were talking about. Toby's abductors.

"Hey, you're awake," the sheriff said from the doorway. "Mitch, Brandie's awake."

There was no way to avoid it. She'd given him permission, and Mitch had taken charge. He'd brought the law back on to the case. She had enjoyed the couple of hours of peace they'd had. Even if she'd been worried out of her mind. There would be no getting rid of these guys. Facing the kidnappers alone would be even harder.

"Feel better?" Mitch squeezed past Cord, Pete and Nick. "I told them to wait to move the jukebox. And for the record, there's no news about Toby."

"What are they doing?"

His hair was wet, still dripping enough to dampen his collar. He'd finally showered—he hadn't had time when she'd left the house so quickly and he'd refused to take one here if she was alone.

"They thought it was easier to move the jukebox out through the garage for the guy to pick it up. Andrea found a restorer willing to take it. I didn't think you'd want it to just hit the landfill. Looks like it's going to get stuck to me."

"That's fantastic, but I meant what are they all doing here?" She answered positively, even though it broke her heart to part with the antique. "Did you say Andrea?"

"Yeah. I was surprised. Your friends came to help clean up and get the place open again." He grabbed her hand, excited for once with a smile as big as a canyon.

She jerked him to a stop and whispered, "Mitch, I can't do this now. I don't think I can pretend that nothing's wrong."

"Your *friends* don't expect you to fake anything. They're here to help. Period."

Friends?

They went through the doorway and met a small crowd. Nick Burke and his fiancée, Beth Conrad, stood near the kitchen. Pete and his fiancée, Andrea Allen, were at the counter. Cord was just inside the door looking at his wife, Kate, who sat in a booth with their son.

"We wanted to help clean up, Brandie," said Andrea.

"I hope you don't mind us just barging in." Kate lifted Danver into her arms.

"It's purely selfish on our part," Beth added. "We don't have anywhere to meet while the café is closed."

She was about to lose it. Fall apart. Her seams were coming undone because of their kindness.

"I really don't think this is a good—"

"No. Just say thank-you and let them help." Mitch squeezed her hand, wrapped tight within his own. "You said you wanted me to make some decisions for you. Well, this is the first. And if either of these guys try to talk to you about Toby, they'll have to answer to me."

"Right. I might. Just so I can knock some sense into you." Cord slowly threw a fake punch at Mitch.

"I forced Nick to leave his beloved cows for the afternoon. But seriously, Brandie. Just say the word and we'll head back to the ranch," Beth said.

"We're not here in a law enforcement capacity," Cord added. "We realize the kidnapper might not see it that way. We've canvassed six blocks and made certain it was clear."

"We just couldn't stand you facing all this alone," Andrea said.

A quick look around the room showed her how valuable their help had already been. Everything was in order, but the friendship they were offering meant so much more. "Please stay. I'll see if I can get some food together."

"Oh, no, you don't." Andrea dashed to her side and gently tugged her to Kate's booth. "We're taking care of food and cleanup. You just sit down and don't worry about a thing. Maybe you can play with Danver so Kate can help me finish the storage room."

Friends.

Mitch slid into the booth next to her, leaning on the table, that grin still on his face. "You're surprised."

"To say the least." She raised her voice so they could all hear her. "I can't say thank-you enough."

"It's the least we can do. We love this place as much as we love you, Brandie." Kate put her son back in his seat.

The memories of Toby at that age swept her back. He'd spent most of his days in a playpen or swinging chair until he'd turned four and started at the day care.

"Oh, yeah, Sadie stopped by." Mitch's smile disappeared. "She said she was here to help, but she sure wasn't dressed for it. Took off when Andrea and Pete pulled up, but she left you a note. It's in the garage office."

He seemed relieved that she hadn't stayed. Come to think of it, at times he'd gone out of his way to avoid Sadie.

"Is that who that was? I thought there was something familiar about her," Beth said through the service window in the kitchen. "I saw those expensive heels and leather skirt and just didn't think of your waitress."

Kate tapped her bright pink nails on the table. "That's weird. I recognized her wig, but the way she was dressed, it never clicked the woman was Sadie."

"Wig?" the people in the room asked together.

Kate looked up, surprised everyone didn't have that piece of information stored in their brain. "You guys really never noticed? It's a very good wig, but it slipped one afternoon a couple of weeks ago. From my angle in the booth I could see her real hair sticking out around her neck."

"How could I have missed a wig? All this West Texas dust has clogged up my detective skills." Beth laughed at her own joke.

Everybody knew she was the DEA's representative in West Texas. She and Pete had both been abducted into Mexico just before Christmas. Mitch moved over to talk with the men and the women gleefully joined her in the booth.

"Like I said, it was a really good wig. But her hair's a beautiful color so I have no idea why she wears it," Kate said quietly.

"Well, I wouldn't know." Andrea played with her multiple necklaces. "She avoids me like the plague. Pete teased that she was afraid of mouthy women."

They all laughed, but Brandie kept her head down, trying to avoid the conversation. She'd seen Sadie without the wig and didn't know if her waitress would want so many people knowing, especially the county sheriff.

"Brandie, you look as guilty as sin. You already knew about the wig, didn't you? Do you know why she wears it?" Andrea asked bluntly, which was her way.

"I shouldn't say anything. It's sort of private."

"Was it breast cancer?" Kate asked.

"That was the first thing I thought until I saw how long her hair was. She told me she had a violent ex-boyfriend." Brandie lowered her voice. It somehow made it feel less gossipy to talk about Sadie if all the guys couldn't hear.

"Oh, my, a waitress in hiding with a mysterious backstory. I'm intrigued." Andrea whispered, too.

The men cleared a path for the jukebox. They joked like it was a normal day. But it wasn't. Their body lan-

guage was sharp and on edge. Tensions were high waiting on a call that may or may not come.

"Did she mention anything else?" Andrea nudged
her in the side.

"Just that she needed the extra money."

"If I knew the tips were that good here, I would have
taken a job months ago. That was a real leather jacket
and skirt. Not to mention the matching Louis Vuitton
bag and shoes." Beth looked around the booth at their
questioning faces. "What? I happen to like expensive
shoes."

"They were probably knockoffs, right? You can't be
certain they were the real thing." Brandie had a hard
time believing Sadie had been dressed so nicely. "She
was constantly suggesting I take off early so she could
close up the café and get a couple of extra tips. Why
would she work here if she didn't need the money?"

The three other women looked directly at Mitch who
was helping maneuver the jukebox through the door.
His lean muscles bulged as he lifted and pushed. He
caught her stare and winked at her.

"She didn't stand a chance even in that burnt-orange
outfit." Beth leaned across the table to pat Brandie's
hand. "The only person he ever smiles for is you. And
honey, I was a foot model. Those shoes were the real
deal."

"Wait a minute. Beth, are you sure about that color?"
Andrea asked.

"Very sure. It was exactly the shade of your college
hoodie, Kate. I wouldn't have noticed if she hadn't been
wearing those studded rolling boots. They're sixteen-
hundred-dollar shoes." Beth twisted her long black hair

around her finger. "Whoever that violent ex-boyfriend was he certainly had money."

"It can't be possible." Andrea grabbed Brandie's hand, gripping it anxiously. "Was Sadie's real hair color platinum-blond?"

"Yes."

"Pete! Oh, my gosh! Pete get in here!" Andrea jumped up from the table, impatient for the sheriff to return. "I think she's that woman who was working with Rook the night he tried to blackmail my dad."

Brandie's heart latched on to the hope that the nightmare might actually be over soon.

MITCH JUMPED BACK into the café with his heart racing. He hadn't heard a cell ring, but he was certain something had happened. Brandie was as white as a sheet.

"Do you have an address for Sadie, and her last name?" Andrea asked.

"I think she said she lives in Alpine, but it would be on her application," Mitch answered, not understanding why they wanted to know about Sadie.

"What's the matter?" Pete asked, finally pushing past the jukebox.

"Remember that blonde I described who was taking orders from Rook? It's Sadie. At least I think she's the same chick." Andrea was as excited as a little kid on their birthday.

"You said she had long blond hair," the sheriff said.

"She does. That's what we were just talking about. Sadie has long blond hair. That's the reason she never waited on me. She knew I could identify her." Andrea noticed Brandie's shaking hands and slid back into the booth.

"There was a tall blonde woman at Bishop's place," Nick added from the garage.

"The woman who took Toby stood just as tall as Zubict on that ridge. That would make her at least five-ten or eleven. It sure looked like she was a blonde." Mitch couldn't believe it.

"Sadie's about that tall with the shoes she wears," Brandie whispered, but everyone was quiet enough to hear her.

"Give me her address and I'll get the local PD to bring her in for questioning," Cord said to Mitch as he came into the café.

Mitch knew where the employee records were. It was a good thing Brandie didn't have to tell him since she looked like she was about to be sick. How could Sadie be involved in Toby's kidnapping or in Beth or Andrea's abductions and still be bold enough to wait tables on the very people she should be afraid of?

Mitch handed Cord the application, and the Ranger stepped out the front door to make the call. Mitch couldn't get to Brandie. Andrea had an arm around her shoulders. Exactly where he wanted to be.

"You really think it's possible that this woman was working with Jones, Lopez and Rey?" Pete asked.

"You mean Rook, Bishop and King," Mitch confirmed.

"Right. They used code names, but their fingerprints match them to the Mexican and FBI criminal database. Rey used both translations of his name. The arrogant bastard went by King King," Pete said.

"They're all chess pieces," Mitch mumbled.

"Both men had multiple chess boards at their haciendas. We know that Rook was working with a group, but he won't give up anything about them."

"She's been playing us all this time." Mitch hadn't been confronted with anything like this during his career. It was hard to conceive, harder to believe it was real.

"What do you mean?" Beth asked.

"She's been playing everybody, us, these chess men. But what's the most powerful playing piece in chess?"

"The Queen," the group answered.

"Sadie, or whatever her name is…" Brandie said with the barest breath. "She's been in charge all along. She considers herself the Queen."

Sadie's message. What had she said?

"Dammit, what did I do with the note she left? Office." He hit the counter with his palm and locked eyes with the man still on the garage side of the jukebox. "Nick, I tossed the envelope—a blue one like for a card—on top of the loose papers on the garage desk."

"Got it." He took off running.

Looking around the room of intelligent people they all seemed baffled, but no one thought his conclusion was wrong. No one argued a different possibility. They were all just waiting, like him.

Nick had opened the envelope. He handed the card across the jagged glass to Mitch using a work glove.

"It's a drawing. I think it's silos."

"That's it? She doesn't mention Toby? Or any exchange? Or demand what she wants? Are you sure there's nothing else in the envelope?" Brandie pulled her hair back, landing her hands around her neck. Cutting herself off from comforting gestures Andrea tried to offer.

"Sorry. Nothing."

"Show it to us," Brandie said. "I don't understand. Is that where Toby is?"

The women tried to calm her down. Cord took a picture with his cell, and Pete grabbed something to substitute for an evidence bag. Nick pulled while Mitch shoved at the stuck jukebox.

Mitch shoved harder. And harder again. Receiving a strange look from Nick when he threw up his hands and backed away.

"Hey, man. Maybe this isn't a good idea right now," Nick said. "You don't want to wreck it more."

"Dammit!" Mitch wanted to punch something. The anger and frustration he felt had nothing to do with a stuck antique. "We're not going to get a phone call. It's a riddle and if we're going to get Toby back, we have to solve it."

Chapter Twenty-One

"That was Alpine PD. No one matching Sadie's description lives at the address on her application. That would have been too easy. I had another message. Your man Gary Zubict was found dead from a drive-by in San Angelo." Cord closed his notebook and stuck it in his pocket.

Mitch had ducked out of the café to wait with Cord. The energy inside had gone from overly excited to flat and pensive. They all realized—especially Brandie—that knowing Sadie was involved didn't change the fact that the woman still had Toby.

"If she was taking care of loose ends like Zubict, why risk coming here? What was so important about this note that she had to deliver it herself?" Mitch was still baffled. The picture made no sense. "What the hell does she want with the kid?"

Cord looked past him, indicating the open door where Brandie stood.

"I want to know the answer to that myself," she said, standing next to him.

Mitch wrapped his arm around her shoulders, drawing her close to his side.

Brandie must have seen the way Cord shot his evil-eye warning. She pulled away to lean on the awning post, hands around the back of her neck, as tense as always.

"Silos in this country are few and far between. It will take us hours to check them all out." Brandie grabbed the drawing. "I don't know what to do."

Cord pulled out the notepad again. "Let's go with your theory, Mitch. If Sadie considers herself the Queen and smarter than us, then why did she set up all her men to fail? Hell, she had King shot in the back in front of you."

"It sounds like she's running the board. Taking out all the major pieces one at a time. She had us do it for her with Rook and Bishop. At each abduction we confiscated what we thought were major gun shipments. While we're dealing with one set of problems—"

"That's when we discover a second shipment heading across the border," Cord finished.

"Wherever she has us looking for Toby…"

"Yeah, you're right." Cord slapped him on the back, took out his cell and started dialing as he walked to his truck.

"What did you two just figure out?" Brandie asked.

"She's using the hunt for Toby as a distraction."

"Sure doesn't feel like a distraction."

"You called your parents? I'm surprised they're not here already."

"We convinced them there might be a message or phone call at home. But everyone knows there won't be." Her cell was still in her hand. "That picture. Does it seem kind of amateurish to you? As if it weren't thought out ahead of time?"

"Yeah, kind of last-minute, which doesn't match

the profile of a meticulous planner." He reached for Brandie, but she paced in the opposite direction. "So maybe Toby's kidnapping isn't a part of her plan."

"I know how to find her." Beth burst through the café door. "The shoes. We can track her by her sixteen-hundred-dollar shoes. There's got to be a record of a sale."

The buzz returned as they went back inside. He waited, holding the door for Brandie. He was just opening his mouth to tell her to ignore Cord when she placed a hand on his chest.

"I think we should put a little space between us. It's hard enough functioning with Toby gone. I can't handle the questions and the looks. Let's keep our focus on finding him. And I mean everyone's focus. Don't you think *we* can and should wait?" she whispered as the group got quiet.

"Sure." He agreed, wanting the exact opposite.

Brandie's whole existence was wrapped around what other people thought. She needed to think about herself and believe that her true friends would love her no matter what. But he'd respect her decision. He had no right not to. No matter what fantasy was in his head about their relationship.

"PETE, AS MUCH as I love you, sweetie, I can't do any research with that archaic computer system at the courthouse." Andrea gathered her things. "We'll be at the house where I have a very competent system and high-speed internet."

Brandie still stood around without a job. She absent-mindedly picked up a few things and made another pile of broken objects. She wanted answers, and everyone was trying to get them. The least she could do was appreciate all their assistance.

"Thanks for helping, Andrea. I'd be helpless researching on a computer." Brandie felt out of her element. Everyone was busy, but her best skill was running a café.

"I'm glad I learned something after three higher education degrees." She laughed and joined Pete. "I'll locate the silos and the future hubby over here will coordinate a search."

While Kate spoke in a low voice to Cord, Beth was hopelessly attempting to strap Danver into his seat.

"Here, let me get that." Brandie took pity on her, but secretly thanked her that she had something to occupy her hands.

"Thanks. I've been practicing and still can't get the hang of this thing. Nick will be the designated car seat guru in our household."

"Are you two…?" Brandie pointed to Danver.

"Oh, no, sorry. The wedding's planned for my mom and dad's summer break at the university. He wanted a short engagement, but I never imagined spring on a ranch could be so all consuming." She looped the diaper bag over her shoulder. "You ready to go?"

"I'm staying here. If they won't let me search for Toby, then I'm staying here."

"That's not what—"

"Right. But *I* decided to stay. I appreciate that everyone thinks I'll be safer there with you. But Sadie's not trying to kill me and if she wants to get in touch, I want to be close. I'll feel like I'm contributing."

Beth cupped her hands around Brandie's shoulders, the most sincere look on her face. "Then I'll stay here.

Is that okay with you? I can do everything with Andrea by phone."

"Sadie pretended to be my friend while she was spying, learning our secrets and doing I don't know what. If she doesn't want anything from me then why hasn't she called? Do you think it's because you're all here? Maybe she still has someone watching us?"

"It's possible, but Pete has deputies patrolling close by. They would have seen someone who doesn't belong in town," Beth said. "I'll stay, okay?"

"I'd cry my appreciation, but I don't have any more tears. They're all gone. I just know I'd go crazy forty-five minutes from town."

"That's okay. You're saving me. If I went with Kate and Andrea I'd be in tears, too. I think Nick asked her to show me how to change a diaper." She laughed.

Beth laughed a lot more now than when she'd first arrived in Marfa. She was good for Nick who seemed back to his old self after being shot over a year ago. Andrea and Pete were good together. Kate and Cord were icons. She wanted that type of love.

The real kind that took in each other's strengths and weaknesses. Her mom and dad loved each other, but it was totally different from what these three couples had.

Mitch looked her direction. She needed to tell him she wasn't leaving. He'd be upset and want to stay. *So let him.* Her inner voice was telling her she deserved him and all the comfort that he brought her. But Toby deserved his skill.

"Everyone knows what to do?" Cord asked. "Pete will handle all the coordination. His deputies are searching for twin water cisterns. There are a lot more of those around here than silos. If they find anything, he'll contact you, Brandie."

"Our primary objective is to find Toby," Mitch said.

Brandie's pocket vibrated and tweeted indicating she had a text message. Everyone held their breath while she slid her finger across the screen. "It's my mom. Excuse me a second." She went into the storage room and called as her mom had asked.

"I know you said you'd call when you had more information, but Sadie asked me to pass along a message."

Her heart stopped. She couldn't feel it beating in her chest. If the woman had called her mother, then she hadn't wanted the people in that room to know.

"What...what did she say?"

"She just wants you to call her when you have a moment alone, but she left a new number."

"Would you text it to me, Mom?" She was glad her mother didn't know about Sadie's betrayal yet. It was the only way they'd both stayed calm.

"Sure. Are you all right, honey? Want me to come to the café? I could fix lunch for everyone."

"No, ma'am. They're about to leave. I'll be... I'm going to...to, um, the courthouse. They think I'll be safe while they follow up on some leads." She fibbed to ease her mother's mind.

"That's good. You shouldn't be alone. I'll text this to you. Just let me know if you need me. I love you."

"Bye. Love you, too."

Brandie did feel alone. As much as she didn't want to make decisions, that's exactly what she had to do. Tell Mitch? Not tell Mitch? She couldn't risk it. After they all left, she'd call Sadie and do whatever that horrible witch said to do if it would get her son back.

"You okay?" Mitch asked. "I was just locking up when Beth said you guys were staying."

"That's right."

"I'd feel more comfortable if I hung around, too, then."

"Honestly, you're taking being in charge of me way too seriously." She had to get rid of him. He'd never leave her alone long enough to make the call or allow her to meet Sadie. "Don't worry about me and just go do your job. You are still a Texas Ranger, right? It certainly doesn't seem like you quit. You probably lied about that so you could keep tabs on me."

"Brandie, what's going on? Who were you talking to?"

"My mother. See? You are not responsible for me. I take it back. I hate other people always making decisions for me. Hate it." She raised her voice and shoved past him back into the dining area.

"Not a problem. But I'm not falling for it. It's too convenient. Let me see your phone."

"We're friends, Mitch. You really don't get it, do you?"

"I don't believe that you got a phone call and suddenly you can't stand me."

"So now I'm a liar and don't know my own feelings?" She had to hold it together. "See for yourself. It was my mom. No one ordered me to do anything. I just came to my senses. I don't like all the looks and everyone assuming we're a couple."

Mitch checked out her call history. Deep confusion was in his eyes when he locked eyes with her and returned her phone. "I'm sorry. I…"

"Should have believed me?" She slipped her finger over the volume button and turned the phone to silent so when the text from her mom came through, no one would know. "I get enough of that at home."

The horrible implied meaning, accusing him of being like her father, was loud and clear to him. He stood straighter. Stiff. Lips flattened just like when he'd first worked for her and watched everything from a distance.

Would he forgive her? If she came home with Toby, maybe he would. If she helped Sadie with drugs or guns…would he forgive her then? It went against everything he'd been working for his entire adult life. But she didn't have a choice. She had to choose Toby even if she loved Mitch.

She drew in a sharp breath at the realization of just how much she loved them both. They'd slowly become a family over the past six months. Mitch was everything she wanted. Nothing like her father as she'd implied. He'd proven that to her, even while doing his job as a Ranger.

"I'm sorry, too. If I had cooperated yesterday we could have prevented most of this misunderstanding. You would have figured out it was Sadie before she came here today." *Remain strong. Don't let him see how sorry you really are.*

She followed him through the door, standing in front of the café. The thing that had been all-consuming until a few days ago. She could lose the family business, but she couldn't lose her family.

"It was Andrea who put everything together, not me. Those women wouldn't have been here to talk if you hadn't kicked us out. I guess everything happened just like it was supposed to." Mitch had a sad look in his eyes. "I know things aren't right between us."

"I think Cord's waiting on you."

"I just want to say that you're, uh… You really are the strongest and bravest person I've met. You'll get through this just fine and so will Toby. We'll find him and I'll be out of your hair for good."

He gently tugged her hand from massaging her neck. He kissed it, squeezed it and walked away.

"WHAT'S THAT ALL ABOUT? Isn't she coming?" Cord asked in the truck.

"Drive around the block and let me out back." Mitch could tell when Brandie was lying. Her mom had called, but something was wrong. Brandie had changed after that.

"You going to tell me why?"

"You need to check on the Quinns or send a deputy. Someone might be in Brandie's house, using their phones."

"You think Sadie was in touch with Brandie? I think she articulated exactly why she didn't want you around."

"Articulate all you want. I've been around Brandie a lot of hours in the past six months. She's lying. I just don't know why." Mitch felt her lack of trust like a knife twisting from his belly to his backbone.

"I told you not to get too involved. It always complicates things."

"You told me not to get involved with a suspect. Brandie's not a suspect."

"And that's part of your problem, Mitch. You weren't and still aren't looking at the facts." Cord stopped the truck on the back side of the garage. "Brandie's given us plenty of reasons not to trust her, to doubt her story. We still don't know how or why King was able to blackmail her."

"It was a legit reason to her."

"She told you." He put the truck in Park, throwing an arm across the top of the seat. "But you aren't going to tell me. Dammit, Lieutenant. I imagine ordering you to disclose the information won't do me a hell of a lot of good? At least tell me if it's relative to any possible shipment that's—"

"No, sir. It's a private matter."

"You're going to follow her?"

"I'm burnin' daylight, sir."

"Get out of my truck." Cord lowered the window as Mitch shut the door. "Pete's got a deputy posted to make sure she stays put. And Beth's inside. Oh, and Mitch? I hope she is lying. You two are good together."

Chapter Twenty-Two

Mitch planned to follow Brandie when she left the garage. He assumed she'd get a phone call blackmailing her to do something questionable. Every part of his investigative ability told him that. His stubborn boss was bound to get herself into a boatload of trouble attempting to get her son back on her own.

It wouldn't take long. Sadie—or whatever her name was—had gotten to her. He didn't blame Brandie for any of it. He'd do anything for Toby, too. Anything.

Mitch heard car tires crunching the gravel lot and ducked to the edge of the building behind some used tires. If he followed in a car, particularly his car, Brandie would see it for miles. That left him with one choice. He had to get inside Brandie's car, which was still parked in the garage.

Luck was on his side that their argument had interrupted him setting the building alarm. He still had his keys. He snuck inside and then was at a loss how to hide his six-two body in the backseat of a compact car. Unless…

Faster than he thought possible, he popped the hood, disconnected two essential wires and dropped his keys on the desk before running outside again. If Brandie was in a hurry, she wouldn't think twice about borrowing his car. He unlocked the door with the spare he had tied under the frame.

The sleeping bag and stuff they'd taken with them to King's massacre was still in his car and easy to toss over him. He pulled off his jacket, balled it under his head and got as comfortable as he could on the floorboard.

It had only been a few minutes when something tapped the side of the car and he heard keys jingling. The engine purred as she gunned it a couple of times. Beth's voice was outside along with a banging against the windows. "At least let me go with you!" she shouted as Brandie sharply turned right.

Mitch should have removed the gun Cord had loaned him from the small of his back. Every bump the car hit jarred a part of it into his flesh. She moved the seat closer to the wheel, which gave him a little relief. He looked at his watch—five minutes and he should reveal that he was there.

Wait. He needed to know that her phone call wasn't with the kidnappers. His phone was already on silent. He slipped it into his palm, swiped open the camera, hit Record and squeezed it between the seat and the door.

It took two tries, but he hadn't seen her phone. She was completely absorbed in driving the car and looking in the mirror.

"Deputy Hardy, you need to go back to town. We just crossed the county line and okay, that's it. Yep. Head on home now."

Mitch hoped she was talking to herself.

The car sped up and then slammed to a halt. The gun pinched, his legs cramped, his head shook but he kept his mouth shut and his body covered in case she was looking over the seat. He'd never thought of his car as small before. Now he did.

"You can sit up now. Nobody's around."

He sat on the seat, stretching his legs in blessed relief. "When did you know?"

"My car was perfectly fine yesterday. And you would never have left your car keys on the desk." She glared at him in the mirror. "How did you know I was lying?"

"You have a couple of tells. Grabbing your neck for one. That's something you do when you're exhausted, though. The real tell is when you twist your mouth a lot."

"Okay, thanks. I needed to know when I meet the chess Queen. Now get out."

"No way."

"Seriously, Mitch. I can't bring anyone with me. She'll know."

"As far as she knows I'm just a mechanic. I'm not letting you go on your own." Nope. He was with her for the duration. Period.

"She was listening to everything in the café."

Mitch shook his head and leaned through the armrest between the front seats. "Not a chance. She's lying. If they had been, she would have known about the drugs and that we didn't have them. That's just my educated opinion, of course."

"You know, I never asked for your opinion. I was quite happy in my life before all this started in my garage. Totally ignorant of drug smugglers and undercover agents."

"Not leaving the car." He stared at her with his head cocked sideways. She could have injured him pretty badly if she'd used her elbow to hit his face. But she wasn't that kind of woman. She didn't react that way. Oh, wait, she had knocked him out with a lamp.

Either way, it made him more determined to stay. She needed him. He could react quicker and before the thought crossed her mind that she was in danger.

"Even if she explicitly said not to bring anyone?"

He was staying. "What are we supposed to do?"

"I have to call her and let her know I lost whoever they had following me." Her hands flexed around the steering wheel. "I just want it all to end. Can we do that? Can we get my son back and get back to normal?"

"Yes." A pitiful remark bounced into his head. Something about how he was a little hurt that she hadn't trusted him. The serious part of himself that he'd discovered since Cord had used the words *daddy crush* held him back. This wasn't about him. They would get back to normal. That's who they were.

"Then let's call the witch and get on with it," she said.

Before she had her cell in her hand, Mitch's pocket was vibrating. "It's Pete."

"Put it on speaker or you're out of the car."

"Yeah?" he said, holding the cell over the seat back.

"Great, you answered. Put me on speaker if you're still with Brandie," Pete said.

"You already are. What do you need?"

"We have an Alpine address for a Patrice Orlando and we're ninety percent certain it's the blonde we're looking for. Her background and timeline fit. She travels across the border a lot. I've got an Alpine unit heading there now."

"She won't be at her place. She told Brandie to lose the tail and call, indicating she's sending her somewhere else. We're just about to do that. I'll mute my phone so you can listen in."

Brandie dialed.

"It took you long enough. If you want your precious little Toby back with all his fingers and toes, then you'll do exactly what I say. I need you to go to the border station in Presidio. When you arrive, you'll verify that the four women who have listed you as their employer are telling the truth. Give them a ride to the post office."

"Will Toby be waiting for me there?"

"Honey." She stopped to laugh. "Toby's safe for the moment. He thinks he's at summer camp. You get those women to my contact and we'll talk again."

Sadie, also known now as Patrice, disconnected, sounding confident that Brandie would follow through with whatever was commanded.

"Those women are smuggling drugs, aren't they?"

"Most likely." He adjusted the phone between them. "Did you catch all that, Beth?"

"Yes. Brandie, do exactly what she says. I've got this end covered. There will be DEA agents there to follow those women. You won't be breaking the law, you'll be helping us."

"She'll probably have someone watching me once I get to Presidio. I should drop Mitch—"

"I'm staying."

"That's ridiculous. Are the women going to sit on top of you?"

"We'll have the building covered," Beth said. "Brandie, drop him off a couple of blocks from the post office."

"Mind if I ride up front?"

"Sure. I even promise not to leave you on the side of the road."

He was in and out of the car faster than a speeding bullet. "This is weird for me, you know."

"What?"

"I've never ridden in this seat before or in the back-seat for that matter."

"Well, you can't drive to—"

"It's fine. Just…different." Mitch stretched out.

"You should put your seat belt on. You can never tell if aliens will be landing on the highway. Or a deer. Be safe."

"So, do a lot of aliens land in broad daylight?" He buckled up whether he thought he needed to or not. It made her happy. And he liked cheering her up a bit.

"Well, they are more likely to land at night, I'll give you that. Do you have any sunglasses?"

"No, but I do have some very expensive shades." He took the case from the glove compartment, wiped the lenses with the cloth he kept them wrapped inside and handed them to her.

"Nice. They really cut the glare. Why don't you wear these all the time? Instead of the ten-dollar pair you usually have."

"We're closing in on Patrice Orlando because of her shoes. I didn't think that a two-hundred-dollar pair of shades fit my nomad mechanic background."

"Smart, but I might just steal these."

"I'll buy you your own pair." He could. He'd been collecting a paycheck for almost three years with no expenses.

She swished her head quickly to the side and the glasses slid down her nose. Instead of the cute O-shaped lips he thought he'd see, she scrunched up her nose to stop their descent.

"You will not spend that kind of money on me for a pair of sunglasses."

"But you like them."

She shook her head and her free hand shot up behind her neck. "Stop kidding around and tell me what I need to know when we get to Presidio. You have about forty minutes to turn me into a secret agent."

He stared at her, surprised by how her words affected him. She'd probably meant it to be funny. But he was suddenly frightened like he'd never been before. He'd had years of driving highways by himself, pulling over drunks or drug dealers. He'd been cautious but not frightened.

The thought that Brandie would be in the middle of everything. That she'd run into any type of fight to protect Toby at any cost… The thought of losing either one of them chilled him to his marrow.

Chapter Twenty-Three

Mitch had talked for the entire drive, and Brandie had listened. He explained that he knew Presidio, having been on assignment there last fall. They'd taken side street after side street until he'd pointed her back in the right direction. With one turn she'd have a straight shot back to the main road. He was about to be on foot four blocks away from the post office, but said he'd be there in plenty of time to make sure her drop-off went smoothly.

"If you act too calm, then whoever's watching you is going to get suspicious," Mitch told her with his hand on the handle ready to jump from the car. "Remember, there's a company of Texas Rangers looking for Toby. Along with troopers, deputies and everyone else they can snag. You do your part here and we've got your back."

"Andrea is really imposing on her father?" Brandie shook her head, still unable to process what they were all doing for her. "I can't believe she asked Homeland Security to track down Sadie's—I mean, Patrice Orlando's possible family or other real estate. I know everything's being done that can be done."

"I know you probably meant what you said in the

café. I'm not trying to be a dictator. What I'm trying to do—"

"Is save my life and get Toby back." She covered his cheek with her hand, and he leaned into her palm, kissing it. "I'm sorry, I didn't really mean it."

There had been very few kisses between them. How could she know that this man was hers? It probably didn't make sense to the normal couple. But they were like two attracting magnets, unable to stay apart. When he was around, she forced herself to stay away from him. She'd said that she wanted their lives back to normal, but that was far from the truth.

Things had to be different. No more boss lady and mechanic. She wanted him as a boyfriend in every way possible. Even on the way to vouch for illegal alien drug smugglers.

"Will ya kiss me so we can get this part over and done?" She smiled hesitantly, wondering how he'd react or if the request was completely out of line. Then he pulled her to meet him halfway.

His lips slashed across hers—full of tension, control and desire. His tongue slid into her mouth completely at home. It didn't seem like their third or fourth kiss. It seemed like something they'd been sharing every early morning and every late night. Both of them were reluctantly pulling away, putting an end to a very precious moment.

"For the record, *that part* will never be over and done with."

He ducked out of the car and was gone before she had both hands back on the wheel. She pressed the gas and would be at the border station in a matter of minutes. Kissing might not have been the appropriate thing, but it had bolstered her resolve. Had some of his courage shot into her?

Mitch had told her twice how brave he thought she was, how strong. Yet, she was always so frightened. She'd always been frightened of losing everything. Since her mechanic had come to work, she'd grown into that strong woman he saw and encouraged her to be. She parked the car and made it inside because of Mitch's faith.

Her hands shook when she handed her driver's license to be copied and completed the paperwork. The women looked like ordinary teenagers. Brandie assumed they'd been thoroughly searched and must have swallowed the drugs. At least none of them looked ill. They actually didn't look scared or concerned about any part of the process.

They were out the door, one calling "shotgun" as they took off running in their pretty heels and short skirts. The tight-fitting T-shirts showed off slim, young figures. They chattered away in Spanish, not caring who she was or why she was there.

It took only a few minutes to get to the post office. She looked around for a car or someone who was Sadie's contact. But as soon as she parked in a spot, the girls were out the door and waving as they walked in four different directions.

Following them wasn't her responsibility. Toby was. She didn't see anyone moving after the women, but what was she supposed to? If they were covertly there she couldn't tell. She didn't see Mitch, either.

She tapped the leather steering wheel cover with a broken nail. If she'd been in her car, a file would be in the change holder. Waiting on the phone call, she tried to even the ragged edge. She needed someone to tell her what to do past this point. She'd kept her end of the bargain—twice. She'd broken the law—twice. Where was her son?

There wasn't a soul in sight. The street had been empty since the four women had gone their separate ways. She hadn't asked specifically about her next step. Maybe they'd meant to go inside the post office. She cracked the door open and her cell rang, making her jump out of her skin.

"Be at the border station same time tomorrow."

"Sadie, please. Please tell me where Toby is. He must be scared. I promise to do anything you need me to do. I'm begging you to give him back."

"You have too many law enforcement friends, Brandie. I'll call tomorrow with an address. For now… he's safe and one more night away from you is just an adventure." She disconnected.

"No!" Brandie threw her cell into the opposite floor-board. "No!" she screamed, hitting the dash with both of her fists. "No, no, no!" She grabbed the wheel and shaking the car. She rested her head on the horn and cried.

She could have sworn that there weren't any tears left, but she'd been wrong. She had to meet Mitch. They had a pre-arranged meeting, and he'd probably been waiting for her a good ten minutes.

The engine of his car reminded her of him. Fine-tuned, quiet and when you stepped on the gas it raced ninety to nothing. He leaned against the wall of the building, head down with a splash of graffiti at his back. She barely braked for a stop before he opened the door and slid down in the seat so he couldn't be seen.

He pushed her phone away from his feet with his boot. "Did she call with a location?"

"No." The single word choked her up, but she kept driving. They were out of Presidio and heading back to Marfa.

"Brandie, pull over. Come on, sweetie, let's slow down."

She glanced at the speedometer. They were going eighty-five. She eased off the gas and slowed, turning to stop on an old overgrown road.

"Sorry."

"I think it's better if I drive us back and you tell me what happened. Let's meet at the hood."

They got out, but all she could think about was wringing that thirty-something-year-old neck. She threw her fisted hands in the air, screaming her frustrations to the late-afternoon sun. A picture-perfect blue-sky day. Ironically, she'd be picking her son up from day care about now.

It was the slowest time at the café so she spent it with Toby.

Mitch handed her a rock as big as her hand. He spun her to face the field. "Throw it."

"What?"

"Just do it."

When she'd let it go like a wimp, he opened her palm and set another giant rock on it. Then another, repeating the process until she was exhausted and tears ran down her face.

Mitch spun her again, but this time he held on to her. She buried her face against the soft comforting cotton of his T-shirt.

"She said nothing. If I want my son back I have to

show up here tomorrow. Do the same thing. What if she says to come back again? How many days do I do this? How many times before Toby gives up that I'm coming to get him?"

His strong arms wrapped her tight. The safer she felt, the worse she felt that Toby wasn't there, too.

"I can't tell you that Toby isn't scared or missing you. You'd never believe me anyway." He spoke above her head. The sun blazed its descent in the sky. "But you know that he loves you. He'll heal. We'll make sure of that."

The sound of a telephone ringing was faint in the background. It took a second for her to realize her cell was in the car. Mitch's cell buzzed in his denim jacket.

"Yeah? Wait and slow down a second. Putting you all on speaker." They ran back to the car so they could hear the conference call.

THEY NEEDED A BREAK in this case. Toby had been missing long enough. No matter how strong Brandie acted, it was still an act. He'd hate to see her shut down like she talked about that morning. He couldn't bear that.

Everyone was finally connected to the call, lots of voices talking to others around them. Mitch and Brandie were silent. Waiting. He tried to be patient and was about to take the phone when she frustratingly spoke up.

"Excuse me. What's going on?"

The voices quieted.

"We've found her. Believe it or not her real name is Patty Johnson aka Patrice Orlando, aka Sadie Dillon. She owns a lot of property. One is a newer place where her mother lives in Presidio, 642 Bledsoe Boulevard," Andrea said.

"Do you really think Toby's there?" Brandie asked from the passenger seat, holding the cell between them. "Does anyone know if that's where my son is being held?"

"We're less than ten minutes out." Mitch put the car in gear, the tires spun dirt and dust into the still air. "We'll look. It's worth a try. Sadie, Patrice or Patty—whatever her name is—she doesn't know we're onto her or she would have upped the stakes for Toby's return. She thinks she has all the time in the world. That's why she thinks she can order you back here tomorrow."

"She did what?" Andrea asked.

"We're sending county backup." Pete's connection wasn't as strong, but they still heard him give commands. "You can't go in until I get a team there. If I call Presidio PD they'll go in hot and we'll lose the advantage. We don't want that. You got it?"

"I'm obtaining a search warrant," Cord told them. "We need to be sure about this. Once we go in, our target is going to know everything."

"Okay, we'll watch the place to see if there are any signs of Toby," Mitch told them, knowing in his gut that he wouldn't wait if they saw him. Screw the case. He and Brandie weren't taking any chances with a delayed rescue.

"Mitch, I'm repeating myself," Pete said clearly. "I want you to hear me. Do. Not. Approach. That. House."

"I hear you, Sheriff." They'd do what was needed.

"But—"

"Hang up." He cut Brandie off before she could ask about any exceptions. It was better to ask forgiveness than break a direct order. He knew that it didn't matter.

Pete knew he was lying through his teeth. The man had gone against Homeland Security to protect the woman he loved.

"You can wait if you want to. I'm getting Toby." Brandie tossed his cell on the dashboard and crossed her arms.

"I know."

She wouldn't be silent for long. There weren't many streets in Presidio. He knew where to head and even knew what side of Main Street the house number indicated. He didn't know what they were heading to, but one thing was certain. He'd protect them both. They needed a fast, safe way to do it.

"A simple way to check out the house and not alert them is to get invited inside."

"How do you suppose we do that? And don't you think they know who we are? She worked at the café for over two months."

"We can hope that whoever is inside doesn't know what you or I look like." He wasn't crazy about this next part, but waiting for Pete's men and the warrant would be harder. "I can raise the hood, act like we're having car problems. Do you think you can go to the door and ask for water? I can hang back, cover you and cross my fingers they ask us both."

"Can we go in without a warrant? I thought that was illegal."

"Not if whoever's in that house invites us. We'll take a look around, see if we need to tip our hand to our opponent. I'd hate to lose that advantage if we don't have to. If we get inside and Toby's there, we don't need a warrant, either." He coaxed her hand into his, getting her to really look at him.

"What if Sadie is inside?"

He shrugged because she knew the answer. "We can wait around the corner for Pete's men. It's your call."

"You know I'll do anything for my son."

"So will I."

Chapter Twenty-Four

"Iron gates, three sides iron fence, brick wall on the east with a twenty-foot easement. The windows give them a pretty good view of anything on the street."

Brandie heard cussing as Mitch gave the report. He'd left the speaker on without Brandie asking this time. When circling the block, they'd made notes from a distance and parked on the far north side of the house. They'd talked themselves out of approaching the house.

"No way to observe who's inside. Garage is closed. Can't tell what type of vehicles it's holding. Curtains closed, dark. There are lights on. I'm not close enough to determine shadows if anyone passes."

"What you're telling me is that they've got a 360 degree view. There's no possible way we'll get surveillance on the inside to see if Toby's there."

"It gets worse. There's a field at the back of the house."

This time Brandie wanted to join in on the cussing.

"Then that means we serve the warrant. ETA for my deputies is nineteen minutes. We're right behind them. They'll be there by the time we determine what to do," Pete said in the background. Cord was in the same vehicle heading to Presidio. "Don't do anything stupid."

They disconnected, and Mitch looked through his binoculars again.

"I don't know where either of those men get off telling us not to do anything stupid. They've both put their lives at risk more than once for the ones they loved." Brandie refused to cry and lose her determination. "Isn't it my decision? Don't I have any say in what happens?"

Mitch set the binoculars in his lap. "They're being overly cautious."

"They want to do everything by the rules and they're forgetting that the most precious thing to me in the world may be in that house."

"Dammit. There's a car pulling out of the driveway. I can't see the tag number, but it looks like the make and model of the blonde Queen's."

The woman had so many names, they'd given up on using any at all. It was ironic because Brandie felt like she'd been doing nothing except bowing to the woman's will for the past two days.

"I'm not waiting." She reached over and turned the key. "Let's go."

And just like that they were on their way. It was a knee-jerk reaction needing to do something herself to get Toby back in her arms. Mitch stopped at the first corner, a worried look clouding his eyes.

"Remember, you'll have to leave your cell phone in the car. Think of a reason why neither one of us would have one or they couldn't be used. Be mad at me—it'll cover the nervousness."

She nodded. They'd been over this several times, but as soon as he'd mentioned nerves, she'd realized how horribly nervous she was. "What do I need to look for? Besides the obvious, that is."

Her hands were shaking even with her fingers laced together.

"Listen for other people. Someone trying to keep Toby quiet. See if you can get into the kitchen. Look for kid food. Ask for a map or to use the phone. You're a smart woman, Brandie. You got this."

"You're sure this is the right thing?"

"No. I'm not. I'm impatient to get this over with, too. Look, if you have any doubts…it's fifteen minutes. Just fifteen minutes." He shook his head and reached for the key. "I shouldn't have suggested you do this. It's too dangerous. We'll wait."

"What if she's leaving with him right now, taking Toby to another location that isn't one of her properties? If no one follows her we might lose him forever. I'll stay here and watch the house. You go after the car." She opened the door. He caught the back of her jacket as she swung her legs outside.

"I'm not going to let you do something so—"

"Stupid?" She relaxed her arms and came free of the jacket as she got out and slammed the door. "You don't control my actions, Mitch Striker."

She pointed in the direction the car had left, hoping and praying that he wouldn't jump out and throw her back inside. She was no match for his strength or up to another debate on what was the right or wrong move. She turned and ran down the edge of the street. She'd watch the house from behind the brick wall. It was beginning to get dark and there were no streetlights to expose her.

Mitch's car engine seemed loud, but no one inside would pay any attention to it. He drove straight, and she headed back to the house. It was a relief not to argue with him. Making a decision and moving forward was scary but she'd done it.

Brandie hadn't realized that the wall was just a little shorter than her. She had to stand on tiptoes to peek over it. She walked even with the backyard, searching it again for signs that a little boy had been playing there.

Nothing. And no movement in the house. She ran back to the opposite end of the wall straight into a very large man with a very large shotgun pointed at her. He jerked the barrel toward the house. So much for her secret agent training.

The man shoved her inside the garage door. "Sit. Cross your legs. Keep your hands behind your head."

She complied since she didn't really have a choice. He had a gun and she had nothing. He slid his hands across her sides as she sat, removing her cell and smashing it under his boot.

The two-car garage looked new with neatly stacked boxes on metal shelves against the back wall. It was unusual that there were two windows, both barricaded with bars. No tools, either, for yard work or for a car. And no escape as he pushed a button, shutting the door and closing it at her back.

He stood silently in the corner, gun pointed at her casually. She wasn't a threat. They both knew it, just like they both knew she couldn't talk her way out. Her legs were beginning to cramp when the door leading to the house opened.

"Sadie, where's Toby?"

"Well, hello to you, too." Her son's kidnapper acted like they were long-lost friends. She was still in her chic outfit, beautiful studded shoes clicking against the concrete floor. "This could have been so easy. You do as I say and Toby would have mysteriously turned up tomorrow. You could have created any story and everyone would have believed it."

She was wrong, but Brandie wasn't going to argue.

"I go by Patrice, and if you found this place, then you already know that."

Her palm stung Brandie's cheek without warning.

"You have complicated my life beyond your small comprehension level.

"*Mamacita*, pack only what you need. ¡*Vámonos*!" she called through the door then took the shotgun away from the man standing guard. "Go help her. Only essentials. Remind her of our talk."

The man stepped inside.

"I don't have time for you." She rested the shotgun against the wall near the door button, replacing it with a handgun she pulled from one of the open boxes.

"Just give me Toby and we'll sit here out of your way long after you're gone."

She flipped open another box and began loading the pistol. "I'm afraid we both know that won't work. If you're here, I can assume that Mitch is chasing after our decoy. Was he hiding in the trunk when you picked up the girls? I should have known that he wouldn't keep his nose out of your business. He's clearly got a thing for you since he wouldn't look twice at me." She spun around, gun at her waist. Her long blond hair was free, straight and past her shoulders.

Although she was very beautiful, her face was full of hatred. Gone was the woman who happily waited on tables, smacked gum and brought Toby Mexican jumping beans. The evil seemed to ooze from every motion, but especially her eyes. Brandie knew what the gun was for. Her.

"You can use us as hostages. I'll cooperate. I swear. Just don't hurt Toby."

"Don't be ridiculous. *Mamacita* would kill me if I hurt your little boy. She's taken quite a shine to him. We can raise him to use his pale skin to our advantage. Don't doubt that. But you, on the other hand. You are just a sacrificial pawn. I might let you say goodbye to your son if you tell me what they know."

"I have no idea. It's just me and Mitch, exactly like you said. He came to help me. We saw your car leave so we split up."

"Don't lie to me!" she screamed. "I had everything planned to perfection, every move carefully calculated. Then you came into the picture and hired a mechanic who would never leave. Rey screwed everything up by kidnapping your kid."

"That wasn't a part of the plan?" Brandie asked, genuinely surprised that her son was an afterthought, but had brought down this woman who thought of herself as the queen of an organization.

"Of course not! Too many variables." She paced back and forth. One, two, three steps, then back. Mumbling to herself. "Magnus Carlsen. Think like Carlsen. His end game."

Brandie was at a loss, not comprehending the conversation, witnessing the demise of a desperate woman. She paced erratically, mumbled and tapped her temple with the weapon.

She finally looked up, pointing the gun at Brandie like an extension of her finger. "That's what I need. One of Carlsen's famous endgames. I have the strongest pieces. I should move them into position and be able to take out no matter what opponent shows its face. Like your knight mechanic."

Sadie still didn't know that Mitch was an undercover Ranger. That fact had to be in their favor. Her knight? Images of a giant game board with life-size playing pieces sped through her mind. Rey sat as the king. Sadie next to him. But in what game would the queen take down her own? That was just it. Sadie was the dark queen and the rest of them were playing opposite her.

"This isn't a game," she said, trying to bring Sadie back to reality.

"Of course it is. I make a move and someone counters. You're simply a passed pawn, something to exchange for what I want."

"If you exchange someone, exchange Toby. He—"

"Shut up and let me think."

Mitch had to be outside by now along with Pete, Cord and the rest of Presidio County's sheriff's department. If she knew for certain, she could run to the button on the wall and open the garage door. She uncrossed her legs, getting life back into them before making a mad dash. She gained only a momentary glare from her captor who still paced.

Trying to reach the opener was useless until she knew someone was outside. She hadn't heard anything. Nothing from inside the house. No cars leaving. How was everyone escaping?

"Can I please see my son? You said he was inside, right?"

Sadie stopped in her tracks, eyes clear and evil. "Do you think I'm stupid?" She pointed the gun, it didn't waver like when she was thinking. "You're staying exactly where you are."

Brandie really wished that Mitch had given her some physical secret agent training. She desperately wanted to know how to leap forward, take the gun from Sadie and find Toby.

The doorbell rang. And rang again. The doorbell did multiple rings until Sadie/Patrice/Patty Johnson lost her temper at the annoyance. She threw her head forward, flipping her hair with an irritated growl.

This was Brandie's chance. She pushed up from the floor as quickly as she could and threw herself at Sadie as she lifted her head. They toppled backward, tumbling into the metal shelves, knocking the boxes to the concrete.

Guns and boxes of ammo fell in every direction. They continued to spin across the smooth surface while Sadie yanked, tugged and jerked on all of Brandie's clothes, trying to stop her from getting to the garage opener button on the wall.

Brandie's boots slipped on the slick surface, and she fell to her knees. Sadie was on top of her. They rolled. Sadie pulled hair and clawed. All Brandie could do was protect herself.

Then Brandie's head cracked to the right, reacting to the butt of the gun hitting her jaw. She saw shards of light and felt the world sort of phasing out.

Toby!

She couldn't let this witch take her little boy. If she wanted a fight…she'd get a fight. Brandie fought the haze gathering in her head, pushing, punching the blonde madwoman in her scrawny sides.

Kicking out from under her, Brandie rolled, then

crawled until she could get her feet under her. Sadie had hold of her boot when there was a loud crash. They froze.

Brandie turned and scooted away, but Sadie didn't care. She was on her feet and running inside. Brandie should wait on Mitch. She knew that. The lack of sounds within the house earlier frightened her. There had been others in the house. She'd heard them moving, talking. Then she hadn't.

If she wanted Toby…she should go after wherever that crazy woman had taken him.

Chapter Twenty-Five

The deputies couldn't just shatter the front door with a ram. They had to pry the iron bars off the front, then crash through. The car he'd followed was a decoy. Some sixteen-year-old kid had been hired to drive it to the border. As soon as Mitch had gotten a look and verified the car was empty, he'd headed back to the house.

There was a chance that during that time, Brandie had been found and everyone inside had driven away. He swallowed hard, controlling his emotions as Cord crushed his ribs holding him back from entering the house first.

The sheriff's department searched. No shots were fired. Pete walked out the door, shaking his head, and Mitch was finally released. He ran, jumped the short iron fence, ignoring the gate.

"Are they in there? Are they…?" Mitch doubled over. His head dropped below his belt before he fell to his knees. "This is my fault. I shouldn't have left her alone. I shouldn't have waited on warrants and procedure."

The pain shooting through his heart was unbearable. He didn't want to live without Brandie and Toby. They'd become his life, the most important things to him. He couldn't imagine losing them to a waitress he'd always call Sadie Dillon. It was so bizarre, he couldn't wrap his head around their deaths.

"Mitch, they aren't inside, man. No one is," Pete said, grabbing Mitch's shoulder to get him to stand.

"Then there's a chance. What do you want me to do?"

"I've got my men canvassing the neighbors. I doubt they'll give us any workable information. We'll set up to watch her other properties, but I think she's smarter than that."

"Until she resurfaces or makes demands," Cord said.

"You want me to sit and wait? That's why we're in this mess." That was the last thing he'd do. "I waited on the right way to do things. I waited and gave her time to make her chesslike moves. I can't do that now. I need to find my family."

The men looked at each other. Neither seemed surprised.

"I'm going inside." He stuck his hand out to Cord. "Give me my sidearm."

Cord complied and stayed in the dry, lifeless yard. Mitch shoved past a deputy who said "hey" and attempted to stop him while Pete shouted the okay.

Mitch didn't care about anyone else. They could all assume they'd all cleared out. But he'd been on the major road in town. He hadn't seen many cars. He'd looked at every face. And his gut told him to keep trying. He'd keep searching until he found them. Period.

Men were in different rooms looking for anything the warrant allowed. Someone was coming down from the attic. "Nothing there."

Mitch secured his weapon at the small of his back when he realized none of these men knew he was a Ranger. He straddled a dining-room chair. How could they have gotten out of this house? It looked every bit like a normal house. But it wasn't. It belonged to a smuggler.

What did smugglers have?

"Tap on the walls and move furniture. There may be a hidey-hole." He yelled loud, told some twice as he pulled the china cabinet to look behind it.

Nothing. He searched every inside wall and started for the garage. There had to be something.

"Striker!" Deputy Hardy called. "I found something. I looked inside after I saw the laundry basket in the bathtub. I mean you wouldn't do that, right? Laundry goes to the— Anyway, it looks like it goes under the house."

At the bottom of a bathroom linen closet was a panel with a small finger hole. It looked like extra access to the water pipes and it might be. Except this was wide enough for a man twice his size to fit through. He pulled his weapon and reached to lift the wood.

Hardy jerked his arm back stopping him. "I understand why you have that weapon, but I'm going to have to ask you to hand it over to me, sir."

"I'm afraid I can't do that."

Hardy drew his sidearm. "Damn it, Mitch. I can take care of this. Hand me your gun."

The youngest deputy in the sheriff's department was shifting nervously. Mitch hated what he was about to do, but he couldn't tell him he was undercover. Hell, he might not be. He had resigned and not proceeded back to Austin like his orders had stated.

He wasn't taking a chance. He was heading down that hidey-hole.

Hardy readjusted his grip to reach for his radio. Mitch

slammed his forearm up under Hardy's gun, knocking it to the floor. He ripped the radio from the stunned deputy's belt and shoved him backward through the door. Locking it while Hardy recovered and began shouting and turning the knob.

"Run, tell Pete," he mumbled. "I'm going to need backup."

Mitch quickly pulled the hole cover only to find it spring back into place. He lifted again, wishing he'd grabbed Hardy's flashlight. He unlocked and cracked the door open. No reason to delay the cavalry. He propped the panel open with a stick located on the underside, secured both weapons, then lowered himself through the hole.

As soon as his feet hit concrete, his gun was back in his hand. He took a second to let his eyes adjust. But immediately he could see light at the end of a long tunnel. Then he heard voices. Arguing.

His heart raced as fast as his feet wanted to move, but he held himself in check. His fingers felt a rough, concrete block wall behind him. This place had been specifically built for smuggling.

The tunnel led to the back of the house. Judging from the voices and the far sliver of light, it probably led the full distance of the field behind the house, too. Three feet wide and at least fifty yards long. There was no way to find the exit without walking through this end. He had a few minutes before the sheriff could follow.

He hugged the wall, staying flush to it as best he could.

"Shoot her and be done with it. We've taken much too much time here," Sadie said, her distinctive voice shrill as it bounced through the tunnel.

"I thought I was a pawn to be traded for a better playing piece."

Brandie!

There were at least three people standing in the light. Sadie and whoever she'd been demanding shoot Brandie.

"We lift the door. She screams. We might as well put a bullet in our own heads."

The Spanish that followed was a deep bass and too fast for Mitch to catch all of it. The pool of light grew larger until it was apparent there was another small area about ten feet wide like under the house. He could make out Sadie with one hand on a ladder rung. A figure was on the floor—Brandie. And a large outline with a hand extended as if to shoot.

The gun drooped back to his side. This time Mitch could understand the Spanish. "You shoot her then. I take care of your mother."

As the man handed Sadie the weapon, Mitch ran forward. "Drop the weapon."

"Mitch?"

Sadie did the opposite. She snatched the gun and fired. He dove, sliding across the pavement on the elbows of his jacket. The lightbulb shattered, spinning the room into darkness.

"Get next to the wall and don't move, Brandie," he called out as the large man kicked his thigh.

He heard a door or hatch open. Then a scream of frustration. By the sound of Sadie's curses, Brandie hadn't listened to him. She must have yanked Sadie's ankle and latched on in order to keep her from escaping.

The yelling continued while he stood. Fighting blind was nearly impossible. The man could be heading back down the tunnel for all he knew, but then a big fist connected with his kidney.

"Mitch, help! We can't let her go. Toby's already gone."

He headed toward the voice. She was right. They had to get Sadie off the ladder.

But a direct hit to his right kidney again made him spin and fire off a couple of punches—including one using the gun still in his fist. "You stop hitting me and you can take your chances out of this dark hole, man. All I want is your boss lady." He hoped he'd said the right words in Spanish.

"Mitch, I'm slipping."

"Okay," the big man answered.

Mitch pulled out his cell with his left hand and pressed on. It was a blinding light after so much complete darkness. He fixed everyone's positions in his head, stuck his phone back in his pocket and climbed the bottom two rungs to get Sadie. He wrapped his arm around her waist, and she immediately began clawing at his head.

Brandie fell to the floor as Mitch was rammed in his side. Obviously, the big man changed his mind about his freedom. Mitch didn't let go. He pulled his arms close against his ribs, taking another punch.

"Stay still, you rotten woman," Brandie said. Her hands tried to control the frantic flaying Sadie achieved while screaming at her man to kill them both.

He'd never hit a woman in his life and never intended to. Sadie was quickly changing his mind. He rolled several times, taking her with him in order to stop being her man's punching bag.

"Hang on to her, Mitch. Someone's coming," Brandie said from farther away, maybe down the tunnel.

"That should be the sheriff."

"Go! Kill the boy!" Sadie shouted.

"What?" Brandie cried. "You can't!"

Sadie was no longer as important as stopping the big man from leaving. Mitch shoved her off, got to his knees and leaped away from the lights coming through the tunnel. He grabbed the ladder rungs, just behind the big man making his escape.

"Send the men up after me, Brandie. I'm going to need their help." He didn't wait for an answer, but he heard another scuffle begin below and shouts of the deputies approaching.

The big man threw back the hatch, leaving a square patch of dark bluish sky pinpricked with stars beginning their nightly West Texas reign. Mitch's ribs ached and his muscles tensed at the thought of seeing the big man's boot aiming for his head. He climbed, grabbed on to the top rung for his life and prepared his left forearm to block a kick.

Sure enough, the kick came. Mitch swung his arm around, locking his hand around the big man's ankle. With all his strength and a loud growl, he yanked, twisted and then pushed. His opponent tripped to the ground, and Mitch hurried out of the hole.

His opponent was lighter on his feet than he'd hoped. Mitch had both feet on the brittle grass and dirt just in time for another whack to the side of his head. He'd had enough and reached for his weapons…

"STOP! I SAID, STOP!" Sadie screamed with flashlights honing in on her face.

Their short scuffle for the loose gun had once again

resulted with Brandie on the wrong end of the barrel. She was breathing hard, but at least on her feet.

"I swear I'll shoot her and you'll never find Toby."

The men behind the beams stopped. Sadie nervously shifted the gun between Brandie and the tunnel.

But most of the woman's focus was on the deputies. She didn't seem to notice Brandie inching a little closer along the wall when Sadie faced the tunnel. Brandie didn't know any defensive moves, but she put everything she had into a vicious kick against the back of Sadie's legs.

The blonde fell to her knees, the gun flew from her hand and landed across the tunnel. The men swooped in, pinning her to the ground while they cuffed her.

Pete pulled Brandie from the ladder, but she clung to it. Her son's life was at stake.

"Let me go! She told someone to shoot Toby. Mitch went after— You've got to help stop him."

Pete grabbed his radio from his belt. "We've got Brandie. Can you see the hatch exit?"

"Negative."

"Head north from the house. Mitch is there. I hear him fighting above me." Pete's eyebrows arched, asking an unspoken question.

Brandie let go of the rung and stepped to the side. "I'm fine. Please go help him."

Pete headed up the ladder.

"It doesn't matter," Sadie said with her face in the dirt. "You will not find that boy. He's gone. Without me you will *never* find him."

MITCH HEARD SADIE'S screeching words. His backup would be surfacing at any minute. He shrugged out of the denim jacket, needing the flexibility. He reached for one of the guns he'd had entering the tunnel but changed his mind. He couldn't shoot him or take a chance of accidentally wounding him in a fight over the weapon. The man he fought might have different ideas about negotiating a deal than his boss.

The man had at least fifty pounds on him. Mitch's strongest punches barely made him wince. He wove his fingers together and swung. The backhanded blow made the man stagger. Mitch threw one from the opposite direction. The man's head snapped to the side.

He fell backward like a tree toppling to the ground.

Pete's head popped out of the hatch. "Need some help?"

"Just cuff him." Mitch rested on his knees, catching his breath. His eyes were peeled on the road. "You have units headed here yet?"

"On their way. This thing—" he stomped on the hatch "—is blocked from the street by that storage shed. Fairly smart on their part. Now where do you think they all headed?"

Pete slowly turned, searching the perimeter. He was too calm for Mitch's comfort. He joined him, nudging his shoulder when the unconscious man began to moan. The sheriff rolled the man to his stomach and added handcuffs to his wardrobe.

"Where the heck were these two planning on going?" Mitch asked, staring at the open lots.

"Do you think there's another tunnel?" Pete asked.

"Sir?" the radio blared into the quiet night.

"Go ahead."

"Brandie's demanding to come up the ladder now. That okay with you?"

"I'd prefer that she return to the secured house, but I take it that's not an option?" Pete looked at the hatch and leaned down to help Brandie up.

Mitch walked toward the road. Toby was still out there. They'd missed him by minutes and needed to find him. Not later. Right now. Nothing against Pete, but they didn't know what they were facing.

The entire neighborhood had to be watching. They all had to be aware of what was going on. Somebody had to have seen something. The people in the house had to have gone somewhere.

"Vehicles," he mumbled. "To get away, they needed vehicles, but we're watching the roads. So how would they get past your roadblocks?"

"They didn't," Pete proclaimed.

"Then where are they? Where was he trying to run?" Mitch asked.

Two driveways to the west there was a mobile home with a carport. Two trucks and two cars parked and ready to pull onto the street. But no lights on inside. Not even the glow of a TV. Too early for anyone except the elderly and those souped-up trucks didn't belong to anyone who went to bed at seven at night.

Could it be that simple? He didn't wait to explain himself. He didn't wait to follow procedure. Or the letter of the law. Or wait for backup.

He jogged along the side of the road, hanging close to the edge of the pavement because of the darkness. He heard the squawk of the radio behind him. He'd dropped Hardy's a long time ago. He patted his pockets. No jacket meant no cell or extra clips. But the cold steel of a gun was secure against his back.

He skirted the wall of the mobile home. Listening. The

front of the trailer had a direct line of sight to his fight at the tunnel. They probably knew their battle was lost.

"Mitch," Brandie whispered directly behind him. "Pete said to wait on him."

"No. Go back and give him my answer. This is too dangerous."

"I'm staying. This is Toby."

He knew that look and heard the determination in her voice. She couldn't kill him with niceness—he wasn't a customer, but she would be stubborn.

"Stay here. I'm going to the front door." He squeezed her hand. "They might not know my face, hon. Please stay here."

"Since you said please."

He saw all her hope that Toby was inside that trailer. Maybe he recognized it because he felt every bit as anxious for all of it to be over. If he weren't here...

Mitch turned the corner of the trailer and lightly stepped on the wooden porch leading to the door. The little glass panels used for the windows were raised. Whoever was inside could hear him.

"Toby, son," he raised his voice. "Can you hear me?"

"Go away," said a heavily accented woman. "No want."

"All I want is the boy."

"No boy here. Go away," she said.

"It's over." Brandie's eyes searched his from the corner. Pleading. "You don't want to hurt the *niño*. Just send him out and that'll be it."

He'd lie if it got Toby out of there. *What if you're wrong? What if they've already left and you're wasting time?* He could see the same questions in Brandie's movements.

A county vehicle, lights flashing, stopped about fifty feet away. Cord stood behind the door, the radio mic in his hand. "Rosita Morales, we know you're holding a little boy. Send him out to the officer, then follow with your hands up. If anyone's inside with you, have them do the same."

Cord said it in English for everyone to hear and then again in flawless Spanish. Before he finished the second time, the door creaked open. At Mitch's position on the short porch, he was trapped behind the door. He saw the joy and relief on Brandie's face and heard the running down the steps. It was Toby.

Chapter Twenty-Six

Each of Toby's feet hit the big steps, and he ran across the stepping stones the same way. He had a big, laughing smile on his face and didn't seem scared or abused. Brandie wanted to run to him, but Pete held her back, weapon drawn and pointed at the door.

She scooped her son into her arms, and Pete pushed them behind him, away from the mobile home and into another county vehicle farther down the street. He tapped on the hood, the car was put into gear and they left. She didn't see how everything ended. She didn't care.

Toby was chattering away. Brandie wanted to listen to him, concentrate on his words, but she stared at Sadie and the man who'd kept her son. They were facedown, hands cuffed behind their backs by the tunnel entrance.

Defeated.

"Are you okay, sweetie heart?" she asked.

"You had to work a long time, Mommy. I want to stay with Gramma Ollie next time. 'Kay?"

"Sure thing, absolutely."

"Ma'am?" Deputy Hardy interrupted. "We'd rather proceed to the station unless you think Toby needs a doctor."

"He seems fine. Why the police station?"

"We don't know what—if any—retaliation there might be. My orders are to protect you and the boy."

"Thank you."

Toby was safe, but the apprehension wouldn't leave her alone. Mitch was still there. He'd been behind the door when she'd left. They hadn't acknowledged any goodbye. If something happened...

But nothing was going to happen. He was just as safe as they were. She had to hold on to that thought, concentrate on Toby. She held her five-year-old so securely in her lap that he wriggled to be free.

"Too tight, Mommy."

"I'm just so happy to see you again." She wiggled her nose against his, unable to get enough of him. She was relieved, grateful, thankful.

"It's okay. I had an all right time. But I like my room."

"Sure you do." She kissed his forehead. He even smelled clean, like soap.

The deputy drove the two miles to the Presidio Police Station and escorted them both inside to the chief's office. A local officer stood outside the door as if they were fugitives. But they weren't.

One by one the Queen's men paraded by her. When the man Mitch had fought with staggered past, Toby smiled and waved. The man may have worked for a drug smuggler, but he'd obviously treated her son with kindness.

She heard Sadie coming through the main doors before she saw her. The expensive shoes were back on her feet. Brandie rubbed the side of her head where one had hit her during their fight. The leather skirt had been ripped and there was dried grass stuck throughout her long hair. She couldn't flip it and be beautiful. Her horrible true nature oozed out, screaming with every foul word that escaped her lips.

Then she saw Brandie. Her eyes darted to Toby drawing at the desk. She smiled by tilting the corners of her mouth and narrowing her eyes. It was so evil Brandie had to turn away. She wanted to protect Toby, to get him out of a building where this vile woman would be.

They couldn't leave. Mitch hadn't come through the doors.

She lifted Toby and sat him in her lap. She couldn't see the door, which made her even more nervous. Was he walking through it or on his way to a doctor?

"What are you drawing there, Toby?"

"See, this is the black tunnel we had to crawl through. Not really crawl, but they saids I could pretend. Mommy, I didn't get to brush my teeth. You aren't mad, are you?"

"No, no, honey, I'm not mad."

"Javier said you wouldn't be, but I didn't know for sure because of the mean lady." He touched her chin, drawing her attention to his wide-eyed baby blues. "I love you, Mommy."

She kissed his forehead again. She'd never get enough of his sweet smell and loving arms. She buried her face in his little neck until he giggled. "Toby Quinn Ryland, I love you right back."

"So do I."

"Mitch!" Toby jumped off her neck and ran to be scooped up into her knight's arms.

Not that horrible woman's knight. No, Mitch was hers. She knew she wanted to spend the rest of her life with him. The question was, did Mitch want a life with a ready-made family?

"The supposed Queen involved her mother, Rosita, and other family members. They're bringing in quite a few from her operation including the young women from this afternoon. All in all, I think we made a pretty good team out there." Mitch shifted Toby to his side and held out a hand to her. "Come on, let's get out of here."

Sitting handcuffed to a chair, Sadie didn't look as important or threatening any longer. "You know she really did think of herself as the Queen. She said her whole operation was thrown off because of the unknown variable of Toby's kidnapping. She is a horrible person."

"Don't think you're safe, Brandie. You'll never be completely safe," she spat from the other side of the room.

"Pipe down," an officer said, dropping the duffel of cocaine on his desk.

Brandie was no longer nervous. Her family was safe and they'd stay that way. She was never a person who spoke her mind, but this time, she had something to say.

"You should probably be more worried about yourself. You're a captured Queen. And I think you're wrong. I'm not your passed pawn to be traded for a more important piece. I'm on the winning side." Brandie didn't flinch when Sadie threw herself forward, attempting to stand. "I think that's checkmate."

Chapter Twenty-Seven

Toby fussed about having to take a second bath, but then Mitch said he'd take one, too, right after his mom. So they'd played with the toy soldiers and dinosaurs marching in two by two formation on the racetrack carpet. Toys and carpet had been moved to the living room so Bud and Olivia could enjoy the fun, too.

Once they were all clean, they ate grilled cheese sandwiches and tried for the best chocolate milk mustaches. Olivia and Brandie tucked Toby in bed, giving Mitch time to speak with Bud on the porch.

"You spending the night again, Ranger?"

"Yes, sir. I don't think she needs to be alone."

"You're right about that. I guess you'll be moving on to your next assignment then?" Bud stretched, smiling like a man with a secret.

"Actually, Bud, I, um…"

"You want to hang around here awhile?"

"If she'll have me, sir. Yes."

He clapped him on the shoulder. "I don't think there's a question about that. You take good care of them or you'll answer to me."

"Yes, sir. I know."

"Come on, Ollie. I'm yearning for a good night's sleep."

Mitch secured the doors, checked over the windows so they'd both sleep sounder. While Brandie dried her hair, he pulled the couch cushions and stood them behind Toby's door. He took the blanket and pillows off the bed, looking at it longingly, imagining what might actually happen there one day.

But not tonight.

The drier went off as he pulled the covers back over Toby.

"He still asleep?" she asked from the doorway.

"I think he'll sleep at least until six, maybe six-thirty if we're lucky. You ready to hit the hay?"

"Yeah, but I don't think—"

"Brandie, I can't—" They both began, both grinned. "Check out behind the door. I sort of thought you'd want to stay in here, too."

They pushed the cushions together and leaned against the pillows. He was ready to wrap his arm around her when she pulled back, taking a deep breath and letting it out on a long sigh.

"I love you." She closed her eyes and leaned her head on his shoulder. "Not just for everything you've done in the past couple of days. It happened months ago. After one of those long, protective looks you gave me standing in the doorway to the garage."

"I think I've loved you since I met you. I never saw anyone after you and I honestly felt more at home on the cot in the garage than I have in years anywhere else."

"If you stay, will you still be a Texas Ranger?"

"I don't think they'll let me run the garage in my spare time, so no."

"Is that going to bother you?" she whispered.

"No. I like working on engines. And I like washing

dishes after a bus has come through town. But there's a bigger question, Brandie... Will you marry me?"

"Absolutely."

Mitch pulled her across his body, their mouths sparking a passion he didn't think possible with anyone else. But not tonight.

He wrapped his arms around her body, keeping her close, watching for shadows. She rested her head on his shoulder, and he wrapped a hand in the long silky locks. He softly kissed her good-night, thinking about how good they'd be together. But that was their future.

Tonight was the first as a family.

Epilogue

Five weeks later

Brandie opened the door to the café, expecting business as usual. Toby ran through while she waited on Mitch a few steps behind them.

It was their first day back since returning from their honeymoon, and she'd been apprehensive about getting back to normal. Her parents had convinced them to sleep late. They'd open up like they had for the past week and take in Toby home with them when they swapped places.

"Surprise!" Multiple shouts and waving hands, then laughter and loud conversations.

It was standing-room only in the café. The bar was full of cake, sandwiches, a punch bowl and behind it stood her mom and dad. Her father had his arm around her mom, looking very proud and happy.

"Oh, my gracious," Honey and Peach said in unison. "You two should have seen your faces."

"I thought I was seeing double. It's so unusual for you sisters to be together and away from the sheriff's office. Who's minding the dispatch desk if you're both here?" Brandie hugged them both. "Thank you for coming."

"We couldn't miss it. We're so glad there's nothing wrong with Toby. He thought it was a sleepover. That's great. Just great." The sheriff's department dispatchers faded into the crowd.

Mitch wrapped his arms around her waist and whispered in her ear, "I think you have some friends, Mrs. Striker."

"I'm so very lucky." She did feel very lucky that there had been no lasting effects from the kidnapping. She turned her face to his, giving him a quick kiss. "And so are you."

"It's after the fact, but the two of you took off so suddenly to get married, no one had a chance to give you a shower. Or a reception, so surprise." Andrea explained the party faster than Brandie could take it all in.

Neighbors, friends and café patrons crowded more to the edge of the room, leaving a path straight to the far wall. "I can't believe it." Brandie ran to the shiny, refurbished jukebox. "You all shouldn't have. It was much too expensive."

"We didn't," Kate said, nodding to Mitch on the other side of the room. She handed her two shiny quarters. "Bride's choice."

Brandie's hands shook, but she got the coins through the slot. Her vision was blurry from happy tears, but she found her favorite song. She dabbed at the corner of her eyes and then extended her arms in an invitation. Her husband of one week wrapped her tightly and kissed her to a round of "awws."

They danced to her favorite song with only Toby talking in the background. The other couples swayed, but it was mainly them. It really was the reception she'd dreamed about. Held in her favorite place, with her favorite people.

At the next song everybody danced with them. Her dad dug the next quarters out of the cash register to keep the music going.

"I can't believe you got the jukebox fixed," she said to her husband during the next slow dance.

"I might even buy you those expensive sunglasses if you don't behave." He winked, then held her closer. He nibbled her neck. Something they'd both discovered she loved. "Do you get the impression that Toby isn't all that excited to see us?"

Toby was sitting on a bar stool, turning back and forth, but not spinning. He knew that was against the rules. "He's upset about something."

"Let me try." Mitch led her to the bar. "Hey, kid, why the long face?"

"Gramma Ollie said I need to wait."

"If there's a problem, then you should probably tell your old man. That'd be me now."

"I want a new name like Mommy."

"Well, now. That's not a problem. Your present came while we were on our trip. We've got papers at home to prove your name is now Toby Ryland Striker." Mitch announced the news of the adoption loud enough that her parents heard. They both stopped and hugged each other.

"For real?" Toby said with a brilliant smile, completely happy again.

"Want me to tell everybody for you?" Mitch asked.

"Naw," he whispered. "I think we need to eat cake."

"You got it." Mitch messed up Toby's hair, then smoothed it back down.

"I love you more and more every day," she told him. "You truly are my shining knight. Think you can keep that up for a while?"

"Sounds like the plan of a lifetime."

* * * * *

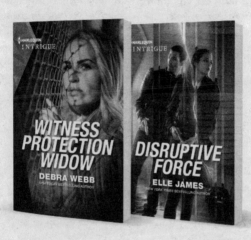

He was challenging her already and they hadn't even really started working together, but if they were going to survive several weeks of training, honesty was going to be the best policy.

"My husband was a marine," Piper said, but didn't make eye contact with him. Instead, she whirled and started walking back in the direction of the outdoor training ring.

He turned and kept pace beside her, his gaze trained on her face. "Was?"

Challenging again. Pushing, but regardless of that, she said, "He was killed in action in Iraq. Four years ago and yet…"

Her throat choked up and tears welled in her eyes as she rushed forward, almost as if she could outrun the discussion and the pain it brought.

The gentle touch of his big, calloused hand on her forearm stopped her escape.

She glanced down at that hand and then followed his arm up to meet his gaze, so full of concern and something else. Pain?

"I'm sorry. It can't be easy," he said, the simple words filled with so much more. Pain for sure. Understanding. Compassion. Not pity, thankfully. The last nearly undid her, but she sucked in a breath, held it for the briefest second before blurting out, "We should get going. If you're going to do search and rescue with Decoy, we'll have to improve his obedience skills."

Rushing away from him, she slipped through the gaps in the split-rail fence and walked to the center of the training ring.

Shane hesitated, obviously uneasy, but then he bent to go across the fence railing and met her in the middle of the ring, Decoy at his side.

"I'm ready if you are," he said, his big body several feet away, only he still felt too close. Too big. Too masculine with that kind of posture and strength that screamed military.

She took a step back and said, "I'm ready."

She wasn't and didn't know if she ever could be with this man. He was testing her on too many levels.

Only she'd never failed a training assignment and she didn't intend to start with Shane and Decoy.

"Let's get going," she said.

Don't miss
Decoy Training *by Caridad Piñeiro,*
available April 2022 wherever
Harlequin Intrigue books and ebooks are sold.

Harlequin.com

Love Harlequin romance?

DISCOVER.

Be the first to find out about promotions, news and exclusive content!

[f] Facebook.com/HarlequinBooks

[twitter] Twitter.com/HarlequinBooks

[instagram] Instagram.com/HarlequinBooks

[pinterest] Pinterest.com/HarlequinBooks

[You Tube] YouTube.com/HarlequinBooks

ReaderService.com

EXPLORE.

Sign up for the Harlequin e-newsletter and download a free book from any series at **TryHarlequin.com**

CONNECT.

Join our Harlequin community to share your thoughts and connect with other romance readers!
Facebook.com/groups/HarlequinConnection

HSOCIAL2021

HARLEQUIN

Heartfelt or thrilling, passionate or uplifting—Harlequin is more than just happily-ever-after.

With twelve different series to choose from and new books available every month, you are sure to find stories that will move you, uplift you, inspire and delight you.